The kitchen lights l   ved
away from the do   ava
against the bugs.

At that moment, something stabbed me between my shoulder blades.

Stab might be too strong a word. On the other hand, if the mosquito was big enough that its proboscis had gone through my track suit and jabbed my back, it might exactly the right word. It felt like I needed to reach the spot between my shoulder blades and pull it out before I passed out from blood loss. Damn, that hurt. How big was that sucker?

During that half second of distraction I tripped over a freaking lawn chair. It was one of those cheap ones with nylon webbing and thin aluminum tubing that makes a big racket when it falls over with almost 60 kilograms of startled private investigator tangled in it. That would have been bad enough, but the deck also had a built-in, recessed hot tub. I fell onto the cover.

Evidently, Collin didn't approve of rigid pool covers. They probably cost too much for his taste. Instead, he'd bought one of those cheap, floating bubble-wrap things with no structural integrity. Water leaped for joy, and made a big splash as it went everywhere. My top half was soaked, my feet were still tangled in the chair, and my head was underwater.

At least the water was warm.

I floundered for entirely too long, trying to do a reverse sit-up while my hands scrabbled to find the edge of the tub. I managed to grab it, and push myself out. By now, there was not much point in trying to be stealthy, so I kicked the chair free of my legs. Inside the house, a male voice was bellowing. This was not going as well as I'd hoped.

I sprinted up the path to the fence, cooling water trickling from my soaked top down the inside of my trousers. I pushed my way through the tree branches, and jumped for the top of the fence.

Despite the adrenaline fuelling my jump, I wasn't even close. I slid down the fence boards, and another branch caught me in the same kidney.

On my second jump I didn't even get that high. My clothing got caught on a branch, and I was knocked off balance. I fell backward, and rolled down the slope toward the garden.

It was a good thing that the glass cold frame broke my fall.

To Josh,
Are you pondering what I'm pondering? ☺
G.W. Renshaw.

THE PRINCE AND THE PUPPET AFFAIR

Book Two of The Chandler Affairs

by

G.W. Renshaw

Javari Press
Calgary, Alberta
2015

The Prince and the Puppet Affair

Javari Press,
Calgary, Alberta, Canada.
http://www.javaripress.ca/

ISBN: 978-1-895487-07-7 (pbk)

First paperback edition, April 2015.
Modified cat cover model "Lilith" used under following terms:
https://creativecommons.org/licenses/by-sa/2.5/legalcode

Set in Gentium Book Basic
Printed in the United States of America

DEDICATION

To all those women who have rejected, sometimes at great personal cost, the imposed limitations of those who would make you less than you can and want to be.

ACKNOWLEDGEMENTS

This novel was written with the generous help of these experts who gave up their valuable time to answer just one more question from a sincere, but sometimes clueless, author.

Those people whose names are in italics are fellow members of the Imaginative Fiction Writers Association (IFWA).

In alphabetical order:

The lovely and talented Peggy Adams, retired criminal prosecutor, bon vivant and a rich source of knowledge about both the Calgary police and RCMP.

Renée Bennett, editor and linguist, who corrected Sitri's 17th century grammar, and howled with anguish over Collin's.

Harold Cardona, whose native knowledge of Colombian culture and language provided me with much-needed authenticity.

Paola Andrea Galindo Cuervo for her assistance with Kali's more colourful dialogue.

Sandra Fitzpatrick, my lovely wife, and financial, tax, and science consultant, without whose love, ruthless editing and encouragement I might have been another wannabe.

Det. Darren Hafner (ret.), truly one of Calgary's Finest, who provided a lot of rather obscure details about the Calgary Police Service.

Cheryl Meeder, with her professional understanding of locks and lock picking.

Jenna Miles, who continues to educate me in the finer points of being a young woman, as well as beating me up in aikido, Krav Maga, and baton class. The cake is a lie; the popcorn is true; the porchetta is delicious.

Rosy Rondot, RN, for her help with ER procedure.

Anthony Stark of Mountainview Safety, for help with ambulance procedure.

Any variances between the information given to me, and what appears in my writing are mine. All mine. I refuse to share the credit with anybody else.

If they want credit, let 'em make their own mistakes.

WORKS BY G.W. RENSHAW

Stand-Alone Books:
Hic Sunt Dracones: Being a True Account of the Rescue of Professor George Herbert Endeavour from Misadventure

Odd Thoughts: A Collection of Speculative Fiction

The Chandler Affairs:
The Stable Vices Affair
The Prince and the Puppet Affair
The Kalevala Affair
(coming in 2015)
The Daddy's Girl Affair
(coming in 2016)

CHAPTER 1

Rêve Noir

The offices on this floor were the last stop for people who had reached the end of the line.

There was the doctor who would tell you not to bother making any holiday plans. The accountant with bad news about those guaranteed investments. The PI who might be able to help, if only he wasn't in a monogamous relationship with Jack Daniels.

The corridor stank of pine cleaner, dry rot, and years of quiet desperation. In both directions it stretched away from me, barely illuminated by the cheap, low-wattage bulbs in their wall sconces. The red runner carpet underfoot had seen better days, the threadbare corpse of its once opulent life struggling to pad my footfalls as I approached my destination.

The door before me was dark wood enclosing a frosted glass panel. Slightly worn gold-leaf lettering on the glass read "Chandler Investigations." A round, faceted-glass knob was set in a brass face plate with a hole underneath it for a skeleton key.

Under my trench coat, my bare legs felt a slightly cool breeze. The faint smell of ammonia, probably from a leaking compressor in the basement, told me that this was what passed for air conditioning in this dump.

For some reason I don't remember the door opening, or the reception area inside. The next thing I saw was the inner office.

Sam Spade would have felt comfortable there. A cluttered, cheap wooden desk sat in front of a grimy window that looked out onto the street. Outside, a neon sign intermittently flashed its lonely message of "H__EL" to an uncaring world. I wondered how far down life had to have dragged you when you were willing to take a room there. If you needed a flop house, there were better ones elsewhere for the same money. At least this place didn't have a rat problem. The cockroaches ate them.

Battered filing cabinets lined one wall of the office. The door was closed, the golden lettering spelling out "Veronica Chandler, Private Investigator" in reversed letters on the frosted glass. A stained old couch, still comfortable-looking, but long since due for a one-way ride to the dump, faced the filing cabinets from across the room.

I was sitting at the desk, in a slat-backed wooden chair with no padding. A mostly empty bottle of cheap whiskey sat on the desk in front of me. The bottle cap was nowhere to be seen, probably having wandered off in disgust. Beside it, a well-used Colt 1911 handgun acted as a paperweight, anchoring the scattered mess on the desk against the efforts of the labouring fan in the window. It was doing its Sisyphean best to circulate slightly less warm and humid air into the room from the naked city outside. There was no air conditioning in here. I figured that the duct was probably clogged with rat bones.

The glass I held in my hand was half full of amber rotgut. I toyed with it casually, thinking of how disappointed my father would be if he could see that I wasn't drinking a good wine.

My vision of the world matched my mood. Everything looked grainy, and painted in colourless shades of grey like a black and white film. That didn't worry me as much as the thought of me drinking scotch before breakfast. I didn't even like scotch. Had it really come down to this?

A blurred shadow appeared through the window on the office door, and whoever it was tapped on the glass. I was too busy brooding to react. Maybe they'd take the hint, and leave me to searching what passed for the remains of my soul.

No such luck. The door opened, and David entered. A silver ribbon around his neck kept his black bow tie in place. His black swimmer's briefs hid very little, and accentuated the rest. Just the way I liked them. My secretary's dark hair was artistically mussed, and the look in his eyes was smouldering, awaiting only a gesture from me to erupt into the flames of passion, as he had so many times before.

"Ms. Chandler, there's a man here to see you. Would you like me to show him in?" His voice was silky, reminding me of his warm hand working its way down the smooth skin of my belly.

"A client?" I couldn't bring myself to care, and another hit from the glass burned a caustic trail down my already scarred throat.

"I hope so. You'll want to see him anyway – he's a knockout."

That got my attention. The man who followed David into my office was indeed a sweet papa with a classy chassis. His leather trousers were so tight they squeaked when he walked. An open leather vest and copper's cap completed his ensemble. His chest was, if anything, even better than David's, with just the right amount of hair and muscle. A dame could get lost exploring that chest. Maybe I should take the last of the office petty cash and invest in a pith helmet.

"Are you the gumshoe?" He said with a voice like sweet wine cut with honey, "I desperately need your help."

I played it cool, though parts of me were warming up.

"They all do."

"Please, you don't understand." His voice held the desperation of a man who might do himself an injury if his hopes were dashed. That would be such a waste. "The mob's after me. If I don't have a threesome by noon I'm a dead man." He ripped off his vest, revealing that perfect chest in all its glory.

What the hell, they don't call us private dicks for nothing. I've always been a glory hound.

"Fifty bucks a day plus expenses," I said, casual and smooth. "If you can last that long."

The two men licked their lips as I rose, my wooden chair creaking, and the steel casters scraping on the scuffed wooden floor.

I headed for the couch, hips swaying out from behind the desk. A shrug of my shoulders made the trench coat fall away, revealing nothing but my own glory for them to seek. The first man reached for me and, as I sank back onto the cushions, something gouged my bare leg.

My eyes snapped open. For a moment I was confused as to why my thigh hurt. Yoko Geri was lying on my lap, his black-furred face looking up at me. His green eyes were fixed on mine, and again he flexed the claws that were resting on my jean-clad leg.

I had been dozing in my comfy chair before Yoko decided that I should be awake. He kneaded me again, and I was forcibly brought the rest of the way back to consciousness by the sensation of being tattooed with a wire brush.

I disengaged his talons from my flesh, then scratched the side of his neck. My offering of affection pleased him. Rewarding the predator who was trying to excavate my femoral artery did nothing to cure my suspicion that all cat owners are insane.

Like most humans belonging to cats, I'd picked up the habit of talking to him. The day he answered back would be the day I would know it was time to give up, and get myself a nice holiday in a psychiatric ward.

"Holy crap, where did that dream come from? Either I need to get laid more, or I need better meds." He tilted his head, and I moved my scratching to his throat. "Maybe both. Next thing you know, I'll be reading romance novels in bed." I stroked his ears, and his eyes closed in bliss. "Again."

The deep rumble of his purring expressed his appreciation of my wise choice. Whether I was insane was of no interest to him, as long as he received regular food and affection. I stopped petting Yoko, and he bunted my hand to remind me of my duty.

"Come on, sidekick, let's get some lunch."

In the cat universe, food trumps everything else.

My phone rang as I was scraping a lump of wet cat food off the spoon, and into Yoko's bowl. Being in the kitchen or the bathroom almost guarantees that my phone will ring. The phone, of course, will be elsewhere. This time, it was on the coffee table in the living room.

I scooped the glop off with one finger, put the can and spoon on the counter, and managed to get to the phone before the caller gave up.

"Chandler Investigations."

"How's my favourite daughter?"

"I'm good, Dad. Wait, you have a favourite?"

"You know I love Kali, but you'll always be my Princess," he said.

I sighed. I could *hear* him capitalize Princess. My father has some unshakable delusions about girls. This had better not lead to him buying me anything pink. Again.

"So, what's up?"

"Your mother and I are going away for a holiday."

"You mean an actual holiday? Not just puttering around the house, and worrying about the restaurant on your time off? That's fantastic! Where? When?"

"I can tell that you're heart-broken to be rid of us, but it's only for three weeks. We're going to Northern Ireland."

"Wow, any room for stowaways?"

"Why, do you think your cat would like to come?"

"I'll ignore that. This seems kind of sudden for a major trip. Why right now?"

"Your mother is competing in the World Police and Fire Games. She's forcing me to go as her cheering section."

"You're kidding! When did that happen?"

"It's a last minute thing. One of the guys on the Calgary team broke his arm while chasing a bad guy over a fence, so they asked her to fill in."

"Which event?"

"Pistol shooting, as well as some kind of martial art thing."

"She is *so* going to kick ass. You are *so* going to record every moment for us. When do you leave?"

"Tomorrow. The games start on August first, and we want a day or two to acclimate."

"You weren't kidding about last minute. Do you need a ride?"

"Yes, please. Unless you are busy."

"At the moment I'm between cases. What time?"

"The flight leaves at nine, so we need to be there around seven."

Given a choice, I like to pretend that there's only one seven o'clock per day: the one right after supper. The things we do for our parents.

"All right, I can do that. Have you let Kali know?"

"Not yet."

"I'll call her. We'll see you at six A.M."

I had never thought of my mother as an international athlete. I wondered what kind of "martial arts thing" she'd be doing. I pictured her in a *Mad Max* arena, dressed in a Princess Leia bikini, with moves like River Tamm from *Serenity*. What can I say? I'm a product of my time. At least, at 44, Mum has the figure for it.

I called Kali, my sister-by-choice, and let her know that the parental units were going off to have fun without us. She lives a few minutes up the road from their place, so she said she'd meet me there in the morning. She sounded perky about it. She's a morning person but I love her anyway. We'd met six years previously in high school when I thumped some girls who were bullying her.

Yoko's bowl was empty, and he was subtly hinting that I'd forgotten to fill it in the first place. I went back into the kitchen to give him another spoonful. As the food hit the bowl, the phone rang.

See? You thought I was exaggerating, didn't you?

"Chandler Investigations."

"I, um..." The woman's voice was small, suggesting someone who completely missed the line when assertiveness was handed out.

I waited patiently, leaning with my back against the kitchen counter while Yoko devoured the second helpless blob of Chicken Feast. Eventually the woman continued.

"I think my husband is having an affair."

"I'd be glad to look into that for you," I said. "If you wish, we can meet at my office this afternoon."

"Okay."

"What's your name?"

"Alyssa Blakeway."

"All right, Ms. Blakeway, do you have my address?"

"No, um, I got your number from the telephone book."

I don't list my office address for a good reason. It's also my apartment. Drop-ins are not welcome.

"I'm at 2246, Twenty-second Street North West, Suite 404. Would two o'clock be convenient?"

"Yes. Thank you."

"Please bring any relevant documentation about your husband, his job, hobbies, or other activities. Also bring a recent photograph of him. My fee is $60 an hour plus expenses with a thousand dollar retainer."

"Okay." She paused, clearly unsure that we were done.

"Excellent," I hinted. "I'll see you then."

"Okay." She hung up.

"Congratulations," I said to the predator who was now washing his face while sitting by my feet. "It looks like you get to eat next month."

Things weren't really that bad. Unlike fictional investigators, whose entire lives seem to be lived hand-to-mouth, I was comfortably solvent. My parents had started an investment portfolio for me when I was nine that was doing well. I even had enough income from my business to add to it.

True, the first couple of months as a PI had been lean, but things had picked up with my first two cases. They were bizarre, involving, I kid you not, a mysterious dwarf (or pair of dwarfs, a matter that had never been completely settled) named Beleth, and people doing dressage while dressed as horses.

After that, things had settled down. For the past eight months I'd been living on a steady mixture of erring spouses, insurance fraud, runaway kids, and a silver tea service.

It was the tea service that was responsible for my dream-filled, late-morning nap.

When Kendra and Darrel moved into a basement suite together, Kendra's grandmother gave her the family's antique tea service as a housewarming gift. There was no room in the basement for the silver, so they'd packed it carefully in a cardboard box, and stored it in the garage along with the rest of their surplus belongings. Unfortunately, they didn't think to put their names on the box.

When the upstairs guy moved, his buddies loaded all the boxes into the truck with a profound lack of due care and attention. I understand that a premature and unregulated ration of domestic beer may have been involved.

There were two reasons for my lost sleep. Firstly, Kendra's grandmother was coming for a visit. The tea service was expected to be on display. Tomorrow.

The second reason was that, although the landlord had been able to give me the upstairs tenant's name, he didn't have a forwarding address, or any idea who his friends or family were. Still, how many Michael Li's could there be? After all, Li is only the most common Chinese family name. Michael is only the most common boy's name in North America.

There were two silver linings to the case, if you'll pardon the expression. One was that Michael had mentioned that he had a new job, but was staying in Alberta. The other was that for some reason he hated cell phones. He was a land line kind of person, and Kendra hadn't missed the tea service for two months. By now he would have a new phone.

I spent nine hours calling every M. Li, Mike Li, Micky Li, and Michael Li I could find, starting in Calgary, and working my way outward. To my everlasting joy, I found him in Red Deer, 90 minutes north of Calgary, instead of in Indian Cabins, 13 hours north. He checked his basement while I stayed on the line, and there was the box, still unopened. He was apologetic about the mix up. Kendra was panicking about needing the tea service right away, and Michael said he was going to be up late anyway, so I drove to Red Deer that night to get it.

In person, Michael was not only polite and charming, but also really hot. Unfortunately, his girl friend came home just as I was getting around to asking personal questions such as relationship status. Not every case involves derring-do, sex, or sleep. If they do, I prefer them in that order.

After a nice lunch of prosciutto with fresh basil, sliced tomato, and smoked Gouda on ciabatta, I did my usual pre-client clean up of the apartment. That's the one drawback to using your living room as an office: all socks, underwear, books, and cat toys have to be out of sight.

The up side is that my commute time is manageable, and renting one place is cheaper than renting two.

At 1:45 I exchanged my usual flannel pyjama house wear for something more professional, brushed my hair into a pony tail, and sat down to wait.

The intercom buzzer sounded at exactly 2:00. My laptop showed the image of the person at the building's front door. The woman certainly looked more like a nervous client than a burglar, so I buzzed her in.

The security system was new. My building didn't have one when I had moved in, but after the previously mentioned dwarf had appeared without warning at my front door, I decided that it needed one. There was no chance of convincing the building owners to spend money on a professional system, so I went to a friend of a friend, Keith Barager-Bonsell, who owed me. His solution was cheap, elegant, and didn't require the owner's permission.

I explained the idea to the other tenants, and took up a collection. Keith turned the $350 into a web camera, a wireless router and a used laptop computer. Nice Mrs. Schauwecker, in apartment 201, let us mount the camera on her balcony with a homemade weather shield. The laptop and router sat in a corner of her living room, out of her way, beaming the pictures to the rest of the building. Any tenant could see who was at the door just by logging on to the web server. Everybody was happy with the added security. Our building manager pretended not to know about it in case the owners asked.

My final preparation before the arrival of Mrs. Blakeway was sticking the tastefully small "Chandler Investigations" magnetic sign on my front door.

I was open for business.

Mrs. Blakeway was about a century out of date.

Brown hair in a side French braid bun made her look far more severe than necessary. Her green blouse had double frills across the front, and pearl buttons up to the high neck. The full skirt went down to her ankles and she clutched a smallish handbag before her like a shield. I wondered if she was also wearing button-up boots and silk stockings, but decided that they might be too kinky for her. All she needed was brass goggles to complete her Steampunk look. Underneath her worries, and lack of self-confidence she was probably pretty.

"Mrs. Blakeway?" I said, extending my hand. She smiled nervously. Her handshake was moist, but moderately firm. "I'm Veronica Chandler. Please come in."

When I turned from the door, I found her gazing out my balcony window. She was already remarkable among my clients in that she had not yet mentioned that she expected me to be older. Nineteen year old private investigators get that a lot.

I headed for the kitchen. "Can I get you anything?"

She shook her head as she stared out at nothing in particular. Sad to say, that's a good description of the view from my apartment. The most interesting thing at the moment was the small park across the street where people were playing catch. I suppose that the abandoned Mystery Bicycle, chained to the lamp post out front since before I'd moved in a year ago, also counted as local colour.

I brought two bottles of water back with me, just in case she changed her mind. By then she was looking at my investigator's course certificate and provincial PI license on the wall bracketing my 1941 Maltese Falcon poster.

I invited her to sit on the couch. She sat primly; she was wound way too tightly. I took my place in my comfy chair, and opened my computer on my lap. I had to prompt her to say anything.

"You mentioned on the phone that you are concerned about your husband."

"I...," she said tentatively. "He's been out late at night. He says he's working, but..." She stalled. I gave her another nudge.

"You suspect that he may be seeing someone?"

"Maybe it's nothing. I don't know. He seems more distant lately, like he's lost interest."

Her hands were in her lap, nervously trying to macrame her fingers together. She sniffed delicately, and I saw tell-tale glistening in her eyes. I pushed the box of tissues closer to her, and she took one to dab her nose. That was all it took for the waterworks to start. She was not one of those people who can cry prettily.

I took the moment to enter what little she'd said so far in the case file. Most PIs use a paper notebook. I have one of those too, for use in the field. The problem is that, as a child of the computer age, my handwriting is on the far side of awful. If I keep my notes on the computer it's actually possible for me to read them later.

When Alyssa stopped sniffling, she pulled a large and rumpled manilla envelope from her purse. I wondered how she'd managed it. Maybe the purse was larger on the inside than on the outside.

"I wrote down everything that I could think of," she said as she passed me the packet. Inside were hand-written notes in a precise hand. They covered when her suspicions started, background, and his schedule. There was also a photograph of her husband. The dossier was impressively thorough. Most people in such an emotional situation don't have that kind of focus. The elegant handwriting did nothing to dispel her Edwardian vibe.

I finished entering the details into the contract template, and sent it to my printer. She jumped at the sound of the machine in the corner whirring to life.

Although I encouraged her to read it carefully, she barely glanced at the contract before signing it.

"I'll start tomorrow," I said. "If you have that retainer?"

She pulled another envelope from her Gallifreyan purse. The good news about carrying that much cash is that the new, plastic $100 bills seem to stack better than the old paper ones. A thousand dollars barely takes up any room at all.

There's probably an economic moral in there somewhere.

I showed her out a few minutes later, removed the sign from my door to keep the superintendent happy, got a cup of coffee from the kitchen, and went back to my chair to review the file.

From his picture, Collin Blakeway looked to be about 45 although her notes put him at 36. He had a pointed nose, thin lips, and small eyes. It would be a miracle if this guy was having an affair, unless he had a really great personality. Given the circumstances that seemed unlikely. Looks are often deceiving, but his photo gave me the impression of someone who was cruel and self-absorbed. Her nervousness also pointed in that direction. Somebody had her badly spooked, and to my mind he was the prime suspect.

I wondered why she'd married him, and it made me sad to think of the obvious answer: He'd asked her. Her low self-esteem had caused her to grab the first offer she got in case there wasn't a second one. According to the file they'd been married for six years.

His life seemed to be fairly boring. The notes said that he spent most of his time either at home, or at his office. Curiously, she also listed skiing, snowboarding, and hiking as his hobbies, although she also noted that he hadn't done any of them in over five years.

It looked like his life had changed significantly since their marriage. Although it wasn't strictly part of my job, I was curious as to what had caused the alterations.

This might be a more interesting job than it appeared on the surface.

CHAPTER 2

Social Life

According to his file, once Collin Blakeway was home he never went back out to "work", so there was no point to starting surveillance until the next day.

That was good, because I had plans for the evening. I had to get up early to take Mum and Dad to the airport, but with any luck I'd be in bed before it got to be too late. Whether I'd be sleeping or not depended on a number of things.

My evening plans involved an interesting pair of jeans that I'd seen in the baking goods aisle earlier that week.

All right, it wasn't the jeans that were interesting so much as what was inside them. The wearer had strong legs, a great butt, and a really nice set of shoulders. His back was slender but muscular without being gross. Yum.

Just to frustrate me, it seemed like every time I tried to see his face he turned the other way. He was moving down the aisle slowly, examining almost everything as if he was a tourist trying to take in all the sights that an unfamiliar country had to offer.

It took me a while to manoeuvre into a position where I could see what he looked like. It was well worth the effort. He was about my age, and very definitely attractive. I'd go so far as to call him cute. From the selection of nuke-and-eat items in his cart I could tell that he was single. The strange thing was that he was in the baking aisle. From his furrowed brow, it was obvious that he was not clear about what these mysterious products were.

He stepped back, and stared at the sugar for a long time, like he expected the packages to tell him some great secret. As I pulled my cart up beside him, he automatically took a step to one side to make room. He didn't really notice me. I walked in front of him, and took a package of ginger that I didn't need off the rack.

That got his attention. I smiled at him. He smiled back.

"Hi. Looking for something in particular?"

He frowned.

"Do you know anything about baking?"

Some men can have fragile egos, so I tried to be modest. Telling him that I'm a chef might scare him away. "A little," I said. He looked uncomfortable, like he was about to ask me something deeply personal. When he spoke, his volume was much lower than it had been, as he voiced his secret shame.

"What kind of sugar do you use in a cake?"

"It depends. What kind of cake?"

"My sister is making a birthday cake for her friend. She sent me to buy some sugar, but I don't know what kind to get."

"For the cake, or for the icing?"

"Um, I don't know. The cake, I guess."

If she was making a cake from scratch, his sister probably would have known to ask specifically for icing or brown sugar if that's what she wanted. I picked up a package of plain, white sugar.

"This should do."

"Thanks." He put it in his cart, and I continued smiling at him until he got the hint. "My name is Brian."

"Veronica," I said.

"So," he said casually, "are you in university?"

I'm told that there are proprieties to be observed in dating. The guy shows interest by asking questions that he won't remember the answers to. The girl shows interest by giggling, and tossing her hair. Both parties pretend that they don't know exactly where the whole thing is going.

I've never mastered the hair toss, and I hate giggling.

"No, but I am free for dinner." He looked shocked. "Come on, you were going to ask me out eventually. I think you're attractive, so I thought I'd save some time."

"Okay. Sure." I could see his brain trying to adjust to a woman picking him up instead of the other way around. "Um, well, I am in university, and I have an exam tomorrow. I really should study tonight. How about tomorrow night?"

Darn, I'd already made arrangements for a girls' night with Kali. Maybe the delay would make me seem more appealing. You know, that whole hard to get thing. However that works.

"I'm tied up. Are you free on Thursday?"

"After seven. I have a late class."

"Great. Do you know Nick's Steak House?"

"Sure."

"Shall we say 7:45?"

"Sure. I'll make the reservation." I hoped that he was a better conversationalist once his brain had caught up with current events.

I pulled out my phone, typed in "Brian", and handed it to him. He looked at it for a moment before my outstretched palm suggested to him that he should hand me his phone in return. We each typed our phone numbers, and handed the phones back.

"I'll see you on Thursday," I said, as I pushed my cart down the aisle.

At the end of the aisle I turned and glanced back. He was still checking me out. Excellent. My chest is too small, but I've been told that I have a world-class butt. I gave him another smile, then disappeared around the corner.

This just might be interesting.

Nick's is less than a fifteen minute walk from my place. The weather was nice, so I left my car at home. I arrived at the restaurant with a good five minutes to spare, waiting for my date between the inner and outer doors.

Brian showed up at exactly 7:45. Being on time for appointments shows respect. I liked that. It gained him immediate brownie points.

"Hey," he said as he opened the door. "Have you been waiting long?"

"Only a minute or two."

He gave his name to the hostess, which let me know that his last name was White. We only had to wait a minute or so before we were seated.

We spent the next while with the usual small talk about what looked good on the menu, and what we'd tried before. I'd been looking forward to a steak all day, preferably with a big baked potato smothered in sour cream, chives, and bacon bits. He decided to have the same. He got another brownie point for ordering his steak medium rare. My professional opinion as a chef is that, if steaks were meant to be well done, the process would be called cremation instead of grilling.

He asked if I wanted wine with dinner, and seemed pleasantly surprised when I ordered beer instead. Big Rock Brewery is an excellent reason for living in Calgary.

I begin my interrogation before he could start on me.

"Tell me everything about Brian White."

"Hmm. I'm nineteen, in my first year taking Kinesiology at the U of C. My goal is to be an MMA fighter for a couple of years to build a reputation, and then become a coach."

No wonder he was in excellent shape.

"That's different. Which martial arts have you studied?"

"Tae Kwon Do, Wushu, boxing, and wrestling. I've been taking lessons in one form or another since I was fourteen. Did you mean different good or different bad?"

"Different good. It's nice to see someone who has a plan, rather than just doing general studies until they figure out what they want to be when they grow up. Do you live near here?"

"Just over on 25th Ave. My sister and I rent a house together. She's in second year women's studies."

A live-in sister might be a problem. We'd have to see. Oh well, adapt and overcome. If all else failed I could always take him back to my place. In the meantime, having a plan for his life earned him more brownie points.

Eventually, he slipped past my questioning.

"Enough about me. Who is Veronica...?"

"Chandler. I'm a private investigator."

He didn't even blink. More brownie points.

"Really? I thought PIs were all fifty year old guys with an alcohol problem."

"Only if you habitually wear a trench coat and fedora." My mind flashed back to my dream for an instant. *Down girl.* "I decided to buck the trend. I took the investigator's course while I was still in high school, and the licensing exam as soon as I turned eighteen."

"Don't you have to have been a cop or something first?"

"In some other provinces, but not in Alberta. I did do an internship with the Calgary Police, but I was never a sworn member."

I told him, in general terms, about some of my cases. In common with doctors, lawyers, and other professionals, I was careful not to mention anything that could identify anybody involved. There were still some good stories.

One case that I didn't mention was my first one. If he was going to run away, I preferred it not to be because he thought I was crazy or a liar.

We were getting along really well. Brian had a wicked sense of humour, and we made each other laugh.

Nick's main dining room in built on two levels, and there was a party of about 20 people on the upper level of the restaurant. Apart from noting their existence, I didn't pay them much attention until the singing started. It was not your usual drunken, off-key, unsynchronized chorus.

It was one man, and he must have been classically trained. He sang *Old Man River*, and his deep tones effortlessly filled the restaurant.

We stopped talking. So did the rest of the diners. I think that even the cooks in the back paused to listen. When the unknown singer finished, everybody applauded.

"That was impressive. You didn't arrange that, did you?" I asked my date.

"I wish I had."

Another brownie point: We both opted for a dessert of cheese cake. I wondered if he was trying to impress me with how compatible we were, or whether it was his honest choice. It probably didn't matter that much.

When we had both gotten to the last bites, our eyes met. He slowly nibbled his cheesecake from the fork. I licked mine off with the tip of my tongue. By that point in the evening, that was as subtle as I was willing to be.

He refused to let me pay my share, which lost him a brownie point. Now and then I had detected a whiff of unattractive machismo in his attitude. It could be that he had been brought up by traditional parents, but was still trainable.

Still, he was way ahead on points when we went outside.

"May I walk you home?" He asked. I'd already made my decision.

"How about if I walk *you* home? It's closer. As long as your sister doesn't mind."

"Remember that birthday cake? Tonight is the party. She won't be home for hours."

It was only ten minutes from the restaurant to his place. We held hands as we walked, which was brownie-point neutral. I was feeling like I wanted his arms around me, and he was trying to be a gentleman.

I'd have to do something about that.

There's an old movie called *Conan the Destroyer*. My favourite part is when the girly-girl princess asks Grace Jones' character how to let a man know that she's interested in him. Grace's answer is "grab him! And take him!"

I have medical problem that sounds funny and isn't. My hormones can spiral out of control on a moment's notice. When they do, Grace Jones is the spokeswoman for their moderate wing.

Brian barely had time to get the front door open before I attacked him. Some guys freak out if a woman is sexually aggressive. I figured that it was better to know if he was like that sooner rather than later.

He didn't have time to freak out before he was on his back on the living room carpet, watching me pull my sweater over my head as I straddled his hips.

After two months of trying to be a good girl, taking my meds, and keeping my libido under control, it felt good to just let her out to let her do her own thing.

Three hours later, both his and her things were exhausted. I was lying on my back on the carpet, amazed and a bit worried about whether he'd think I was a slut, whether *I* thought I was a slut, and how bad the rug burns were that I could feel on my knees, elbows, shoulders, and butt. Not to mention my heels. I rolled toward him to snuggle. I'd just rest for a minute, and then find my clothes.

I woke to the sound of the front door closing, followed by a painful blast of light as the overhead living room fixture came on. I rose up on my elbows, blinking a few times in the sudden illumination.

Between the clothes that were scattered everywhere, and two very naked people, the living room was a mess. A bowl of chocolates that must have been on the coffee table was all over the floor. I'd wondered what the squishy lumps were. My purse was open, and the contents spilled out, the result of Brian telling me that he didn't have any condoms on hand. Four of my emergency stash were lying around us, the open ends tied closed. For some reason, I've always found used condoms creepy. In the light from the overhead fluorescent bulb, they looked like we were surrounded by dead slugs whose necks had been wrung.

Brian's sister was standing by the front door, looking at us in disgust. At me in particular.

Just in case you were wondering, situations like this can *always* get worse.

Brian woke up, and saw his sister. He yelped, and grabbed the first piece of clothing he could find to cover himself. Unfortunately, it was my underwear.

I'd worn a thong.

"Uh, hi sis. Um, you're home early." He frantically reached for another piece of clothing. This time it was his shirt.

I just sat up, hugged my knees, and crossed my ankles. There was no way to maintain dignity while sitting naked in a stranger's living room surrounded by used condoms, and melted chocolates squashed into the carpet. I tried to be suave and look comfortable with the situation.

I'm not that good an actor.

"It's not that early," she said, still staring at me.

"Oh, sorry. I guess we, uh, got carried away."

Her brown eyes just stared. Brian decided that introductions were in order.

"Uh, Veronica, this is –"

"Hello, Judy," I said. "Sorry about the mess."

"Veronica," she acknowledged coldly, then turned back to her brother. "I didn't know you had company."

"You two know each other?"

"We were in school together," I said, leaving out the details.

"Sorry, sis. I didn't have time to put the sign out." Brian seemed oblivious to the tension between Judy and me. I noticed that he'd also just made this awkwardness my fault. *Thanks, Brian.*

I should have stayed quiet, but my curiosity got the better of me. "Sign?"

"If one of us has someone over, we put a 'Do Not Disturb' sign on the door."

"I see."

Judy angrily kicked off her shoes.

"I'm going to bed." She stomped off down the hall, and I winced as I heard a door slam.

"Well," I said with as much dignity as I could under the circumstances, "that was awkward."

"She'll get over it." Wonderful. Now he was dismissing his sister's feelings.

I tugged my thong out from under Brian's clutching hands, and started getting dressed. There was a minute of embarrassed silence. Somehow, getting dressed in front of a man I barely knew was more difficult than getting naked had been.

"Judy's my half sister," he finally said as I tried to find my other sock. "Her father was black."

"No, really?" I said with some sarcasm. Judy was a rather beautiful shade of brown with black hair. Brian looked like he could be Norwegian. He sighed.

"Yeah. We're twins."

That stopped me.

"How can you be... oh."

"Yeah. Our mother was screwing around, and Dad caught her. He left before she knew that she got pregnant by both of them at the same time. Well, probably not at *exactly* the same time, but close. Now you know our dirty family secret."

"I know that she blames Judy for everything that's gone wrong in her life. It must have been tough for you, too."

"Judy's father was at least decent enough to pay support. Mine wasn't. I bought into mother's BS until I was old enough to realize that our mother wasn't being persecuted because she had a black child. Judy was just an excuse so she could get sympathy instead of being exposed as an ass hole."

Memories of the times I'd met Mrs. White came back as I pulled my sweater on. Although I completely agreed with him, I decided not to comment. "How come I never met you in school?"

"Judy didn't want anybody to know we were related. Our mother really did a number on her mind. I've probably done a number on yours, too. This wasn't how I expected a first date to go. So, do you want to keep seeing a guy from such a screwed up family?"

"Only if he doesn't mind seeing a girl whom his sister doesn't like. Judy might never get over our school history."

Brian grinned.

"I've had girl friends she didn't like before."

"I don't need to know the details, as long as none of them were named Ashley."

"Ashley Borenstein? Oh, hell no! She makes our family look normal."

"You know her?"

"Unfortunately. Ashley is Judy's BFF, except that she alternates between telling Judy how cool she is, and putting her down. I keep telling her to drop the bitch, but Judy will do anything for her. That's where she was tonight. I've tried introducing Judy to new friends, but it's like she's addicted to Ashley's line of bull."

"Ashley and I have some seriously unpleasant history. It might get ugly if we met here."

"You don't have to worry. She won't lower herself to visit Judy. It's always the other way around. What kind of history do you have?"

I sat on the rug beside him to put my socks on. Brian didn't seem at all interested in getting dressed. I tried to remind myself that I was tired and sore.

"She screwed my boyfriend, and supplied him with cocaine. Or maybe she gave him the coke first. I'm not sure which."

"Ouch. The only drug I ever do is the occasional beer. I have to stay clean for the fights."

"I'll hold you to that."

"Speaking of holding, I don't suppose you'd be interested in seeing my bedroom before you leave, would you?"

Another brownie point. Didn't this guy ever run out of energy? My brain tried to responsible while the rest of me perked up with interest.

"Sorry. I'd love to, but I have to get up early tomorrow."

"Today."

"What?"

He pointed to a wall clock. It was almost one thirty.

"Crap. I *really* have to leave." I finished dressing.

"Will I see you again?"

"Definitely." To be a smart ass, I held out my right hand. "Thank you for dinner. I had a nice evening."

He took my hand as if he was going to shake it, then drew me closer. There's something about being kissed by a naked man. Especially one who knows enough to kiss slowly and sensually instead of going after your tonsils like a starved Great White shark. Not to mention the unsubtle pressure against my belly that let me know he was still interested even after four bouts of non-stop fun and rug burns.

Ah, the joys of dating young men.

The walk home was peaceful for the first block. Once I got away from Twenty-fourth Avenue the streets were completely deserted, and it was perfect for introspection. In the near silence, I did the Walk of Shame as the aliens and I had a debate about what I'd done.

I couldn't believe that I'd screwed my brains out on a first date, especially with a guy I'd known for only about two hours before that. Doubly so when he turned out to be Judy White's brother.

I wondered if I needed to talk to my doctor. It was possible that my medication needed adjusting again.

Girls, like boys, lie so much about sex that I'd never really felt like I'd gotten a good idea of what was normal. My therapist wasn't helpful by suggesting that I had to find a sexuality that I was comfortable with. Maybe I wasn't a slut, and it was normal for a healthy girl to jump on the first nice guy after a two month dry spell.

After all, Brian was handsome, funny, and a great lover. What was wrong with having sex with him?

If my slight trouble walking was any indication, my body voted for there being nothing at all wrong. For some reason, I'd never completely let myself get my freak on before. It had felt wonderful. It wasn't just the physical release, though.

I felt free. For once I hadn't worried that my breasts were too small, or that I might be weird for being the Queen of Libido. Brian had kept up with me the whole time. Maybe this was a relationship that could last for a while.

By the time I got home I'd decided that it was far too late in the morning for advanced soul searching.

I set the alarm, let my cat under the covers to snuggle, told my doubting self to shut up, and left it at that.

For now.

CHAPTER 3

Thrills

At 5:30, I woke with a yell. Yoko Geri had, as usual, been snuggled up against my side under the covers. I think he forgot where he was, and panicked when he couldn't immediately get away from the obnoxious buzzing sound of my seldom-used alarm clock.

In a movie, it might have been hilarious: him trying to escape from the evil blanket monster, and me trying to avoid four kilos of startled, fur-coated razor blades. In real life it was considerably less funny. At least I was out of bed on time. I tossed my pyjamas into the bathtub and let them soak with water during my shower so the blood stains wouldn't set.

I had cunningly set up the timer on my coffee machine before I left for my date the night before, so the elixir of life was ready when I zombie-shuffled into the kitchen. Four hours of sleep wasn't anywhere near enough, especially after an athletic night. I was able to infuse some life into myself while nuking one of the breakfast wraps I keep in the freezer for such occasions. By the time I made it out to Binky, my faithful, white Chevrolet Cavalier, I was mostly awake. Not happy, or high-functioning, but awake.

The morning air was cool and still. Most of the million people around me were still sensibly unconscious so the traffic was light.

The sky was still dark, the sun still being about 45 minutes from making its scheduled appearance when I arrived at Mum and Dad's place. Kali's Audi was already there.

"Good morning," she carolled, not at all put out by the hour. Some days I feel a very sisterly desire to strangle her, and hide the body in the garden. Mum and Dad might object, though the flowers would probably like it.

I yawned as I took one of the suitcases to the car. When I tried to heave it into the trunk, a muscle in my inner thigh painfully reminded me of last night. I fumbled the luggage, and it slid to the ground as I leaned against the car.

"Are you all right?" Dad asked as I rubbed the inside of my left leg.

"Late night," I said. "I pulled a muscle."

Dad accepted the explanation at face value, and put the suitcase in the car for me. Mum and Kali looked at me with badly concealed smirks as Dad went inside for the last case.

"Late night," Kali said.

"Pulled a muscle," Mum said.

"Bite me," I said to them both.

"I'll bet that's what he said."

"*Guarde silencio, hermanita.*" Kali stuck her tongue out at me.

I glared at them, daring them to continue the taunting. The effect was spoiled when I yawned again. Dad had no idea why they were laughing as he put the last of the luggage in the trunk and closed it. Over the years, living with three women, he's learned that it's sometimes better not to ask.

Considering that they were going on a three week trip to another country, our parents had remarkably little luggage. All of it fit into the back of Kali's car without anybody having to bounce on the trunk lid to close it. I would have offered to put some in Binky, but in all the excitement I'd cleverly forgotten to clear out all my PI gear.

Dad and Kali were both cursed with morning perkiness. They chatted excitedly as she drove to the airport. Mum and I sat quietly in the back seat. We silently bonded over our shared opinion about the pre-dawn hours.

We were almost at the airport when the sun finally made its way above the horizon. A graded wash of orange faded upward until it met a band of clouds that also turned a deep orange. Above that, isolated clouds were pink in the increasingly blue sky. It was beautiful.

I yawned again.

We did the usual airport dance of finding a short term parking space, hauling the luggage into the terminal, and then finding out where we had to be. Things went smoothly once we'd identified the correct place to check their luggage, and to obtain the all-important boarding passes.

Half an hour before flight time we did our hugs and goodbyes before the parentals vanished into the restricted boarding area. Kali drove me back to Mum and Dad's place so I could get Binky, then was off to work at her occult shop.

I'd lost a chunk of the morning, but that probably made no difference. Once they are out of bed most cheating husbands are inactive before noon.

Depending on who you ask, the Beltline district is either just south of Calgary's downtown, or is part of downtown. The main streets are lined with various small businesses, while the side streets are crammed with apartment buildings, and scattered pockets of old houses. The back alleys near the businesses tend to be grungy.

Collin's office was in a two-storey building that might have started life in the 1920s as a boarding house. Maybe it had been converted to offices before anybody thought to put it on the historic register. Or possibly it had been too ugly to conserve. Either way, it was now a suite of small businesses with a common receptionist. I'd looked at it back when I was shopping for my own office space. I might be Collin's neighbour if the rent hadn't been so expensive. At least my current place has free parking. Collin's office did not. According to Alyssa he took city transit to and from work every day.

As soon as I'd parked near his building, I did a walk-by of the back alley. Collin's office couldn't have been more ideal for surveillance if I'd designed it that way.

There was a back door, but a large, black rubbish bin partially blocked it. If there was a fire the tenants were in big trouble. I made a note to call the fire marshal's office when this case was over. At one time, there had been an iron fire escape, now long gone; I could see the scars on the brickwork where the brackets had been attached to the building. From the smell, drunks from the nearby bars used the back alley as a urinal. All the windows looked like they were painted shut. Collin wasn't getting out that way unless he broke the glass.

The front of the building was much different. The brick had been sandblasted at some point, making it look almost new. Modern windows and glass doors had been installed. Well-tended planters full of flowers stretched across the width of the facade just under the window sills.

Directly across the street from the office was a coffee shop where I had an early lunch. Through the glass front doors of the office building I could see the receptionist sitting at her desk. To the left were the windows of Collin's ground-floor office. If he had something to hide, it didn't make him paranoid enough to close his blinds. The coffee shop's south-facing windows were covered with silvered film to keep the sun from blinding customers. As I crossed the street, I was happy to see that it also made it impossible to see inside the cafe from the outside.

So far in my career I've discovered that most cheating husbands are really considerate. They usually tell their wives in advance that they will be "working late" in an attempt to cover their tracks. Of course, that really means that they are going straight from work to their girlfriend's bed. Still, it makes it much easier for me to surveil them efficiently. I was here now in case he was seeing someone during the day. Some people like quickies during lunch. As far as Alyssa knew, he wasn't supposed to be "working late" that evening.

One of my pet peeves is people who live up to their obviously ridiculous cultural stereotypes: Newfoundlanders who are brainless; Americans with no grasp of geography; blondes who are airheads; Calgarians who wear Stetsons despite never having seen a live cow.

Collin was a stereotypical accountant.

His day consisted of sitting at his desk like Scrooge, staring at his computer screen, or sorting through tall stacks of paper. At exactly noon he put his brief case on his desk, took out his lunch, and ate it.

Half an hour later, he finished eating, closed the case, put it on the floor beside him, and went back to work. According to his wife, the brief case was never used for anything other than a lunch box. I wondered what he did when he visited clients. Maybe they always came to him.

The receptionist led an only slightly more interesting life. Apart from trips to the coffee machine and, presumably, the washroom, she didn't move from her desk all day. She also appeared to have brought her lunch. That shot down one theory as to who the mistress might be, unless the two of them were being super-humanly careful about being seen together at work. She certainly never went to see Collin, and the only time they picked up the phone at the same time was when she notified him of a pickup or delivery.

Messengers were the high points of Collin's day. Several of them arrived to ferry files boxes or envelopes to and from his office. He never got out of his chair when they entered his office. None of the messengers were female. I never saw him interact with an actual client.

After a while it was like watching paint dry, but without the spine-tingling excitement. It didn't help that I was so tired from my late night and early morning that I could barely keep my eyes open.

Most people assume that the "plus expenses" part of my fee schedule means paying shadowy informants, or travelling to Azerbaijan to interview ex-KGB agents in smoke-filled taverns run by Russian mobsters. This close to downtown, it meant shovelling handfuls of money into the maw of a voracious parking meter.

My mind drifted, and I had a mental image of high priests in parking authority blue-green cutting the loose change out of helpless victims. They would fling the tribute into the gaping mouth of a massive parking machine idol. Every time they did so, a small parking receipt would blow out its nose to be held aloft by a priest as the crowd cheered.

Man, I was starting to hallucinate. I really needed to get some sleep.

"More coffee?" The shop guy asked me for the hundredth time. He was lost somewhere in his thirties, and he hadn't seen a barber for at least four months. He was completely bald on top with an overly long fringe around the sides and back; not a good look for him, or anyone else outside of the Rocky Horror Picture Show. It's not that I have anything against bald men. I wouldn't mind at all if Vin Diesel wanted to save my privates.

I smiled at the thought as my cup was refilled, then dropped the smile as I realized that this guy probably thought I was flirting with him. I saw him react to my former expression. Damn.

"Whatcha doing?"

I lowered the lid on my laptop so he couldn't see the screen. It would have been difficult to explain exciting spreadsheet entries like "11:52 – C answered phone."

"Writing a novel."

"Wow, you mean, like, that woman who wrote Henry Potter? You know, she wrote that whole thing in a coffee shop like this."

I winced internally, and wondered if he thought Henry's best friend was Rob or Herman. I didn't bother correcting him about the coffee shop story either.

"Something like that but completely different." I glanced across the street, hoping that I'd see something that would require me to spring into action. Nope. I wished the coffee guy would get to the point so I could get rid of him.

"What's it about?"

"Sorry, it's a secret. If I told you, I'd have to kill you."

He laughed too much, like somebody who wanted to impress me with how amusing he thought I was. The least he could have done before trying to pick me up was to brush his teeth. Brian had brushed his teeth, and his hair. Damn it, my mind was wandering again.

"That's funny," he said, in case I was unaware of my own hilarity.

I put my chin on my left palm, displaying my fingers to him as prominently as possible.

"No, really. I'd have to kill you."

The grin slowly faded from his face.

"Uh, yeah. Okay. Anyway, I was wondering what you're doing later?"

This guy was so dense he made lead look like a souffle. I gave him a look so cold that the other patrons should have started shivering.

"Going home to my husband." Since he was having difficulty with such advanced concepts I used a visual aid, wiggling the fingers of my left hand accentuate the gold ring I was wearing.

He got up silently, and returned to his lair behind the counter to nurse his wounds.

I was shocked when I'd gone shopping for a wedding band, and found out what they cost. A couple of hundred dollars is a bit much for a prop. The fake wedding band I was wearing had been made for me by an art student who needed a class project. Under the electroplated layer of gold it was brass, and it had cost me $30.

The ring was there to keep people from hitting on me, and to keep my libido honest. Even if I'd found coffee boy attractive (shudder), I had to keep my professional and personal lives completely separate. Otherwise, there could be big trouble. Even with medication, my hormone problem has me thinking about sex more than most teenage boys do. That's fine when I can find a recreational partner to help scratch the itch (*mmm, Brian*), but it's an incredibly bad idea when I'm on the job.

Besides, I was now in a relationship. At least I hoped I was.

Just before six o'clock, while my attention was on Collin, my phone started buzzing and dancing on the table. I almost jumped out of my seat. My half-finished, thousandth cup of coffee sloshed in its saucer, but didn't quite spill. Maybe I needed to cut back on the caffeine.

"Ms. Chandler? This is Alyssa Blakeway. Collin just called me to say that he'd be working late tonight."

See how considerate they are?

"Good. I'm outside his office now. I'll let you know what I find out."

Coffee boy had been willing to let me run a tab (at least, until I had sliced off his manhood with my laser wit), but I had made sure that I was paid up anyway in case I had to leave quickly. Sure enough, I could see Collin putting on his jacket, and turning off his computer screen.

A few other people exited the building, and I noticed that they all spoke to the receptionist on the way out. She generally returned their greetings with a smile.

By the time Collin got to the front desk the receptionist was also preparing to leave. They came out the door together, and he waited while she locked it. He said something to her, but I didn't see her make any response. I wished I had a parabolic microphone, not that I could have used it without everybody in the area noticing. When she left, she crossed the avenue almost directly toward me.

The looks on their faces were instructive. As she brushed her shoulder-length black hair back from her eyes, she had an expression like she'd just stepped in something nasty, and was thinking about whether to clean her shoe, or just burn it.

Collin's expression was disturbing. When a man is casually enjoying the sight of a pretty girl, he usually has one of two expressions on his face: either a slightly dopey look like he's on good drugs, or a look of lively interest with a slight smile. Collin looked more like the creepy uncle that nobody in the family talks about, and whom you would never dare ask to babysit for you. He followed her across the street, closely enough for a good view of her butt, and far enough that he didn't have to obviously look down to watch her.

Beltline is famous for its high density housing, with about 95 percent of the buildings being apartments. There was a good chance that his mistress was in the neighbourhood. Since he hadn't brought his car to work I expected him to walk to her place. I packed up my laptop, and followed him. As far as I knew, he'd never seen me, but just in case I walked half a block behind him on the opposite side of the street.

At the next intersection the receptionist kept going north. Collin, with a final look at her retreating figure, turned right, crossed the street onto my side, and walked along Twelfth. I was beside a school yard, and he was clearly visible through the chain link fence. I slowed my pace to delay having to turn the corner.

A bus sailed through the intersection, and stopped just as Collin got to the bus shelter.

Crap. I ran toward the intersection, and at least caught the route and bus numbers on the back as it pulled away.

This was not good. There was an excellent chance that a bus in Beltline would go through the downtown core. In the core, pulling over in a vehicle is absurdly difficult, and the traffic makes following anyone next to impossible unless you are right behind them and are willing to run traffic lights. There was a superb chance that I was going to lose him unless I got on the bus with him. That had its own dangers.

I sprinted back down toward where I'd parked Binky. I had to duck and weave around pedestrians who were not happy with me. It felt like it took forever.

I pulled my car door open, almost getting hit by a motorcyclist, then really took my life in my hands by pulling a U-turn in the middle of the street. Collin's office was on a relatively minor street so at least the traffic wasn't bumper-to-bumper. Nevertheless, horns blared as I forced everybody to stop while I did a three-point turn with complete disregard for anything but my need to follow that bus. Luckily for me, the other motorists' sense of self-preservation overwhelmed their road rage. They let me in.

Once Binky was pointing in the right direction, I had to catch my prey. I turned left at Tenth Street, and caught a break. A bus was stopped at the light. The light turned as I got there, and with a snort of black smoke from the exhaust, it moved through the intersection. With a magnificent display of precision driving, and luck, I crammed myself in behind it. The guy who had been behind the bus had to slam on his brakes to avoid rear-ending Binky. He was not amused. I didn't really blame him.

The bus signalled a left turn. People were grudgingly willing to let a bus in. I had a more difficult time, but managed it before the number seven turned left on Eighth Street.

I wasn't familiar with the route, so I had no idea where it was going. Trying to drive in rush-hour traffic while checking online would have been suicidal. All I could do was to blindly follow the leader.

Somebody else cut me off, and I was two cars behind when the bus stopped for the lights at Tenth Avenue. At Stephen Avenue it turned right, and I was directly behind him again.

Every time the bus stopped, I pulled in behind it. It must have been obvious to the driver that I was following him, but the passengers were occupied with thoughts of getting home, and weren't interested in what was happening outside the bus. Besides, only passengers in the rear seats could see out the back. At each stop, I looked for Collin while simultaneously trying not to lose the bus as it pulled away. He never appeared, so unless he'd gotten off while I was going back for Binky, I was confident that he must still be on board.

Now that there was nothing between me and my quarry, I celebrated my cleverness by lowering my voice in an alto imitation of Darth Vader. "I have you now." I drew the line at making asthmatic breathing noises, partially because I'd have had to take my hands off the steering wheel to cup my mouth.

When will I learn not to tempt fate? We turned left on Fourth Street, and I knew I was in trouble. Sure enough, a block later the bus turned right on Seventh Avenue.

The only traffic allowed through the downtown core on Seventh Avenue is the C-Train, buses, and emergency vehicles. Private vehicles are strictly forbidden. If I followed, the very least I could hope for was being ticketed for terminal stupidity. Otherwise, I'd either be crushed between two buses, or pancaked by the C-Train.

There was exactly nothing I could do about it. Some stops on Seventh serve nine different routes, so there was no way to tell where he'd come out, if he came out at all. For all I knew, his destination was somewhere in the core.

After a thrilling day of drinking coffee, fighting off a Transylvanian look-alike, and trying to stay awake, all I'd learned about Collin was that his work day was boring, he had a creepy stalker thing going on with his receptionist, and he took the bus to where ever he was going when he lied to his wife.

I was going to have to step up my game.

CHAPTER 4

My Dinner with Andrea

It was going to take time to implement my alternate plan for keeping track of Collin. Meanwhile, there was another lead I could follow.

The next afternoon, dressed in a suit, I was lurking across the street from Collin's office at quitting time. Binky had been left at home.

At six o'clock, I watched the same scene play itself out. Collin, as usual, was staring at the receptionist's retreating figure like a hyena studying its prey. For some reason, I thought of serial killer Gary Heidnik who had abducted six women, and held them prisoner in his basement. Collin wouldn't do that, would he? Maybe he'd done this before, and this was just the first time Alyssa had suspected something. I tried to believe that I was being paranoid, but there was something in his expression when he looked at his receptionist. He looked like someone who was close to the edge. It was important that I find out what the edge was, and how near he was to it.

Whatever their relationship, it was a reasonable bet that the receptionist might have some information I could use.

This evening he was going home, so he followed her to the C-Train station. Again, I stayed half a block behind on the other side of the street until I was ready to make my move.

When we got to the Eighth Street station Collin waited for the Crowfoot train that would take him home. The receptionist went to the east bound platform without buying a ticket.

Downtown is a free fare zone, so either she was going somewhere downtown, she had a transit pass, or liked to live dangerously. I bought a transit ticket, and stood nearby, out of sight of Collin behind the shelter.

A few minutes later the east-bound train for Saddletowne arrived. This being the extreme west end of downtown, there actually were a few completely empty seats despite it being rush hour. She sat in one, and I was able to slide in beside her.

I let out the sound that is the universal female signal for, "I've been in these shoes all day, and I need someone to rub my feet."

"Rough day?" She asked.

"Has it ever," I said. "Job hunting is brutal."

"I can believe it. What are you looking for?"

"Secretarial. I don't suppose there are any openings where you work?"

"Sorry, I'm the only one there."

I pretended to misunderstand.

"You have your own business?"

"No, I'm the sole receptionist for five offices in the same building."

"That must be hard. Maybe they should hire someone to help you."

"Good luck convincing that bunch of misers to do that. A couple of years ago they remodelled the outside of the building – but only the front. You don't want to know what a dump the back is."

I smiled, knowing exactly what it was like.

"It was worth asking. I had six interviews today, and three of them were men who were more interested in my bra size than how fast I could type."

"I know what you mean. Most of the guys where I work at least took the hint when I said I wasn't interested. But there's this one guy..."

"Creepy?"

"Like you wouldn't believe. He more than makes up for the other ones being gentlemen."

I put two fingers and a thumb to the side of my head in imitation of every bad psychic on TV.

"My spirit guide tells me that he's married."

She laughed. It looked good on her.

"You're amazing. I can't imagine going home to somebody like him, even if he was my type. I'd be afraid of hearing on the news that he was molesting children, or he had women chained up a storage unit some-where." Hearing her echo my imaginings about Collin did nothing to make me feel more at ease about Alyssa's husband. I made a mental note to get the number for a women's shelter, preferably in another city, just in case Alyssa needed to disappear quickly.

"I used to work for a guy like that," I said. "His wife wasn't chained up, but she might as well have been. She had to get up before six every morning just to make his lunch. He controlled everything. As far as I know, she had no job and no friends."

"Holy shit, that sounds like the guy where I work. His name wasn't Collin Blakeway, was it?"

"No, it was Adam. Is Collin the name of your guy?" She snorted.

"No way that he's *my* guy."

This was going well, so I kept feeding her my theories to see if she could confirm them.

"You know what I mean. Adam used to stay just barely this side of the sexual harassment line at work, then go home and bully his wife."

"I met Mrs. Blakeway once when they were going to some kind of client party. He was too lazy to go home first, so she had to come to the office to meet him. He made her sit out in reception while he finished what he was doing. Then he just walked out, and expected her to follow him like a dog. While she was waiting I got her to talk a little. She sounded like she was happy that he treats her like shit." She shuddered. "It really gave me the creeps. I would never let anybody do that to me."

"I'm with you on that. I think Adam's wife had a really abusive family, and just married the first man who asked her. He had a girlfriend on the side, too. I don't know how he treated her. He'd have me make the hotel reservations for him, so I'd know what a big man he was."

"At least my boss never asked me to do that. Maybe he makes his own reservations."

"So he doesn't have a girl friend on the side?"

"Not as far as I know."

"Amazing. Maybe he's in the market. Is he rich?"

"Don't make me call for an intervention. He's not the kind I'd wish on my worst enemy."

"Actually, I was thinking of taking him for every penny, and then dumping him. It would be easier than finding a job." She looked at me like I was an alien. "Don't worry, I'm kidding. I have more self-respect than that."

"If you met him, you'd know that he isn't worth it. He has the personality of a wet paper towel: a mean, wet paper towel."

We'd been ignoring the station announcements until now. Rundle was coming up.

"This is my stop," she said. There was a moment, not more than a second, when we locked eyes. I got the definite impression that she was trying to tell me something. I just didn't know what it was yet.

"If you don't have to be home right away, maybe you'd like to come to my place for coffee?"

"I'd love to." Maybe she had other terrible secrets about Collin.

"By the way, my name is Andrea Cinotti," she said as we crossed the street on the pedestrian overpass. She pronounced it ahn-DRAY-ah, with a rolled r sound. There was an accent to Cinotti, too.

"Veronica Chandler," I said.

"That's pretty name."

It was nice that she didn't make any kind of pop culture reference. I hate being compared with fictional investigators. You wouldn't believe the number of Sherlock and Raymond Chandler jokes people make, and yes, Veronica Mars too. It wouldn't be so bad if I occasionally heard a new one.

We headed toward the cluster of townhouses that lines that section of Thirty-sixth Street.

"I don't know why these guys get married in the first place," she said, continuing our conversation. "Not if they're going to cheat."

"My guess is that it's security. If you have a wife at home, it's not so bad if your girlfriend can't meet you some night."

"That sounds like Blakeway. He's an accountant. I can just imagine him thinking that women are like pens: always have two in case one doesn't work."

"I'm surprised you didn't say something about double entry book-keeping." She rolled her eyes.

"You're giving him too much credit. He's not much of a poster boy."

"I hope his wife is reconciled to that."

"I wouldn't make book on it."

I found Andrea refreshing. Women who make puns tend to be relatively rare. By then we were both laughing.

"He sounds really romantic."

"What about you? Do you have anyone at home?"

I had a flashback to my conflicting feelings about Brian.

"Just my cat. I had a date the other night but I don't know if it's going to go anywhere."

"Aha, a cat person. Me too. I love pussies." I wondered if she was continuing the double entendres.

We reached her unit, and she unlocked the door. The main floor of the townhouse had only a living room and kitchen. The bathroom and bedrooms must be upstairs. A long-haired tortoise-shell cat trotted to greet us, and jumped into Andrea's arms.

"This is Genvieve," she said, stroking her cat under the chin. "What's you cat's name?"

"Yoko Geri. It's Japanese for side kick."

"That's so cute."

The coffee was excellent. Andrea used a real percolator, the strength was perfect, and the coffee itself was top quality. She even had real cream. I was beginning to like this woman.

At this point I was pretty sure I'd gotten everything I could from her about Collin. As far as I was concerned, I was now off the clock.

We sat on her living room sofa with our coffee.

"Where were you born?" I asked.

"Cosenza, in southern Italy. We moved to Canada when I was ten."

"I thought so. At least, I knew you weren't born here."

"What gave me away?"

"The way you said your name."

"Damn, I've tried to lose my accent for years. Kids in school laughed at anything that's different."

"I think it's beautiful. Lyrical. Say something in Italian."

"*Ciao, Veronica. Sono felice di conoscerti.*"

"Wow. With a voice like that you should have a radio program. Is Cosenza anything like Calgary?"

"Some parts of it are. We lived in the Old Town, which is more like the pictures you see in travel books of ancient European villages."

"Why did you move?"

For an instant she seemed to be considering her answer, like she was afraid to say too much.

"My father thought that it was time for a fresh start. He's a cabinet maker."

"Did you ever work with him?"

"No. While I was in school I worked in an Italian market on Centre Street. How about you? What does your father do?"

"He's a chef. He taught me how to cool, and then I worked in his restaurant while I was in school."

"Oh my God, you don't mean Maison Chandler, do you?"

"You know it?"

"I love that place! My grandmother used to make gnocchi for us that was to die for. Maison Chandler is the only restaurant I've ever found that comes close."

I was particularly pleased to hear that. Dad hadn't had gnocchi on the menu until I gave him my recipe.

"Were your grandmother's gnocchi made with potatoes?"

"No, flour."

"I'm glad to hear that she's a traditionalist. Potatoes are a modern perversion."

Andrea furrowed her brow as she took another sip from her cup.

"Really How modern?"

"Oh," I said, waving my hand with a dismissive flick, "potato gnocchi can't be more than 400 years old. Real gnocchi is made with wheat, and goes back to Roman times. My father uses my recipe at the restaurant. Would you like to learn how to make it?"

You'd have thought I'd given her a winning lottery ticket.

We made a quick shopping trip in her car, getting a block of parmigi-ano cheese (not that pre-grated stuff), prosciutto, and fresh basil. The rest of the ingredients she said she had. I also picked up two bottles of a nice Italian white wine. With gnocchi, beer would have been a sacrilege.

I had her mix the flour with water, salt, and egg.

"I don't think my grandmother used egg ."

"You can make gnocchi without it, but it takes a lot more skill and practice. Cooking is art, but it's also chemistry and physics."

When she had a moderately stiff dough, I had her roll it out by hand on a floured board into ropes as thick as her finger. I cut the ropes into individual gnocchi for her. Then we both pressed them into forks to score the surfaces.

We set them aside while the pot of salted water came to a boil. While we were waiting, I prepared the butter sauce and she grated the parmigi-ano. I was glad to see she favoured a large amount.

The water was boiling, so with great drama I put the gnocchi into the pot, and covered it. A few minutes later, the little white curls had fluffed, and were floating on the surface.

"Don't over-cook them," I warned, "otherwise you get mush."

I strained the water from the pasta into a bowl of cold water to stop the cooking, then put the gnocchi into a frying pan with the herb butter to reheat them. After we'd plated them, I garnished with parmigiano, prosciutto, and finely chopped fresh basil.

By the time I brought it to her table, she'd gotten the wine from the refrigerator, and poured us two glasses.

"*Buon appetito*," I said, nearly exhausting my Italian. I can say *good appetite* in four languages.

The look on her face as she tasted the pasta was worth it.

"That," she said reverently, "is better than my grandmother's. Why aren't you working as a chef if you can cook like that?"

"I *was* a chef, or at least a sous-chef. Restaurant kitchens are way too high stress for me. I have more fun cooking for myself and friends. "

"You could at least teach cooking classes."

"Interesting. That's something I never considered. I'll have to think about it. In the meantime, *buona salute*." We toasted each other's health.

We had chocolate ice cream for dessert. I introduced her to the idea of drizzling Cointreau over it. By then we were well into the second bottle of wine, and were getting a bit silly. We also moved from the table back to the sofa.

"Tell me more about Cosenza," I said.

"It's old," she said after a moment. "When I came to Canada I couldn't understand why people talked about historical buildings that were built only a hundred years ago. Our house in the Old Town was built in the seventeenth century. There are Roman ruins everywhere. People have lived in the area for 40,000 years. Rome and its religion are newcomers compared with us."

Neither of us caught the implication for a moment, then I smiled. She looked worried.

"So you aren't Christian," I said, then sipped my wine. I was careful to sound non-judgemental. It took her a while to decide to answer.

"No. Four hundred years ago my ancestors lived in northern Italy and were *Benadanti*. Those are..."

"...magicians who battle evil witches. The Inquisition decided that they were the bad guys and persecuted them."

"How do you...?"

"I have a friend you should meet. The two of you probably have a lot of things in common."

"Is she Italian?"

"No, Colombian. She owns an occult shop in Marda Loop called Bhad-raKali."

"I've heard of it, but I haven't had time to visit it yet."

"When you do, tell Kali that I sent you."

"I will. Anyway, our family moved south to avoid persecution, and ended up in Cosenza. Some call us *Streghi*, but we predate them."

I realized something that should have occurred to me earlier. Andrea was becoming a friend, which meant that eventually she'd find out that I'd lied to her.

Crap. And the evening had been going so well.

"Andrea, there's something I have to tell you." She drained the rest of her glass and put it down a bit unsteadily.

"Don't tell me you're *Benadanti* too?"

"No, I'm more or less an outsider when it comes to the occult. I wasn't completely truthful with you earlier. I wasn't looking for a job today. I already have one. I'm a private investigator."

It took her a moment to connect the dots. She stiffened.

"So you didn't sit next to me by accident? You're investigating me?"

"No! Not at all. I was hired to find out if Collin Blakeway is having an affair."

She thought about it. "So you were just after information."

"No. Yes, at first. But I could have just stayed on the C-train when we got to Rundle. I came here because I enjoy your company. I really do like you, Andrea."

The sound of somebody riding past Andrea's unit on an overly loud motorcycle caught my attention, and I instinctively turned to look toward the window. When I turned back, Andrea's lips were on mine. They were soft, and the kiss was gentle. She tasted like chocolate and wine. It was nice.

It took my slightly drunk brain a moment to figure out what was happening, then I pulled back sharply. The first thing I saw was an embarrassed and hurt look in her eyes.

"I'm sorry," she said. "I thought maybe..."

I took a deep breath.

"No, I'm sorry. It's not your fault. I knew there was something you were trying to tell me, but I didn't know what."

"You aren't interested in women?"

"Not even a bit," I said, then thought about it honestly. "Well, maybe a tiny bit. It was a lovely kiss. It's just that I really like men."

She looked down at her lap, and I thought I saw the beginning of a tear. I took her hands in mine.

"It's okay, Andrea. I'm not offended. It was just a misunderstanding."

I can be such a moron at times. She erupted into tears anyway. I was comfortable with my sexual boundaries, mostly, but I still felt like I'd done something terrible to her.

Now that I was thinking about it, I realized that she'd been dropping little hints ever since the train. I'd just been too dense to pick up on them.

Despite thinking of myself as completely heterosexual, I had to admit to myself that the kiss was nice because it was a nice kiss. The sensation was wonderful regardless of the source, but for me, trying to imagine doing anything more with another woman was an emotional null. I could imagine it, but there was no excitement to the image. At least, that's what I'd always thought.

Andrea said something nearly unintelligible through her tears. I got the gist of it.

Putting my arms around her, I held her as she cried.

"I know. I get lonely too."

She mumbled into my shoulder again, then started crying harder.

"No," I said, "just because I'm straight doesn't mean it's that much easier. I have a hormone condition that has to be controlled with medication, or I'd be out on the streets attacking every man I could find. I like to think that I'm not a slut, but sometimes it gets so overwhelming."

I thought about Brian. Then I thought about Andrea, a gay woman I'd known for about the same length of time, who had given me a kiss I'd enjoyed, and was now soaking my blouse with her tears. Was it so terrible to kiss a woman? Did I really feel no excitement at all?

Sometimes, life can be confusing.

Eventually, she cried herself out and sat up. She sniffed, and wiped her eyes with her hands.

"I'm sorry."

"Don't be. I'd still like us to be friends, if you want."

She nodded, still wiping her eyes.

"Good. Because I still have to teach you how to make porchetta ."

She laughed, just a little. That was better.

"Would you really attack every man in sight?"

"Probably." Maybe it was the wine, but I felt like confessing. "It can be a bit crazy at times. More than crazy. Sometimes I feel like a complete slut."

"Veronica, I can tell that it bothers you. Do you know what the definition of a slut is?"

"You mean apart from a woman who will screw everything in sight?"

"A slut is a woman who is having more fun than you think she should."

I thought about that for a moment, and got more confused. When I thought of myself a slut, was it because I was having more fun than I thought I *should* be having? What the hell was that about? Why were men who had lots of sex "players," but women who did that were "sluts?"

"I'll have to think about that." I took in a deep breath, let it out, and looked at my watch. It was time to go.

I took out one of my business cards.

"Here's my phone number. Give me a call. I'd really like to stay in touch."

"You're leaving?"

"Believe me, it's not because of you or the kiss. I need to get up early tomorrow to keep tabs on Collin. I'm just glad I didn't drive. That really would not be a good idea right now."

She smiled again.

"If your head feels anything like mine, you're right." She became serious. "Are you sure about this?"

"I'm sure." I put my card on the coffee table. "You aren't getting rid of me that easily."

I held my arms out and we hugged. Her half of the hug was slightly awkward, and I got the feeling that she wasn't very experienced with women. Or anyone else for that matter.

"Wait!" She went into the kitchen and rummaged through a drawer. She came back with a piece of paper and a pen. "Here's my number. Or you can call me at work if you have that number."

"Thanks, Andrea. It really has been a wonderful evening."

Not to mention a wonderful kiss. But I didn't want to say that to her.

Not until I'd had a chance to think about it more.

It took almost an hour for me to get home by train. During the ride, I kept thinking about Andrea. She didn't have much information about Collin, but I'd made a new friend.

I also thought about much I had liked her kiss. Maybe my sexuality wasn't as simple as I had thought. That was just what I needed: a more complicated sex life. If I turned out to be bisexual it would double my chances of finding a good lover, but was that just an easy rationale because I was horny?

I had a lot to think about that, preferably when I was much less drunk. I tried thinking about Brian instead.

But it was a very nice kiss.

CHAPTER 5

Olympic Event

Collin's late nights had started about a month before, and at first they averaged once a week. Their frequency was slowly rising. So far, this week, he'd been "working late" twice. It shouldn't be long until opportunity to follow him occurred, as long as I could solve the problem of the bus.

The obvious thing was to get on the bus with him. It certainly would be obvious to follow him through an unknown number of bus changes, and suddenly jump off when he did. If he started to suspect that someone was following him I'd lose a major advantage. It's much easier to shadow somebody who doesn't know that you exist.

My age and sex gave me certain advantages as an investigator. As my recent evening with Andrea illustrated, most people didn't suspect me of being a professional snoop until it was too late. More than once I'd used my fluttering eyelashes as a gentle form of enhanced interrogation. During surveillance of straight men, however, those same attributes made me more noticeable when I wanted to remain unseen. There was always the chance that Collin was secretly gay, but the way he'd looked at his receptionist made that highly unlikely. Getting on the bus with him had too great a probability of blowing my cover.

If I had a big agency with several investigators, we could have arranged rotating surveillance. That wasn't going to happen any time soon.

There was a better way, if I could pull it off. The big problem was getting Alyssa to help me with it.

During the past several months I'd reinvested some of my hard-earned money in toys. My most recent purchase was now lying on my coffee table. Alyssa was staring at it like it was a snake.

She was terrified that we'd be caught, and it took me almost an hour, sitting beside her on my couch, to convince her that nothing bad would happen. The mere fact that she was so afraid of her husband told me that, whether he had a mistress or not, there was something not right about him. By definition, people in normal, happy relationships aren't terrified of their partner.

"But what if he looks inside?" She said for the fifth time. I repressed the urge to break something, and used my reasonable voice.

"You put his lunch in the brief case every day, right?"

She nodded.

"How long have you been doing that?"

"Six years."

"In those six years, have you ever seen anything else in the brief case? Papers? A pencil? Lint?"

"No," she reluctantly admitted.

"Trust me, he's not going to start searching his lunchbox now."

"But, I don't understand computers and things."

Once again I resisted the urge to sigh deeply and growl. I tried be patient, but it wasn't one of my strong suits.

"It's easy, you don't have to know anything technical."

From the coffee table I picked up what looked like a USB drive and a small battery pack.

"Plug the battery into the logger, like this. It only goes in one way, so you can't make a mistake. Then peel the coating off the tape, and stick it into the bottom of the file pocket of his brief case." I demonstrated on the case I used for my laptop, then pulled the logger free. "Got it?" I asked as I replaced the piece of two-sided tape with a fresh strip.

"I think so."

Talking to her was frustrating as hell. She seemed to have no will of her own, which meant that getting her to do something was like pushing a car uphill. With enough effort you could start it rolling, but as soon as you stopped pushing it stopped. Placing the GPS logger in her husband's brief case was something that a moderately bright five-year old could have handled.

That a normally intelligent woman in her thirties was terrified of making a mistake, and was so deep into learned helplessness, told me a lot about how much she'd been psychologically abused over the years. I wondered if her husband had started the process, or if he'd just continued what somebody else had begun.

The thought of anybody being that abused really pissed me off, and I fully intended to introduce Alyssa to my favourite psychologist as soon as we settled what was happening with her husband. She deserved a much better life than this.

At the moment, however, Alyssa was useless to me. I unplugged the logger, and put it on the table.

"All right, I'll do it. You said that you make his lunch at six A.M.?"

"Yes, he likes me to do it in the morning so it doesn't get as stale by the time he has lunch."

"Great. I'll be in your back yard at six o'clock tomorrow morning. Just place the brief case outside the back door for a few moments, and I'll do the rest. Can you do that?"

"I think so."

I resisted the urge to shake her. "Good. It'll be easy. Nothing will go wrong."

Covert operation was perhaps too grand a term for sneaking in and out of a suburban back yard before dawn. Regardless, I dressed in a dark grey track suit. In low light, most objects appear grey: someone dressed in black can actually stand out. My balaclava was rolled up to look like a toque. Rather than boots, I also wore my sneakers. They have more grip on smooth surfaces.

The Blakeway yard backed onto John Laurie Boulevard, a major four-lane, divided road running east-west across Calgary just south of Nose Hill. Along this section, the city hadn't bothered to install the concrete noise-abatement walls that were used elsewhere along the boulevard. Instead, the houses in this area were separated from the road noise by a uniform line of two-metre high wooden fencing. There was a good five or more metres of grass between the fence line and the road to allow vehicles to pull off in an emergency.

Or when doing covert ops.

Unless a resident heard you screaming, the unbroken fence prevented a motorist without a cell phone from getting help from a homeowner. The nearest accessible help was at least a kilometre away. That would make it less suspicious for Binky to be left on his own for half an hour or so.

There wasn't much traffic at 5:30. After a night of minimal vehicle exhaust, and industrial pollution, the air smelled mostly of spruce trees. It was just cool enough to be invigorating, something I desperately needed. Despite having two cups of coffee in me, it still felt like, once again, I was up before dawn.

The sky was still dark as I pulled off the road, and onto the grass. I turned on Binky's hazard lights, and raised the hood so it would look like I had car trouble. By my calculations, the Blakeway house should be right behind the fence.

The fence was almost half a metre taller than I am. I took a running jump, and my grippy sneakers actually gave me a little extra height on the boards. I was able to grab the top of the fence. Pulling myself over was another matter, but it only took a few seconds. It wasn't easy, but not uncomfortably difficult. I shouldn't have any trouble climbing back over.

My first hurdle (if you'll pardon the pun) was getting down again. Alyssa hadn't mentioned that balsam poplars had been planted along the back fence. I couldn't just drop down without crashing through branches and possibly impaling myself. I had to lower myself until I was hanging full length, then let go and hope. It mostly worked. One branch stuck me in the back but was springy enough that I was just bruised instead of gored.

I rubbed the sore spot on my back, and looked around before proceeding. There was one other tiny detail that Alyssa hadn't thought was important when were discussing the layout. The yard sloped down toward the house, with a small retaining wall under the back fence to keep the ground from subsiding. It also meant that the fence was effectively another half metre higher on this side with no room to take a run at it.

Crap.

It shouldn't be an insurmountable problem (sorry) as long as I could climb a tree to make up the height difference. Poplars aren't known for their strong branches, so I'd have to be careful not to snap one off and leave evidence that I'd been there. Balsam poplars also weren't known for being easy to climb, but it shouldn't be too bad. After completing my mission I'd have plenty of time for a leisurely exit.

It would have been a lot easier to come into the yard through the side gate, but when I asked about it Alyssa told me that her husband always kept it locked. Of course, Alyssa didn't have access to a key. I'm sure that he thought it would have given her too much control of her life to be able to go from the front yard to the back without going through the house.

Once on the ground, I carefully made my way out of the crisscrossing branches, across some landscaping boulders, and onto a brick-paved path. The path wound its way from the back deck, and up through the garden. In the darkness I could barely see that it terminated at the back fence: a path to nowhere.

The patio door opened onto the deck, just as she'd described it. I cupped my hand over my watch to hide the light when I pushed the illumination button. The faint green light made me blink. It was still an hour until sunrise, but I was a few minutes behind schedule. The lights in the kitchen were on, so Alyssa must be up. The brief case should be waiting for me by the door.

It wasn't.

Maybe she was too scared to risk it, or she might have put it out earlier, and already brought it back inside. Collin should still be in bed so she should be alone. Maybe I could attract her attention through the glass.

I looked into the kitchen. It was empty. Perhaps she was in the bathroom or getting dressed.

Collin wandered into view, wearing a tartan flannel bathrobe. I ducked back from the door, my heart pounding. What the hell was he doing up at this hour?

Off to my left was a small gazebo with a cedar shingle roof and wooden lattice sides. It was out of range of direct light from the house. Inside I would be hidden even if Collin came outside, and I still should be able to see most of the kitchen.

As I peered through the lattice, Collin got a cup of coffee from the automatic machine on the kitchen counter, then went back the way he'd come. Maybe his conscience was bothering him, and he couldn't sleep.

A faint, rosy hint of sunrise was visible in the east. If something didn't happen soon I'd have to leave. It was a pity that I'm not a morning person. There was a gentle calmness to the air at this hour that seemed to encourage quiet contemplation.

The only thing to spoil this pastoral moment was the cloud of mosquitoes. As soon as I stopped moving they were everywhere. For added concealment, and as armour, I lowered my balaclava over my face. That left my eyes and ankles as targets. It was also far too warm.

Through the back window of the house I could see something moving in the kitchen. Alyssa was now standing at the island, her back to me, while she did things that I couldn't quite see from that angle. The brief case was now standing open on the counter beside her. From the movement of her arms, it looked like she might be slicing something. Every so often she'd look off to one side. Maybe Collin was watching her.

Ten minutes later, she closed the case, and furtively brought it to the back door.

I was up like a shot, not wanting to waste a second if Collin was around. Fortunately, she was the kind of person who freezes when startled, instead of screaming when a masked figure appeared before her out of the darkness.

"Alyssa, it's all right, it's me," I whispered, pulling up the balaclava.

She said nothing, so I took the case from her, popped it open, took the GPS logger and battery from my pocket, connected them, pressed the tape into position in the file pocket, and handed back the brief case. The whole procedure had taken less than fifteen seconds.

"Remember," I whispered, "remove the logger when you make lunch after he's had a late night. I'll get it from your later."

She was still petrified, so I manually turned her around, and gave her a small push into the house. I slid the glass door closed behind her with one knuckle to avoid leaving fingerprints.

The kitchen lights had ruined my night vision, so I carefully moved away from the door to let my eyes recover. I lowered my balaclava against the bugs.

At that moment, something stabbed me between my shoulder blades.

Stab might be too strong a word. On the other hand, if the mosquito was big enough that its proboscis had gone through my track suit and jabbed my back, it might exactly the right word. It felt like I needed to reach the spot between my shoulder blades and pull it out before I passed out from blood loss. Damn, that hurt. How big was that sucker?

During the brief distraction I tripped over a freaking lawn chair. It was one of those cheap ones with nylon webbing and thin aluminum tubing that makes a big racket when it falls over with almost 60 kilograms of startled private investigator tangled in it. That would have been bad enough, but the deck also had a built-in, recessed hot tub. I fell onto the cover.

Evidently, Collin didn't approve of rigid pool covers. They probably cost too much for his taste. Instead, he'd bought one of those cheap, floating bubble-wrap things with no structural integrity. Water leaped for joy, and made a big splash as it went everywhere. My top half was soaked, my feet were still tangled in the chair, and my head was underwater.

At least the water was warm.

I floundered for entirely too long, trying to do a reverse sit-up while my hands scrabbled to find the edge of the tub and get leverage. I managed to grab it, and push myself out. By now, there was not much point in trying to be stealthy, so I kicked the chair free of my legs. Inside the house, a male voice was bellowing. This was not going as well as I'd hoped.

I sprinted up the path to the fence, cooling water trickling from my soaked top down the inside of my trousers. I pushed my way through the tree branches, and jumped for the top of the fence.

Despite the adrenaline fuelling my jump, I wasn't even close. I slid down the fence boards, and another branch caught me in the same spot on my back.

On my second jump I didn't even get that high. My clothing got caught on something, and I was knocked off balance. I fell backward, and rolled down the slope toward the garden.

It was a good thing that the glass cold frame broke my fall.

Do you have any idea how much noise breaking glass makes in the silent hour before dawn? It's a lot more than the noise of an angry man screaming inside his house.

The outside light came on. I could see Collin looking out the patio door.

I was stunned for a moment, then something sharp poked my leg, encouraging me to move carefully. The track suit was thick enough that I didn't think that I had been cut. I didn't dare dust myself off in case there were splinters of glass sticking to me. Most likely, the only thing that had saved me so far was the time it took him to put his shoes on before coming out in hot pursuit.

I struggled to my feet without using my hands to avoid the pieces of glass, and tried climbing one of the trees, heedless of whether I was leaving traces or not. At this point that was the least of my worries. A few snapped twigs would make no difference when I was leaving a trail of water, broken glass, and possibly blood.

Just as the patio door slammed open, I got high enough that I could throw myself at the top of the fence. For an awful, painful moment, my ribs balanced on the top, then I got one foot onto the boards. Before I could swing around, and let myself down gracefully I fell head first. It wasn't elegant but at least I landed on the correct side of the fence, albeit on my back. The wind was knocked out of me, and all I could do was lie there, and try to will my diaphragm to work.

Covert operation was definitely too grand a term.

From inside the yard I could hear Collin yelling things like "who's there?" interspersed with various obscenities, threats of police action, and bodily harm.

That didn't bother me. Although I'd made a mess in the yard, I was almost certain that, mostly by good luck, I'd left no identifying evidence behind. Even if he'd seen me, all he had for a description was a dark grey on dark grey figure whose face was covered with dark grey. Unless he was an Olympic athlete, it was unlikely that he could follow me over the fence. I'd gotten away, although not very cleanly.

As I limped toward my car, I heard the rattle of a gate being unlocked.

The rising sun was beginning to illuminate things, and with the sound telling me where to look, I could see an outline on the fence. It was more like a door than a normal gate. On this side, the only clue was the faint outline which I'd missed in the earlier darkness. That must be why the path led all the way to the fence. In hindsight it was obvious. Also obvious, in hindsight, was that I should have tried jumping the side gate on the way out. I could have immediately disappeared into the residential streets, even though it would have left me with a two kilometre walk back to Binky.

Well done, Veronica. You should write a book on trade craft.

There was no time to start Binky and escape. My license plate would easily be visible to Collin as I drove away. As long as he didn't know that the car was mine, I was safe. The only problem was that I needed to get under cover, and apart from Binky the nearest cover was at least two hundred metres away on the other side of the boulevard. It sounded like I had about three seconds before the gate opened. Nobody could run that fast. My only chance was to vanish into thin air. I threw myself down on the ground and tried to burrow as far under the driver's side as I could, hoping that he wouldn't check the car too closely.

The gate banged open, and from under the car I saw his legs standing in the opening, dimly back lit by his house. I could feel him staring at the car, looking for the intruder, while the occasional vehicle whizzed past on the road. The morning traffic was beginning to pick up. All I needed was for some sharp-eyed and kindly motorist to see my body lying on the ground, and stop to help. Then there'd be all sorts of fun.

A third leg joined his other two. That made no sense at all until I realized that he'd brought along a weapon. From the width it was probably something like a two by four or a baseball bat. I had no doubt at all that, rather than taking me into custody, he'd break it over my head, and claim self defence. Maybe he had a knife with him that he'd plant on my unprotesting corpse as justification for my murder.

I really must do something about my imagination.

I lay in the grass, trying to breathe quietly through my mouth as Binky's hot engine made small, metallic noises above me. Tiny prickles of glass poked me in the stomach. The legs moved toward the car.

There wasn't enough room for me to turn my head to look. All I could do was lie there, waiting for him to look under the car, and haul me out. Mosquitoes jabbed me where ever they could and sucked blood. I didn't dare to twitch, let along slap at them.

Several thousand years went by. I could hear engine noises, my own heart pounding, and the occasional vehicle. What I couldn't hear was anything that gave a hint as to what Collin was doing.

Two legs moved into view, accompanied by some really impressive swearing as he walked back to the gate.

He stood there for a while, leaning on his weapon. Then the third leg disappeared, the feet turned, and the gate slammed behind him.

The sensible thing to do would be to take off the top of my track suit, and wring it out before getting in the car. It wouldn't take long, and if I squatted on the passenger side my semi-naked state would be out of sight of other drivers. I wiggled out from under the car, losing my balaclava in the process. Every move I made squelched.

That's when I noticed the blue and red flashing lights illuminating Binky's side.

My only consolation was that the police officer couldn't possibly be my mother. Not only was she in Ireland, but as a homicide detective she drove an unmarked car, not one with a roof-mounted light bar.

The dazzling white beam from a flashlight caught me just as I stood up.

"Is everything all right?" Oh hell. I knew that lovely Yorkshire accent. "Veronica?"

"Hi, Stan, fancy meeting you here. Can you lower the light, please?"

The death ray immediately shone on my feet while huge purple spots danced before my eyes. "Sorry about that," he said.

Stan Watkins was one of the Yorkshire policemen who had been recruited by Calgary a few years before. I'd met him while doing my internship at the Calgary Police Service. He also went to the Krav Maga classes I attended. Stan, Nick Holley, and my mum also got together for practice at the gum. Now that I was older, I'd joined what I called their Abuse Club. It was far from unusual for all four of us to have vivid bruises the day after, despite our use of full body armour.

"Did Binky let you down?" As a Brit, he approved of my car's name. I'd taken it from a Terry Pratchett novel.

"No, some piece of junk get caught underneath. A piece of metal." I looked at the car as I said it to hide my face. I'm a good liar but Stan has been a policeman for a long time. "I pulled it free."

"You seem a bit damp."

I looked at my dripping sleeve like I'd never seen it before, desperately trying to think of a good reason why I looked like I'd just been swimming fully clothed. Apart from the truth, of course, which was that I'd just been swimming fully clothed.

"I was doing surveillance for a case, and the damned automated lawn sprinklers came on."

He looked at me for a full five seconds while I sweated, then he raised one eyebrow.

"Right, then. If you're good to go, I'll see you later."

He watched as I got in the car and drove away, carefully signalling before pulling onto John Laurie. In my rear view mirror I saw his silhouette against his car headlights. He was bending over to pick something up.

Oh crap, my balaclava. Maybe he'd think it had been there for a while.

Right. My freshly laundered, still smelling of fabric softener, wet from the hot tub, and warm from my head balaclava.

My name wasn't in it, so technically he didn't know for sure that it was mine. He wouldn't do anything official about it.

However, with that and the soaked top, he'd know that I had been up to mischief, and I'd never hear the end of it.

I drove home with the heat on full, trying to warm myself as the now cold water trickled down my legs and soaked the car seat. It probably would take a week to dry out. In the meantime I'd have to remember to drape towels over the seat so I wouldn't have a wet back.

What a lovely start to a new day.

CHAPTER 6

Tempest Fugit

The morning after his next night of "working late," Alyssa actually managed to get the GPS logger out of Collin's brief case without having a nervous breakdown. I was frankly amazed that she'd done it, and slightly proud of her.

Despite her fears, he didn't catch her and, clearly, he suspected nothing. If he had, we both knew that he wouldn't have been slow to express his anger.

I went to her place to pick it up.

Back at home I plugged the logger into my computer. It had worked as well as I could have hoped, which is to say, not as well as these things do on television. The trackers on TV always show exactly where the subject is, even if they are inside a building, a subway station, or anywhere else. In real life, GPS requires a clear line of sight between the satellites and the receiver. A hundred things can screw that up, including trees, vehicle roofs, being indoors, tunnels, and signal reflections from surrounding buildings. Some of these will completely interrupt the signal, while others just cause the reported position to be vague or wrong.

That's why I was waiting for him at this bus stop. The GPS track across the city was vague at times as the receiver lost its satellite lock, but this point was firm, and it seemed to be the last time he was in a vehicle. At least, it was the last time he was travelling at vehicle speeds. From here, it looked like he had gone to his destination on foot. All I was sure about that was that it seemed to be several blocks south.

The weather had been lovely when Binky and I had left my apartment: a sunny, warm, and dry early evening in September. Everything was perfectly safe and sane.

By the time I got to Forest Lawn, and was approaching the co-ordinates, the clouds that were forming above me looked like the Red Sea scene in De Mille's *The Ten Commandments*. The sunlight took on a surreal, golden quality as the rapidly darkening masses of cloud churned overhead. The radio weather report gave no indication that a storm was brewing.

A few minutes later, with no other preliminaries, the storm began. No light patter of droplets warned people that they should get under cover. The sun vanished, eaten by the black clouds, the temperature dropped by at least ten degrees, the wind suddenly blasted across the road carrying billowing clouds of dust. Cars swerved as they were pushed to the side by wind gusts. Pedestrians staggered, and I saw a man fall down. Then the heavens opened.

I'd never appreciated that phrase before. This wasn't a metaphor, it was a literal description. Unbelievably, even guys in muscle cars abruptly slowed to twenty kilometres per hour. Most people, including me, were going slower than that for the excellent reason that the visibility was the next best thing to zero. At one point I couldn't even see the end of Binky's hood. I'd have pulled over except that I couldn't see well enough to make sure I would be out of oncoming traffic, and not hitting a light pole or pedestrian. It was actually safer to keep crawling forward.

Next time you are at a cocktail party, here's a fun fact with which to amaze and astonish your friends: During an average year, Calgary receives about a third of a metre of precipitation, almost 11% of it in September.

Here's a more important fact: Calgary weather is notoriously unpredictable. When I was a child, I remember running back and forth between the front and back windows of our house. At the front it was raining and thundering. In the back it was sunny. This is not a city for people who can't handle whimsy in their lives.

If somebody had told me with a straight face that our entire year's worth of rain was falling that night, I would have had a hard time disbelieving them. Within seconds, all I could see was the blurry ghost of the car in front of me, and that only because the driver was smart enough to have put his lights on. I did the same, hoping to avoid someone smashing into my back bumper.

I almost missed the turn into the Sobey's parking lot, spotting the illuminated sign on the side of the building only at the last moment. The building itself was invisible. I found an open stall in what should have been a perfect position, about 50 metres from Collin's bus stop. The moment I looked toward the road I realized my mistake.

In this rain, I could rarely see the massive grocery store, let alone the bus shelter. As I watched, the rain came down harder. Seventeenth Avenue was turning into a swirling, grey lake that was rising above the curb as the storm sewers overloaded. The water was so deep in places that cars were beginning to stall out as the water drowned their electrical systems.

I crept out of my parking spot, trying not to run over shoppers who were frantically running with their heads down, trying to reach their vehicles before they needed an outboard motor to get home. I parked as close to the bus stop as I could, about 15 metres. The glass enclosure of the bus shelter was only occasionally visible.

The rain pounded vehicles and pavement; the water jumping knee high into the air when it hit. The street was officially a river as I watched a Canada goose float by about five metres in front of Binky. I wondered how I was going to get home. During the lulls, it sounded like someone was doing a particularly energetic drum solo on Binky's roof. When the downpour resumed, the drummer was swept away by someone dropping a million dead chickens onto the car in batches of a dozen. I'd treated Binky's windshield with a coating that was supposed to repel water. It worked well in rain, but in this stuff I could barely see anything outside the car.

The good news was that I had a perfect surveillance situation. The only way Collin would notice me is if he was standing on the roof of my car, and then only because his feet would have been slightly drier than they would be anywhere else.

Binky's trunk contained all kinds of cool PI stuff that I'd been accumulating. At that moment, the most important thing to me was that, among the disguises, surveillance equipment, emergency supplies, snow shovel, and a bucket of gravel, was a rubberized military-surplus poncho. Its lovely, fashionable shade of olive drab made for great camouflage in everything but a big field of snow. It was heavy as sin, made for someone much taller than me and, if I had to leave the car, it might stand some chance of keeping me partially dry even in this torrent.

One of the things I like about Binky is the way I can get into the trunk through the back seat without going outside. I wiggled into the back, then did some athletic things to pull the seat down without sitting on it. Watching me put the poncho on in the cramped space would have been entertaining to someone looking in, if they could have seen anything through the fogged and water-streaked windows. A few minutes later, I was back in the front seat, decked out in the height of covert rain fashion. It's amazing the way skills gained during back seat make-out sessions can prepare one for a career in law enforcement.

Fifteen minutes later, and way behind schedule, I could see a smear of light in the distance that gradually resolved into two widely-spaced headlights. Tonight "in the distance" meant about half a block. A moment later, what I assumed to be the Route One bus appeared. It pushed a wave of water ahead of it as it slowed to a stop. The back doors opened, and a passenger got off. The water was level with the back step of the bus. Whoever it was immediately went into the bus shelter. The bus slowly pulled away, leaving an impressive rooster tail behind it.

I started the window wipers and, in the fraction of a second between the wiper's passing, and the windshield becoming a distorted blur again, I was almost sure that I recognized Collin. In the shelter, he struggled to open his umbrella, then staggered away through the rain and gusting wind.

Now all I had to do was find out exactly what he was doing here, on a night when anybody with any sense whatsoever would have been heading for high ground. Preferably in the Sahara.

Collin, apparently unaware of the irony of carrying a red umbrella, and wearing a bright yellow rain coat while trying to be sneaky, was making his way south through the Sobey's parking lot. How the hell had he known to bring the umbrella and coat to work? Either he'd heard a weather report I hadn't, or he was psychic. I never did find out for sure, but from what came later, I had my suspicions.

On any other night, it would have been ludicrously easy to follow him. Tonight, I had difficulty seeing the bright colours more than five or ten metres away. For once, that was good. If I could barely see him in that outfit, he'd never see me in my Canadian Forces ninja poncho.

Just to be sure, I skulked around the edge of the building as he waded through the swirling puddles. As I lurked, the cold spray beat against my chilled face. Despite the hood, enough of it got through to plaster my hair to the side of my head before it trickled down inside the poncho, leaving a cold shiver on my ribs. Lightning flashed, on average, about once every thirty seconds, followed very closely by mighty peals of thunder that seemed to shake the ground. The storm was right on top of us.

Sometimes, such as when I was watching Collin from the coffee shop, or being eaten by bugs and drowned at six A.M., being a private investigator sucks. At other times, like right then, it is pure exhilaration. I felt the joy of the hunt, inherited from a hundred thousand generations of ancestors trotting across the African plains, tracking their next meal with their stone-tipped spears. Yes, I know that traditionally, the men hunted and the women gathered. Who cares? I am woman, hear me roar! It was a night just made for playing *Ride of the Valkyries* at top volume on a gigantic stereo, and daring the gods to do their worst.

Maybe somebody already had.

I wiped my eyes to clear them of water, and tried to pull the poncho further over my face. Through the rain, I saw Collin abandon the parking lot for Fiftieth Street. I hurried to catch up, the hammering rain covering all other sounds. I hid behind a post box on the street corner, just peering over the top to keep him in sight. The rain pounding on the metal surface sprayed in my eyes, so I had to wipe my face again and move back from the box. His blurred image was still walking, innocent as could be, along a street lined with industrial outfits.

When his image became too blurry, I moved up to a line of bushes beside a loading dock. Collin continued south, not even bothering to look behind him as he crossed the next avenue. Who would be following him on a night like this? Certainly nobody sane.

Abruptly, the street lights flared and went out, the bulbs showing a residual orange glow that slowly faded to black. The sharp crack of an explosion sounded a moment later, briefly competing with the thunder. Somewhere nearby, a power substation had given up the ghost in the rain. Maybe it had been hit by lightning.

Now we were both in the dark, so I moved in closer. The next block had a building with an awning on the corner where I could hide for a few seconds. I was effectively deaf due to the rain pounding down on my poncho. I'd heard the explosion. I doubt that I'd have heard a car horn unless it was beside me.

Shortly after that, we crossed an unpaved lane that marked the end of civilization. The city didn't think it was reasonable to install sidewalks in a commercial area where only lunatics would walk instead of driving. Collin was following a footpath worn through grass beside the street, then crossed the road where at least there was gravel underfoot.

I had nothing but a chain link fence for cover on either side, and the rain looked like it was tapering off.

The business on his side of the street was some kind of industrial supply yard. My side was a mobile home park.

I stuck to the east side of the street. At least there I could find occasional large bushes along the fence separating the street from the mobile homes. When Collin reached the next intersection, he turned right.

The rain picked up again. I had to hurry across the street to make sure I didn't lose him. That meant wading through a puddle the size of Lake Superior that came up to mid-calf on me. It was a pity that my boots only came up to my ankles. My feet were wet and cold within seconds. Despite my best efforts, my poncho was dragging through the water, and there was actually enough of a current to make walking difficult. I was no longer quite so exhilarated about the chase.

The avenue where he'd turned was lined on both sides by commercial strip malls. He crossed to the south side, and disappeared into an unmarked doorway between a printing shop, and an auto parts supplier.

It was odd place to meet a mistress. It certainly wasn't a particularly romantic location, although there was a hooker stroll a few blocks north. I hoped the women had gotten under cover before they caught pneumonia or downed.

Maybe something more was going on. I wasn't stupid enough to take my phone out of its nice, dry pocket, so I made a mental note to check later for any on-premises swing clubs in Calgary. Even if there were, it was unlikely that he'd be attending alone. From what I'd heard, they preferred women or couples as members, not single men. Especially not ones as personable as Collin.

The side street was drier, with streams of water only as deep as the curb swirling along it. I waded across, heedless of my sodden feet. It wasn't as if they could get any colder or wetter. The door he'd entered was a blank, industrial steel one, not intended for public access. At this point he was probably two minutes ahead of me.

I was surprised when I tried the door; it was unlocked. Once inside, I fought to ease it shut against the competing pulls of the door closer and the wind gusts. Fluorescent lights on the ceiling partially lit the grimy corridor, except where tubes were burned out or missing. Stacked cardboard boxes and miscellaneous equipment lined the walls, making it a death trap in case of fire. Collin was nowhere in sight. The corridor was silent except for the annoying buzz of old fluorescent fixtures, and the muted pounding of rain on the roof.

I didn't need Mantracker to tell me where Collin had gone. There was a trail of obvious drips and wet footprints to a door at the end of the hall. It was industrial grey like the rest, and marked with a stencilled number 12.

I put my ear to the door – nothing. The loudest sound, apart from the storm, was the squishing as my feet redistributed the water in my saturated boots. They sounded like somebody trying to sneak through a particularly muddy swamp.

The gap at the bottom of the door seemed promising. I knelt down with my ear as close as possible, and could hear muttering from inside. I couldn't make out what was being said. It sounded like only one person – a man. The floor smelled like old concrete, machine oil, and some kind of solvent.

The gap was at least a finger wide. I had no interest in coming face-to-face with Collin, and as long as I wasn't disturbed, I should be able to get a video of what was going on without having to confront anybody. He seemed like the type that was too likely to become violent without warning. There was no question that I could take him in a fair fight. Sadly, I'd learned that it was far too easy for unfair things to happen. Easy money is always the best money.

My trusty inspection mirror showed movement inside the room, but the gap was too small for me to get my eye close enough to the door to get a good viewing angle. I shook my cold, wet hands rapidly to try to get most of the water off them, and some warmth in. Then I carefully took my phone out of my inside pocket. I positioned the camera lens by guessing, and let it record for five minutes. I hit the playback button with a prune-like finger tip to see if I'd made a sex tape good enough to get Alyssa out of her marriage.

What the hell?

The view from floor level was suggestive rather than revealing. Collin was visible up to his thighs, or waist when he moved further from the door. As far as I could see, he was alone, wandering back and forth in the middle of the room and reading aloud. The object in his hands might have been a big book; I only caught glimpses of the bottom edge of it. Assorted furniture was pushed back against the far wall to give him space.

All of that was inexplicable, but it wasn't strange. The strange thing was that it looked like he'd removed his clothing, and donned some kind of robe. It was covered in a variety of symbols, and was too small for him. The hem was far up his skinny calves.

The other things that were obvious were four candles sitting on the floor. They looked like they might have been set in a circle.

In practice, I knew next to nothing about the occult. Just a bit of Wiccan stuff I'd learned from Kali. This didn't appear to be Wiccan, but at the same time the general flavour was similar.

I had to decide whether to stay, and try to get better video, or bug out before there was a real chance of me getting caught. Unless I found another location to shoot from, the video I had recorded was probably as good as it was going to get for now. It looked like I might need to invest in a fibre-optic snake for these kinds of situations.

The corridor was fairly warm, and the wet footprints were drying, albeit slowly. He looked like he'd be at this a while, so I found a cleanish rag in one of the boxes and used it to erase my trail as I went down the hall backward to the exit. By the time he was done he wouldn't know that another person had been outside his door.

The wind almost tore the door out of my grasp as I opened it, but as I waded back toward Binky, the rain eased up enough that I thought there was some chance of me getting home alive. The only person I saw was leaning against the corner of the building where I'd hid before. He was lighting a cigarette in his cupped hands, and the lighter showed a brief flash of a man in a fedora and trench coat. He looked annoyingly dry, like he'd just stepped outside. Already soaked to the bone, all I wanted was to get home, get dry, get warm, and consider what I'd discovered.

Collin wasn't having an affair. Instead, there was something weird was going on involving a religious or magical ritual, and it looked like the money might not be so easy after all.

All I could hope was that there would be no dwarfs or ponies involved this time.

CHAPTER 7

The Player

The next morning was sunny and mild, with no sign of the previous night's storm. There was moderate interest in the phenomenon on the TV weather station, but the comments from experts boiled down to two types: "Hey, it's Calgary. What do you expect?" and "Global Warming! We're all doomed!" In other words, nobody had any idea why one small area got pounded while the rest of the city was dry.

Alyssa wasn't allowed to drive the Blakeway's only car, so to save her time, effort, and bus fare, I met her at her home after Collin had left for work. I hadn't probed too much, but from what she'd said Collin discouraged her from making friends. He expected her to stay home, clean his house, make his meals, and provide sex when he wanted it. It was fortunate for her that he was too lazy to give her a household allowance. It meant that she had access to the bank account so she could pay me.

It never seemed to occur to either of them that she could clean out the account and run.

I've noticed that same curious hypocritical behaviour in others. The accountant who doesn't keep track of his domestic finances. The doctor who doesn't have a first aid kit at home. The musician who is angry with people who pirate music, and then downloads movies. I don't let it bother me. If people were rational I'd probably be out of business. At the very minimum my job would be much harder.

Alyssa insisted on making tea for us before she'd get down to business. We took it in her perfect living room.

The mantel of the faux-fireplace had a central clock with an arrangement of pictures of the happy couple spread to either side. There were generic landscape pictures hung tastefully on the walls. The carpet was thick enough that we left footprints in its otherwise pristine surface. There was one odd thing: Bits of masking tape peered out from under the legs of a chair. Once I started looking, I could see the tape under all the furniture legs.

I asked to use the washroom, and pushed my chair slightly as I rose. When I returned, the chair had been moved so that its feet were back in the depressions, covering the tape squares. Apparently all the furniture needed to be in their exact positions at all times. I added OCD to Alyssa's list of problems.

I showed her the video of her husband that I'd transferred from my phone to my laptop. As she watched, the look on her face was interesting. For a brief moment she seemed angry. That quickly changed to a look of docile bewilderment.

After the video, she insisted we drink tea from her silver tea service. Collin wasn't the only one who was governed by ritual.

"I don't understand. What's he doing?" She asked.

I answered her question carefully. It would be easy to spook her.

"Maybe it's a surprise. Has your husband ever been in theatre, or expressed an interest in acting?"

"No, never. Do you think he's rehearsing something?"

"Perhaps, but if he is I'd expect other actors to be there. I don't know why he'd need to rent a space just to practice a monologue." As if it had just occurred to me, I added, "does he have an interest in magic?"

Again there was that flash of something else before she just looked perplexed. "You mean, like children's parties? Balloon animals and disappearing rabbits? No, not that he's ever told me."

"I was thinking more of the robes, candles, and chanting around an altar kind of thing."

She traded her perplexed look for one more appropriate to a society matron who had been propositioned by a homeless leper.

"Good heavens, no! He'd never do such a thing. His parents are strict Baptists. They'd disown him if he ever got involved with anything like that."

"It must be something else, then," I said, all the while thinking *no, that's exactly what it is*. Collin was too rigid to do anything without what he considered an excellent reason, and I couldn't imagine anybody taking up ritual just as a hobby. He was planning something. It had to be important if it overrode the threat of parental disownment.

She was terrified enough as it was, so I said nothing. I didn't need her imagining black-hooded figures with sharp knives gathering around her bed in the middle of the night. Unless she was willing to move out, right now, there wasn't much that I could do to protect her until I had more information.

"Maybe he's gone mad," she said, looking at her hands in her lap, "he keeps saying that I'm driving him to it."

"Alyssa, have you ever thought of leaving him?" I spoke gently, hoping that I wasn't overstepping the bounds of our professional relationship.

She stared at me like a deer in headlights. "Where would I go? What would I do?"

Like a sneeze triggered by the smell of a cheap perfume, the urge to quote Rhett Butler in *Gone with the Wind* was almost overwhelming. Her continual helplessness aggravated, frustrated, and generally annoyed the hell out of me. I exhaled slowly, and reined it in. She was still my client.

"You could go where ever you want. Do whatever you want. You'd be free." All she gave me was a scared, helpless look. Well, I tried.

"Very well, I should be able to get a camera into the room so we can see exactly what he's up to. It's your choice."

After a pause, she nodded unhappily.

Even though she was about fifteen years older than me, I thought of her like a handicapped daughter. She tended to agree with anything I suggested, which to my mind made me responsible for her. It was a stupid thing for me to allow myself to feel that way. She was just a client, nothing more. I should do the job, get paid, and move on. Still, I promised myself that, if anything happened to her, Collin would get what was coming to him, one way or another. He was a bully, and I have long-standing issues with bullies.

I finished my tea, and got up to leave.

"I'll keep you informed."

The mission to place the camera was meticulously planned, despite having an abysmal success rate lately for having such operations stay on track. I still had bruises from falling over the fence at the Blakeway house. The general who said "no battle plan ever survives contact with the enemy," would be so proud of me.

The first step was to scout the area. By that afternoon, the puddles had receded, with a little help from city workers who were removing the debris that had plugged the storm sewer grates.

The hooker stroll had been invisible, and probably empty, the night before. Now it was revealed in all its depressing lack of glory. At this hour, only a few women were out, dressed for display rather than warmth. Some of them were well beyond supermodel thinness, and into refugee emaciation. A depressing number of them looked like they had terrible acne, a result of scratching the itches caused by nerve damage from street drugs. Between the starvation, the scarring and the vacant expressions, I had no idea how old most of them were. Somewhere between fifteen and fifty was my guess. I wondered what had led these girls and women to this life style. Just when I thought I couldn't find it more horrible, I wondered what kind of men would pay for sex with women in that state.

The whole scene emitted an emotional stench of desperation and hopelessness.

Two blocks south I reached Collin's hideout. After counting units at the front of the building I drove around to the service alley. Fortunately, it was paved and mostly dry.

There was no access to room 12 from the alley, but there was a window. It was high up on the wall – over three metres to the sill. The good news was that the glass was clear rather than frosted. I could plainly see the ceiling inside from my car. If I could somehow get up that high, I should be able to look in.

A possible solution was right in front of me. There was a wooden utility pole within a metre of the building, and it was almost centred on the window. A ladder was the obvious answer, but it would be difficult to transport, awkward for me to handle by myself, and impossible to hide in case anybody saw me. For a brief moment I considered standing on Binky's roof, but that wasn't as high as I'd like, and I doubted that it would hold my weight without denting. Still, this should be easy.

All I had to do was learn how to climb.

I didn't want to hang around any longer than necessary in case I was seen, so I drove west until I got to a residential area before pulling over to make a phone call.

It took me a few minutes to chase down the friend of my father's whom I wanted. I didn't remember his last name, and I didn't quite remember the business name, but it was obvious once I'd brought up a list of tree care specialists.

I'd heard Dad talking about Jean-Mathieu, but I didn't remember ever meeting him. When I called him, he sounded nice, with a slight French accent.

"This is Veronica Chandler, Quin's daughter," I said.

"Good heavens, I haven't seen you since you were a very little girl. How are you?"

"Great. I don't know if Dad told you, but I'm working as a private investigator, and I was hoping to get your help. I need someone to teach me how to climb a pole." There was silence for a moment, then he laughed.

"I assume you don't mean a dancing pole."

"No, but I'd rather discuss it in person."

"All right, do you know where my shop is?"

"Unless your directory listing is outdated, I'm looking at your address right now."

"When would you like to come over?"

"I'll see you in half an hour."

I seemed to be spending a lot of my time lately hanging around industrial bays. At least this one was pleasant. The sign above the door read "Hyla Arborea Tree Services." The inside of the reception area was tastefully decorated in earth tones with artistic photographs of forests on the walls. A corridor led from reception to the office, and the shop itself.

The man who appeared in response to me ringing the bell on the desk was somewhat younger than I'd expected and quite handsome. I tried not to think that way about a friend of my father's.

"Hi, I'm Veronica."

"Jean-Mathieu. Tell me, what kind of pole do you want to climb?"

"A wooden utility pole." He frowned.

"That can be very dangerous, not to mention illegal."

"I won't be going anywhere near the top, just a couple of metres up."

"Still, you can get in a lot of trouble."

"I appreciate your concern, but I need to perform surveillance, and this is the only way."

"I don't know..."

"Dad says that you love and respect women." He smiled, acknowledging what I'd said but unsure of my point.

"The man I need to surveil abuses his wife. I need proof of what he's doing so I can stop him." That wasn't strictly true, but it was close enough. Jean-Mathieu's smile dropped.

"Come with me."

We went into his shop where he selected several pieces of equipment from shelves.

"Step into these loops," he said, holding a complex-looking collection of heavy nylon straps. The harness went around my thighs and waist. He adjusted the large buckles until he was satisfied with the fit.

He picked up two things that looked like leg braces and an enormous belt that he slung over his shoulder.

We went outside, me waddling slightly, and he led me along the alley until we got to a utility pole. He handed me the braces, and showed me how to buckle them to my lower legs. They had spikes on the inside edge of my feet. The belt he threw around the pole, then clipped it to sturdy rings on either side of my harness.

"Throw the belt up the pole as far as it will go." I did so and the rough nylon clung to the wood.

"Now, in one motion, raise one foot and kick sideways into the pole, then bring the other foot up beside it and kick." I tried to get my foot as high as possible, and he corrected me.

"This isn't a race. Take small steps so you can maintain control."

The spikes dug into the wood, and soon I was standing slightly above the ground.

"Now pull yourself toward the poll, throw the strap up again, lean back again. No, not that high with the belt. Remember, small steps."

At first I had trouble trusting the strap to hold me, but after it slipped a couple of times I realized that I had to lean back on it to keep it in place. I leaned forward only when moving it up. The most unnerving thing was that my hands were always on the belt. My instinct to hold onto the pole was completely wrong.

When my feet were at the height of his head, he told me that was high enough.

"To come down is the same but in reverse. Bring the strap down no further than your chest. Move one foot down, and then the other."

Once I let the strap drop too far down and almost overbalanced. He was ready with a hand at my back to steady me while I recovered. After a minute I was on the ground.

"Good, now do it again."

He ran me up and down the pole at least ten times before he was satisfied that I wouldn't kill myself. I took the equipment off, and we went back to his shop.

"How long will you be up the pole?"

"Just long enough to place a camera. I'll also need to retrieve it a couple of days later."

"All right, I can lend you the equipment for that long."

I eyed the harness, strap and climbers that were intended to last a professional through years of daily use.

"Is there any way I can get by with lighter equipment?"

He looked at me, and one eyebrow went up.

"I know that what I want to do isn't usual for your business, but I'm not going very high, and I'll probably only be using it twice."

He gave me a look that suggested that he'd heard similar things from people who were now extremely and messily dead.

"All I need is to climb a couple of metres." I tried looking flirtatious, but apparently that didn't work on Jean-Mathieu when he though death was a possibility.

"You climb one metre, your strap breaks, maybe your neck does too if you can't free your feet," he said. "I don't want to have to explain that to your father. Why don't you want to use proper equipment?"

"I need to be able to conceal it in case someone interrupts me. There's no way I can put all that in a bag, and have it mistaken for anything other than industrial equipment." He thought about it for almost a minute. For once I stayed quiet.

"All right, come with me."

We went to his office where he sat behind his desk and phoned someone. Their conversation was in French, and I understood about one word in ten. So much for three years of high school French. After a couple of minutes he hung up, then wrote on a piece of paper which he handed to me.

"That is the address of a friend of mine who is a rock and ice climber. She is willing to lend you a strap, harness and crampons. They will work much the same but are lighter. You can pick them up after six this evening." He leaned forward, and looked very serious. "You will *not* take any risks. I will *not* explain to your father why we have to go to your funeral. Do you understand?"

"Yes. I'm not anxious to go to my funeral either."

He smiled.

"Let me know how it works for you."

My closet does not scream "girl." It's divided into two sections, a small one for my actual clothes, divided into lots of "every day," some "business," and one "formal." I have one pair of good shoes, runners, and a couple of pairs of boots.

The much larger section holds my growing assortment of professional costumes. As I stared at the selection, I thought about the technical requirements of the mission.

Strictly speaking, I wasn't going to put a camera *in* the room. That definitely would be illegal, a shortcut to me losing my license if I was caught, or the camera was traced back to me.

However, there was nothing illegal about setting up a camera in a public place that just happened to face Collin's window. As long as he didn't announce his intent to want to block the view by putting up curtains or something, he had no legal recourse if someone just happened to look in. Of course, this ignored that climbing the pole was illegal all by itself.

I made my decision. My graduation dress was hung on the border between the two closet sections. It had never quite been the same after I'd hiked across Nose Hill in it in the middle of the night. The top was fine, so I'd hemmed it shorter for undercover work. It would do nicely.

During my scouting trip I'd noted that the businesses neighbouring

Collin's hideout closed between five and six P.M. His usual arrival time was around seven thirty, so theoretically I had ninety minutes to place my camera with a low probability that anybody would see me. I got there at six thirty, my gear stuffed into a huge handbag. I parked at the side of the building, so anyone seeing Binky wouldn't associate him with a specific unit, and walked to the pole. I looked around, just in case. The only vehicle in the alley was an old beater next to the door of the neighbouring unit.

I walked around the pole, trying to decide far up to place my camera for the best view.

"Hi."

I spun to face him, fully prepared to rain down death and destruction. It is not a good idea to sneak up on me while I'm working. The guy was in his twenties with grubby hands, wearing a shop apron, and a stupid grin. Damn, I'd forgotten my fake wedding ring at home. Fortunately, I had other weapons.

Mum had spent some time doing undercover work in her earlier years, so when I was old enough she took me aside to explain the Undercover Facts of Life. Typical of my Mum, she used a military metaphor to explain her point.

"If someone has fired a missile at you, you deploy ECM, electronic counter measures, to distract its brain. The missile gets confused, and forgets about blowing you up. FCM does much the same to straight men."

"FCM?"

"Female Counter Measures. Take your pick of two varieties: short hemline or plunging neckline. Either way, it can give you at least a momentary advantage."

Now I was seeing the FCM effect in real life. His eyes were inexorably drawn to the legs below my extremely short black dress, even before I turned around. My legs may not be long, but they have curves, and go to all the places they need to.

"Oh," I said in my best bimbo voice, "do you know where there's a washroom?" I waved my arms vaguely to disguise the fact that I'd dropped into a defensive stance when I first turned toward him. I also jiggled a little, and squeezed my thighs together as if I needed to pee. He smiled at my legs as if they were smiling back. He wasn't bad looking. Under other conditions, I might have been interested, except for the cigarette pack under the sleeve of his tee shirt. My hormones may urge me to be less monogamous than I would prefer, but I draw the line at kissing an ash tray.

"Sure, you can use ours," he said.

He led me inside, through the back door of the printing shop. There were boxes of t-shirts stacked beside a machine, so I assumed that they did silk screening too. The washroom was nasty, although I'm sure that the people who worked there thought that they kept it clean. In fairness, it's hard to be spotless when you work with ink. The sink was lined with soap scum in various colours. The toilet bowl had a brown ring around the water line and other, unidentifiable things under the rim. On top of everything else, the plastic seat was cracked.

I waited a timed two minutes as cover, then pushed the toilet lever with my foot, and kicked the stall door for sound effects. I ran the water and, after another count of thirty, I came out.

"Thanks, you're a life saver," I said coyly. Despite the faint smell of cigarette smoke, it struck me again that he was cute, and looked to be in excellent shape. Damn it, I had work to do, and no time for this. His eyes glanced at my face, probably curious to see if I actually had one, but were immediately deflected again by the FCM. It was doubtful that he'd ever be able to describe me accurately.

"My name's Adam," he said, casually moving to get between me and the exit.

Oh, that was *so* the wrong thing for him to say. My first boyfriend, the one who'd cheated on me, was named Adam. Sure, I'd gotten over it, but the name still gave me a twitch response. I nonchalantly moved my hand to the outside pouch of my handbag where my tactical baton was stored.

"Hi, I'm Cindy."

"I'll be done in a few minutes. Can I buy you drink?" *Only if I get to pour it over you and light it*, I thought. I can be uncharitable at times. So sue me.

"Oo, I'd love to, but I have to meet some people, like, ten minutes ago. Can I give you my number?"

It was a tribute to the FCM scrambling his brain that he never once questioned why a girl was waiting for friends at the back of a grubby industrial area, nor where they could be going in that area that would require clubbing clothes.

He gave me an over-confident grin, and handed over his smart phone. I punched buttons, and then fumbled while handing it back to delay him checking it.

"Oops, sorry. I think I turned it off."

"No sweat, I'll call you tomorrow."

Swivelling my hips on the way out to enhance the FCM, I wondered if he'd see the humour when he checked his phone and found that, instead of getting my number, he'd made a $50 donation to breast cancer research.

See, I *can* be charitable.

As soon as the door closed behind me, I ran to the nearest rubbish bin with open lids and hid behind it. It didn't take long.

Less than a minute later the door banged open, and he came out with his phone still clutched in his hand. He looked up and down the alley, seeing nobody, then screamed "bitch!" at the top of his lungs. I was peering out through the gap in the hinge of the bin lid. He looked around for another few seconds, then went back inside. He angrily slammed the steel door behind him.

He'd said that he would be leaving soon, and I couldn't afford to have him interrupt me while I was placing the camera. I waited, fidgeting, for him to leave. It was nearly 7:30, another forty minutes gone, when he drove away in the beater I'd seen earlier.

Jogging back to the utility pole took a few precious seconds. There was no time to be coy. I hiked my dress up to my waist so I could put the harness on, then strapped the crampons on over my low-heeled boots and flipped the strap around the pole. The nylon chafed, and I was really glad that I'd worn underwear.

The trick was to get the camera high enough to cover as much of the room as possible. The pole was close enough to the window that, by leaning out in a way that I'm sure would have given Jean-Mathieu a heart attack, I could stick a tiny contact microphone onto the corner of the glass so I'd get audio as well. I had to guess at the camera angle since the window was currently dark, and nothing inside was visible.

The blast of light was blinding.

Collin had arrived. He was facing toward the window, but wasn't looking up. I was fully illuminated, so all he had to do was lift his eyes to see a woman dressed in what appeared to be a black T-shirt and panties hanging off the pole directly outside. I didn't dare move. At least I had a front row view of the room.

As I'd suspected from the video, it was normally used for storage, with assorted office furniture pushed back against the walls. Most of his stuff was lying on an old desk.

The most obvious thing was a huge book. I could just read the gold title: *Lemegeton Clavicula Salomonis*. If fantasy stories were any guide, it was *not* a good sign when a ritual book had a Latin title. There were various carved candles, an incense burner like the one you see being swung on a chain during Catholic mass, a knife that Kali would call an athame with symbols on its black handle, and some kind of neatly-folded black cloth. There was also a flat metal pendant, sized to fit the ego of a rap star, that looked like a soup bowl with three crosses growing out of it. The middle of the room was taken up with a complex circular design painted on the floor. I had no idea exactly what any of it meant, but I knew who I could ask.

I risked moving my hands slowly to get my phone out of my bra so I could take some pictures. Even if the video malfunctioned, at least I would have something for my efforts. As soon as Collin turned away, I scurried down the pole as quickly and quietly as I could. My heart was racing.

One last check showed that the camera was well-positioned, all but unnoticeable unless somebody was improbably nosey. The microphone wire was thin enough to be effectively invisible.

I put my climbing equipment back in my handbag, pulled my dress down to cover myself, and vanished quietly into the growing darkness.

CHAPTER 8

Antisocial Life

I was still feeling strange about Brian. I liked him a lot, but my head-long leap into his bed (or, at least, onto his living room carpet) made me feel – weird. Maybe it wouldn't matter if things worked out between us.

I recognized that I'd just used one of the most popular rationalizations in the world: the ends justify the means. I didn't want to be a slut who had sex with guys she didn't have relationships with, so if I developed a relationship with Brian, then having sex with him on the first date wasn't a problem.

Yeah, sure. Tell yourself another one, Veronica.

I was still working on how I felt about Andrea's definition of a slut. Was it really that simple? Just feel comfortable with the amount of fun I was having?

Apart from the hot sex, Brian and I had an interest in martial arts in common. It would be good to see if we could have a date that didn't involve rug burn or bruises, so I invited him to an Abuse Club meeting.

Don't look at me like that. It made sense to me at the time.

The next one was the day after I'd tracked Collin to his lair. While Mum was still in Ireland it was just me and the boys: Stan Watkins and Nick Holley. Stan wasn't a regular, so I asked him if he'd like to spar with me first.

"I think I'll warm up a bit. Brian, would you care for a go?"

Brian had been warming up on his own, dancing around like a boxer and throwing lightning fast jabs at the air.

"Afraid Veronica will hurt you?" He said to Stan.

"You'd better believe it."

Brian laughed as if he thought that Stan was kidding, which irritated me. The others took me seriously. If Brian didn't, he'd learn.

They went out onto the mat while Nick and I watched, and Brian held

out his glove. I was more familiar with Krav Maga courtesy, which had
been borrowed from the Japanese. Stan had done some boxing in school,
so instead of bowing, he and Brian touched gloves.

Our club rules were simple: don't permanently injure your partner,
and observe the courtesies. We wore full body armour while sparring so
we didn't have to pull our blows. Brian insisted that he didn't need it.
That seemed foolish to me, no matter how good he was.

They started out slowly. I saw that Stan was just warming up, so he
moved deliberately, and pulled his punches at contact. Brian was also
moving much more slowly than he had been on his own. At first I
thought he was also warming up, but he seemed hesitant, like he was
afraid to hit Stan. It occurred to me that he might be intimidated by
fighting a police officer, even though Stan and Nick were off duty.

"Come on Stan," Nick called out, "quit dancing and start fighting."

"Hit him, Brian," I called.

Stan sped up his attacks, hitting Brian more forcefully. Brian was still
pulling his punches, which was ridiculous with Stan in armour. After five
minutes of that, we called time.

"What are you doing?" I asked Brian as he removed his mouth guard
to take a sip of water.

"What do you mean?"

"You looked like you were afraid of breaking him. This is supposed to
be full contact."

I was trying to be reasonable. Perhaps Brian had misunderstood the
rules.

"I'm a professional. I don't go full out against amateurs."

I dropped my voice so Stan and Nick wouldn't hear.

"I can't believe you said that. In other words, we're beneath you, and
you only came here because you and I had sex."

He seemed genuinely surprised by my attitude.

"Hey, don't be like that. I just don't want to hurt anybody."

"Nick," I said more loudly, without taking my eyes off him. "Brian and
I are next."

Nick made sure that my armour was properly fastened, and I went out
onto the mat. In the meantime Nick helped Stan out of his gear.

"Shall we?" I said before putting my mouth guard in. Brian stood a
good head taller than me, and he obviously spent a lot of time at the
gym. Like the boys, he probably had a good 30 kilos on me.

In the ring, or the octagon, there are weight classes for a good reason.
I would never be able to win against someone his size. A smaller person
can't absorb the punishment that a larger person can when you are
fighting by the rules.

There's a way around that in real life, where the only rule is to survive. You fight like a girl. That is, you fight dirty, using every trick you know. You use your lack of size to move quickly, skipping out of range to tire your opponent, and you never stop. It was what Mum called being a honey badger on crack.

Brian grinned at me, and I got the feeling that he was thinking that I was cute when I was angry. I'll bet he even thought he'd let me land a few little punches just to make me feel good about myself. I knew that I was working myself into a rage without much evidence, but I didn't care.

I saw Nick say something to Stan, who smiled and shook his head.

All right, Mr. Cocky Professional, meet Ms. Badger.

When Nick called for us to start, Brian held out his glove. I ignored it and bowed. My gym, my rules.

He started dancing around me like a boxer, shuffling back and forth out of range.

My anger was now on the back burner as I put my game face on. The crack-fuelled honey badger waited for him to commit himself.

He threw a few feints, but they were too far away so I ignored them. I stood relatively still, relaxed and waiting.

He jabbed at my midsection. He was still too far away to hurt me, even without the armour, but at least it was an honest punch. I brushed it aside with one hand, and simultaneously burst forward, using both legs to launch my attack, and caught him with two rapid jabs to his unarmoured face.

The third punch missed as he ducked and covered – to meet my knee coming up into his chest. There was a satisfying *woof*, and he ended up on his knees. If it had been one of my regular partners, I'd have hit him harder, then gone in for the figurative kill. I figured that I'd made my point. He wasn't the only one with skills.

In fact, I expected him to be better. I turned away, intending to get a drink. I heard a slight scuff on the mat, and turned as he lunged at me.

Under our non-rules, that was fair enough. Nobody had said we were taking a time out. I fell backward to absorb the blow, and he rode me down while grabbing for my wrists.

We landed with him astride me, trying to pin my arms to the mat. His mouth guard distorted his grin, but it was obvious to me that he thought my previous strikes had been pure luck. I let him lean into my wrists, then applied a move I'd used on his sister several years previously in the school yard. He wasn't expecting it, and flew off to the side.

I rolled with him, landing astride his hips. Immediately I put three good punches into his face before he could raise his arms to protect himself. As soon as his arms went up, I put another set of punches into his ribs. As his arms came down to protect those, I arm barred his throat.

I don't know whether it was the lack of oxygen, or his reaction to my game face a few centimetres from his, but his eyes were definitely bugging out. The grin was gone, replaced by a sudden realization that I wasn't being cute. If I had dropped the arm bar straight onto his throat instead of onto his sternum to slide it up into place, he'd be gagging to death with a crushed trachea.

I let him up. This time I kept my eyes on him. Again he started bouncing while I waited calmly. He looked pissed, and seemed more cautious this time. Good, he was learning respect.

I'd expected better of him. For a budding MMA professional, he was falling for things I never would have. He was fast, and if he managed to connect with a real punch or kick I'd be in trouble, but he was relying on his speed and weight rather than cunning. It occurred to me that, while he'd said he'd studied a couple of martial arts, he'd never said what ranks he'd achieved.

On the other hand, I was fighting like a girl. Ms. Honey Badger don't care.

He'd had enough of close contact. This time he tried a roundhouse kick to the side of my head. It was fast, but I didn't have to go far. I stepped into it, wrapped my arm around his knee from the outside, brought that hand down like I was reaching for the ground while pivoting to one side. I vaguely heard the sound of somebody starting to laugh in the background, then choking it off.

I could tell that Brian had never seen that technique before either. His entire body spun in mid-air as his one planted foot lost traction. Since his other foot was currently held a metre and a half from the floor, he landed head first on the mat. It was not a pretty landing: he almost didn't get his hands down to prevent his face from being the first point of contact. From that I suspected that he'd never really learned how to fall properly either.

Immediately I dropped down, and jammed my calf behind the knee of the leg I was holding. The weight of my body leaning forward folded up his leg, trapping my calf. In that position, if I leaned too far forward I'd rip his knee out of its socket, my own leg acting as a fulcrum. Since both my hands were free, I grabbed one of his arms to keep him from twisting around. All I had to do was maintain my hold. The harder he tried to pull his arm away, the harder he pulled me into his pinned leg, and the greater the pressure trying to dislocate his knee.

After a few seconds of trying to get out of the hold, he slapped the mat for release with his free hand. As he stood up I bowed to end the match.

He ignored my bow and lunged forward. He drove a kick into my mid-section, intending to follow it up with punches.

What the hell? That wasn't in the rules. I brushed the kick aside across his body, scooping his leg up as I did so, and burst forward. His body pivoted, and by the time I lost control of his leg he was facing in the opposite direction. Being much bigger and heavier than me, he could probably have stayed upright if I hadn't pushed my foot into the back of his knee as I pulled down and backward on his shoulders. I danced back as he went down instead of kneeing him in the back of his head, as I would have with my friends.

He hit the mat flat on his back, in a perfect reverse belly flop. He did not have his arms in position to help him land.

Okay, enough. It was time for Ms. Badger to go to sleep again before someone got hurt. I started to pull my armour off as I walked away. I'd gotten as far as my gloves and arm guards when there was a growl from behind me, and the slap of a foot on the mat. I heard one of the boys yell, "stop!"

Seriously? I was now supremely pissed off and done playing nice. This time, I dropped down right in front of his shins. He tripped over me, and I helped him along by standing again just as his legs were going over my back. He headed for the ground nose first. Again.

His landing was hard enough that Transport Canada should have been called to investigate the crash.

"What the fuck do you think you're doing?" I said very quietly. By that time Ms. Badger wished he'd try to get up again, so she could mop the floor with his MMA professional ass.

He, on the other hand, was a yeller. "I've spent my whole life training for this. I won't be beaten by a little girl!"

Brian was obviously a *very* slow learner.

I took a step toward him, and Stan caught my arm.

"Don't do it, love."

"Butt out," Brian said, getting to his feet. He was favouring his left leg, and he wiped the blood from his nose. "If she wants to take a shot, let her try."

"How's that working for you so far?" I said.

"Calm down," Nick said to everyone, approaching Brian with his hands in front of him in a gesture of peace. It's also a ready stance. Nick isn't a fool.

Brian took a wild swing at him. Nick redirected the arm around in a circle while pulling Brian's head around and down. Brian stumbled and went to one knee, then came at Nick again. Was this guy stupid or insane? I saw Nick get ready for serious mayhem.

Nobody hits my friends if I can help it. His eyes were on Nick. I don't think he even remembered that I existed at that point.

I tackled Brian's shins with my legs collected under me, making a good try at lifting him off the mat. I didn't get far, but it threw him off balance and he went over like a tree. He thrashed around, trying to rise, but I was already standing over him.

I should have let the boys do the rest, but Ms. Badger demanded one more shot before I sent her back to her room. I dropped, putting my full weight behind an elbow strike to the back of his head.

Damn, that was stupid of me. I'd forgotten that I wasn't wearing arm guards. The pain in my elbow was excruciating, not that I'd ever admit it to the boys. Brian collapsed, unmoving except for his ribs. He was still breathing, although at that moment I'd have been happy either way.

"You shouldn't have done that," Nick said. "It was a police matter." I was still pissed.

"Sorry, next time I'll let the bad guy beat on you."

"I could have handled him."

"You're just pissed because a civilian saved your ass."

Nick shook his head, and knelt beside my former boyfriend to see how badly he was hurt.

Once Nick had become involved in the fight, Stan had gone to his duffel bag, pulling out a pair of handcuffs and his cell phone. He tossed the cuffs to Nick who put them on Brian. Meanwhile, Stan called dispatch for transport and an ambulance.

I sat on the bench, sucking at my water bottle, and letting the anger drain away. I ignored the crowd that had gathered around our mat. I couldn't decide whether I was more angry at Brian for being a jerk, or myself for thinking that he was a good guy. One thing was for sure: I was *so* done with dating jocks.

Nick sat down beside me.

"Are you all right?"

That was not a conversation I wanted to have at the moment.

"Fine." I took another swig of water. "What were you and Stan talking about just before the fight started?"

"I bet him twenty dollars that your boyfriend –"

"*Ex*-boyfriend."

"Ex-boyfriend would lose. For some reason he wouldn't take the bet."

I held his eyes for a moment, then managed a grim smile.

"Clever boy."

Nick put his hand on my shoulder, like he would with another cop.

"Remind me never to get you angry."

My smile this time was slightly less grim.

"You're also a clever boy."

Nick left me alone. *Very* clever boy.

Now that the fight was over, I started shaking from the adrenaline. It was the first time I'd ever been in a real fight, against a real opponent who could have really hurt me. Beating up girl bullies in school didn't count. Neither did friendly matches with friends.

I'd been bruised, winded, and even knocked out in these fights, but I trusted that whatever they did would eventually heal. Brian was big enough, and strong enough, that he could have severely hurt me if I'd let him.

Although she'd believed it before, Ms. Badger now *knew* that she could win a serious fight. I took a deep breath and stopped shaking. Damn, my elbow hurt. I wondered if I'd broken it.

Stan and Nick came back a minute later, and sat down on either side of me. They were wearing their badges on the waist band of their sweat pants.

"When do we get to meet your next boyfriend?" Stan asked. Jerk. I gave no warning as I punched him in the upper arm, hard, with one knuckle extended.

He gave a surprised yelp, and grabbed the spot where I'd hit him.

"You're lucky she didn't rip it off and beat you with it," Nick said while trying not to laugh.

"You two are hilarious," I said quietly. The boys finally realized that it was too soon for me to see the light side of this.

"Sorry, Veronica. I apologize," Stan said sincerely."

"For what?" I wasn't letting him off that easily.

"For being a gormless, insensitive idiot."

"Me too," Nick added.

"Noted. I'll forgive you both later after you've bought me dinner."

"Who said..." Nick started. I raised my fist again, knuckle extended.

"I mean, where would you like to go?"

We all looked up as a man in gym clothes approached us. He was around 40 years old, and had a young girl with him who looked to be about ten.

"Excuse me, officers."

"Yes?" Stan said. They were his cuffs, it was his crime scene.

"If you need a witness, I saw the whole thing."

"Great," Stan said. "Come with me." He led the man over to his duffel, where he pulled out his notebook. The daughter stayed behind, staring at me. I took another pull from my water bottle, and tried to ignore how much of a bruise I was going to have on my elbow. She kept staring.

"Can I help you?"

"There's this bully at school, and I want to take some self-defence classes. What kind of martial art do you do?"

"Krav Maga. It's Israeli."

"Do you teach classes?"

I smiled at her. She looked so serious.

"No, but I can give your father the name of my teacher if you like."

"Yes, please."

I led her over to my duffel, where I printed *Madrich* Ish-shalom's name and phone number on the back of one of my business cards. Fortunately, it wasn't the elbow of my writing hand that was in pain.

By then Stan was done with the father, and I handed him my card.

"Your daughter mentioned she wants to take classes. This is the contact info for my teacher."

"Thanks. It's hard to figure out who's real and who's a scam without a recommendation."

"Trust me, my teacher is real: he was in the Israeli special forces. He doesn't have a separate class for kids, but he'll take your daughter if she's serious."

"She's serious."

"Good. Tell him I sent you."

They started to walk away, then the girl turned back.

"I want to be like you when I grow up."

"Brilliant," Stan said. "We arrest the guy, and Veronica gets a fan club. Where's the justice?"

"That would be when I beat you senseless for being a smart ass again," I said.

Nick, wisely, said nothing.

CHAPTER 9

BhadraKali

The next morning I woke up to a distinctly strange sensation. It took me a moment to realize that Yoko Geri was sniffing my eyelids. Just as I became aware of that, one of his whiskers inserted itself up my nose. He seemed offended that I batted him away as I madly rubbed my nose to get rid of the itch. My arm did not appreciate that at all.

I'd spent a couple of hours the night before, putting alternating hot and cold on my elbow. It was no longer swollen, and no longer felt like I had broken it. It was, however, an amazing shade of purple. The ibuprofen helped too.

I didn't know what time it was, but I did know that it wasn't yet time for Veronica to be conscious. I rolled over on my side. Yoko circled around my head, stepping on my hair as he went, then patted my nose with his paw. I covered my nose with the blanket. He put his paw out anyway, then flexed his claws slightly. There were sharp pains in my nose. I really needed to trim his claws.

I opened my eyes to see him staring at me, his nose only a finger length away from mine, beaming his kitten mental control signals into my brain. *It's past time for breakfast, human.*

I gave up.

The clock agreed with my cat. My brilliant plan to miss rush hour by oversleeping had succeeded. It was around 10:30 when I stumbled out of bed, and fed the predator. It was after eleven when I left the apartment to see my occult expert.

Kali, real name Liliana Marina Hernández Rojas, and I had been best friends since grade seven when I saved her from a bully. She was a Colombian, Wiccan Romantigoth. While my dream in school was to become a private investigator, hers was to open an occult shop.

Never call her Liliana Marina if you value your life. Only her parents and older sister ever called her that. Or, occasionally, my parents if she was in trouble. Now that her biological family are all dead, she is just Kali. Thanks to a trust fund left to her by her parents she's also rich.

After graduation she opened her shop, BhadraKali, in the Marda Loop area. And by "opened," I mean she bought the whole building out of petty cash so she wouldn't have to pay rent. Yeah, that kind of rich.

Of the two of us, despite her love of black, pseudo-Victorian dresses trimmed with blood-red lace, Kali is the conservative. I'm the wild child.

The shop has a state-of-the-art electronic security system with video cameras. It also has an antique bell on a spring over the front door. It jingled merrily as I entered the shop, and I was greeted by the wafting smell of jasmine incense. Kali is smart about it. The scent is subtle rather than knocking her customers over as they come in.

Once you are inside, there is no doubt as to what kind of shop you have discovered. The book section displayed works on Wicca, New Age, Eastern Philosophy, and High Magic (whatever that is – is there a Low Magic too that nobody ever talks about? I wonder if Low Magic is ever invited to family reunions), as well as dozens of other occult topics. An entire shelf section was devoted to various decks of tarot cards. Other areas held candles, incense burners, silver jewellery, bins of crystals and stones of various types, and a clothes rack with sample robes beside a poster showing the portrait of a local seamstress with red hair and mischievous eyes, whose speciality was making you the ritual robes of your dreams. Behind the counter, various ritual knives and swords hung on the wall. There were wands of all kinds in the display case, from plain wood to ones adorned with feathers, crystals, and carvings. A notice let the customer know that custom items could be ordered from local artisans. A cork board on the wall had advertisements for classes, psychic development groups, concerts and lost pets. I always felt like I'd entered Diagon Alley when I came here. A CD was playing in the background.

Behind the counter, Keith Barager-Bonsell was explaining the differences between tarot decks to a customer who was having trouble deciding which to buy. He glanced in my direction, then smiled and waved. Keith used to be a computer programmer before the company where he was working had gone bankrupt. Kali had given him a job in the shop to tide him over, and he found that he liked it better than writing computer programs for clients who kept changing their minds. That was around the time that he'd hired me to investigate his then fiance, Parker. They had gone through a rough patch while both of them came to terms with the still largely unknown hold that the self-proclaimed demon, Beleth, had gained over Parker and others. Explaining the circumstances to Keith had been awkward and tearful, but Kali, Parker, and I had finally convinced him that Parker was in no way responsible for what had

happened. Their love and friendship was strong enough that they managed to repair the damage in time for their scheduled wedding this past
June.

I'm not a big fan of parties, but the wedding was a lot of fun, and I got
to meet some of their friends and family. Apart from the one, obligatory
anti-gay uncle who came for the free alcohol, glared at everyone, and left
in a huff, they were all cool. A Unitarian chaplain, herself married to her
childhood girlfriend, was the officiant for the legal wedding. After that,
Kali and her boyfriend George performed a Wiccan handfasting for the
boys. That's a Pagan wedding followed by a lot of food and dancing.

I saw Keith push the button under the counter to let his boss know
that she was needed up front.

Kali's office was a tiny cubbyhole next to the stock room. A few moments after the button was pressed she glided out through the beaded
curtain. Given her Colombian ancestry, looking dark and mysterious
wasn't at all difficult for her. As usual, she was dressed in a black Romantigoth gown like a Steampunk vampire costume. All she was missing was
the brass goggles and top hat.

"Hey, it's Veronica the Spook," she said in her deep, lightly accented
voice. She always sounds like a sexy coffee commercial announcer.

"Hey, Kali," I responded, "how's my favourite Satanist?"

"Wiccan," she growled, "not Satanist. Satanists have no sense of humour. Wiccans, on the other hand, would find turning you into a newt
quite humorous."

"A newt?"

"You'd get better."

We hugged as she came around the end of the counter.

"I miss you," she said. "When are you coming over for dinner?"

"I don't know. Have you learned how to cook yet?"

She stuck her tongue out at me. Dad and I had been teaching her how
to cook for years, and by now she was very good.

"I'm afraid this isn't a social call," I said. "I have a professional question for you." She glanced at the customer, who had narrowed her choice
down to four decks. It looked to me like the traditional Rider-Waite deck,
the only one I recognized, was the front runner.

"Let's go into my office."

She held the beaded curtain aside, and I ducked through. Kali's office
is always fairly tidy, but there were still stacks of invoices everywhere,
including on top of her filing cabinets. Regardless of all that paper, a
computer sat on her desk. The browser was open to a site about wedding
planning.

She realized her mistake, and casually closed the browser. Kali was thinking of marriage? That would be a big step for her. If she wasn't ready to say anything about it, I wasn't going to ask, even if it killed me. I pretended to have been looking elsewhere, and ignored the blush that spread over her dark cheeks.

Instead, I opened the envelope I was carrying, and spread the stack of pictures I'd printed from my phone camera.

"Have you ever seen anything like this?"

She took the pictures from me, and skimmed through the stack. Her eyes widened.

"Holy Mother Isis," she said. "Somebody is into some seriously bad shit."

"What kind of seriously bad?"

She pointed to the picture of the book. "You've seen this book before under its English title: The Lesser Key of Solomon."

Oh no, not again.

The Key is a seventeenth century text for forcing demons to do your will, based on material from about 300 years earlier. Assuming that you can perform the ritual properly, each demon listed in it has a speciality for granting wishes. Beleth, the gender-confused dwarf from my first case, took his/her name from one the demons listed in the book.

Kali waved her finger at the other items on Collin's desk. "These tools are used for the conjuration." She leafed to the picture of the floor design. "This looks like the standard protective magic circle, at least if you are into summoning demons."

She opened a new browser, did some clicking on bookmarks, and then scrolled to a picture of a magic circle. When we compared it with Collin's, the parts we could see seemed to be identical.

"I think the triangle part outside the circle is where the demon is forced to appear."

"Aren't you sure?"

"Summoning demons isn't a Wiccan thing, and it certainly isn't my thing. You're just lucky that I read a lot. Especially with the cases you take."

"Can you tell which demon this guy is summoning? What does he hope to accomplish?"

I had an uncomfortable feeling about this. I didn't for a moment believe that Collin would get a meaningful response from doing his 700 year old ritual. That was why I'd bowed out of practising Wicca with Kali a couple of years previously. The whole concept of being able to do cool things just by waving a wand didn't make sense to me. Not only did it violate the laws of physics, for me it violated the laws of common sense. She'd explained that, unlike the flashy hocus-pocus in stories, real magic was in the heart, and that the changes one made were to oneself. Still, it seemed to me like a waste of time when a good therapist could do the same thing for you. Maybe I'm just more in tune with my shrink than with cosmic forces.

She leafed back to the picture of the tools, and pointed to the soup-bowl pendant. "That will be the demon's seal. If it's in the Key, we can look it up."

She went back to the website again. That made me think of another question.

"Why would he buy the book if he can get the whole thing online?" I asked as she slowly scrolled down the page.

"Maybe he just likes paper. Besides, a lot of people find it hard to get into a proper ritual head space if they're reading their lines from a tablet. It's too modern." She stopped scrolling. "Got it."

There was a paragraph, and a picture of the familiar soup-bowl symbol.

"Prince Sitri?"

"Oh yeah, seriously bad. Worse than Beleth."

I read over her shoulder. It was a short read; more of an outline rather than a full dossier. "He doesn't sound too bad."

"You have to learn to read between the lines. She quoted from the text: 'Inflames Men and Women with Love for one another, and causeth them to shew themselves Naked, &c.' His deal is forcing someone to fall in love. In theory, he can cause anyone the magician chooses to do anything he wants by convincing them that they are madly in love with him. In other words, he forces them to volunteer for their own rape."

I looked at her sceptically.

"I have a hard time believing that such a thing would work, or every idiot teen boy would be doing it."

"They probably would be if they could. First they'd have to know that the ritual exists. Then they'd have to create the ritual tools. That's not easy or cheap, and generally takes months. Then they'd have to have the patience and discipline to do the ritual. Teenage boys aren't noted for their focus. That alone would make it a rare problem."

"You don't really believe this stuff, do you?"

"The jury's still out. As I said, I haven't tried it myself. I've met people who claim that the Key is all superstitious rubbish, and people who claim that they've made it work. Granted, the ones who say they've done it also tend to wear their black-dyed hair over their eyes, and live in their parents' basement. As I said, I've never tried it myself. Either way, I hope whoever is doing this isn't your client."

"He's her husband."

She looked back to the screen, and I could hear the wheels turning in her head.

"I don't suppose you've seen any dwarfs hanging around this guy? This seems like a familiar story."

"Not even close. All we have here is a husband who has rented a space where he can fool around with a ritual. Nobody's been given any mysterious silver coins, and there isn't a horse to be seen anywhere. Besides, Sitri isn't Beleth. Two separate things."

"You don't see the similarity?"

"I don't want to have this argument again. You've just proven that anybody with access to the internet can get this information. Beleth was just a con artist with a good scam who was preying on people. This guy is a solo nut case with delusions of grandeur."

"I hope like hell that you're right, because if this case has anything at all to do with the other one, it's going to get nasty. Beleth was fairly mild as demons go, apart from the whole 'killing those who fear her' thing. If possible, I'd get your client into a women's shelter, and recommend a good divorce lawyer. If he's summoning Sitri, the only possible intention he can have is to try turn somebody into his own personal sex slave. Even if it doesn't work, she doesn't want to be around a guy who thinks that this is a fun way to spend an evening."

"*Now* we agree. From what I've seen of him when he isn't summoning demons, he's a controlling, abusive bastard with anger management issues."

"He sounds like a real charmer. Can you convince her to leave him?"

"I've tried, but she's pretty well under his thumb. It's a miracle that she had enough initiative to hire me when she thought he was having an affair."

"Ah," Kali said like a prosecutor jumping on an inconsistency in a witness's testimony. "So there's that in common with the Beleth case as well."

Sigh.

"Yes, and you'll remember that I've had a couple of other infidelity cases in the meantime with no hint of demonic involvement of any kind. No matter how much it might pain me to say it, not every guy who can't keep it in his pants is in league with Satan." My brain took the opportunity to remind me of Brian. I told it to shut the hell up.

"Absence of proof is not proof of absence," Kali said in a good imitation of my mother lecturing me on investigative technique.

"*Eres una molestia, miquita*," I said firmly.

"I am not annoying," she said, "I'm cute. George told me so. And who's a monkey girl?"

"Fine, just to make you happy I'll keep a look out for the scent of brimstone. Thanks for your help, *hermanita*."

"*De nada*," she said, then smiled evilly. "*Miquita*."

CHAPTER 10

Revelations

I was determined that retrieving the camera from the pole outside Collin's hideout was going to be as boring as possible. I was tired of my well-planned operations going sideways at the last moment.

As before, I had to wait until after business hours. Of course, then I might run into Collin, or Adam the Second.

My preparations started that morning. I called Alyssa and, as far as she knew, her husband would be home at the regular time that evening. I knew he'd called her at the last minute before, so I made her promise to let me know immediately if his plans changed.

This time I was leaving nothing to chance. At 5 P.M. I was sitting in the coffee shop, just in case he forgot to tell her he'd be late. The back of my neck twitched as I felt my least favourite coffee shop worker staring at me. I ignored him, watching the office like Yoko Geri watching invisible Martians.

At 6:00, Collin packed up and left, again watching Andrea walk away with a look that made me want to have a bath on her behalf. As usual, he waited a few moments, then followed her across the street. The three of us formed a little parade, heading north along Eleventh Street toward the West End of downtown. When we got to Seventh Avenue, Andrea boarded the C-Train heading east to her townhouse. Collin waited until the number 201 bus came, then took it north toward his home.

I went back and retrieved Binky. Now that Collin was safely on his way home, it was only a matter of waiting until the workers in the area of his hideout left for the day. I went home to have supper.

At 10 P.M. I arrived at the strip mall wearing boots, jeans and a dark sweat shirt. I slowly drove around the building twice. There was no sign of anybody. In particular there was no sign of my buddy Adam's car.

The camera was right where I'd left it, and by now I was an expert at pole climbing. I went up, unstrapped the camera from the pole, and leaned over to pull the contact microphone from the window pane.

Below me, the door to the print shop banged opened, and I almost lost my balance. Adam came out, tapping a cigarette out of the package he habitually wore inside his shirt sleeve. He leaned against the base of the pole to smoke it. We were close enough that I could have kicked the top of his head.

This was freaking ridiculous. His car was nowhere to be seen. Where the hell was he hiding, and why did he have to be here at this moment?

This could take a while. I carefully slid the strap further up the pole a bit at a time so I could stand more upright. I didn't dare move my feet.

The cigarette was almost gone when the glow of approaching head-lights appeared, bouncing around on the facing building as the vehicle went over a speed bump. A moment later, a pickup truck with a crappy sound system came around the corner, and skidded to a stop by my pole. By then my muscles were aching from the strain.

Adam stood up, flicked away the remains of his cigarette, and put his head inside the cab. I couldn't hear what they were saying over the badly distorted rap song that was thumping from the truck. He went back in-side the building for a few minutes, then came out and hopped into the truck.

When they were gone, I shimmied down the pole, slid into my car without bothering to take off my climbing gear, and got out of there be-fore anything else happened.

I had to stop a few blocks later to remove the crampons. Driving with big, spiky, metal things attached to your feet isn't as easy as you might think.

Driving home through the darkness, the most famous quote from *Goldfinger* ran through my mind: "Once is happenstance. Twice is coincid-ence. Three times is enemy action." My planning skills did *not* suck as badly as recent history would suggest. There was no way that everything to do with this case could go wrong, unless somebody was out to get me.

Who? Why? And how?

There were two, no three, possibilities for the first question: Collin, friends of his, or enemies of mine.

If Collin knew about my investigation, I couldn't see him being subtle in his response. He might scream profanity, and come after me with a baseball bat, but I couldn't imagine him playing games from the shad-ows.

Assuming that he had any friends at all, he might have some who could be looking out for him, and trying to throw me off my game.

Maybe there was a demon worshippers' club working together. Just because I hadn't seen them around his hideout didn't mean that they weren't there at other times.

Bad guys in the private investigator genre who were traditionalists would have had anonymous thugs corner me in an alley, making eloquent but vague threats about what would happen if I kept investigating Collin. Maybe these were avant-garde ritualists who didn't believe in tradition.

Enemies of mine seemed the most likely culprits. Perhaps people I'd pissed off during other investigations were trying to play with my head. It was just possible, but again, why be so indirect that it took me this long even to suspect interference? The whole point to revenge is that your target should know that you've gotten them back for whatever they did. Anonymous revenge just didn't feel right. Besides, how would anybody I'd pissed off know I was investigating Collin Blakeway? And why would they care?

Of course, it was possible that the whole thing was a conspiracy. Alyssa and Collin might not even be married. I could have been set up.

That led to the possibilities for why: screwing with my investigation, or screwing with me. The evidence was biased toward the former since Mr. Murphy had come calling at the start of this case, and didn't seem to be interested in my private life. At least, not yet. Unless Brian was in on it too. That was being really paranoid of me, considering that I'd approached him, and not the other way around. Only a crazy woman would suspect that there was a conspiracy to seed hot guys around me so I'd be tempted to pick one of them up.

What was the purpose? Throw me off the track of what was really happening? Did that mean that something *else* was happening? Or was this just to make me so ineffective that I'd drop the case? Anybody who knew me should know that putting obstacles in my way wasn't the way to get me to give up.

It was the *how* that made my head spin. I *almost* could imagine somebody booby-trapping Collin's back yard. After all, that was a logical place that I might visit sometime. Maybe that mosquito bite in the back was a dart of some kind to make me trip over the chair. It seemed rather – silly – and not very likely or practical. I couldn't imagine somebody lurking within sight of his back yard with a dart gun just in case I showed up. That was really unlikely, as only Alyssa and I had known that I'd be there and when. Maybe somebody I'd investigated was connected with Alyssa. Whoever was responsible couldn't be setting traps everywhere that Collin went on the off chance that I showed up. Could they? That would be ridiculously wasteful for them. Now I was talking about a conspiracy of dozens of people with an unlimited budget.

I didn't believe it for a second. A conspiracy of that magnitude would be almost impossible to pull off unless you were a government agency. I simply wasn't important enough for anybody with enough resources to be interested in playing tricks on me.

Then there were the other situations. I'd left Alyssa with the impression that I'd be putting a camera in the room, not outside it. Adam was a bozo, but not a credible threat. He couldn't be hanging out in the print shop 24 hours a day waiting for me to show up. Given that someone in the print shop had no way of looking out back without opening the door, there would have to be a spotter somewhere outside either radioing or phoning Adam to come out. But why did Adam never look up if he knew I was there? Catching me in the act would have been the way to screw with me, not just *almost* catching me.

I remembered the Sam Spade look-alike I'd seen the night of the big rain. Maybe he was in on it too. Wow, I really was going crazy.

The fact was that there was no way to arrange all the misadventures I'd had on this case. They had to be just coincidence and happenstance.

Somehow, though, I had a gut feeling that they weren't.

Back at the office, I poured myself a homemade beer while the video from the camera was downloading to my computer, then settled in to watch with Yoko Geri sitting on my lap.

The video was – freaky. That, coming from a girl who had surveilled a naked fat guy doing a dressage routine while being ridden around on all fours by his dwarf girlfriend.

The camera was triggered by movement, and Collin's hand was still on the light switch when the recording started. He took off his boots and coat, throwing the coat onto the desk. The boots he put to one side. The moment when he turned toward the door to make sure that he'd locked was the moment when I managed to climb down the pole and make my escape. Everything after that was new to me.

He set out the fat candles, four of them, around the circumference of the magic circle. From the way he casually stepped on the lines and symbols, they had to be painted rather than drawn.

He put a charcoal brick in the incense burner and lit it. While that was getting going, he stripped the rest of his clothes off. Seeing him naked was an experience I could have lived without. The folded cloth turned out to be the calf-length robe with a cowl. I wondered if the seamstress who advertised in BhadraKali had made it. If so, why had he ordered a robe that was at least a size too small? Maybe he'd washed it and it shrank.

He hung the soup-bowl pendant around his neck, and opened the book to a marked place. Clearing his throat, he began to walk around the inside of the circle, reading aloud from the book.

The contact microphone didn't capture the best audio in the world, but at least it was mostly understandable.

"I invoke and conjure you, O mighty Prince Sitri, and being armed with power from the supreme Majesty, I thoroughly command you by Beralensis, and Paumachi, and the most powerful princes of the Tartarean seat..."

I wondered who the people, or things, were that he named, but at least the gist of it was clear: I'm being polite, but I'm a well-connected bad ass so you'd better show up, blah, blah, blah. I tuned out most of it, but I couldn't fast-forward because I needed to know if he named any actual, human accomplices or maybe victims.

Two insanely boring hours later he was still at it, although he'd stopped asking politely, and was now demanding that Sitri appear on pain of Bad Things Happening. My impression was that it's pretty hard to threaten someone who spends his time living in Hell. Who'd have thought?

At two hours fourteen minutes I was stroking Yoko, and he was purring. Between the ritual and the cat, I was close to falling asleep. Then the shit hit the fan, the leopard changed its spots, there was a revelation, and my life changed forever.

I hate it when that happens.

Outside the circle, above the triangle, a mist appeared that rapidly formed an outline, and then solidified into a humanoid figure. Sitri had finally shown up.

As demons go, I guess he wasn't too bad looking. At least he had the usual number of eyes. There were no Hollywood snapping mandibles or slime-coated tentacles.

Start with a naked man almost two metres tall, all bulging thews and rippling pecs like a classical Greek statue of perfect manhood. Transplant the head of a leopard onto him, and give him wings like Pegasus. Apart from those details, he had the hottest body I could ever have imagined. You could have grated cheese on his six pack, and had fun doing so. Garnish with a pointy gold crown. Give him the personality of serial killer Ted Bundy, and the voice of Idris Elba smothered in honey.

He was completely inhuman, a demon with wings, and the head of an animal. I still had an urge to know what it felt like to run my fingers through the treasure trail of hair on his lower abdomen.

That's the vibe that came through on a recording made through a dusty, unwashed window, under poor lighting conditions, and with a crappy microphone. I wondered what the effect was like in the room it-self, and a shudder went through me. Logically, I did not want to know. Emotionally, I couldn't wait to find out.

I wondered if he had this effect on all women, or whether I was just particularly susceptible to his influence. Either way, he terrified me.

There were only two possibilities: Collin had found my camera, and hired Pixar to do an extremely expensive rush job on the special effects as a joke, or I was looking at something completely real and utterly im-possible.

Again.

This sort of thing had happened before, during my first case. When I'd had *that* video analyzed, it bore all the evidence of being a real video of real happenings, even though an entire house full of furniture had inex-plicably materialized out of thin air, and then vanished again.

Now I was in my living room, sitting in my comfy chair with a purring kitten on my lap, and I wanted to throw up I was so panic-stricken. I was all out of sane explanations, rationalizations, and just plain denial. My nice, rational world collapsed around me.

If the book was right, this *thing* could turn anyone into a drooling love slave. What frightened me even more was the strong, undeniable attrac-tion I felt towards it.

I was used to the movie demons who were all unflossed teeth, claws, scales and drool. Nothing prepared me for the reality, which was that he was the sexiest thing in the universe. My emotions didn't care at all about the wings or the cat's head.

A moment ago I had been concerned that Alyssa should pack some things, and move to a women's shelter before Collin started using her as a punching bag. Now she might be in the deepest trouble imaginable. If Collin wanted to dump her and get a new plaything, she might still be all right. But if Collin was going to have Sitri do a number on her, simply running away wasn't going to cut it. How do you defend yourself against a demon?

I had terrible fear that the solutions that worked in movies were probably completely useless to me. I didn't have any magical artifacts or weapons. Nor did I have some long-lost ritual that would send him screaming back to Hell. Assuming, of course, that demons actually fol-lowed *any* of the rules that they did in stories.

I wondered if there was some kind of occult police I could call. I hoped so, because I was completely out of my league. I could just imagine call-ing on any of my cop buddies for help:

"Hi Nick, how are you doing? Say, I've got a bad guy here who is sum-moning demons to turn somebody into a sex slave. What part of the criminal code can we charge him under... hello?"

In all honesty, my buddies would probably listen to me. They would even take me seriously. But listening and believing were two different things. It was yet another thing to be able to do something about it.

Legally, getting a demon to subjugate someone should be the same as hiring a goon to assault them. In practice, I couldn't see any judge believing that Collin had done any such thing, or that it was even possible. All Collin had to do to get off was *not* to summon Sitri in the courtroom.

The next fifteen minutes on the video were filled with Collin arguing back and forth with the demon in excessively wordy, and truly terrible, King James English. Collin wanted something. Sitri demanded something in payment. Collin seemed confused by that, like he wasn't expecting anything but blind obedience. Sitri insisted that he be paid. Collin insisted that Sitri do what he was told. Neither side would budge.

By then it was late, and Collin wrapped it up to be continued later. Collin was treating magic like it was a business meeting – scheduling a block of time, and when that was done, moving on to other business. I doubted that demons saw things the same way. Even I knew that Collin's approach was wrong.

Like any preliminary business meeting, the deal was hammered out in principle with no details. The nature of the payment, the reason for it, and the names of any other involved parties, were to be determined later.

Crap.

It took another hour and a half for Collin to banish Sitri. It didn't take much imagination to picture demons building up a lot of resentment against people who forced them to drop whatever it was that demons do in their off-hours, and come like trained dogs. No wonder magicians needed an elaborate protective circle around them. I wondered why demons didn't just show up on their own, when the magician wasn't protected by a circle, and nuke the magician's ass. Maybe it was against the rules. Whatever those were.

I'd have to find out what those rules were in a big hurry, and the information would have to be absolutely accurate. This was no time for fooling around with online "sources" written by wannabes wearing a black goatee and eye-liner, pretending to be all-powerful sorcerers while living in a friend's basement with their 4000 D&D miniatures. I needed the real deal. Kali wasn't an expert in these matters, but she was all I had at the moment. Maybe she knew somebody.

There was a horrible moment of clarity when I realized that I'd just found out the answer to some of my questions about the interference with this case. Specifically, the "how," and also likely the "who." There was still no real evidence as to "why," but I had a sickening feeling that I could form a theory about that based on my previous experiences with Beleth. If Sitri was anything like her/him/them, and was behind my plans falling apart, he probably did it just for kicks.

The video ended when Collin clicked off the light, and left for the evening. Yoko Geri, confident that the affairs of mere demons were beneath his notice, decided that I was boring, and went off to investigate his food bowl. I softly closed the lid of my laptop.

Half an hour later I was still curled up in my chair. I was too scared to move, and felt humiliated. Yoko came back, and sat by the chair, meowing at me. When I ignored him, he jumped onto me, and started purring. Rather than bunting me to get me to pet him he curled up and put his head on my throat. After a minute he licked my neck, giving me a couple of kitten kisses.

His love probably wouldn't protect me from demons, but for now it was enough. I uncurled, and got ready for bed.

Yoko snuggled in beside me as usual, and after a few minutes of purring he fell asleep.

As I stared at the blackness, my mind kept trying to figure out what I was going to do next. Some time during the endless night, I had an idea that I could try. Its advantage was that it wouldn't involve putting any of my friends in danger.

That didn't mean I got any sleep.

CHAPTER 11

The Priest

The next morning I dragged myself out of bed, and spent time with Google maps while drinking far too much coffee. Not all the shaking of my hands was from the caffeine overdose. The good news was that help was only a few blocks away.

The Catholic church closest to my apartment was St. Pius X on Twenty-fourth Avenue. I'd walked or driven past it many times, but I'd never really noticed it. Apart from two weddings, I'd never been in a church. This was going to be completely outside my experience, and I suspected that it wouldn't be an everyday occurrence for the priest either.

After parking on the side street beside the obvious doors, I took a moment to try to prepare myself. My expectations were built on every movie with a church scene. I'd go into the whatever-it-was-called where all the pews were, a priest would notice I was there and come out to talk to me, I'd explain the problem, and he'd either give me a solution or point me toward somebody who knew how to handle demons.

I walked up the steps, grabbed the handle of the big wooden door, and pulled. It was locked. This was not according to plan. Weren't churches always open?

I walked around the south side where I thought I remembered there being another door. This one was labelled "Parish Offices." Even more promising, it opened when I pulled.

Inside was a small corridor. There was an open door on the left.

"May I help you?"

I almost jumped out of my skin, even though there was nothing startling about the woman who had appeared through one of the closed doors on the right. All my carefully prepared dialogue vanished from my brain.

"I need to talk to a priest," I blurted as I followed her into the office. It was small: a desk covered in papers, filing cabinets, and several chairs.

"He's quite busy. You'll need an appointment," she said as she moved behind the desk.

Just as I was about to tell her that this was an emergency the phone rang. She held up one finger as she answered it. Whoever was on the other end seemed frantic.

"That's all right, Noel. It isn't your fault. You can just reschedule." She flipped through an appointment book. "How does 10:30 work? No? How about nine A.M. tomorrow? Good. Thanks for calling."

The inner office door opened just as I was about to open my mouth again.

The priest was younger than I'd expected – no older than forty. In movies they're always about eighty years old unless celibacy is a plot issue. He glanced around the office and fixed on me.

"Noel?"

"She just called. Her car won't start so she rescheduled," the secretary said. "This young lady would like to see you."

"No time like the present," he said. "Please come in. I'm Father Cole."

We shook hands.

"Veronica Chandler."

His office looked like a lawyer's. The only real difference was that the books had more to do with sermons and saints than with law. Also, most lawyers don't have a crucifix on the wall. He closed the door, and offered me one of the guest chairs. He sat opposite me on the same side of the desk.

"What can I do for you, Ms. Chandler?"

Now that the moment had come, anything that I could say seemed completely stupid.

"Um, it's kind of difficult to explain."

"You needn't feel uncomfortable. Everything you say to me is completely confidential, unless there's immediate danger to yourself or another person. Over the years I've heard just about everything."

"I'm not sure where to start."

"How about the beginning?"

I let out a long breath.

You asked for it.

"I'm a private investigator. A client hired me to find out if her husband was having an affair. During surveillance something else happened that I hope you know how to handle. It turned out he's not cheating. It's worse."

His eyebrow went up as I handed him a USB drive.

"What's this?"

"Surveillance video. It'll be much easier if you just it before I answer any questions."

"Is there anything criminal on here?"

"No. I wish there was. Then I could just call the police.."

He plugged the drive into his laptop, and turned it so we could both see the screen.

Collin started to take off his clothes.

"Um, you can fast forward half an hour," I said quickly.

I watched the priest's face harden as he watched Collin doing his incantation.

"I see what you mean," he said. "He's performing black magic."

"There's more," I said. "Skip to about 2:12."

He fiddled with the computer, and the video resumed with Collin threatening Sitri to make him appear. I had my eyes on Father Cole as Sitri materialized.

At first he was startled, then he smiled as he paused the video.

"I didn't know that amateur film makers had access to special effects that good."

"This isn't a joke. This is the raw footage from my surveillance camera last night."

"That's enough. This isn't funny any more."

"Believe me, it never was. I'm asking for your help because this guy really, actually summoned a demon. Not a guy in a costume. Not CGI. A real, honest to God demon." I realized what I'd said. "If you'll pardon the expression."

"Somebody must be playing a trick on you. The Church teaches us that demons are purely spiritual beings. They can tempt and sometimes possess, but they have no physical being. They don't show up on video."

"I wish you were right, but if this was a hoax it would cost hundreds of thousands of dollars, and weeks of work. I placed the camera two nights ago, and collected it last night. There wasn't time to plant a fake."

He looked at me for a long time. I tried to be patient.

"I believe that you believe this," he said. "But you have to understand that what you are showing me contradicts everything that I've been taught. Demons are not physical entities."

"I'm sorry, Father, but t doesn't matter what you've been taught. Prince Sitri is real. He's standing right there in front of Co-... my client's husband. He's casting a shadow, for heaven's sake!" I took another deep breath and tried to calm down. "Please, I can't think of anything else to do. Can't you do an exorcism or something?"

"Exorcism is the act of casting a demon out of a person who is possessed, and doesn't apply in this case. Even if it did apply, it's rarely done these days, and then only after a thorough investigation to eliminate all other possibilities such as the person being mentally ill."

"Isn't there something else you can do?"

"I'll have to research the options and get back to you."

"All right. You can keep the video." I passed him one of my business cards. "Please call me as soon as you have something."

I went home, worried, played with my cat, worried, and made lunch. While I was in the kitchen the phone rang. The caller got right to the point.

"Ms. Chandler, this is Father Cole. If you are serious about this problem, I'd need to see the demon for myself. There will need to be clear proof that this is real. After that, I'm not sure how we will proceed."

It sounded like the best deal I'd get. The trick was to guarantee that there would be no tricks.

"All right. Do you have a video camera, a long cable, and some way to hook it up to a monitor?"

"I'll have to check. I know that the church has a camera."

"The windows where the ritual takes place are at least three metres above ground. My camera was mounted on a utility pole, and it recorded the scene for later. If we run a cable from your camera to your monitor we can watch the whole thing as it happens. As long as nobody but you touches the equipment, will that satisfy you?"

"I'll think about it, and consult with our A-V person. When do you propose doing this?"

"It depends on him. It's always on a weeknight starting around 7:30. I usually find out from his wife whether he'll be 'working late' around 5:00 to 6:00 on the day."

"That's extremely inconvenient. I have duties most evenings." He thought for a moment. "How often does this happen?"

"Once or twice a week. Sometimes more."

"Without fail?"

"So far."

"All right. I can get someone else to cover my evenings for a few days. If this is a joke or a trick I warn you that I will not be at all amused."

"Believe me, Father, I'm sincerely hoping that it *is* a trick."

Alyssa called me the next day at 5:30. I immediately called Father Cole, who said he'd pick me up at my place at 7:00.

Somehow, I expected a priest to drive a small, older car. Maybe a Citroen. Instead, he was driving a late model, dark blue cargo van with a sun roof. My assumptions about priests were taking a beating.

"Nice wheels," I said as I got in with my equipment. This time I was wearing my surveillance sweats.

"We borrowed it from one of my parishioners. I thought it would be useful, especially with three of us."

"Who else is coming?" I said as I tossed my bag into the back. There was a distinct, "ow."

"You remember our church secretary, Ruth?" I turned to look. The older woman was sitting on what looked like a futon in back.

"Oh. Sorry about that."

"Ruth is here as a witness," he said sternly. "I'm here because I have given you the benefit of the doubt, but I don't know you and I'm not a fool. Again, if this is a trick..."

"It's not. The more witnesses the better," I said. "Shall we go?"

We were silent during the drive, except when I gave directions. The van had rear windows but they were covered with what seemed to be aluminum foil held on with masking tape. From the brief glimpses I got, lit through the windshield, the good Father had borrowed somebody's make-out vehicle, complete with what looked like a refrigerator. Despite the thick futon in the back, Ruth did not look at all comfortable.

When we pulled up to the back of the building light was shining from Collin's window. There was no sign of Adam's car, but that didn't mean anything.

"I'll get my climbing gear on," I said as we parked.

"There's no need," he said, opening the sun roof half way.

Ruth passed the camera to him. It was mounted on the end of what looked like a painter's pole. Sitting in the comfort of the van, he ran the pole up through the sunroof. The cable snaked to the back where his laptop was plugged into a power inverter. We could watch the show sitting on the futon. All the comforts of home.

It took several tries to aim the camera properly. The sun roof was mostly closed to help hold the pole in place.

It was somewhat weird sitting in a make-out van with a priest and a church secretary. The foil on the windows turned out to be the Father's idea so we could turn the interior lights on without being seen. He also drew a black curtain that he ran on a rail between the sides of the van to block the front view. It wasn't perfect, but it would do.

"You seem comfortable with surveillance," I said once we were settled.

"I wasn't always a priest. Before that I was an RCMP officer for eight years."

"I don't suppose you know anybody in the Calgary Police?"

"No. Why?"

"My mother's a homicide detective, and I have a lot of friends on the force. If I'd known you were an ex-Mountie I could have had somebody confirm that at least I'm not some air head joker."

He managed to smile and look slightly guilty at the same time.

"That's why I decided to believe you. I called my own contacts to find out who you are, and if you are really a private investigator. You'll be glad to know that you have a good reputation. I heard about your run-in with the crack head."

I looked away from him.

"I don't want to talk about it."

"I wouldn't expect you to."

The van had overhead spot lights like the ones in aeroplanes. Ruth turned one on, and began reading a book. I don't think she approved of me.

On the screen, Collin was doing his incantation. The camera had a good microphone, but without window contact the sound from inside was faint at best, and sometimes obscured by outside noises. Father Cole watched the screen of his laptop while she read.

I pulled a book out of my bag, and leaned against the opposite wall. It would be at least two hours until something interesting happened.

The priest caught my attention when he sucked in a big breath. It caught Ruth's too, and I could see her eyes widen. She dropped her book, crossed herself, and clasped her hands before her as she began reciting in a whisper.

"Hail Mary, full of grace, the Lord is with thee..."

Father Cole crossed himself as I scurried over to their side of the van.

The screen showed Collin in his robe, his arms outstretched. Sitri was standing in the triangle, his arms folded across his chest.

The sound was now turned up as far as it would go. I could make out some conversation. Enough to know that they were continuing the negotiation for a sacrifice in exchange for sexual favours.

Father Cole put the laptop down on the futon, and went forward to the sunroof. He peered upward, and wiggled the pole slightly.

"Stay here," he said. He turned off the engine, removed the key so there would be no noise from the warning buzzer, and quietly opened the driver's door. He used the seat to climb onto the roof.

I could hear him carefully making his way across the van staying close to the edges. Meanwhile, Ruth was into her third of fourth repetition of the prayer.

"...and blessed is the fruit of thy womb, Jesus. Holy Mary, Mother of God, pray for us sinners now, and at the hour of death. Hail Mary..."

Despite his instructions, there was no way that I was missing whatever action was happening. It also occurred to me that I might be better off in the open rather than trapped inside a van if something weird happened. I went out through the same door. Ruth didn't budge.

Father Cole was standing on the roof near the front of the van, and holding onto the building's tiny window ledge. His knees were slightly bent so that he was just high enough to peer through the bottom of the glass.

He stayed there for a few minutes. Then he slowly made his way toward the back of the van while keeping his eyes on the ritual. Nothing else happened, so as far as I could tell Sitri wasn't aware of us.

I went back inside, and looked at the computer screen. It was business as usual in the circle, with Collin obviously trying to convince the demon to see things his way. One thing that was different was that Sitri was holding what looked like a small photograph. From that angle I could see that it was a portrait, but I had no idea of who the person was or even whether it was a man or woman.

The van rocked slightly as Father Cole climbed back inside, and pulled the door closed as quietly as possible. When he got into the back, he returned to watching the screen. I tried to go back to my book, but gave up and watched the screen too.

Eventually, Collin started his banishing.

"We should get ready," I said. "Once the demon is banished we won't have long before he leaves."

Father Cole didn't say anything as he got into the driver's seat. He put the laptop on the centre console where we could see what was happening. I rode shotgun again. Ruth was still praying in the back behind the black-out curtain.

I really wanted to know what he was thinking, but this seemed like a time for me to pretend to be patient. He was having to process a lot.

As soon as Sitri disappeared, the priest opened the sun roof. Rather than taking the time to collapse the pole all the way, we just tilted it into the back. I grabbed the laptop while he started the engine and drove away. Once we were on the street, he thumbed the switch to close the sun roof.

We were silent for about ten minutes. He drove. I watched the traffic. Ruth was quiet in the back, although I could still hear an occasional muttered word.

"I apologize for doubting you," he suddenly said.

"No problem. It's a lot to believe. What did you see when you were on the roof?"

"I wanted to see it with my own eyes. To make sure that reality agreed with what the camera was showing." He paused.

"You also got multiple points of view," I said.

"Yes. At first I thought that the scene might be a projection of some kind. If so, it was remarkably three dimensional."

"What was that Sitri was holding?"

"A photograph. The magician tossed it to the demon to look at. It was the picture of a woman. I don't know who."

"Can you describe her?"

"Caucasian with dark hair. That's about all I could make out."

"It could be his receptionist. Or it could be half the women in Calgary. I assume this means you'll be talking to your bishop?"

"I don't have a choice. Handling the photograph proved that the demon is physical. The whole thing is recorded on the computer. I have proof of what we saw. Do you mind if I also show him the recording you made?"

"Not at all. Anything to get this solved."

We lapsed back into silence, each with our own thoughts.

"I'm sorry," I said.

"For what?"

"Screwing up your world view, I guess. This is going to change the Catholic view of reality, isn't it?"

"We've survived changing our views before."

"Yeah, but it looks to me like we're moving from demons can make you unhappy to demons can literally chew your leg off. How's that going to change things? I can really imagine it causing panic when this gets out. Personally, I'm terrified."

"I don't know. Maybe demons were physical beings all along, and they fooled us. Wiser heads than mine will have to figure that out."

"I don't know how you are so completely cool about this. When I first saw my video I completely freaked out."

"As a member of the RCMP I saw things that nobody should. The way you handle it is to focus on the job at hand. You take pictures, collect evidence, and help load body bags into the ambulance instead of thinking about what they represent. Believe me, I won't be sleeping much tonight."

The good Father dropped me off at my apartment. By then Ruth had stopped praying. I didn't think that sleep was in the cards for any of us.

It would be tomorrow morning at the earliest before he could contact his bishop, and the church started to change its mind about demons. While failing to sleep, I did some research about the history of the Catholic church. They were not in the habit of changing their minds quickly. While I admired their attention to detail, in this case it wasn't good.

Whoever was in that picture Sitri was looking at didn't have years to wait for help to arrive.

My phone rang at eight o'clock while I was having breakfast. I was still in my clothes from the night before, and Yoko Geri was peeved that I hadn't come to bed. The caller was literally the last person I expected to hear from.

"Ms. Chandler, this is Father Cole. I have some news for you."

"That was fast."

"I'm told that this is not the first time that this has happened. It is, however, the first time that we've caught the summoning ritual in progress. It's also the first time we've gotten a demon on video. I'm told that the Roman Curia has a course of action already planned that should solve the problem."

"I'm not sure why, but knowing that this isn't just happening here makes me feel a bit better," I said.

"I feel the same way. Even if terrible things are happening here, at least we know that we aren't being singled out. We do, however, have the honour of being the test subjects for the proposed solution."

"Great. What do you need me to do?"

"My bishop has delegated me to bless the ritual site. Demons are known to be repelled by religious symbols, so that should make it impossible for it to appear in that location again. Can you get us into the room?"

"Probably. We could go in the middle of the night. Nobody should be around then. Even if it's one of his ritual nights, he's done by eleven or so. Let's say two A.M."

"Good. I'll let the bishop know."

I picked up Father Cole at the church. It was exactly one A.M. as he threw his kit into Binky's back seat and climbed in. His kit consisted of a military-looking cubic duffel about the size of a beer cooler.

"What's the plan?" I asked once we were underway.

"I have to bless the space and say Mass. That will sanctify the space, and make it impossible for the demon to appear there."

"What about elsewhere?"

"This style of ritual constrains the demon to appear in the triangle. If that is unavailable the demon can't appear at all until the magician creates a new circle elsewhere."

"Sounds good, as long as Collin doesn't figure it out. Otherwise we'll be playing spiritual Whack-a-Mole as he changed locations."

"May I assume that you'll be keeping him under surveillance?"

"For a while. I can't do it for the rest of my life."

"Sufficient unto the day are the evils thereof. We can only cross each bridge as we come to it."

Sometime, it would be nice to be a normal teenage girl.

We circled the whole building first. Except for the lights at the front, it appeared that nobody was home. No vehicles were parked anywhere nearby.

I was prepared to pick the lock on the utility door, but there was no need. Either someone had been careless, or nobody worried about the junk in the hallway being stolen. There was no such luck with the door to room 12.

The keyhole was on the right side, which meant most people would open it with the key in their left hand. The natural way to turn the cylinder would be counterclockwise.

I gently felt for the pins with my pick, breathing quietly and slowly so I wouldn't get overexcited. Anxiety would only slow me down.

Picking common locks isn't rocket science. It's an art, a delicate one, requiring one to visualize what is happening inside the mechanism by tiny differences in touch. Being an art, it takes as much time as it takes. Somebody with experience will, on average, be faster than a beginner, but these people in movies who walk up to a door, jiggle some tools for a few seconds, and then walk in have the script writers on their side. That's only happened to me once, during practice, and I was so startled when the lock opened immediately that I almost let it lock again.

This lock was cheap and easy. Gentle tension, stroking the pins like a lover's hair. Who wants to be the first one to set?

One by one, the pins fell to my mechanical seduction. The cylinder moved a little. The lock was open after ten minutes of gentle effort. As I turned it with the wrench I smiled at Father Cole and – nothing. Some idiot had installed a lock that required turning the cylinder the other way. I would have to lock it, pick it again, and move the cylinder clockwise to open the door.

Shit. So much for looking like a professional.

Okay, no sense in getting upset. I allowed the cylinder to move back to its centre position, and heard the rapid-fire rattle of the pins resetting. Starting again, at least this time I had some feel for the mechanism. It only took me eight minutes to coax the cylinder to move for me again. This time the bolt retracted, and the door opened.

"How long will this take?" I asked as he went in with his kit.

"An hour or so."

"Do you need me for anything?"

"No. You can observe or wait outside."

I took out my phone.

"Put your phone on vibrate. I'll stand guard, and call you if anybody shows up. You call me if you run into any problems. I'll be about fifteen seconds away."

Binky was parked on the street out front, positioned so that nobody could approach the building without me seeing them. At least, that was the theory.

An hour is a long time when it's past your bed time, and you have to be paying attention. Reading was out, not only because I might miss something, but also because I'd have to turn on the overhead light. Not exactly stealthy. I was really feeling the lack of sleep from the night before too.

I'd forgotten to heed my own advice. When my phone rang out loud I almost had a heart attack.

"What's wrong?" I said as I jumped out, and ran for the door.

"Nothing," he said. "I'm finished."

I slowed down and stopped running just as I reached the utility door. Inside, I caught the priest just about to close the door to the ritual room.

"Wait a moment." I did a quick check of the room. He'd been careful, and I couldn't detect anything out of place. There were some splash marks, apparently from water, but they'd be dry well before morning. The smell of incense wasn't that strong, and likewise should be gone before anybody else noticed it.

We put the kit in the car, then I drove around the back. He watched with some amusement as I climbed the pole to place my camera and microphone.

"You do realize that climbing a utility pole is illegal?" he said when I was down.

"If you don't mention it, I won't mention anything about you breaking and entering."

"Fair enough."

I was beginning to like Father Cole.

The next day dragged, even though I wasn't out of bed until the afternoon. Mostly I read, drank coffee, and petted Yoko Geri. Around 4:30 Alyssa called. Collin certainly was busy with his project.

The suspense was killing me, so I drove over to his lair around ten P.M. The light was still on. I had a brief desire to climb the pole so I could watch him being frustrated, but I wasn't that stupid. If he looked up at the very least I'd have an old fashioned crazy man after me.

Twenty minutes or so later the window went dark. I peeked around the corner of the building as he walked away heading for the bus to take him home. Retrieving the camera took very little time before I headed home myself.

I downloaded the video as soon as I got in. It was malicious of me, but I wanted to watch him get frustrated. I sampled the action every few minutes starting at two hours to see when he figured out that his pet demon wasn't coming.

Sometime between two samples, Sitri showed up.

I watched from that point onward. It was all very much according to plan. Collin's plan at least.

What had gone wrong? This should be impossible. Of course, so was the whole situation. Yet here we were.

All right, so getting a Catholic priest to prevent the demon from showing up didn't work. I'd been sure that it would keep it away, and didn't have a plan B.

I really needed a plan B.

The phone rang four times before picking up.

"Hi, this is Kali. I'm probably doing something that doesn't involve answering the phone, so please leave a message and I'll get back to you sometime."

Beep.

I cleared my throat and swallowed. The lump in my throat migrated to my stomach.

"Kali, it's me. Please call me back as soon as you get this. I'm in really big trouble."

CHAPTER 12

The Elder

The night had passed with agonizing slowness, as I alternately tossed and turned, and stared at the dark ceiling. Yoko Geri actually gave up on sleeping with me, leaving the bed around two o'clock to sleep on the sofa. I know that, because I got worried about him and went to check. He was not amused when I turned on the light.

After a few hours of subjective eternity, a beautiful, sunny autumn morning arrived. On the trees outside, the leaves were beginning to turn to their fall colours. Kids not much younger than me walked by, laughing and awkwardly flirting on their way to the nearby school, unaware that there were more serious matters in the world than what colour of iPod to buy, and whether it was still cool to like Justin Bieber.

Self-absorbed adults parked on our street where there was no time limit, before walking over to the Banff Trail C-Train station to go to work downtown. It was cheap for them, and annoying for the residents. They had no idea what was going on either.

I got up with all the enthusiasm of a zombie faced with a vegan buffet, and sat in my comfy chair. The beer I'd poured for myself the previous evening was still sitting on the side table, warm and flat. I put my feet on the coffee table, and Yoko Geri stretched out along the trough formed by my extended legs. He purred, his black head occasionally bunting against one of my hands to remind me to pet him. Maybe he sensed my mood and wanted to comfort me. *Hey, human food dispenser, how bad can it be? Rejoice! You have me lying on you!* I ran my fingers behind one of his ears. The fur felt incredibly soft and silky.

I'd never lived on my own before getting this apartment. When Kali told me I should get a pet, I thought of a gold fish, like the one I'd had as a child. Instead, she took me to the Humane Society, where she forced me to wander through the cat cage area. I'd never had a cat. Neither had my parents. Cats were okay but, really? A cat? Me?

Yoko Geri was one of a litter of six, all of them black and devastatingly cute. I stopped to watch five of them playing together. He was off to one side chasing his tail. I'd never seen that before in real life. He looked so serious as he hunted his prey that I laughed.

He stopped his circling, and trotted over to the glass that separated us. He just sat there, watching me, his green eyes looking deeply into my sort-of-hazel ones. He sneezed, stuck one hind leg straight up in the air, and started licking his foot, his toes spread wide. Then he overbalanced, and fell on his back. He lay there, his tummy exposed, looking at me as if to say, *what are you looking at? I meant for that to happen.*

It was inexplicable to anyone who hasn't experienced such a moment. I was in love. Half an hour later we were on our way home together, the two of us cuddling while Kali drove, a smart-assed smirk on her face.

I thought of calling him Miles, after Sam Spade's partner in *The Maltese Falcon*, but Miles Archer dies early in the story. That didn't seem like a good omen. Every good PI needs a sidekick, so that became his name.

My nostalgic memories were interrupted by the phoning ringing. Yoko Geri teleported off my lap leaving several puncture marks in his wake. Ow.

"What's wrong?" Kali said as soon as I picked up. Just the sound of her voice, her concern, chased away a lot of my fear.

"Can you come over right away? There's something I have to show you."

"I'm already in my car. I'll be there within ten minutes."

She looked worried when she let herself in, and she didn't even know what was happening.

I put my laptop on the coffee table so Kali and I could sit on the couch as we watched the video together. At least I was able to save her from looking at all three plus hours by fast-forwarding to the relevant parts.

It was a mistake to have given her a beer. It now sat beside her, matching mine on the flat and warm scale. When the video ended I cleared my throat.

"I should just give my client the videos and notes, then pick up my final pay cheque, and walk away. Preferably to someplace exotic where I can lie on a beach for the rest of my life, and get skin cancer."

Our eyes met over Yoko who had returned to lie on his back between us. *Rub my tummy, humans. At your own risk, of course.*

"There are problems with that," Kali said as she gently stroked his chest. He extended his chin in kitten bliss.

"Like what? It sounds like an ideal solution."

"You mean, apart from leaving somebody to a target? It could be his wife, or his receptionist. Maybe it's both. Or someone else."

I scratched Yoko's throat.

"Anyway," she continued, "even if she divorces her husband, that won't stop Sitri."

Something occurred to me.

"Damn, should we even be saying the name out loud?" Another thing to worry about.

"Don't worry, magic requires intent. Despite what you see in movies, just saying names out loud won't do anything. Even if you say them three times."

"Are you sure? I don't know what the rules are for this kind of thing, and if I'm not running away to Bora Bora I need to learn them fast. Anyway, if Collin wants her, whoever she is, he'll get her. How am I supposed to stop a black magician, let alone a demon? I don't suppose you have the number for some secret council of white wizards on speed dial?"

"Sorry, I've never heard of one outside of fantasy novels. And you mean *we*."

"What?"

"How do *we* stop a black magician."

"Oh, hell no. You are not going to be anywhere near ground zero when this goes down. I don't want you risking your life."

"Don't be an idiot. One, I'm already involved. Two, you're my sister, not my boss. Three, you didn't abandon me when my parents died, and I'm not abandoning you now, and four –"

"Four," I interrupted, "we're asking the wrong question,".

"Oh?"

"Forget the black magic, how do you stop any bad guy?"

"Normally, I'd say that you call the police."

"That won't work. They'd never believe the video, and there isn't any other evidence. Even after the fact, the only evidence will be that one or more women change their minds about how attractive Collin is."

Kali leaned back, and rested her head on the back of the couch.

"So how do you think we stop a bad guy who's beyond the law?"

"It's simple," I said. "Someone steps up to the plate, and does whatever is necessary."

Kali sat up, and turned to face me so fast that Yoko bolted. I didn't want to look at her, so I watched him trot into the kitchen.

"Are you freaking nuts? You aren't a killer, and neither am I."

"But I *am* a killer. If you'll remember, I have already shot and killed a man. This isn't so different. If Collin goes away, I assume that the problem does as well. Unless there's some rule that Sitri has to avenge him, or something." I thought of something unpleasant. "Or is this one of those 'kill the sorcerer and free the demon from his binding' situations?"

"You are insane. The situation you mentioned isn't at all similar to this one. The guy you shot was coming at you with a baseball bat. You reacted in the heat of the moment to save lives. This would be a cold-blooded execution. Besides, where are you going to get a gun?"

"I know the combination to Mum's gun safe."

"Oh, that's brilliant," she said, dripping with sarcasm. "You're going to murder someone with Mum's service weapon. Have you ever heard of forensics?"

She had a point but I wasn't giving up. She can be stubborn but so can I.

"There's no problem if I don't leave a bullet behind. I could dig it out –"

"If you can find it. I understand that can be difficult at times."

"– or I don't have to use a bullet at all. Putting the gun to his head, and using a blank will blow his brains out just as effectively."

"That's a little personal, isn't it? If you're going to get that close, why don't you just stab him? Or better yet, strangle him so you can feel the life leave him."

"Stop it! I don't like it either, but I'm low on options."

"On the other hand, isn't Mum's service weapon in Ireland at the moment? That makes things a little more difficult, although it would be a great alibi."

I hate it when she's so bloody logical and wise.

"It was just a thought."

"Yes, a bad one, even for you. How about confronting him? Maybe if you tell him that you know what he's up to he'll realize it isn't worth it now that somebody knows his plan."

"Possibly, but if I'd gone to as much time and effort as he has I'd just advance my timetable. My guess is that spooking him will cause him to give Sitri whatever he wants immediately. He can just get the demon to take me out later. Or sooner."

"Okay, I admit that would be bad."

"I'm glad we agree. I don't know what else to do, though."

"For one thing, you can remember that I own an occult shop, and this is an occult problem."

"You said you didn't know of anybody who could help."

"No, I said I didn't know of an occult police force. That doesn't mean I don't have contacts. Let me make some calls before you start murdering anybody."

Kali did the driving later that afternoon. Our destination was on the shoulder of the Nose Creek Valley overlooking Deerfoot Trail. We pulled into the small parking lot near a building that was surrounded by grass and trees.

A Native man walked out of the building to greet us. By my standards he was tall, but in truth he was about the same height as Kali. He had the rolling gait of someone who has spent most of his life on a horse.

"Remember," she said as we walked to meet him, "he'll test you. Just be honest in your answers."

He went directly to Kali, and shook hands with her.

"Kali," he said quietly. I got the feeling he didn't talk much. "Who's your friend?"

"Wilburn, this is my sister, Veronica."

He shook my hand. Wilburn Crowchild looked like he was a hundred years old. In spite of that, his handshake nearly crushed my fingers. On the way to the Native Addictions Centre, Kali had told me that he'd been a rancher all his working life, which explained his gait. Now he was a councillor at the Centre.

"I'm pleased to meet you," I said.

He tilted his head quickly, like a crow regarding a shiny object whose value was yet to be determined.

"Why?"

If he responded to honesty, that's what he'd get.

"I need your help."

"But do I need to help you?"

"I think so. Yes."

"Good," he said, nodding quickly like a bird, "then we have things to say. Let's walk."

The three of us left the parking lot, and walked south along a pathway toward Deerfoot Trail.

The old man suddenly stopped, and sat on the grass. We did likewise.

"Tell me what you think you need."

I started more or less at the beginning. I'd uploaded part of the video of Sitri being summoned to my phone. When I got to that part, I handed him the phone.

He watched the video in silence, then handed it back to me. For a moment he was silent.

"His English is terrible. He should take classes in Shakespeare."

I couldn't help it. I laughed.

"I know. It's shameful."

Again, he gave me that crow-like look.

"Why?"

I took my time before answering.

"I'd expect someone brought up speaking English to be better at it."

"But people haven't used English like that for four centuries. Should he be responsible for something his people did four hundred years ago?"

This wasn't the way I'd expected the conversation to go, so I kept silent.

"That's your way of thinking. The world has changed. What my ancestors did seemed good to them at the time. What I do seems good to me now. Are you ashamed of what your ancestors did to my people?"

"I believe that it was wrong."

"Not from their point of view. Not at that time. Do you feel that you should atone for their sins?"

"No. I was born here, so in that sense I'm as much a native as you. What people who may have been my ancestors did has nothing to do with how I choose to live my life. All I can do is what seems right to me."

"Good. Maybe you aren't completely white. Why do you believe that I can help you?"

I looked at Kali.

"You know that I do not share your ways, but I honour them," she said. "Everything I have seen leads me to believe that you have more power than I do with the spirits. If you will not help, I will do what I can. But to stop this man from doing harm to others, I think that you are our best hope."

He gave her the crow look.

"Why do you care?"

"A person is in trouble and we can help. Why don't you?" She shot back.

Crowchild laughed.

"Good one, Kali. All right, I'll see what I can. Do you have a file on this asshole?"

I raised one eyebrow. It wasn't quite the language I'd expect from a Wise Old Native Elder. I had the feeling that very little about him was conventional. At least, in my sense of the word.

Kali nudged me. I handed over a USB drive with all the case information on it.

"Thanks. I'll let you know what happens."

He stood up like he was my age. He'd dusted the grass off the back of his trousers by the time I was on my feet. He held out his hand.

"Veronica, it was good meeting you."

This time, when he squeezed, I squeezed back. He still might have been able to crush my hand, but at least I made him work for it. He grinned again.

"Kali, I like your sister. She could almost be an Indian."

He leaned closer to us.

"Don't tell anybody I said that. These days we're supposed to be First Nations Peoples, but I grew up an Indian."

"What would you like to be called?" I asked. My generation has been taught to be careful about labels.

"You can call me Wil," he said. "Just don't call me late for supper."

He laughed at his joke, and Kali smiled. He really wasn't what I'd expected, which told me something about how little I knew about Canadian Natives.

I wanted to know what he was going to do about the demon, but I stopped myself from asking. If Wilburn wanted me to know, he'd tell me. Otherwise, I was going to respect his ways. Whatever that meant, exactly. We walked in silence back to our car, and Wil waved without looking back as he went into the building.

"I can see where he'd be an effective counsellor," I said as we drove home. "How did you two meet?"

"A few months ago a Native woman came into Bhadrakali. She'd been a prostitute and drug addict for years, and was pretty messed up. She saw the shop as she was walking past, and she said it called to her. We talked for a while, then I phoned the addiction centre to see what help was available for her. She came back the next day to meet with Wilburn. I hear she's been clean ever since."

"I just hope he's as good with demons."

She looked toward the door that Wilburn had gone through.

"I wouldn't bet against him. You only saw the surface. He's like a force of nature when he decides something needs to be done."

Three days later I got a call from Kali. There'd been no messages from Alyssa in the meantime.

"Wilburn Crowchild just called me. It's done."

"Wonderful. Any idea what he did?"

"No, none. The whole New Age White Indian crowd has made the real Natives cautious about discussing anything to do with their culture, even with people they consider friends. They've been burned too many times by poseurs."

"I get that. Did he at least say what the effect should be?"

"He said he asked the spirits of this place to drive away any foreign spirits, so Sitri shouldn't be able to show up, or if he does, he won't stay long."

"I guess we'll see."

I don't know why Collin was lying low for a couple of days, but I didn't hear from Alyssa until the next Sunday. Collin told her that he'd be working late on Monday night. I was still debating how much to tell her about what Collin was doing.

I waited until after 11 P.M. to place the camera. There was no way that Adam, or anybody else, would be working that late, especially on a Sunday.

Sure enough, there were no other vehicles around. Just to be sure, I parked Binky across the alley, behind one of the dumpsters, for a quick get away. In deference to paranoia, I also covered his license plate with a towel. I walked back, put on my harness and crampons, and went up the pole. Attaching the camera and microphone would take only a few seconds.

I heard the thumping bass before I saw the car. A moment later, headlights bobbed drunkenly across the building, as a beater with bad shocks turned into the alley. It ground to a halt only a couple of metres from my pole. Literally, ground to a halt. It needed new brake pads too. The music cut off with the ignition, although the engine rattled on several times before finally giving up. Adam got out, a cigarette dangling from his lips. He took one more long drag from it before flicking it to one side. He unlocked the back door to the shop and went in.

As soon as the door started closing I completed my installation, and got out of there as fast as possible. What the hell was with this guy and working late? I wondered if Sitri was controlling him somehow, but if Adam was the worst Sitri could do we were in good shape.

The next night I went back at two A.M. to retrieve the camera. For once, my little friend wasn't around.

Despite the hour, I downloaded the video as soon as I got home. Fast forwarding through the boring parts, I started watching around the two hour mark. As usual, Collin was threatening Bad Things if Sitri didn't show up Real Soon.

By two hours fourteen minutes nothing had happened yet. 2:20. 2:30. It looked like Wilburn had put the hex on Collin's working. I had a bottle of my best milk stout to celebrate.

At 2:43, as I was rubbing Yoko Geri's ears, Sitri appeared. He didn't seem to be under attack, or in any distress whatsoever. He certainly stayed longer than a few seconds. Crap.

"Oh Great Prince Sitri, mightiest of Hell's infernal legions, I doth commandeth thee, that thou obeyest mine wishes," Collin said.

"Nay, Magus," Sitri responded. "It is not mete that thou makest demands without proffering payment."

"Forsooth, I needeth to pay thee nothing. Thou must obeyeth mine every commandment!"

"Again I say nay, Magus. Speech is of little value, and action commands defrayment."

Under completely different circumstances, I could have found Sitri amusing. What he'd just said sounded suspiciously like the King James version of "talk is cheap, action costs money."

"What is it that thou demandest? And by makingeth such an enquiry, thou mayest not assumeth that I am required to provideth whatsoever thou asketh."

When I processed Collin's bad grammer, I realized that he was spouting standard legal disclaimers. Would lawyer-speak would cut it with a demon? Hell, for all I knew that was part of the rules.

"Thy demands require great effort on my part. It shall require the sacrifice of a female human."

What is it with things that want a human sacrifice? Why do they always want a woman? Why not a fifty year old guy, or a box of chocolate?

Collin paced back and forth within his circle. The next few moments would pretty much define him, as far as I was concerned.

"Dost thou requireth that she be a virgin?"

And he failed. Instead of drawing the line at murder, he was dickering about the details. What the hell was so great about being a virgin, anyway?

"It matters not."

See, Collin, even demons don't give a rat's ass about virginity. Welcome to the twenty-first century.

"Thy request be unreasonable. Mine situation is such that killing for thee wouldst put me in peril of discovery."

"Thou needst not do the deed thyself."

Collin looked at his watch and frowned.

"I shalt considereth thy request, and shalt contact thee when my decision hath been made."

Collin opened the book to a marked place, and began trying to get Sitri to leave. At one point during the threats Sitri yawned. I got the impression that he wasn't as affected by the ritual as Collin thought. That was another troubling line of thought. Finally, he turned into mist and evaporated.

Clearly, for some reason, the shamanic approach to the problem hadn't worked.

I finished off the milk stout without really tasting it. I foolishly had thought this case couldn't get any worse.

I was wrong.

Not only did I have to find another way to stop Collin from summoning a demon to make someone his sex slave, now I had to prevent the murder of an unknown woman as well.

CHAPTER 13

The Coven

This was a situation demanding a lot of strong drink, so we were sitting close to the tea pot in Kali's kitchen. "Does he have any idea why it didn't work?" I asked, as she poured me another cup of lapsang souchong.

"Not in the way you mean. Native ceremonies ask the spirits for help, they don't command them. He just said that the spirits must have chosen not to intervene for some reason."

"I'm out of my depth here. Is spirit indifference a normal thing?"

"In the sense that it isn't abnormal, yes."

"Damn, I was hoping that this was over. Any ideas about our next move?"

"I have a group I work with who can help me to do a binding spell. That should make it impossible for Collin to do anything bad."

"Holy shit, you can do that? I never knew you had that kind of mojo. You've been holding out on me."

She had the decency to look embarrassed.

"I've never done anything like this before, but the theory is straightforward. It should work."

"*Hermanita*, I don't think we have time for *should*. If it doesn't work then somebody dies. Sitri demanded a human sacrifice before enslaving whoever Collin is after."

"It will work."

I didn't want to introduce any self-doubt, so I didn't contradict her. Privately, I was thinking *that's what Wilburn said.*

I called Kali the next morning at what, by my standards, was an uncouth hour. The call went straight to voice mail. That was unusual unless she was concentrating on something. George, her boyfriend was back in Toronto, so it wasn't that. I took her lack of answering to be a good sign for the binding project.

Next I called BhadraKali. Keith told me that she was in her office, and didn't want to be disturbed unless it was an emergency. I took that to be an even better sign.

Around noon I made some sandwiches, grabbed some cheesecake squares I'd made earlier, and went to see how the spell was progressing.

I was trying to act cool, like I'd adjusted to the new reality of spirits, demons and magicians.

I hadn't.

Internally, I was still having big issues with the whole concept. It seemed like everything I thought I had known about the way the world worked was a lie. Oddly enough, not once in the investigator's course was there mention of using magical spells. I could easily imagine the Pope having similar feelings to mine if aliens landed at the Vatican, and proved conclusively that Jesus was one of them, and God was the name of a used car salesman from the Barada Nebula.

And I thought my sex life was confusing.

Kali didn't even look up as I pushed aside the beaded curtain to her office.

"Go away," she said without looking up.

"I love you too." I got a grunt in reply.

"I brought lunch."

That got more of a response. She looked at me like a starved mongoose. I tossed her a sandwich before I lost an arm.

"Have you slept since you saw the video?" I asked as she inhaled the food. She swallowed quickly so she could speak.

"I think so." Another shark-sized bite of sandwich disappeared.

All of her food, and half of mine, vanished before I could get more from her.

"The theory is easy enough. It's just difficult to find the right ritual elements so that we can do this properly."

"Aren't there some kind of standard spells you can use?"

"This isn't the kind of thing that Wiccans do on a regular basis. It takes really special circumstances like these before we'd even consider curtailing a person's free will this way. There are plenty of cheesy books that pretend to have working rituals for getting people to do your will. Love spells are particularly common. Fortunately, the published ones are useless."

"When are you going to do this?"

"Tonight, around eight, if I can get the ritual done. I want you here when we do it."

I took the hint, and packed up the debris from lunch.

"I don't know what good I'll be, but I'll be back then."

A little before eight o'clock I parked Binky next to several other
vehicles outside BhadraKali. Parker Barager-Bonsell, Keith's husband,
opened the of the shop door for me.
  "Hi Parker, long time no see." I gave him a hug.
  "Not since the wedding. How have you been doing?"
  I sighed. "Mostly okay. Lately, not so much."
  "Yeah, Kali gave us the short version."
  I took my coat off, and threw it on the pile that was accumulating on
the counter.
  "That's why we're here; to make things better."
  "We'll see," I said. "How are you doing?"
  "Great. Thanks to you we're really happy."
  "Well, look what the cat dragged in." The voice reminded me of Sam
Gamgee in *Lord of the Rings*. I turned around to see Stan Watkins grinning
at me.
  "Stan, I didn't know you were Wiccan."
  Constable Watkins, late of the West Yorkshire Police, and now of the
Calgary Police Service, shrugged.
  "I didn't know you were a demon hunter. I'd say we're even."
  I moved closer and spoke quietly.
  "I hope that you aren't going to say anything about tonight to Nick or
my mother, are you?"
  "Don't worry. What happens in circle stays in circle. Come meet the
rest of our crew."
  I was introduced to three more women I'd never seen before. Iona
Faulkner was in her thirties, and looked like a soccer mum. Nichole
Laraby, complete with black-rimmed glasses, was a high school librarian.
Stan called her Giles, which she put up with. The most colourful member
of the group was Yolanda Alcindore, a small woman from Puerto Rico
wearing a bandana dress. She had been born in Jamaica and, in addition
to being a member of the Wiccan group, she was a Santera, a Santeria
priestess.
  There was the sound of the bead curtain, and Kali appeared from her
office carrying a stack of paper.
  "We're ready," she said.
  One of the reasons why Kali had chosen this building was the basement. She'd had it renovated into a boiler room, a couple of rooms for
classes and meetings, and the ritual room.
  The ritual room was used exclusively by Kali and her group. There
was a circle painted on the floor, the design being much simpler than the

one Collin was using since it delineated sacred space instead of trying to keep demons out. A small, sturdy cabinet, acting as an altar, stood in the middle. It was covered by a white cloth embroidered with a pentagram. The space under the altar held the group's ritual tools when they weren't being used. There were pegs along one wall for ritual robes, although not all members wore them. Wicca was a lot more relaxed about the details than the magic Collin was using.

Tonight, I was the only one not wearing a robe.

I'd never been in this ritual space before. The walls, furnishings, and robes were saturated with the faint smell of sweet incense.

Kali had tried to get me interested in Wicca shortly after we met. I went along with it for a while, but I just couldn't get over the feeling that it was playing make-believe. Regardless, the religion gave Kali a lot of comfort after her parents died, so I was the last person who would ridicule it. I'd better be wrong about Wicca if we were to have any hope of stopping a murder.

Once people were robed, or in my case at least barefoot, Kali started giving out scripts.

"Don't I get one?" I asked when it was clear that I didn't.

"You've had more contact with our target than anyone else. Your part is to be our link to him. Did you bring the picture?"

"Of course."

It all sounded very important, and probably true, but I also suspected that I was also being left out of the inner workings because of my lack of faith. It wasn't easy for me to be a by-stander, and for a moment I was annoyed. Then I told myself to suck it up. If this is what it took to make the binding work I'd do my part.

The first part of the ritual was standard. Kali was acting as the High Priestess. She took a broom and swept the perimeter of the circle to clear it of any unwanted spiritual influences. Since George wasn't here, Keith was acting as her High Priest. He used a sword to "cut the circle," establishing the boundaries of the ritual space. Kali added salt to a bowl of water, and consecrated it.

"Spirits of Earth and Water, I consecrate thee in the names of the God and Goddess. Aid us in our work tonight. So mote it be."

Everyone in the circle, including me, repeated "so mote it be."

She went clockwise around the circle, sprinkling the boundary and the participants with the consecrated water. When she was nearly done, Keith lit a charcoal brick. It was smouldering nicely by the time she returned to the altar. Keith added a pinch of frankincense.

"Spirits of Air and Fire, I consecrate thee in the names of the God and Goddess. Aid us in our work tonight. So mote it be."

Again we repeated "so mote it be."

He walked around the circle, censing the area, and each person individually, then returned to the altar.

There were two unlit candles on the altar, one gold and one silver. Kali positioned herself before the silver one.

"Parvati, Great Mother of us all, come to us and give us aid that we may help one of your children to return to the light." As she spoke she lit the candle. "Hail and welcome."

We all repeated "hail and welcome." Parvati I'd encountered before in Kali's circle. Depending on which aspect you were talking about, she was the Hindu goddess of pretty much everything female. Kali, the demon slayer, after whom Kali the BFF is named, is one of her aspects. Confusing, but true.

Keith stood before the gold candle.

"Ganesha, Great Father of us all, come to us and give us aid that we may help one of your children to return to the light." Again, he lit the candle. "Hail and welcome."

Ganesha I'd also heard of. He was the Hindu god of obstacles in charge of both removing them and creating them. I hoped that he'd be willing to lend a hand tonight to put up some really good ones.

I had a sudden, freaky thought. If the ritual for summoning a demon actually worked, what was to prevent the invocation of the Wiccan gods from working as well? One was a long, drawn-out ritual involving coercion, the other was a short, gentle invitation. What if the invitation was extended? Would the gods physically appear like Sitri did?

A long time ago, like, last week, I would have laughed at the thought. Now I seriously wondered if Kali and her group realized just how close to our reality the powers they were playing with were.

I dragged my focus back to the here and now. This was not the time for my imagination to be running away.

Kali and Keith held their athames upward in salute. The others with athames did likewise. I used my pointing finger.

"We stand between the worlds, between light and shadow, between the realm of man and the realm of the gods. By all the powers of the sacred, we call thee to guard and witness our rite, mighty Ganesh and Parvati. So mote it be."

All the athames came down as one, to point at the floor in the middle of the circle. For a moment, I could almost feel the energy surround us.

"Veronica, the photograph," Kali said.

I pulled out a picture of Collin, and handed it to her. It was probably my imagination that he looked to be scowling even more than usual.

Kali put the picture on the altar, and sprinkled it with consecrated water.

"By water and earth, we consecrate this image as a true likeness of Collin Blakeway."

She then held the picture over the smoke from the incense.

"By air and fire, we consecrate this image as a true likeness of Collin Blakeway."

On the altar were several skeins of embroidery thread in different colours, and a small pair of scissors.

Keith took the photograph, and wrapped the yellow thread around it like he was wrapping a parcel, then cut it so that it was somewhat longer than needed. He tied the thread around the picture.

"By the power of air, we bind Collin Blakeway so that his mind will be too confused to perform the invocation ritual should he attempt it. So mote it be."

"So mote it be," we all repeated.

Kali measured a similar length of green thread and tied it around the picture.

"By the power of earth, we bind Collin Blakeway so that he will lose the ability to perform the invocation ritual should he attempt it. So mote it be."

"So mote it be."

Keith cut and tied the red thread.

"By the power of fire, we bind Collin Blakeway so that he will become a loving husband who respects his wife, and treats all women as aspects of the goddess. So mote it be."

"So mote it be."

Kali cut and tied the blue thread.

"By the power of water, we bind Collin Blakeway so that he will feel the shame of his actions, and use that emotion to fuel his change for the better. So mote it be."

"So mote it be."

Keith cut and tied the purple thread.

"By the power of spirit, we bind Collin Blakeway so that he will act with good conscience, and the moral awareness of the consequences of his actions. So mote it be."

"So mote it be."

Nichole was standing next to me. I glanced at her script and saw that the next step was "charging the token." I was glad we were moving on. I tried to get into the ritual, not wanting my lack of faith to screw things up, but the "so mote it be" responses were starting to make me feel like I was in a cult or a sales meeting.

Kali had us all sit on the floor. Despite it being concrete, it was warm.

Keith took a square of black silk from the altar, and placed the picture on it in the centre of our group. Kali held out both her hands, and the people on either side grasped them until we joined in a circle.

"Close your eyes and pass power around the circle. Take it in your right hand and pass it out your left. When it reaches maximum, I will put it into the picture to seal the spell," Kali said.

It still made no logical sense to me. I told myself to shut up and do it. I sat with my eyes closed, trying my best to help with something I couldn't feel.

We sat quietly for some time, the only sound being people's breathing. After a while I did feel something. At first it could have been my imagination, but the intensity built up in time with my breathing. I could feel something flowing into my right hand as I breathed in, then out my left as I exhaled. I had no idea what it was, but I could feel it like a flow that slightly tingled. Part of my mind was in awe that I was actually experiencing something magical. Another part was amused that I'd convinced myself that I was feeling something that didn't exist.

The possibly imaginary feeling built, and I had to breathe through my mouth to keep up with the volume of the flow. I no longer questioned it.

There was a sudden change. The – whatever it was – drained from me like I was a pumping station, and someone had dynamited the supply pipe.

I opened my eyes and Kali's left hand, fingers extended, was a centimetre from the picture in the centre of the circle. There was a strong shock like I'd shuffled across a carpet, and touched a door knob, as her finger touched the picture.

What the hell had just happened? Nobody was moving, the picture was lying on a piece of cloth on bare concrete. We were all holding hands, which should have grounded any stray static electricity. There was nothing to create the shock I'd felt.

Stan let go of his partners and shook his hands.

"I hate it when that happens."

Had Stan had felt it too?

"Did anyone else feel..." I started to say, then I felt foolish.

"Don't worry, it's just what happens when Kali breaks the circuit with all that power running through it," Yolanda said in her Jamaican accent.

Apparently Veronica the Sceptic had just been zapped with a magic spark. Holy crap.

If I was very, very lucky, that might be the weirdest thing that would happen to me in this case.

The next afternoon, I got a text from Alyssa that Collin would be working late. That was a bit disturbing, but I tried to maintain a positive attitude. Maybe the binding wouldn't kick in until he actually tried to do his ritual. Or maybe it was taking time to change his mind. It wasn't my field. I didn't want to tell Kali, and have her worry. At least, not yet.

If I ever got tired of being a PI, I could become a pole climber. I wore the climbing harness in the car to save time, and from the moment I parked until the camera and microphone were back in place was a total of 90 seconds. For once, nothing went wrong, and I took that as a hopeful sign. Even my buddy Adam seemed to have the night off for once.

I didn't bother following Collin. Instead, I cruised 17th Avenue looking for somewhere to have supper. There was a ma-and-pa Thai place nearby that looked good and was. They closed at eleven, which was late enough that Collin should have gone home.

After leaving the restaurant I went to check on him. No light was showing through the window, so he must have given up. I retrieved the camera and went home.

As I drove away, I saw a man was standing by the side of the road, leaning against the mail box that I'd used as cover a week earlier. The nearest street light was behind him, so all I could see was a silhouette. I could have sworn that he was wearing a fedora and trench coat. He put one hand to his mouth and I saw the tip of a cigarette flare as he drew on it. He gestured with his hand, acknowledging me as I drove past. I glanced in the rear view mirror, and he hadn't moved. Maybe he was a pimp.

I'd be glad when I no longer had to hang around this freaky neighbourhood.

Yoko Geri was glad to see me when I got back to the apartment. He seemed to know that things had been rough for me lately, and was being more affectionate than normal.

I downloaded the latest video to my laptop, and settled in to watch my least favourite reality show. With any luck, we had finally Collin off the island.

By now I was truly bored with the ritual, so I skimmed and only made occasional checks of the action. Collin seemed to be having more trouble than usual. He was dropping things, and was generally clumsy. A couple of times I dropped back to normal speed to check where he was in the invocation, and caught him flubbing lines. It looked like we finally had a winner. The binding had worked.

Or not. Three hours in, Sitri showed up. Again, Collin treated the whole thing like a meeting with someone he hadn't been able to e-mail.

He informed Sitri that he wasn't feeling well, and needed time to recuperate before they could conclude their business. Sitri had business of his own.

"Hurlyburly reigns within the Power. One of great gifts seeks to interfere with the conclusion of thine affairs."

"What the hell – I meanest, hath thee the name of this person?"

"Look to Iberia, wherein men battle the bullock, and the swirling *muleta* alloweth the soap-maker to prosper. I can say no more."

Collin couldn't get anything else out of him, and did the ritual banishing. Sitri bugged out shortly after. That was it for the night.

Sitri's warning meant nothing to me. It sounded like one of those prophecies in stories that nobody understands until it's too late.

I looked up hurlyburly: tumult, confusion, disturbance. The only place I could ever remember hearing the term before was in Macbeth. What was this Power that was mentioned? Obviously something cosmic. Maybe.

I tried putting it into more modern English: disturbance within the Power? It didn't make much sense. I'd work on it later.

Unless there was somebody else going after Collin, I must be the "one of great gifts." Since I was working backward, the next riddle was easy.

Iberia was the ancient name for Spain. The next bit was a reference to bull fighting. I looked up *muleta* and found that it was the cape used to distract the bulls. Swirling it before the bull was called a *veronica*. I already knew that a soap-maker was called a chandler because I'd looked it up once to find out about my family name.

Collin wasn't supposed to get it. The message was directed at me, and it read, "*I know who you are and what you are doing. Signed, Prince Sitri.*"

My stomach did flip-flops, and I felt that electric rush that comes from a squirt of adrenaline. It took a while for me to get my body to settle down.

There had been too many shocks. I just accepted that Sitri knew my name without any real panic. If he'd wanted me dead, and was able to act directly against me, I'd already be dead.

The binding hadn't worked, at least not completely. It was time for Plan, what? D?.

I sure wish we had a Plan D.

CHAPTER 14

The Highlander

The next day at lunch time, the mulligatawny soup simmered as I thought about my next move.

During my first case I'd been approached by my former psychotherapist, Dr. Trinity MacMillan, with an offer of assistance in processing physical evidence. She had a network of forensic and other experts who whimsically called themselves the Baker Street Irregulars. They did pro bono work for those who couldn't afford the time or expense of legally-approved facilities. Of course, the results were rarely admissible in court, but it allowed those police officers who were in on it to get fast turn-around that let them look at suspects who would otherwise get away. The BSI also had information resources that should *not* have been available to them. I hadn't asked how they managed that.

At first I'd call Trinity directly to make my requests. A few months previously I had been given a high-security, encrypted cell phone for future communications. It even had a red case. I called it the Bat Phone, and kept it in my night table.

It was time to send up the signal.

The big difficulty was deciding how I was going to phrase my request. Sitting in my comfy chair where I did most of my thinking, I knew that, no matter how I did it, this was going to be awkward.

My lunch was already on the coffee table, so to put off the moment of truth. I tore a piece of bread off the freshly baked French loaf, then dipped it in olive oil and balsamic vinegar. Delicious. Never let it be said that the mixing of culinary cultures holds any terror for me.

What the hell, dramatic flare might get me extra points. I unlocked the phone, and started composing my text message.

Need an expert in Lesser Key of Solomon to combat sorcerer.

I re-read the message, then pressed the send key. An anonymous response came back within a minute.

Are you joking?

I expected some incredulity, so I had an answer ready.

I wish I were.

There was another pause, then the phone chimed as a new text message appeared.

Stand by.

I didn't know whether to be happy or worried that the BSI call centre had barely blinked an eye, and had such a resource in its directory.

The soup was gone, and I was down to the last piece of bread when the phone rang. It had never done that before. It took me a moment to figure out how to answer it.

"Hello?"

"Good evening, Miss Chandler. This is Dr. Hull. I understand that you require assistance?" The voice on the other end was male, cultured and had an educated Scottish accent. He probably *was* in Scotland if he thought that it was evening. The scope of the BSI never ceased to surprise me.

"Yes. I have a man who is summoning a demon, and I need to know how to stop him."

The Scot chuckled. "An admirable summary. I take it that you yourself are not a Practitioner?"

"No, I'm not. My best friend is Wiccan, though."

"Very well. Are you sure he's using the Lesser Key?"

"Yes, I've seen the book. The exact title is *Lemegeton Clavicula Salomonis*."

"Do you know which demon it is?"

"Prince Sitri."

"Oh my. Is this man working alone or in a group?"

"Alone. I don't think he plays well with others."

There was a pause.

"How far along is he?"

"He summoned Sitri a few days ago."

There was another pause.

"Do you know who his victim is?"

"Not exactly, although I suspect that it might be the receptionist at his office. Sitri has demanded a human sacrifice before going further, and they're dickering over the details."

"Interesting. What magical resources do you have?"

"Not much. I got a Catholic priest to bless the ritual room. That didn't work. We also got a Native shaman to ask the spirits to keep Sitri away. That didn't work either. My friend's Wiccan coven did a binding spell on the magician that seems to have worked a bit, but Sitri still showed up."

"Hmm," the man said, "at least you have been moving in the right direction. What is this man like in his everyday life?"

"At work, he's a stereotypical, boring accountant. At home, he's an abusive, controlling SOB who won't let his wife have friends, or leave the house. Oh, and he has an anger management problem."

"Charming. I take it that he hasn't done anything legally actionable?"

"Not yet. Certainly nothing I can prove."

"How do you know that the demon has been summoned?"

"I had a camera on him through the window."

"You have a *video* record of a demon?"

"Yes."

"That does put a different colour on things. Can you get access to his ritual space and tools when he's not there?"

"No problem."

"Good. You said that you've seen his book. Have you seen a black-handled knife with symbols marked on the handle?"

"Yes. He leaves all his tools on a desk in his ritual space, including his athame."

"Ah, so you do have some knowledge of the Art. How often does he perform his ritual?"

"Sometimes there is a day or two between them, other times not."

Dr. Hull snorted.

"Then he's an amateur, not that it makes him any less dangerous. Your best bet is to take the athame to a Masonic Lodge for deconsecration. Such a tool has been specially consecrated to conduct and direct energy during the ritual. Once it's deconsecrated it would be just a knife. He should find himself inexplicably unable to make his ritual work. If he's working alone and is self taught, it could take him a very long time to find the problem, if ever."

"I don't think I know any Masons."

"Don't worry, I'll make some calls on your behalf. It will be faster if I explain what it needed. All you have to do is deliver the athame to them, and then return it to the ritual area."

I'd been keeping my scepticism at bay during this admittedly bizarre conversation, but this was too much.

"Are you telling me that the BSI has *Masons* on call?"

"No," he said. I could hear the amusement in his voice. "But I do."

"All right. Is there anything else in case that doesn't work? Sitri knows my name, and I'm pretty sure that he's been sabotaging at least some of my non-magical efforts too."

"Ms. Chandler, you didn't mention that your sorcerer was aware of your efforts."

"He isn't. At least, I haven't seen any sign that he is. Sitri is doing it all on his own."

There was a long pause.

"Really? That's most unusual, and somewhat disturbing. There is one more thing that you can do, but it could be personally dangerous. If replacing his athame is akin to cutting the power, this would be akin to baring the wires, and pouring water on the floor. If he restores power, the results will be unfortunate for him, so be certain that you can live with the outcome before you do it."

Pondering the moral questions involved made me pause for all of five seconds. Collin needed to be stopped.

"All right, what do I do?"

"Does he draw his circle anew each time?"

"No, he permanently painted it on the floor."

"Excellent. Spoil his circle by making small changes. Interrupt some lines by removing flakes of paint. Subtly change the spelling of some of the Names. It shouldn't take much. Do the same to the Triangle of Evocation."

"That's where Sitri appears, right?"

"Correct."

"Gotcha. What will spoiling the circle do?"

"As you might guess, demons tend to be very angry about being summoned, and the only thing protecting the magician is the circle. A spoiled circle and triangle will no longer act as barriers to it. Given the physical nature of the demon, your magician will probably be torn apart."

"You mean that literally, don't you?"

"I'm afraid so. The Lesser Key is not a toy."

Wonderful, more blood on my hands. The fact that he might deserve it didn't make me feel much better about it.

"How do we proceed, Doctor?"

"I believe you are in Calgary? The Canadian one?"

"That's right."

"I'll have someone from a local lodge get in contact with you. Good evening, Ms. Chandler. And good hunting."

I wish I could have thought of something terribly clever and heroic to say, but nothing came to mind.

"Bye."

Later that afternoon, the Bat Phone rang again. A flashing red bar told me that the call wasn't encrypted, and an actual phone number showed up on the call display.

"Veronica Chandler?" It was another man, this time with a Canadian accent.

"Yes."

"A mutual Scottish friend asked me to contact you. When could we meet in person?"

"Any time is good for me."

"Are you familiar with Central Memorial Park?"

"That's the one downtown with the library?"

"Yes. There's a Masonic Hall across from the north side of the park."

"All right, it should take me about fifteen minutes to get there."

"Good. What kind of vehicle do you drive?"

"A white Chevy Cavalier."

"I'll let our people know, so you can park in the lot beside our building. When you arrive, come in the front door, and ask for Larry Jackson. I look forward to meeting you."

I found the hall without any problems. It was a three-storey brick building with sandstone trim. According to the corner stone, it was built in 1928. The only obvious changes to the architecture since then were the addition of a wheelchair ramp at the front, and the replacement of the doors and windows with modern ones. I wondered what the originals had looked like.

I parked in the lot beside the hall, and went in the main entrance.

Inside the glass doors, a kiosk faced me bearing a sign that read "Information Services." A man, probably in his sixties, sat behind the counter.

"May I help you?"

"Veronica Chandler to see Larry Jackson."

He picked up a phone, and punched a button.

"Sir, a Ms. Veronica Chandler is here to see you." He hung up. "He'll be right down."

I wandered a bit, looking at the architecture. Although the building had been kept up to date, the interior of the lobby was still rich wood panelling and custom carpeting. There were real potted plants, not the plastic things you see in most offices.

I heard footsteps behind me.

"Ms. Chandler?"

Larry Jackson was easily in his sixties, and everything about him radiated a deep, peaceful joy in life. He managed to make a golf shirt and slacks look like a high-end business suit. His silver hair did nothing to hide that he must have been a real lady killer in his younger days. I found myself wanting to flirt with him just for the fun of it, without having the urge to jump him. It was a nice change from my usual state.

"Shall we go up to my office?"

His office was on the second floor, and great pains had been taken to preserve the 1928 ambiance while providing all conveniences of a modern technology. He closed the door behind us. I got right to the point.

"Did Dr. Hull explain what's going on?"

"Yes, and I was quite startled to get the call. Do you know much about Freemasonry?"

"Not a thing, other than a couple of references in movies. I'm guessing that you have something to do with magic."

His eyes twinkled.

"Yes, no, and maybe. Masonry is a generic term for a collection of organizations that use Biblical allegory and metaphor to teach good people how to be better people. Some branches are open only to men, some only to women, and some are co-educational. Most Freemasons understand only that they are members of a fraternal organization. In the upper degrees, that understanding is clarified to include what, in this context, you are calling magic. However, we certainly don't summon demons, or do many of the other things popularly associated with the term 'magician'."

"I think I understand. My Wiccan friend once told me that magic is mostly psychological, that real magicians are concerned with changing themselves internally."

"Your friend is right. In what is known as the Western Esoteric Tradition that is called the Great Work. There are some external applications, however. That's what we've been asked to do for you. I understand that you need us to deconsecrate a ritual object?"

"That's what I was told. Have you known Dr. Hull long?"

"I've never met him, although he has a considerable reputation in the international occult community. Getting a call from him was much like a village priest getting a call from the Pope wanting a favour. I wasn't inclined to refuse."

"Can I watch the deconsecration?"

"Sorry, the Lodge workings are open only to initiated Brothers. However, it shouldn't take long. I take it that you'll be returning the object to its owner afterwards?"

"That's the idea, and the sooner the better. My plan is to grab it, then call to let you know I'm on my way. When I get here, you do your thing, then I take the athame and put it back."

"Simple and elegant. I like it. When do you want to do this?"

"The owner always does his rituals in the evening, usually around seven or 7:30. How long will your ritual take?"

"About an hour, I think."

"Give it half an hour from there to here, an hour here, half an hour back, plus an extra hour just in case. That's three hours. How about tomorrow afternoon? I'll get there around 2:00, and it'll be all done before he gets off work."

Jackson consulted his computer.

"That's doable. There's nothing else scheduled in the Blue Room at that time. It'll be tight getting everyone together in time, but we'll manage. We aren't in the habit of letting innocent lives be lost if we can help it."

We stood up and I shook his hand.

"Thank you, Mr. Jackson."

"My pleasure, Ms. Chandler. We'll see you tomorrow."

For good reason, I was becoming paranoid about planning. Keith was completely unknown to Collin, and hopefully Sitri, so I borrowed him to keep an eye on Collin's office that afternoon. All he had to do was sit in the coffee shop, and phone me if Collin left for any reason. It would take at least half an hour for Collin to get to his hideout even if he took a cab, so there was no point in following him, trying to delay him, or engaging him in any way. I wanted Keith completely out of harm's way. Assuming, of course, that such a thing was possible with a demon involved.

A little before 2:00, I boldly entered the service corridor wearing jeans and a work shirt with my usual boots. My jeans were held up by a belt with assorted toys attached, including my baton lightly disguised as a flashlight holder.

If anybody noticed me going in, they must have thought I belonged there. At least, nobody came to investigate. Everybody in the surrounding businesses should have been back from lunch by then, and be busy with the afternoon's activities.

Every second spent in the corridor brought me that much closer to detection, so I moved as quickly as possible. Just to err on the side of caution, I was also wearing my hipster glasses, a blonde wig and bright green lipstick. Binky was parked on the street instead of in the parking lot. I got busy on Collin's door with my lock picks. Having done this twice before, it only took about five minutes.

The room was just as I'd seen it on the video. I locked the door behind me in case somebody tried it. The ritual tools were methodically laid out on the desk. Before touching the athame, I took several pictures so I'd be able to put it back in exactly the right place. I wrapped it in a handkerchief to avoid fingerprints, and stowed it in an inside coat pocket. I got out my cell phone, and dialled the number Jackson had given me. It only rang once before he picked it up.

"I'm leaving now," I said, then hung up.

I opened the door, and taped a piece of plastic over the strike plate so I wouldn't have to pick the lock it when I returned. I had some scrap paper with me to wedge the door closed if necessary, but it wasn't. The door closed, and the extra thickness of the plastic shim kept it there.

As I left, a door opened in the corridor. Guess who it was? Go ahead, I'll just stand around while you think about it.

Give up yet? I told you I don't like waiting.

On the plus side, I'd chosen the green lipstick to be distracting. Last time Adam had seen me up close I'd had different hair, no glasses and he wasn't looking at my face. On the minus side, I hadn't deployed FCM this time. There was nothing to prevent him from staring at me above the collar.

This guy was like a bad penny. Did he live here? I stood still, hoping that he'd do whatever he came here to do without seeing me.

I thought he'd have a heart attack when he looked in my direction. He jumped and squeaked, almost falling over backward, and losing his cigarette pack. I began to think he had a guilty conscience.

"Shit, you scared me." No, really?

"Sorry." I tried to get past him.

"Hey, that's cool. You wanna share a joint?"

I looked at all the junk piled in the corridor. He wanted to smoke dope in this fire trap? I couldn't believe that he was actually stupider than I'd thought.

"No, thanks." I took a step but he moved in front of me.

"What's your name?" For once I had a snappy answer.

"Nemesis."

"Hey, that's different. I like it."

Don't they teach kids anything in school these days?

"You won't like it for long if you don't let me past."

"Hey, don't be like that." He put his right hand on my shoulder. My shirt was clean. His hand wasn't. He made me angry. You know the rest.

I put my right hand on top of his. He grinned, thinking that I was encouraging him. Grabbing his hand, I dragged it down toward my waist and twisted. The pain made him open his mouth to yell, but he'd really pissed me off this time. I did something to his elbow with one finger of my other hand. I love that move. It looks so gentle from the outside. The sudden agony that shot through his entire arm froze the yell in his throat. He gurgled, and his eyes bugged out.

I leaned closer to him, and spoke quietly.

"My wife doesn't like it when men touch me. Neither do I."

I pushed him away from me, and he stumbled over the pile of boxes.

They survived the impact; he landed on his ass on the floor as I walked away. With any luck, my parting comment would put me in his "bitch-dyke" file instead of wandering around what passed for a brain until it bumped into his "hotty I met before" file. Being a real man, he waited until the outer door was almost closed before yelling "dyke!" I smiled. Got him.

The entire way back to the Masonic Hall, I constantly had to remind myself not to speed. It was not part of the plan for me to be stopped by a traffic cop. The way things had been going, Sitri would probably have him go over the car looking for other infractions just to delay me. The Masonic parking lot was full, so I parked in the middle of the lane. The party was in my honour, so I had to trust that nobody would call a tow truck.

I ran to the front door, and yanked it open. Jackson was waiting for me just inside. He was dressed in an expensive suit this time, and wearing a fancy collar, a pendant around his neck, and a very fancy apron like a dress version of the one that a carpenter would wear.

For a moment he stared, and I realized he didn't recognize the panting blonde with radioactive green lips. I pulled off the wig and glasses.

"Ah, Ms. Chandler, you have it?" He said. I handed him the athame, still wrapped in the cloth.

"Wait here." He went down the hall toward a sign that read Blue Room. Outside the doors, a man in a similar outfit was standing guard with a drawn sword. I guess Masons take their perimeter security seriously. I approved.

They spoke for a moment, then Jackson went inside and closed the doors. The guard remained outside. He did not look like the chatty type, so I sat on one of the padded benches along the corridor wall. Either Masons were a quiet bunch or the soundproofing was excellent. I couldn't hear anything that was happening inside.

The hour crawled by. I fidgeted. The nice man behind the information counter introduced himself as Sean, and brought me a box of juice.

The doors opened, and Jackson came out carrying the knife wrapped in my handkerchief.

"It's done," he said. I glanced at it but it didn't seem any different. I don't know what I expected to see.

"Thanks," I called as I hurried out the door.

I caught several green traffic lights on the way back to the hideout, and made it in record time. This time Adam didn't interfere. The door was slightly stuck but opened when I pushed hard on it. I carefully wiped the knife to eliminate any finger prints from the Masons, put it back in its place, checked it against the pictures I'd taken, and minutely adjusted its position.

My phone rang. It was Keith.

"He's leaving his office. I'm following him."

"Damn it, I told you not to get involved."

"It's okay, I'm a block back. He's just passing a school yard."

"All right, stop there. Just let me know if he continues north, or turns east to the bus stop."

"Just a minute."

I waited. I'm sure it wasn't even a minute, but it felt longer. I had to fight to keep from picturing Collin spotting Keith.

"He's going to the bus stop."

"Okay, I'm out of here. Thanks, Keith. I owe you. Go home, and give Parker a big hug from me."

I was about to leave when the circle caught my eye. Just because we'd deconsecrated the athame didn't mean we'd necessarily stopped Collin. Too much had gone wrong for me to believe that.

From what Doctor Hull had said, sabotaging the circle wouldn't have any effect as long as the knife was malfunctioning. It wasn't as if I was rigging an IED on the door or something. *Yeah, Veronica. You just keep believing that.*

I quickly searched the room, and found the can of paint Collin had used. It was on a shelf with a package of a dozen small, cheap brushes for touch ups.

Collin would be here somewhere between 30 and 60 minutes from now. I gave myself 15 minutes.

With my multitool, I scraped a small gap in the actual circle itself, erased a couple of lines in the symbols and a letter from one of the Names of Power. They were in Hebrew, and Collin probably didn't speak it any better than I did, which is to say, I could recognize the alphabet. The paint was solvent based, and should dry quickly. I made up some things for the symbols, and then copied a different Hebrew letter from some other word in place of the one I'd erased. My Hebrew penmanship wasn't great, but then neither was his.

The flecks of scraped paint I dusted under the furniture with a tissue.

I finished touching up my work, then put the paint and brushes away. There was no way for me to clean the brush I'd used, so I took it with me. Collin probably wouldn't notice one brush missing. I sniffed. The solvent smell was already fading. It should be gone by the time Collin got here.

I opened the door just as some big guy was about to knock on it.

"Are you the one who almost broke my guy's arm?"

"Are you the one who hires stoners?"

That wasn't the response he was expecting.

"What?"

"Your boy offered to share a joint with me, and when I said no he grabbed me, and tried to stop me from leaving. I bet your insurance company would *love* to know that you have employees who are working with machinery after doing drugs. You want to make something of it? I was going to let it go, but let's get the police in here so I can charge him with sexual assault." I pulled out my phone, and made a big show of punching numbers. It's easier to bluff now that we have ten digit phone numbers. It gives the other guy more time to fold. 4-0-3-2-6-6-1-

He put up his hands like he was surrendering.

"Are you sure about the joint?"

"He didn't look too bright. I bet he's got it in his cigarette pack. Check it out."

"Adam," he bellowed, "get your ass out here."

I knew where Adam kept his pot because I'd seen him take it out. As soon as Adam appeared, Big Macho Boss Man grabbed the pack from his shirt sleeve. By the time Adam started to protest, the boss was holding a half joint.

"Hey, Carl, it's just a joint..."

"You know I run a clean shop. She says you grabbed her after she said she wasn't interested. Is that true?"

"What? No. I just put my hand on her arm. You know, being friendly."

Carl was the size of a linebacker, and it didn't take much for me to imagine steam coming from his ears.

"Pack up your stuff. You're fired."

"What for?"

"For endangering yourself and others in my shop. But mostly because I won't tolerate disrespect. What part of her saying no did you not understand?"

"Aw shit, Carl. I didn't know she was a dyke..."

For a moment I was actually frightened. Not for myself – for Adam. I thought Carl was going to break him in half. He slammed Adam against the wall so quickly that I almost missed it.

"I have a wife and two teenage daughters. Do you think it would be all right for you to put your hands on them if they said no?"

Carl had grabbed Adam's coveralls near his throat. He had to relax a bit before Adam could speak.

"N-no."

"Damned straight. That goes for anyone. Remember that." He let go. "Get out."

Adam showed his intelligence by asking for his joint back. I thought the boss was going to deck him, but apparently the big guy had slightly more impulse control than I did. Adam went.

"I apologize for the problem."

"Thank you," I said, walking past him and, with luck, out of their lives forever.

I watched Adam leave in his car. He tried to burn rubber to show how pissed of he was, but his car didn't have enough power and stalled. That made my day.

There were now maybe ten minutes until Collin arrived. The businesses were closing down for the night, and I waited as long as I thought I could before going up the pole, and placing the camera. After all this practice I'd have a fair shot at winning if I entered one of those lumberjack competitions.

Instead of waiting around for Collin to become frustrated, I went back to the Thai restaurant where I'd had dinner before.

When I got back, just for fun, I timed how long it took me to retrieve the camera. Thirty seven seconds from feet on ground to feet on ground.

Score one for the girl with the green lips.

Yoko Geri was not amused at the hour when I got home. *Oh, it's you. Forgot my supper did you? Not to mention the time. You should be in bed by now. Good staff are so difficult to find these days.*

I downloaded the video while feeding my sidekick. I fast forwarded through it just to see what happened. Wave the athame, say the words, blah, blah.

What I didn't expect was for Sitri to show up right on schedule.

Despite the best advice from world experts in the field, today had been a pointless exercise in running around for no reason. I had no idea what had gone wrong, and I had a sick feeling that nobody else would know either. Collin and his demon buddy seemed to be making up their own rules.

We were so completely, utterly screwed.

CHAPTER 15

Biker Chick

I rubbed my eyes and sighed as I let me head fall back to rest on the back of my sofa. "But it *had* to work," Kali said. Yoko didn't like all the negative energy in the room, and had left us for the bedroom some time previously. I didn't blame him. I wanted to go to bed, pull the covers over my head, and forget all this.

"I've heard that a lot lately. I called Jackson. He was horrified, confused and apologetic. He had no idea what could have gone wrong. When I spoke with Dr. Hull I got the same speech. I even called Trinity. She said that Hull is the top man in the field, and if he said it would work, it should have worked. She even suggested, ever so politely, that either I hadn't followed his directions, or hadn't noticed that it had worked."

"I have a really bad feeling about this," Kali said. "It looks to me like everything anybody ever thought they knew about demons is wrong. At this point, I'm not even sure that Collin is actually summoning Sitri. Maybe he just comes when he feels like it just for laughs. If that's the case, what are we going to do?"

I was exhausted, and I had a big knot of pain behind my eyes. This whole "fate of the world rests on you" stuff sucks. In movies, heroes may get banged up, but they always conveniently find the Inverse Protonic Infindibulator or whatever the hell it is that beats the bad guys. It may require some tinkering, but it always defeats the evil overlord before he destroys Earth's bacon supply. Usually with 2 seconds to spare on the self-destruct timer.

In real life, it seems, not so much.

"Maybe there's some way we can slow Collin down," I said. "Give us time to come up with something else."

We sat for about five minutes saying nothing. My mind wandered to ways of killing him. It was pleasant to consider ways of disposing of the body, at least as an abstract exercise. Then another thought drifted by and waved hello.

"I have an idea."

"Do I want to know?"

I thought about explaining my idea, listening to her reasonable counterarguments, countering her reasonable counterarguments, justifying myself anyway, having her yell at me, and finally either convincing Kali that I was right or that I'd given up. Then I decided that my grade twelve English teacher had been right. Simplicity and economy of expression was the best policy.

"No."

"Does it involve you facing him alone?"

I thought about that for a while. Technically, it did, but it was reasonable to assume that Kali meant "does it involve you getting into a situation where you'll be killed and/or eaten?"

"No."

"There'd better not be. Otherwise, I'll bring your spirit back, and make it live in a Hoppip."

"A what?"

"It's a Pokemon. A pink one."

I stared at her, shocked that she'd come up with something like that.

"You are one sick, twisted individual." She poked me in the forehead with one finger.

"I had a good teacher."

That afternoon I put on another wig, a pair of sunglasses, more lipstick (red), a hoodie, and went shopping with a pocket full of cash. I went to several stores, buying only a few things in each. If anybody asked questions later about suspicious behaviour, I didn't want some clerk to say, "well, there was this woman who bought all 20 cans of penetrating oil that we had in stock."

How easy it is to slide down a slippery slope. Only a few days ago I'd been a law-abiding private investigator. Now I was technically a thief, a vandal, and I was about to slide even further down hill with the assistance of the penetrating oil. My sole consolation was that, if this worked, I'd have bought us time. I might not even have to kill anyone. At least, nobody important.

Remember that abandoned bicycle near my apartment building? It wasn't an expensive bike. Curious, I'd even asked my superintendent, Mr. Kornblatt, about it. He thought it belonged to a previous tenant, but it wasn't on the property that was his responsibility, so he didn't care. Neither, apparently, did anyone else. It had sat there, chained to a lamp post, for at least a year.

Late that night I cut the lock. The tires were almost flat and it squeaked as I wheeled away. Most of the moving parts were rusted. That didn't fit with my plans for stealth, so I picked it up and carried it. My guilty conscience was sure that everybody on the block must be watching. The back door to my building had no security camera because there was no need. Only tenants with keys could get in.

I brought the bike into the elevator, and hoped that nobody else would be up at two A.M. I made it to my apartment unseen, and got the bike inside. The damned pedal kept digging into me as I carried it along the hall.

I felt like a serial killer preparing to get rid of a body. I'd moved the furniture in my living room to the walls, and spread a heavy plastic sheet on the floor. My newly bought tools were on the kitchen counter.

The bike lay on the sheet, waiting for a skilled mechanic to bring it back to life. Unfortunately, I was all it had. I'm not totally useless around tools, but I'm not an expert. Still, the bike appeared to be all in one piece. Rust and flat tires were the only real problems. I hoped.

The bike and I became intimate for a few hours. Then I gave up, and went to bed on the theory that the instructions on the cans were right. Letting the parts soak in oil overnight would help to free them from their rusty prisons.

Late the next morning, the apartment smelled like an oil tanker had exploded in my living room. Yoko was not happy, and stayed as far away from the mess as possible.

The soaking had done the trick, and I was able to work the various parts until they moved freely. By the end, the rust made my hands look like they'd been dipped in old blood. It took another soaking in oil to free some of the most badly rusted pieces. I used the opportunity to go on another shopping trip to a sports store.

Why is it that when you have no idea what you are doing you can't find a salesperson anywhere? When you know exactly what you want, they swarm around, trying to be helpful by asking what you are doing, and explaining that the item you've selected isn't at all what you need. Miserable creatures. It must be the same law of the universe that dictates that the only person on duty when you go to buy tampons is a cute guy that you knew in school.

The bicycle was in remarkably good shape after I'd soaked, scrubbed, wiggled, and otherwise tried to adjust it. I even rode it over to the Calgary Co-op where I could fill the tires until they didn't feel like they were hitting bottom.

Binky would not be coming along on this mission. I hoped he didn't feel left out, but a car would only be overkill.

What a sense of humour I have.

Part of my preparation took place behind the Co-op. I put on the cheap garden gloves I'd just bought, then went over every part of the bike except the chain and gears with a rag and a big bottle of rubbing alcohol from the pharmacy. When I was done, I was sure there were no fingerprints anywhere on the bike.

I got home, cleaned up the living room, and threw the plastic sheet into the dumpster of a neighbouring building. My new outfit took some time to put on and felt awkward. Better to be uncomfortable than dead.

The ride down to Beltline was enlightening. Bicycling uses different muscles from everything else I did, and I could tell that tomorrow I'd be paying for this exercise. Especially considering what was coming. I was also hot from all the layers. Fortunately, it was all downhill from my place.

This particular plan had to work perfectly the first time with no wiggle room. I spent at least an hour on site, looking at all the potential problems from multiple angles, and figuring out how I was going to pull this off. Timing was everything, and I only had one shot at it.

At the Salvation Army store I'd bought a cheap hoodie with some football logo on it, sweat pants, and sneakers. They were lovely with the gardening gloves I'd gotten elsewhere. To complete my ensemble, I had a cheap pair of hideous sunglasses meant for a man, and a bright orange wig.

At 5:30, Andrea left the office building. As usual, Collin was close behind her. I was a block away.

As soon as I saw them at the door, I got onto the road, and pedalled as fast as I could.

As usual, she crossed the street first. He followed about five metres behind, watching her butt to the exclusion of all else. I was counting on his lack of situational awareness. I was 50 metres away, starting to suck air like a vacuum cleaner, and wondering if my legs would fall off.

Collin stepped off the curb. My timing was slightly off, and I adjusted by swerving between two cars so that I was between the lanes instead of by the curb. Just as I reached the intersection, Collin appeared in front of me.

He saw the motion at the last moment, and turned slightly toward me just as I hit him. That made it better. I purposely ducked to shoulder check him as low as I could as we collided, the second-hand athletic armour under my clothes absorbing much of the impact, at least for me. It also meant that he was hit by 60 kilos of hard plastic shell instead of relatively soft woman.

The whole experience reminded me unpleasantly of being in the car accident with Danielle, with the added creep factor of doing it on purpose. My advantage this time was that the armour spread the shock somewhat, and I was expecting it. He wasn't. We both went down and slid a good five metres as the bicycle skidded out from under me. I couldn't tell how badly he was hurt, but if he felt worse than me, then I'd done my job. My sweat pants and hoodie didn't fare so well after becoming intimate with the asphalt. The plastic armour took care of the abrasion, but also provided much less friction than skin so I skidded further.

Sometime during all this, the light had changed. Brakes squealed as drivers whose attention had been solely on the light stopped to avoid running us over. I got up as soon as I could, and tried the bike.

The front forks were visibly bent, and the balance was off, but it still worked. The front wheel wobbled badly as I pedalled away as fast as possible before some pedestrian could react to the "accident," and realize that this was a hit and run. Fortunately, the front brakes had been unusable, so I'd removed them. The wheel was free to wobble without slowing me down.

In the solid rush hour traffic no vehicle could chase me, and the drivers I was passing didn't know what had happened behind them. It felt like I was doing a snail's pace, but I was still going too fast for pedestrians to catch me, especially ones in suits. That was all I needed.

If you've never committed vehicular assault, then tried to make a high speed escape through rush hour traffic on an old bike with bent wheels while you are swaddled in plastic armour, and have no bicycling muscles, then I have a word of advice for you.

Don't.

By the time I'd gone five blocks I was ready to lie down and surrender to the police. I swerved into a side street, then immediately turned again into the alley. Running solely on adrenaline, I threw the bike into the first rubbish bin I saw, tossed some flattened cardboard boxes on top, and walked away. My muscles were so rubbery that my legs almost buckled just from walking on the gravel lane.

A few blocks later I had dumped the helmet and armour, a piece at a time, into more bins. I pushed them under whatever junk was available. Some pieces I dropped into residential wheelie bins just to confuse things further.

By doing an advanced variation on the technique that allows women to remove their bra without removing their outer clothes, I was still wearing the hoodie and sweat pants. By that time, a lot of the adrenaline had left my system, and my body was feeling even less happy about having hit an obstruction at somewhere around 30 or 40 kilometres per hour. I felt like hell. I probably looked like it, too. I made a mental note to see my chiropractor as soon as possible.

Crossing the street, I took to another alley. I lost the hoodie and sweat pants in separate bins. Underneath the armour, I was wearing yet another layer: a long-sleeved flannel shirt and jeans. They were sweaty but undamaged. I dumped the wig, and put on a baseball cap that had been stuffed into my inner pocket. I pulled my hair out the hole at the back of the hat in a pony tail. Looking at myself in a store window as I went by, I appeared almost normal. I could hear a siren a few blocks away. With any luck it was an ambulance for Collin.

The last things to go were my gloves. I'd scrubbed everything that could hold fingerprints before starting the operation. It might be possible to tie me to the clothing by DNA, but that assumed that they had the resources to do the lab tests, a sample of my DNA to match it to, and a reason to do so. For such a low priority crime I wasn't worried.

I walked east for a while longer, then turned north to eventually reach a C-Train station. Just in case, I pretended to be a normal teen and stared at the ground in front of my toes. The baseball cap visor should help shield my face from the security cameras at the station. A few minutes later, I was on my way to the Dalhousie station, two stops past my destination. I got off the train, and walked over to the Dalhousie Station mall.

In a public washroom, I lost the shirt, hat, and sun-glasses. Under the shirt I was wearing a tank top. I fluffed my hair to get rid of the hat head, went back to the station, and waited for the next southbound train. It had only been about half an hour since I was downtown, so my original train ticket was still valid.

I almost froze to death waiting for the train. The tank top was sweaty and the temperature was low, especially in the shade. A guy on the platform was trying to be subtle about staring at my cold, braless chest: another form of FCM. Twelve minutes later, I was heading back to Banff Trail station, only four blocks from home.

With any luck, Collin wouldn't be summoning anything but a nurse tonight. A description of the lumpy, androgynous bicyclist wearing dark glasses would be in people's minds for a few days, but it wasn't a serious enough crime for the police to be able to allocate resources to a big manhunt. Within a couple of days, most of the dumpsters would be emptied, taking the physical evidence with them. Even if the pieces of armour and clothing were found, there was nothing to connect them with a hit and run a half dozen blocks away, let alone the rider.

At 9:30 that evening, after a long, hot bath, and some pain killers, I called Alyssa. My excuse was that I wanted to ask if she'd noticed any further developments in her husband's alleged affair. It was a risk but I had to know how successful I'd been.

"Oh, Ms. Chandler, it's horrible. I just got back from the hospital. A bike courier ran over Collin on his way home from work."

Apparently, witnesses had assumed that every bicyclist riding like a psychotic lemming near downtown must be a courier. It was such a good piece of misdirection that I wished I'd thought of it.

"That's awful. Is he badly hurt?"

"They don't think so. He has a lot of bruises and cuts, and he hit his head. They're keeping him overnight in case there's something wrong with it."

Damn, I was hoping for a dislocation, or maybe some broken ribs.

"How long will he be laid up?"

"The doctor thought it could be a week or more."

Personally, I thought that it was obvious that something was wrong with his head, but then I knew him better than his doctors did. At least Collin was out of the game, but not permanently damaged. That had been my plan, so I supposed I should be happy.

My years of hanging around cops had paid off. In the name of justice, I'd just committed a perfect crime. Of course, a good part of the reason why I wouldn't be caught was that it was a relatively minor crime. If Collin had been killed then the Ident technicians would have gone over everything in the area, including dumpsters. The brutal fact that the police didn't have the resources to mount that big an investigation was a major part of what let me get away with it.

I felt proud for a moment, then remembered that I was supposed to be on the side of the law. Maybe I should consider another brain tune-up from Trinity.

I think it was the guilt that convinced me that I needed to tell my client part of the truth.

"Alyssa, there's something I discovered about your husband's activities. I know you said that he'd never become involved with anything occult, but I'm afraid that's exactly what's happened. I have surveillance videos of him trying to summon a demon. I believe that his goal is to have the demon get another woman to find him desirable."

I paused to let her process what I'd said. I expected any one of several possible reactions: disbelief, anger, fear.

"I see," she said calmly. "Do you have any idea which demon?"

"No," I lied. It felt like there was something funny going on here. Before all this started, all I knew about demons was what I'd learned from fantasy novels and movies. They were pretty much interchangeable, with a few having weird names that cunning sorcerers would somehow have to discover before the demons could be defeated. The names Beleth and Sitri weren't exactly Betty and Sam, but then the demons themselves weren't exactly like the Balrog from *Lord of the Rings* either. My gut was telling me that a normal person wouldn't ask that question.

"I have to go now," she said.

"All right, I'll call you when I know more."

She hung up, which by her standards seemed like an almost aggress-ive act.

Tomorrow, I was going to have to look at my assumptions about this case more closely.

After seeing Doctor Don and his magic hands, that is.

CHAPTER 16

Welcome Distraction

The next morning, after getting my own, personal, bent forks straightened by my chiropractor, I went for a walk. My stiff legs were almost functional by the time I realized that I'd forgotten to do something important before going out.

By the time I got back to my apartment I was trying to walk with crossed legs. I hobbled as quickly as possible into the bathroom without waiting to take off my coat or shoes.

My phone rang. For the first time I wondered if my history of inconvenient calls while I was in the kitchen or bathroom were due to demonic interference. Being paranoid certainly didn't mean that something wasn't out to get me.

I managed to get the phone from a pocket never intended to be accessed while around the wearer's ankles. The caller ID was unfamiliar.

"Chandler Investigations."

"Good morning, I'd like to speak with Ms. Chandler, please."

I could smell a rich client. It was an instinctive manner of speaking, as if the person was used, from the moment of birth, to being obeyed by servants.

"This is she."

"My name is Clarice Trudeau. Kaleigh Reinkemeyer recommended you as being both efficient and discrete."

Oh, no you don't. I was not falling into that one.

"If you value discretion, Ms. Trudeau, then I'm sure you can appreciate that I am unable to confirm or deny that I know, or even know of, any such person as – Reinkemeyer, did you say?"

"Very well, I believe the recommendation is well merited. I have an extremely delicate and time-sensitive matter that requires your skills. When can I see you?"

Not just now, I thought, sitting on the toilet.

"I'm in the middle of something at the moment..."

"Please, Ms. Chandler. This matter must be resolved in the next 24 hours."

I wasn't sure whether I was annoyed or grateful at being distracted in the middle of the literally unholy mess that the Collin Blakeway affair had become. Now that we had put Collin on ice for a week or more, maybe doing something else that didn't involve the fate of the world would clear my mind. It was a good a rationalization as any.

Besides, what PI worth the name would turn down a rich damsel in distress?

"Very well, can you come by my office in an hour?"

"Actually, I'm on my way now. I can be there in fifteen minutes."

Oh crap, I hadn't had time for housekeeping in the past few days. The apartment was a mess.

"That's somewhat inconvenient –"

"Please, Ms. Chandler. I'm desperate and money is no object." I sighed.

"If you insist. I'll see you in fifteen minutes."

"Thank you."

It was just like one of those movies where the parents are coming home unexpectedly the day after the kids have a wild party. I looked at my watch, then stripped my coat, and pulled off my boots and jeans. I'd be changing into business clothes anyway, and it was faster this way.

Anything that needed cleaning, or was questionable, got thrown into my bedroom. Yoko Geri was a little freaked by my insane running around, and kept running underfoot as he tried to avoid the underwear-clad maniac in his apartment. He was not amused when I started the vacuum cleaner, and ran it around the living room like a germophobe having a panic attack.

T minus eight minutes.

Dirty dishes seemed to be everywhere. It would take too much time to load the dishwasher, so I threw them all into a green rubbish bag, tied a knot in the top, and dumped it into the tub. Drawing the shower curtain put them firmly out of sight, even if my new client needed to use the bathroom.

T minus six minutes.

The various toiletries were tidied by throwing them in the bathtub with the dishes.

When everything obvious was done, I pulled off my underwear, nearly tripping as my feet became tangled, and tossed them into the bedroom.

I must have been a magnificent sight, the poster child for empowered female business owners, as I wandered around the apartment naked, furiously brushing my teeth. When I got to the kitchen, I spat in the sink, ran the water, scooped some into my mouth, and tossed the toothbrush into the closest cabinet.

T minus two minutes.

I ran into my bedroom, and promptly stubbed my toe on something I'd thrown in earlier. I hopped around swearing loudly, and inventively in two languages until the pain became bearable.

T minus one minute.

My business suit was all on one hanger. It only took moments to put it on. My toe hurt as I jammed it into my one pair of good shoes.

Praying that she'd be just a little late, I ran around spraying air freshener. By design, that also stampeded Yoko Geri, who hid in the bedroom. The door buzzer sounded as I closed the door behind him.

T minus zero minutes. All systems go.

Clarice Trudeau was a forty-something woman of impeccable taste, refinement, and desperation. Everything she was wearing was a designer label. I could well believe that she knew my former client, Kaleigh Reinkemeyer.

The look she gave me when I opened the door was one with which I had become well acquainted.

"I know, you expected someone older. I assure you, I'm older than I look."

Or at least, these days, I was feeling it.

"My apologies, it's just that this is a delicate matter and, as I said, time sensitive."

"What can I do for you?" I said as I ushered her to my sofa.

"Last night I was hosting a dinner party for a few people. I was wearing a necklace that has been in our family since the 19th century. The clasp can be somewhat uncomfortable, so after a while, I took the necklace off, and put it in its case. My husband wanted to introduce me to someone. I put the case on a side table for a moment while we shook hands. When I turned around, the case was gone."

"It seems like a straight-forward case of theft. Have you spoken with the police?"

"That would be difficult. Except for the staff, everybody who was present at the party is someone of considerable standing. It wouldn't do to have the police bothering them, let alone suspecting them of theft."

"How many people are we talking about?"

"Thirty six."

"Do you have an appraisal on the necklace?"

"Yes. $326,000."

Kali is the only really rich person I know personally, and I'd sort of assumed that they all had her practical intelligence. I'm almost certain that the thought of putting a third of a million dollar necklace on the table, and then turning her back on it, wouldn't have occurred to her.

"How many staff members were present?"

"Let's see... Six regular staff, and, of course, the caterers."

Great, about fifty suspects, most of whom would be horribly offended at even being asked if they saw anything.

"You mentioned a time constraint."

"The necklace is being loaned to the Glenbow Museum to go on display in two days. They are to take delivery of it tomorrow. If we can't produce it by then, everybody will know that something is wrong. Questions will be asked."

I could smell the money in this case but unfortunately it was pretty much a no-brainer.

"I'm sorry, but the scheduling makes this virtually impossible. If I had a week to interview people I might be able to find your necklace. But twenty-four hours? I don't see what I can do."

"You said it's *virtually* impossible. Is there nothing that can be done?"

"What I can't do is to guarantee that you'll get your necklace back, especially within your time limit."

"Kaleigh mentioned that your usual rate is $50 per hour plus expenses." She drew an envelope from her purse. "I'm prepared to offer you a flat $5000 up front for the next 24 hours, with a $5000 bonus if the necklace is recovered. All I ask is that you try."

She handed me the envelope, and I took it automatically. Inside was a certified cheque for $5000. Damn, that was a lot of money, and it was guaranteed regardless of how successful I was.

What's life without a few challenges?

"Show me where the necklace disappeared."

We convoyed out to her house near Cochrane. She was in a new Mercedes CL65 AMG. I was in Binky. I left a message for Kali that I'd be with a new client for about 24 hours so she wouldn't worry.

I'd seen rich houses in the country before, so this one didn't impress me as much as it might. At a guess, I'd say it was worth at least five million.

Mrs. Trudeau (I never did ask if they were related to the Liberal party leader) showed me the crime scene.

"This may seem tedious, but can you walk me through what happened from the moment you decided to take off the necklace until you realized that it was missing? Any small detail may be important."

We went into the reception room. Cocktails and canapes had been served in an immense space where a hundred people could have stood around chatting without feeling cramped.

"I was over here, by the fireplace. The clasp has an odd shape, and sometimes it irritates my neck. That happened last night."

"Was anybody with you?"

"Yes, the Calgary mayor, one of our senators, and his wife. I excused myself, and went to the door."

She walked over to the open pocket doors. I followed.

"When did you actually remove the necklace?"

"When I reached the table. The clasp doesn't always bother me, but just in case I'd left the box out here."

I wasn't an expert on antiques, but the side table outside the room screamed Louis Quatorze. Beside it was a similarly gaudy loveseat. If they were reproductions, they were damned fine ones.

"I took off the necklace, put it in the box, and then my husband called to me."

"Where was he standing?"

She walked across the Italian marble tile floor and stopped.

"About here. He wanted me to meet a cabinet minister from Qatar."

"You put the box back on the table?"

"Yes, just for a moment, while I was being introduced."

"Where did you put the box, exactly?"

She touched the table near the back on the right side.

"Was there anything else on the table? Before or after?"

"As you see, just the flower vase."

"About how long did the introduction take?"

"I'd say around thirty seconds. My husband took him directly into the reception. When I went back to the table the box was gone."

"Was anyone near the table other than you?"

"No."

"Was anybody looking at you, or seem interested in what you were doing?"

"Not that I can recall."

This was going to take some thought, but already I was getting ideas. I walked back and forth, looking at the table and under it. There was no necklace, but what was there was interesting.

"You said that the event was catered. Where is the kitchen?"

She led me across the hall to the right, beyond the loveseat. Ah ha.

I was familiar with the logistics of catering a high end reception. I'd helped with several of them during my days at my father's restaurant, and I knew the dance and the music.

"Was anybody coming out of the reception room while you were speaking with the cabinet minister?"

"Perhaps a waiter, I think. I'm not sure."

If a waiter was leaving the reception, she would be on her way to the kitchen with an empty tray.

"Was another waiter approaching the room from the direction of the kitchen?"

Her brow furrowed.

"I don't know. It's not something I would normally notice."

"Do you have another box similar to the one the necklace was in?"

"Yes, most of my jewellery is stored in boxes like that." "Could you get one for me, please? If possible, containing something about the same weight as the necklace."

She hesitated, and I could see that I'd lost her. I showed off my Calgary Public School classical education to hurry her along.

"Tempus fugit, Ms. Trudeau."

She disappeared up the sweeping marble staircase. I wondered how many movies that didn't have the budget to fly a crew to New England had used this house as a stand in for one of the Newport mansions. Probably quite a few.

I was forming a theory about what had happened. To confirm it, I needed to perform an experiment.

While my client was upstairs I went to the kitchen. The staff looked at me like I was an alien.

"Where are the serving trays that were used last night?"

A young man pointed to a cupboard. Inside were a stack of silver trays, one of which I pressed into service.

I got back just as my client was coming down the stairs.

"Why do you have that?" She asked.

"Please bear with me. Put the box on the table exactly as you did last night."

She did so. Tray in hand, I went to the pocket doors, then glided out with the tray supported by one hand, mimicking the returning waiter. In my mind, I watched the waiter from the kitchen approaching me, laden tray in hand. It would be faster to switch trays than for me to go all the way to the kitchen. To do that I'd have to put my empty tray on the table.

It's harder than you think to pretend to accidentally let a tray slide into an object that you know is there but are pretending not to see. Apparently, the conditions weren't very exacting because the jewellery box slid off the table, bounced against the arm of the loveseat and landed underneath.

Right in the now empty waste basket.

A party like this would have been using real china and crystal, not paper plates, but all parties generate some debris. It wouldn't take much rubbish in the basket to hide a flat box from sight, especially from someone who was assuming theft rather than mischance. At night the only light was artificial. At the moment the box was obvious. At night the dark blue box against the dark wood of the table would have been much more difficult to see.

The clean up crew would want to be out of there as soon as possible. Nobody would look at what was in the garbage. They were paid to dump the basket and move on.

The whole tray swap would have taken a maximum of five seconds. No wonder Ms. Trudeau missed it.

"Who was in charge of the clean up?"

"I'm not sure. Carlos would know."

Carlos turned out to be their executive chef. I wondered why they'd had the event catered instead of cooked on site. From what little I knew of the guest list, maybe they wanted ethnic items with which he was unfamiliar.

"Has the garbage from the party been picked up yet?"

He looked at the wall clock.

"They should be doing that now."

I ran out the back door, leaving Carlos and my client wondering what was going on.

There was a beeping sound coming from around the side of the house. I damned near slid like a baseball player on the asphalt as I made the corner.

A garbage truck was directly in front of one of two rubbish bins, it's forks advancing to pick up the bin and dump it into the top of the truck. Two bins was a hell of a lot for a private residence. Maybe they rented an extra for the party. I screamed and waved like a mad woman, and the driver finally saw me.

"What?" He looked annoyed.

"Just wait a minute."

"I have a schedule to keep."

"I said wait a minute." I used the Voice of Command my mother had taught me while I was doing my police internship. The driver fumed as I checked the bins, hoping that I'd caught him on the first one.

No such luck. It was empty. I returned to the truck, climbing on the step so I was more or less face to face with the driver.

"Did you empty the first bin?"

"Yeah, and if you'll get off my truck I'll empty the second one too."

"Not happening. Dump it here."

He looked at me like I was insane. I didn't care.

"Are you nuts? Do you know what kind of mess that will make?"

"It doesn't matter. Dump it all right here. Then you can go."

His partner, who had been monitoring the loading from the ground, was watching the whole performance. He was grinning at us like this was the best show he'd ever seen. The driver decided to be stubborn.

"I can't do anything like that without a signed authorization from the home owner."

He waved a clip board at me, and I grabbed it from him.

"Pen."

He almost argued, then gave me a pen. I wrote "dumping of refuse on the driveway authorized by Veronica Chandler for Ms. Clarice Trudeau" then scrawled my signature beneath it.

"Do it," I said, handing him back his paperwork. He looked at it, then looked at me.

"You need to stand clear."

By now, my client and Carlos had caught up with me, and were watching my antics with growing horror.

"Ms. Chandler, you can't be serious."

"I certainly am. If I'm right, the necklace is either somewhere in that truck, or possibly in the second bin."

We watched as the truck backed around so that it was facing down the driveway, away from the house. The back of the truck swung up and a stream of rubbish fell out. The motor revved to power the hydraulics, and there was a sound of creaking inside the truck. The junk that was left inside began to ooze out like particularly disgusting, flaky toothpaste. This house had not been their only stop.

The truck moved forward slowly, leaving a stinking trail behind it. When it was empty, I jumped up to talk to the driver again.

"Pull forward, and give me a moment before you close it up."

This was as much fun as it sounds. I went to the back of the truck, and climbed inside to make sure the necklace wasn't caught somewhere. My suit only accumulated a few minor smears, but it was going need the dry cleaner as soon as possible. The smell was awful. The second sanitation worker watched me, the grin still on his face. I guess you don't get quality entertainment like me every day on his job.

I jumped out and waved at the driver. He closed up the back of the truck, his grinning partner climbed into the cab, and they left.

"What now?" my client said, holding her hand over her nose. Carlos had sensibly gone back inside.

"Now we find your necklace."

She looked at the metre and a half deep pile of refuse with horror.

"You can't be serious," she repeated.

"Call a temp labour agency, and have them send a half dozen men with respirators. It shouldn't take long to sift through the garbage, and put it back in the bins."

We were standing a good ten metres from the pile, and the smell was still disgusting. We followed Carlos back into the cool, sweet-smelling house. She picked up a house phone and told somebody what I wanted.

"I sincerely hope that you know what you're doing," she said as we stood in the hall. I smiled confidently. I hoped that I did too.

"If you necklace was stolen, then there are only two possibilities. Either a member of the catering staff did it, or a guest did it. Can you imagine any of your guests stealing from you? Especially since it would have to be a spur of the moment lark?"

"Certainly not."

"I've worked parties like yours. Everybody thinks that the catering staff are underpaid, and always looking to steal something. The truth is that the staff are paid quite well, and most of them either enjoy what they are doing, or do it because it's good money for relatively little effort. Either way, they'd be stupid to steal. If you'd reported the loss, everyone who was here would have come under scrutiny. Not only that, but any co-worker who even had a vague suspicion about a thief would start talking right away to protect his or her own job. Employee theft in this case would be highly improbable."

"The only thing that made sense was that the necklace was lost, not stolen. My experiment with the tray showed that if the waiter hadn't seen the box, it would have landed in the waste basket where it was probably hidden from view under some refuse. You didn't look in the basket, did you?"

She looked amazed, like Watson listening to Holmes expounding on the solution to a case. Come to think of it, I guess she was.

"Well, yes, I did glance in the basket, but I didn't see it. I looked on the floor, but I thought it had been stolen and – no, I didn't think of digging through the trash."

She was paying me extremely well. I could afford to be gracious.

"It was an easy thing to overlook under the circumstances."

Since I wasn't going to be sitting on any antiques until my suit was cleaned, I spent the next few hours in the kitchen with Carlos. It turned out that he knew both my father and me by reputation. We got along wonderfully.

The workers arrived, and started sifting through the pile. One group would rake the garbage away from the pile, tearing open the bags, and looking for anything even vaguely box- or necklace-like. Another group shovelled the sorted mess back into the bins. I watched from inside the house, quite enjoying my privileged position. I tried not to worry about what would happen if I was wrong.

Three hours later one of the men came to the door, a reeking velvet necklace box in his hand. Carlos wouldn't let him in the house. I didn't blame him. We washed the necklace off in the garden and presented it to Ms. Trudeau while the team outside shovelled the rest of the pile into the bins, and hosed down the pavement. I also suggested that she pay the men a bonus for their hard work.

Her pent up tension released itself in tears as the wedding present given to her great-grandmother was returned to the family.

"Thank you," she said, nothing more. But I could hear the sincerity.

The second cheque for the $5000 bonus that she handed me wasn't bad either.

All I had to do now was to avoid the psychopaths and demons long enough to spend it.

CHAPTER 17

The Final Problem

We were sitting in Kali's kitchen, eating miscellaneous cold leftovers straight from the Tupperware. Her pork fried rice was really good.

"Did you enjoy your holiday?" Kali said. I had to swallow quickly to answer her.

"Yeah, it was nice to have a case where the fate of the world wasn't at stake, despite what my client thought. Not to mention finding a simple, understandable solution."

She picked up a chicken drumstick.

"I hate to spoil the moment, but Collin should be out of his sling in a few days. We're running out of time, and we still don't know how to stop him."

"Believe me, I know. I'm beginning to think that we've been going at this the wrong way."

"In what way *haven't* we been going at this?"

"We haven't tried directly confronting him."

"I thought we talked about that. You said that he'd do the sacrifice immediately if he was threatened."

"Yes, but I've been thinking. It's obvious that Sitri knows what we're doing. Why hasn't he done something to directly protect Collin from us?"

"How do you know he hasn't? So far nothing we've tried has worked. Except that mysterious accident with the bike courier, of course."

The way she said it, I knew that she knew. I could feel my face heat up.

"But he should have been able to squash us like bugs at any point," I said. "Why hasn't he?"

She put down the bare chicken bone, and picked up another piece.

"Why should he? He hasn't gotten his sacrifice yet. Maybe he knows what we've been doing but he's a demon, not Collin's friend. He probably doesn't care what we do to Collin before the deal is sealed. Or after, for that matter."

"I still feel like this is my responsibility, and I should do something to stop it."

"Don't you dare. Even if Sitri isn't throwing fireballs at us, you said that you thought he was causing problems for you. If you go after Collin, I'm coming along. *Nuestra madre* would tell you the same thing. She wouldn't go into a dangerous situation without back up, even carrying a gun."

"Yeah," I said as sincerely as I could, "you're right. We'll figure something else out."

I spent the next day typing my case notes so that they made sense to someone other than me, transferring all the video evidence to several USB drives, and making sure that my equipment was in perfect condition. I paid particular attention to cleaning and oiling my baton so that it opened smoothly with a flick of my wrist.

Now I just needed Collin to co-operate.

Four days later I got a text message from Alyssa: "Collar wokking latte." It took a while to decode the message after I figured out that Alyssa the auto-correct feature on her phone turned on. I phoned her to confirm the message that Collin would be working late. He wasn't losing any time.

Before I could talk myself out of this, I changed into my grey track suit, then loaded my duty belt with all the goodies that I thought I'd need: phone, baton, handcuffs, and multitool, also known as a plausibly deniable legal folding knife.

The case file was printed out. Along with the USB drives, I stuffed it into an envelope that was addressed to Detective Janet Chandler. I hand wrote a note, placing that and the other envelope into a bigger one addressed to KALI – URGENT. As planned, BhadraKali was closed by the time I got there. I stuffed the nested envelopes through the mail slot before heading for Collin's hideout. I tried not to think of the implications of my preparations.

I parked down the street, about level with the far end of his strip mall. Binky was facing toward the service door.

After an hour, I was a nervous wreck. There was not a lot of traffic at this hour, and I tensed every time a vehicle appeared. While I waited for him to show up, my brain started second guessing what I was doing.

In theory, the plan was simple and foolproof. Collin couldn't transport a kidnapped victim by bus or taxi without someone noticing what was happening. That meant that he'd be forced to grab someone, and then use his car to bring them to his rental space. The only problem with that theory was that, during my earlier call to Alyssa, I confirmed that he'd left his car at home. Maybe he was going to rent or borrow one, although that was a stupid idea. If anybody saw the license plate it would be easier to claim that his personal car was stolen than it would be to explain why he needed a second vehicle the day of a kidnapping.

Regardless, once he showed up with a probably unconscious victim, I'd jump him, save the day, and send Collin off to jail for kidnapping, forcible confinement, and whatever else would stick. We'd worry about him summoning demons again when he got out of prison at least ten years from now.

I was hopped up on adrenaline, armed, expecting trouble, and determined not to fight fair. This should not be much of a battle. The one flaw in the plan was that Kali was going to be peeved that she'd been excluded. I could live with her anger if it meant keeping her safe.

By seven o'clock he should have been there. Either kidnapping takes longer than I'd thought, or something was wrong. I hate waiting.

Half an hour later it was officially sunset. Partial cloud cover made it darker than normal, and moonrise wouldn't be until almost midnight.

The tension was making my muscles stiff. There was no sign of him yet, so I disabled the dome light, and got out of my car to stretch. I'd wanted to sneak up on him on foot anyway.

A lot of the units in the mall were industrial suppliers rather than commercial, so they didn't bother with outside lighting at night. I convinced myself that I should wait closer to the door to shorten my response time. At least it was something to do.

I locked Binky, and moved closer to the building with all my senses concentrating on the direction from which Collin would be coming.

Between one step and the next my head exploded, and I had just enough time to see the pavement coming toward my face before everything went black.

This was not according to plan.

Only one eye responded when I tried to open them. My nose hurt. I had trouble breathing. I tried to breathe through my mouth, but for some reason it wouldn't open. I think I was lying on my side. I tried to touch my eye, but my hands wouldn't move. My head ached.

I tried to move my hands again. By the feel of it, they were tied behind my back.

There was a droning noise, a non-stop cascade of sounds that slowly changed from a babble to individual noises to intelligible words.

"...much better than some whore. He'll be so pleased..."

I thought I recognized the voice. I tried opening my good eye again, but all I could see was a blur. I blinked a few times, and saw a pair of hairy bare feet walking past me. Whoever they belonged to seemed busy to the point of mania.

I closed my eye, and things became vague again.

The next time I became conscious, my vision was less blurry. I could make out Collin, standing next to a desk, consulting his book. He had removed his street clothes but hadn't put his ceremonial robe on yet. The videos I had seen didn't show his back. At some point in his life, someone had whipped him. The area from his waist to the tops of his thighs was covered with old scars. There were far too many for one session. I was looking at years of abuse. For a moment, I almost understood him, his need for control, and why he'd married a woman who was so broken that he seemed whole in comparison.

The thing is, a crappy childhood didn't give him the right to ruin other people's lives. Especially when one of the other people was me.

He was muttering to himself, like someone rehearsing their lines before an amateur play. Part of me was cold. I was lying on a concrete floor with lines painted on it. Part of me recognized it, and fired off a shot of adrenaline that seemed to bring a little more of my brain to order.

I was in Collin's magic circle. Nobody would know where I was until Kali saw my envelope in the morning. By then I'd be – I suddenly realized that I had no idea what I'd be. I assumed that I was to be the sacrifice, but the deal was that Collin wouldn't be the one to actually kill me. Or would he?

People use the phrase "a fate worse than death" but they have no idea what that really means. What would Sitri do? Bite my head off? Drag me off to his place for a romantic candle-lit evening? Steal my soul (whatever that was)? Slowly tear me apart with his teeth? Force me to think that I was in love with Collin? The horror of not knowing was so great that I threw up.

The reason I couldn't breathe through my mouth was that Collin had taped it shut. I choked, and my last meal tried to burn its way out through my injured nose. There was searing pain in my throat and nostrils. Breathing became impossible.

Collin was there immediately, ripping the duct tape off my face so I could vomit properly.

"No, no, no, no, no. You mustn't die yet. He won't want you if you're dead. That isn't our deal."

I don't know what had tipped the scales, but something inside Collin had snapped. Before he was just a psychopath. Now he was completely bug-house nuts psychotic.

I tried to stay as limp as possible while he cleaned out my mouth, and then used a rag to clean the mess from the circle. Struggling now wouldn't do me any good, so I saved my strength. When he moved me around I realized that my feet were bound as well.

He hadn't caught on that I was awake. My only hope was to wait for some opening that I could use later.

My stomach was still queasy, and I felt like the room was spinning even though I was lying still on the floor.

I think I passed out again.

Suddenly he had his robe on, and was lighting the candles he'd set around the circle. He'd left the tape off but gagged me with a rag. It almost let me get enough air.

The idiot had left me lying mostly on my back. It wasn't a good position for someone who had been choking. It also meant that, when I opened my eye, all I could see were the overhead lights, and some of his movement our of the corner of my eye. The light was painfully bright. It took a while for me to figure out that I could turn my head to look away.

This time there was definitely a gap in the action. Collin was now wandering back and forth reading the invocation, and waving his knife around. My thoughts moved like tar and kept floating away. It slowly occurred to me that I must have a concussion.

Sometime soon, that would become the least of my problems.

With 20/20 hindsight, my big mistake was expecting Collin to get a victim before coming here. It never occurred to me that he'd come here first, probably to get everything ready before he went trolling for victims.

With his mention of a whore, his lack of a vehicle made perfect sense. The hooker stroll was only a couple of blocks away where he could get somebody to come with him willingly. Instead, he'd found a conveniently close random stranger: me. *Well done, Veronica. You've got him right where he wants you.*

Collin was into his "you'll be sorry if you don't appear right now" routine, so I didn't have that much time.

I cautiously moved my head. My duty belt was missing, and the only other knife was in Collin's hand. It felt like he'd emptied my pockets too. The thought of him putting his hands on me while I was unconscious made my flesh crawl. My only chance was using one of the candles to burn or melt the rope he'd used, and hope that my track suit didn't go up in flames first. At least he hadn't used my own handcuffs on me. Perhaps he couldn't figure out how to get them open.

Talking about it now, things in Veronicaland sound like they must have been very cool. They weren't. I was sweating madly, and almost peeing myself in fear. My brain was stuck in low gear. I was injured, bound, and gagged. There were only a few precious minutes before a demon would come to take me as a human sacrifice so that this psychopath could turn somebody else into his sex slave. If things could get worse, I didn't want to know about it. My heart was pounding, and I had trouble breathing. I tried to wiggle, as quietly as I could, toward the nearest candle.

Things got worse.

There was a swirl of mist, and Sitri appeared in the triangle. It was too late; I'd spent too much time unconscious.

"Oh mighty Prince Sitri, accepteth this, mine offering, that thou mayest doeth my bidding," Collin said.

He grabbed the rope around my ankles with one hand, dragging me away from the candle, and toward the edge of the circle. My hands were under me, and the concrete removed some skin. Thank all the gods for amateur villains. He was looking forward, and didn't notice that I was awake and flexing my knees as he dragged me.

Sitri's golden-green eyes looked down on me, and he smiled with lots of sharp, feline teeth. I couldn't tell whether it was an "oh boy, lunch" or a "I like this one, she has spirit" smile. Collin turned to follow his gaze, and his eyes widened as he saw me glaring at him with one wide eye.

As soon as his eyes reacted, so did I. I had exactly one chance to get this right as I snapped my legs straight. I tried to aim my heels for his gut, trying to take him down so I could kick his head until he stopped moving. At the last moment he dropped my legs, and I caught him low, right in the centre of his pelvic bone. There was a muffled pop as the joint at the front snapped. That was even better. It would hurt like a son of a bitch, and he wouldn't be able to move effectively with a broken pelvis.

He folded in half, and fell backward across the circle's boundary.

His howl of pain was just beginning when Sitri reached down, and grabbed him by the neck with strong, taloned fingers. I closed my eye, and tried to think of something else until the wet, crunching sounds stopped.

When it was over, Collin was gone, and Sitri was licking his fingers. There was no sign that another person had ever been there. From the sounds, I'd expected the room to be painted with blood spatter. The demon looked down at me and smiled again.

"Acceptable. What do you desire?"

The aura of physical attraction that I'd felt through the video was much worse in the room. I didn't care about his inhuman features. I couldn't ignore the gorgeous human anatomy. What the hell was wrong with me?

I heard a mewling noise, and realized it was coming from me. Nothing mattered except the overpowering lust I felt for something inhuman.

The spell broke. My fear rose as the lust receded. In a panic, I lurched and wiggled over to the nearest candle, hoping that the circle would keep Sitri out until I got free. Holding my wrists out blind, it seemed like I burned everything except the rope. Without the use of my mouth to breathe I was never able to get quite enough air in my lungs. It felt like I was slowly drowning.

"A little to your left," the demon said helpfully.

I adjusted my arms, and a few seconds later there was more searing pain as the plastic rope melted, and stuck to my skin. The blistered skin pulled away, and my hands were free. The rag in my mouth was glued to my nose with blood, and it hurt as it pulled free. A moment later I forgot about the pain as I sucked in vast oceans of sweet, sweet oxygen. Nothing else mattered for perhaps a minute as I lay there repaying my body's oxygen debt.

Collin's book, the one that contained the banishing ritual, had fallen outside the circle. There was no way I could reach out and grab it without exposing myself. That brought back the thoughts of the perfect male body just a metre or so away.

For now, I seemed to be safe inside the circle. Maybe I could wait until help arrived.

That was a bad idea. All Sitri had to do was wait until someone showed up, and then eat them, or turn them into sex slaves, or whatever he wanted. My cell phone was on the table outside the circle, so I had no way of controlling him, or banishing him, and no way of warning Kali or the police, the people who were most likely to come bursting through that door next.

Laying on the floor, my head pounding and still working at half speed, it took me a while to think of the obvious.

I'd sabotaged both the circle and the triangle. I was sitting inside a defensive perimeter that should have been as porous as a tennis net.

So why was Sitri still on the outside instead of in here with me?

I had no idea. All I could do was go with the flow. After a couple of tries, I managed to get up as far as my knees, and started to improvise.

"Oh mighty Prince Sitri..."

I stopped speaking as he turned to mist, then re-solidified. Gone were the wings, the leopard head, and the perfect male body. Standing in its place was a much shorter, ruggedly handsome man wearing a trench coat, fedora, and pinstripe suit. He held a lit cigarette in one hand.

Just when I thought this whole situation couldn't get any more surreal he spoke in a very familiar voice."Cut the baloney, doll face. That stuff is for chumps,"

Another piece of the puzzle clicked into place. It was Sitri I'd seen leaning against the mail box the other night. He had never needed Collin to come and go. It was all a game. I think I whimpered again.

"What? You think we care about all that medieval malarkey?" He said, waving the cigarette around. "It's the thought that counts, babe. So, what can I do for you?"

From somewhere, I managed to find enough spit to lick my lips. I tasted blood. At lest the lust had vanished again with his shape change. I still had to clear my throat a couple of times before I could speak.

"You'll do whatever I ask?"

He shrugged. "You slotted the nickel, toots. You get the Kewpie doll. Within reason, that is. I don't really have to do anything, but I'm feeling generous at the moment." The full lips above his dimpled chin smiled, a perfect likeness of Humphrey Bogart from 1941. "Call it a weakness for hot dames like you." He took another drag from the cigarette. "Besides, Blakeway was a crumb. He was going to get me a sporting girl from up the road before he found you. He was a lazy bum who had no sense of style."

"What if I ask you to never answer a summoning again?"

He took a drag on the cigarette and blew a perfect smoke ring while looking up toward the ceiling, considering it. He looked back at me.

"That's pretty hard on me, kid. How about a hundred years?"

"A thousand."

He drew on the cigarette, again looking upward.

"Sure, I can do that. No summonings in Calgary."

I was getting the idea. Talking to Sitri was like talking to a lawyer, but there were no defaults or implied conditions. If something wasn't mentioned, it didn't exist.

"No summonings anywhere on Earth."

"Alberta."

"North America."

"All right, done."

"There's something else."

He took another puff, and gestured with the cigarette for me to continue. The cigarette wasn't smouldering normally. It burned with a quiet blue flame, and the tiny amount of air that still came in my nose held the acrid stink of brimstone.

"Cover up Collin's death so nobody will look into it, and his insurance will pay out."

"Tricky. If you were to reduce my sentence to a hundred years..."

Damn it, I should have seen that coming. "All right. Done."

"You drive a hard bargain, doll, but you got it. I like you, sweet cheeks. You're the bee's knees. In fact, I'll do you a little favour, free of charge." He stepped forward and squatted in front of me. I felt a lingering kiss my forehead. I was too freaked out to protest, but it could have been a kiss my father gave me rather than anything sexy. For a moment I felt dizzy, then he stood upright again.

"Hocus-pocus. I'll see you around, beautiful."

Sitri gave me a casual, two-finger salute off the brim of his fedora and was gone. I guess the banishing ritual was malarkey too.

I was exhausted. I sank to the floor, and rolled over on my back. I must have passed out again.

Some time later, the cold concrete woke me up. It felt wonderful until I woke up enough to start shivering.

Everything from my pockets and belt were on the desk. They were a very long way across the room, and a very long way above me. It took me a while to crawl the distance. Occasionally I forgot where I was going.

Standing was still beyond me. I clawed my way high enough to reach my multitool which made quick work of the rope around my ankles. My head was getting clearer, although I still couldn't open that one eye. A careful exploration with my fingers showed that it was glued shut with blood from a scalp wound. I was extremely careful touching my nose. It was incredibly painful, and felt like it was off-centre.

I tried to think carefully about what I was going to say before I picked up the phone and called the police. The dispatcher had me stay on the line, and cars arrived within a few minutes. Attempted murder gets you premium service.

The police were first in. For some reason the door wasn't locked. Maybe Sitri had done me another "favour."

I told them the truth, sort of. While I was talking the paramedics looked me over, then transferred me to a gurney. When they wheeled me outside there were two cars, a sergeant's van and an ambulance, all with their lights flashing. In my still woozy state, I started giggling. The pretty lights made the area look festive. I was happy that my painful sensitivity to light had gone away. Both of the paramedics were really nice to me. I just lay there and let them work.

One of the medics was young, male, and extremely cute. Maybe it was a reaction to surviving the night's terrors. Maybe Sitri's influence was still lingering. Either way, I had a sudden urge to jump him, and tear his uniform off. It took me a while to figure out that I'd been busy, and skipped my meds that morning. Shit, just what I needed in addition to the injuries: I was high on hormones. He smelled good, too. Fortunately, his female partner was the senior member of the team, and took care of me, bandaging my burned wrists, washing out my eye, and taping my broken nose while he assisted.

She also did a lot of tests, asking me my name, the date, where I was, what had happened. She had me squeeze her fingers, looked at my eyes with a light, brushed my arms and legs with her finger to see if I could feel it, and then did the same with something pointy. She checked my vision and hearing, then asked me to memorize some words, and repeat them back. As a final annoyance, she wanted me to count backward from one hundred by sevens. After all that, they went a few steps away to whisper to each other.

I was feeling better by the moment, and was tired of lying down.

"How long did you say you were unconscious?" The Hunk asked. I tried to ignore his lovely green eyes, and focus on the task at hand.

"I don't know. On and off from a little after 7:30 until maybe half an hour ago."

"You are one lucky woman," his partner said. "You should have some neurological symptoms after being unconscious for two hours."

"I guess I have a hard head."

"We're going to have to take you to the hospital for further tests."

"Not happening," I said firmly. "Apart from some bumps and bruises, I feel fine."

"Then would you mind answering some questions?" A new voice said. I looked up to see Danielle Shuemaker standing by the ambulance doors. Damn, I'd forgotten that we were in her district.

"Hi," I said.

"Are you all right?"

"All my parts are still attached. Apart from some bumps I'm good."

"Maybe," said the female paramedic. I was beginning to dislike her.

"Good," Danielle said. "I'd hate to have to tell your mother that you died on my watch. Or any other."

I told her most of the story. I'd been hired by Collin's wife to find out if he was having an affair. I'd tailed him here, and he'd gotten the drop on me. He wanted to use me as a ritual sacrifice, but he was sloppy. I kicked him and he took off. I thought I might have damaged him.

After we got through the preliminaries, there were some details that didn't make sense to her.

"You said that you were still tied up. Why did he run away?"

"Damned if I know. Maybe I really hurt him. He was limping."

"Did he say why he was doing this?"

"No. I guess not all villains have the decency to monologue, and I was too busy surviving to ask."

"Hmm. Do you know where he went?"

"No idea. Out the door. That's all I cared about."

"And you're sure it was Collin Blakeway?"

"Definitely. Check the fingerprints in the room, and the name on the rental."

Sometimes she'd circle back, and ask the same question in a different way. I knew all the tricks, and was sure my story would hold up. My big advantage was that most of it was the truth. It would have felt really uncool to lie to a friend.

Sometimes it would be nice if Calgary's Finest weren't quite so thorough. After a while, the medics told her that they were still concerned, and she should lay off.

"Okay, I think I have everything. Let me know if anything else comes back to you."

"Will do," I said. She put her notebook away and went to talk to the Ident technicians.

The Hunk took my blood pressure, again, and looked into my eyes with a light, again.

"How do you feel?" His partner asked.

"Just fine, apart from a sore head and nose. Even those are feeling much better."

"We'd still like to take you in for tests. I can't actually find evidence of a concussion, but given what happened to you, you should be in really bad shape."

"I don't need a hospital. What I need is supper, a toothbrush, and a good night's sleep. I promise that I'll see a doctor in the morning."

Neither of them were happy with my decision. Unfortunately for them, I was conscious, in my right mind, and over 18, so I got to decide what would happen to me. It was probably another stupid decision, but I didn't feel like spending the night in an unflattering gown that left my butt hanging in the breeze. I also didn't feel like being poked by doctors who were convinced that I should be a vegetable, and tried all kinds of tests to find out why not.

I wanted to go home and cuddle with my cat. My personal Moriarty had gone over the cliff, I'd just made a deal with a demon where I was the winner, and I was still breathing, albeit painfully. It was long past time for something pleasant to happen to me tonight.

CHAPTER 18

Meltdown

Enough of this, it was time to go home. I sat up and started looking for my car keys.

"Whoa, where do you think you're going?" The Hunk said.

"Home. I have to feed my cat."

"You aren't driving anywhere."

I glared at the paramedic as menacingly as I could. Being used to patients with a poor sense of self-preservation, he returned the glare with interest. I found my keys, and he smoothly took them from me. He was getting less attractive by the second.

"Give those back," I said.

"No. I can't let you drive after a head injury like that. It would be as irresponsible as letting you drive after you'd had ten shooters. If you are too stubborn to let a doctor check you out, at least you need to let someone else drive you home. Otherwise, there's a very real chance that you could pass out and kill yourself, not to mention other people. Am I making myself clear?"

"Fine, you win. I'll call a taxi."

"Don't you have someone else you can call such as friends or family? If you start to crash on the way home, you don't want the first hint of it to be when the cabbie asks for money, and finds you slumped over dead in the back seat." That stopped me.

"Is that likely?"

"I don't know. That's what worries me. You should show evidence of neurological impairment. We can't find it, but that doesn't mean it isn't there. At the very least, you need an X-ray. You could be bleeding inside your brain, and that's fatal."

Danielle was close, so I called her over and asked for a ride home. My EMS guardians explained to her why I needed one.

"Let me have her keys," Danielle said. The ex-Hunk handed them over. I held out my hand, expecting her to give them to me.

"Sorry, these were at the crime scene. They'll have to be held as evidence."

"*Et tu*, Danielle. Will you at least give me a ride?"

"I'll be tied up here for several hours, and doing paper work after that." Damn it, she knew Mum and Dad were out of the country.

That left me with a very short list of whom to call and a dilemma.

Kali would drop whatever she was doing, and come to get me. After our last conversation she'd also ream me a new one, likely in high-velocity Spanish. It didn't help matters that she'd be right.

Keith or Parker would come for me, but they'd also call Kali to let her know that I was okay. She'd be even more pissed off. Andrea might come, but I didn't know her very well yet, and had no idea if she had a car.

"Well?"

"Give me a minute; I'm thinking."

As the paramedic watched I sighed deeply, and made the call.

She was not amused. The Rat-Bastard Busybody, formerly known as the Hunk, insisted on talking to her before he'd approve of me being left in her care. He was the one who hung up afterwards.

"Satisfied?"

He gave me the impression that he thought I was acting like a child, so I sat on the back step of the ambulance and pouted. At least my mind was behaving more or less normally now.

From what the paramedics had said about my injuries, I wondered if the demon had done something to my brain. I was almost certain that I'd had at least a concussion when I woke up. Now it seemed to be gone.

Kali arrived twenty minutes later. Both paramedics intercepted her before she made it to me, and had a chat with her.

This was not going to be as much fun as being fed to a demon.

Once we were in the car, she coldly demanded to know my side of the story. She'd gotten the outline from the medics, but she wanted all the gory details that she suspected had been left out. It was only later that I realized that she wasn't going to drive away from the ambulance until I'd finished my story, just in case I had a seizure or something.

She said nothing through my whole recitation. Once I was done, she started the car, and we drove without speaking until we got to her house. I'd expected her to take me home, but I was smart enough not to argue.

Kali turned off the engine, sat for a silent minute an hour long, then looked at me.

"Listen to me very carefully, Veronica Irene Chandler. You will *never* do anything that stupid ever again. Do you understand?"

Her tone was quietly furious. She must have been building up a head
of steam since I'd called her. I blame my attempt at being reasonable on
the head wound. Or it could have been me being a moron.

"I was just trying to..."

Her fist came down hard on the steering wheel hub and the horn
beeped briefly in sympathy. It was a wonder to me that the wheel didn't
bend. I'd never seen her that angry. The words came out almost too fast
for me to follow.

"*Hijueputa Verónica. No me salgas con esas estupideces. ¿Que mierda te
pasa? ¿Es que no te importa nada la gente que te quiere? ¿Es que tu vida no vale
nada o que? ¡Reacciona! Tu sabes que me moriría si te hubiera pasado algo hoy.
¿COMPRENDE?*"

I understood completely. I'd rarely heard language like that before, in
either English or Spanish. The content was harsh but that wasn't the important part. It was the emotion behind it.

I never wanted Kali to be that angry with me ever again. Especially
when I knew deserved it.

"*Si, pedí perdón,*" I said softly. Kali relaxed slightly.

"If I wasn't so happy that you're still alive I'd kick your idiot ass all
the way around the block. By the way, you're staying here tonight so I
can keep an eye on you. I don't need another dead sister."

I winced. I hadn't thought about that aspect. *Madre de dios*, I'm stupid.

"Yes, Kali," I said quietly. She was absolutely right. The way things
worked out, if I'd taken her along I wouldn't have a headache, and Collin
would be alive in jail.

God, I can be so stupid at times.

Stupid, stupid, stupid.

Muy estúpida.

Morning came extremely early, even if it was into the double digits.

I woke up whimpering like a child whose heart was broken. The pillow was soaked with my tears. I was an emotional mess, unable to figure
out what was wrong with me. Everything was a jumble. It took a minute
for me to make myself wake up enough to understand anything that was
happening.

Usually, I remember a dream for a few moments after waking, and
then it fades away. This one remained sharp and clear.

I was lying on a concrete altar. A hideous creature was standing over
me. At first I was unable to move at all. As soon as I realized that nothing
I could do would help me it started laughing.

As it laughed I became more and more aroused. Now I could move my
hips, and I found myself thrusting them upward, wordlessly asking it to

take me. No matter how hard I tried, I couldn't stop myself.

I was terrified to do so, but I opened my eyes. Where ever I was, it wasn't my bed, and I panicked.

After a moment, I recognized my old bedroom at Kali's house. I cried again, this time relief. I was physically safe.

Waking up in pain in a strange bed reminded me of being in the hospital after I killed Ronald Brandau. For the first time, I understood that my refusal to go to the hospital the night before had been because of that incident. I guess some things never completely go away.

I sincerely hoped that my reaction to Sitri was one thing that would.

That thought gave me a small feeling of comfort amid the rip tides of the emotions from the dream.

Fear, helplessness, shame, anger: I couldn't sort out which was which.

Despite my exhaustion, I hadn't slept well. My burned wrists throbbed under their bandages. My nose throbbed every time I smashed it against something hard, such as the feather pillow. My head ached. I was also stiff and sore from lying on the cold concrete floor for hours. At least my mind was functional.

On the night table I saw a bottle of pain killers, and a glass of water. There was also a chair pulled up beside the bed that wasn't usually there. A crumpled blanket lay on the seat. As if I didn't feel badly enough, I was ashamed to realize that Kali must have sat up all night watching me. Making sure that I kept breathing.

I took two of the tablets with a water chaser, then laid in bed again. I tried not to think of the dream, or the feelings that had gone with it. After half an hour the pills started working. I crawled out of bed to face the music.

The house was silent. I found a note from Kali on the kitchen table. Bless her, she'd gone to feed Yoko, and to get fresh clothes from my apartment.

I debated whether to have a long, hot bath first or breakfast. A loud rumble from my stomach settled the matter. I was starving. As I was hunting and gathering in the refrigerator the back door opened, and Kali returned. She had a copy of the Calgary Herald in her hand.

"How are you feeling?"

"I'll live. Thanks for the pain killers and clothes." I looked down at the two eggs I was holding. "I'm really, really sorry for putting you through this. I'm such an idiot."

She put the paper on the counter, took the eggs from my hand, and shooed me out of her kitchen.

"You should read that, *mi hermanita idiota*."

I looked at the newspaper that had been opened to the local news page. I didn't have to ask which article to read.

Suspect Found Dead.

The account was short and to the point. One Collin Blakeway of Calgary, wanted in connection with assault, kidnapping, and attempted murder, had been found dead in his car. Police believed that he had lost control of his vehicle as he was fleeing the crime scene. The car had been found wrapped around a tree. The death was ruled accidental, and no charges would be laid.

"Well?" Kali said.

"I guess I'm surprised that Sitri kept our bargain. My client will get her insurance money. I just hope that a better life goes with it. I'll have to call her later to let her know I'm okay, and give her whatever closure I can."

"How much will you tell her?"

"Probably everything. Well, maybe not everything. The best thing I can do for her is to give her Trinity's number."

"There's someone else you should call."

Kali gave me that look that every erring child is familiar with, and pressed the button on her answering machine.

"This is Detective Janet Chandler of the Calgary Police Service, calling for Veronica Irene Chandler. You may remember me. It's nice to know that *one* of my daughters lets me know when something important happens before another detective calls to tell me that you were almost killed. Give me a call when you get up." She dropped the sarcasm from her voice. "Please. Kali said you're okay, but we need to hear it from you."

Damn it, I thought as tears ran down my face. Stupidity, the gift that keeps on giving.

For some reason the paper was shaking as I put it down. Oddly, so was the bandaged arm that was holding it. I was gasping for air. Kali put her arms around me, and steered me to a chair. I think she thought I was having some kind of seizure.

"What's wrong?" It took me a while to find my voice.

"A couple of years ago you told me that magic is mostly psychological."

"Yes. It looks like I was wrong. That occasionally happens. I've come to terms with it."

"Well I haven't! The stuff Sitri does is right out of a fantasy novel. I don't care how many legends, myths, and stories are out there, these things don't happen in real life. They can't. There was nothing psychological about what he did. He showed up on the cameras. I saw him change into Humphrey Bogart. Collin was eaten right in front of me. After I asked Sitri to cover things up, Collin magically came back, made it to the car he didn't bring, drove away, and then conveniently crashed at high speed on a deserted road with no witnesses." I paused, breathing deeply to try to calm myself. "Sitri caused physical changes in the real world because some guy followed the directions in a book that's available for free on the internet. Why is this happening? Why here? Why now? This is the second case I've had involving demons. What if this happens again?"

Kali put her arms around me until I stopped shuddering. Then she quietly said something that started me shaking again.

"We'll just have to be ready."

The tears were streaming down my face. Kali handed me a tissue box. I was afraid to try wiping my eyes, the way my broken nose had been hurting. It seemed much better now, so I risked it. My nose barely hurt at all. Those must have been really great pain pills. I blew my nose while the miracle still held.

"I don't want to be ready! I don't want to deal with shape-shifting demons that don't follow any rules. I don't want everything I've ever believed about life turned into bullshit. I don't want any of it."

I paused to take a breath, and try to stop my shaking.

"I want to be a normal teenage girl with normal problems: what to make for supper, what to wear on a date, how to find men who aren't terrified when they find out I want sex more than once a day. I want to be a private investigator, helping people by finding their runaway children, their fucking tea pots, or exposing their cheating spouses. Not some demon hunter from a cheesy reality show."

Mentioning sex made me think of the dream, and those feelings welled up again. It took a while before the new set of shaking and crying stopped.

From outside the circle of Kali's arms I heard another one of her annoying bits of wisdom. Annoying because they tend to be profoundly true.

"I'm not sure that we have a choice."

God damn it, she did it again. In the past year I'd dealt with demons twice. For whatever reason, they were showing up around Calgary, and unless I was missing something, I was the one attracting them. At least, there were no reported sightings in the news, and both Mum and Trinity seemed to be out of the loop as well.

I conveniently ignored the hint that Father Cole had given me that there were reports of demon sightings all over the world. That was for the Catholic Church to deal with, not me.

Again, the questions hammered my mind. Why? Why here? Why now? And why the hell *me*?

I had no idea. That was the most disturbing thing of all.
There was only one thing that let me hold on to any amount of sanity.
At least it was over for now.

CHAPTER 19

Still Waters

Except for the massive storm that I suspected had been caused by Sitri, autumn days in Calgary tend to be bright and crisp. This morning certainly was. It was a morning for rejoicing that I was alive. The blood was washed out of my hair, I was reasonably rested. The bruised face, and neat line of butterfly closures on my forehead, made me look like I'd been to an Abuse Club meeting without my armour.

I was perversely rather proud of my wounds. They showed that I'd survived a close-quarters battle with a demon prince and an evil sorcerer. Of course, I couldn't tell anybody that, but still...

Unfortunately, the bad-ass effect was somewhat spoiled by the bandages on my burned wrists. To me, they made me look like someone who had tried to commit suicide and failed.

It was a good thing that my parents were still out of the country. Mum would have wanted to go over every detail of the fight so I could learn not to make the same mistakes next time. Dad would have gone into his Princess Protector mode. If I'd sliced my hand to the bone in the kitchen he'd have told me to suck it up, and not be so careless next time. Any injury from a bad guy would turn him into a nervous wreck. Fathers can be so unrealistic at times.

I waited two days before I went to see Alyssa. That was enough time for the police to notify her of the circumstances of her husband's death, and for me to feel a bit more human after my abduction. My nose seemed to be back to normal, which was welcome but puzzling to my doctor.

Alyssa would be almost helpless without her husband. He hadn't been the type to encourage his wife to show any independence, or acquire any skills.

I felt a complete lack of guilt for my part in her current situation. Her bastard husband had tried to have me killed, and enslave somebody else. Everybody was better off without him.

On the other hand, I felt like I should try to get her life back on track. Right now she needed a friend who would help her through this.

The Blakeway house was typical of the area: a two-storey with a couple of steps up to the front door, vinyl siding and some fake-stone accent walls.

I pushed the button, and heard a cheerful, traditional "ding-dong." A few seconds later Alyssa opened the door. She looked better than I did.

The first thing I noticed was her eyes.

If my husband had just died, I'm sure my eyes and nose would have been puffy and red from crying. Even if he was an abusive jerk, she'd been with him for six years. I expected some kind of grieving.

Her eyes were normal, but she was looking through me instead of at me.

One thing that's sometimes annoying about being an investigator is that we try not to make assumptions. A normal person would have assumed that she was still in shock, or the reality hadn't hit her yet, or maybe years of abuse had flattened her emotions.

Maybe it was something else. I kept my eye on her, just in case. I still remembered that there was something odd about her previous behaviour that I hadn't explained yet.

She said nothing, but opened the door further. I took it as an invitation to enter.

She was dressed nicely, like she was going out on a date. Maybe the date was with a lawyer, or the funeral home. That would be a good sign. It would mean that at least she was dealing with some things.

We sat in her perfect living room, and once again she made tea. She played hostess, asking if I wanted cream or sugar, not remembering the answers I'd given when she'd asked the same things only a few days earlier. There were a few silent, awkward seconds after I had my tea in front of me.

"I want you to know how sorry I am for your loss," I said.

"Thank you." I waited a few seconds for her to say more, but she remained silent.

"What did the police tell you?" I asked.

"That he tried to kill you. That you hit him, he ran away, and crashed his car into a tree." Her voice was flat, like she was reciting a grocery list.

"That's the gist of it." There was another pause while she sipped her tea.

"Why you?" She asked.

"I'm not sure what you mean."

"Why did he want to kill you? Why not me?"

Whoa, where did that come from? Was Alyssa suicidal? I had no idea how to handle it if she was. I answered carefully.

"I don't think it was personal. My understanding is that his original plan was to grab a prostitute from the stroll a few blocks north. When he saw me almost on his doorstep, he took the easy victim."

"That's not fair," she said, still in her flat voice.

"No, but fortunately I was able to get away. One of the working girls might not have been so lucky." I didn't mention that she might have been street-wise enough not to get into that position in the first place.

We sat in silence for a minute, drinking our tea. Damn, had she meant that it wasn't fair to me, or that it wasn't fair that he didn't offer her up as a sacrifice? I had no idea which direction her thoughts were going.

"Is there anything I can do? This must be nearly overwhelming for you."

"Did you ever find out which demon he was summoning?"

There was that odd question again. Something told me she shouldn't know, although, if Sitri kept our bargain, she wouldn't have to deal with him for a century.

"No."

"Do you have his things?"

"The police would have everything that was in the car. You should be getting Collin's property back in a few days."

She delicately ran one forefinger around the edge of her cup. It looked to me like she was being overly casual.

"What about the items in the room he was renting?"

"They'll have those too, as evidence. From what I saw, there weren't any personal items."

"I still want them back."

"Why?"

She took another sip. It was obviously a bid for time so she could think of an answer, implying that she was hiding the real answer from me.

"Sentimental reasons."

Wow, talk about a generic excuse. This seemed like a great time to lie to my client.

"All right. I have some friends on the force. I'll see if I can hurry things along."

"Thank you."

She offered me the plate of cookies.

"I want you to know that I don't blame you for his death. You were just – convenient."

I waved off the cookies. Her flatness was beginning to creep me out.

"Thanks. I never intended to hurt him, but he didn't leave me much choice."

"Why?" She asked. "What else happened?"

Okay, this was awkward. I tried to dance around the demon issue.

"I'm not sure you want to know. It wasn't pretty."

"Yes, I do. If he wanted to kill someone it should have been me."

I hoped that my poker face was holding up.

"What makes you say that?"

"I was his wife. He should have thought of me first, not some stranger."

I began wish that I'd brought Trinity with me, or at least that I was recording this conversation. This really didn't feel right.

"Believe me, there are things you are better off not knowing."

"You said before that he was summoning a demon. Did he succeed?"

I saw no signs of religion in the house. Maybe she was just curious. Despite my misgivings, she was an adult. If she wanted to know, so be it. I told myself that I wasn't going to bill her more than she'd already paid, so it didn't matter if she thought I was insane. It also wasn't likely that she'd say disparaging things about me to her friends. She didn't have any.

"Yes," I said, "he succeeded. He summoned a demon prince who deals in lust, and was making a bargain to turn someone into his sex slave. The sacrifice was to be the payment."

There was another uncomfortable period of silence. I sat, waiting for Alyssa to react in some normal way to my outrageous statement. Most other people would have been shocked, either because it sounded crazy or because I was speaking ill of the dead. She should have thrown me out. Instead, she picked up her cup, took a delicate sip, and carefully put it down on the saucer.

"I see. Do you have any idea who the slave was to be?"

Could she be jealous? That would seem like a reasonable reaction to the woman who would be replacing her. There was no way I was handing Andrea to her, whatever Alyssa's motives were.

"Not really, although I suspect that whoever it was had no interest in him. I saw no evidence of any kind of extra-marital relationship during my surveillance."

"I see," she repeated. "Perhaps it was his receptionist. It would be nice to think that at least he had good taste."

This was getting weirder by the moment. I dug one of Trinity's cards out of my pocket.

"I have a colleague who is a psychologist. She's helped me a lot. I think that would be useful for you to talk to her about what's happened.

She may be able to give you some practical insights as to where you might go from here."

Alyssa didn't touch the card where I'd put it on the table.

"Thank you." She stood up. "I'm feeling tired now. I assume you'll send me your final bill."

"Of course. Call me if you need anything."

As I went back to my car, I thought about what she'd failed to say more than what she had said.

Her reaction to my revelation about her husband's magical summoning was certainly not what I expected. It's one thing to say that he was trying to summon a demon, and quite another to say that he'd succeeded. Granted, different people have different reactions to stress, but I would have expected something like, "excuse me?", or "you're kidding, right?", or even "holy shit, are you a freaking nut case?" I hoped that she called Trinity. Understanding and fixing Alyssa's mind was way above my pay grade.

When I got home, I did the paperwork to close the case. I'd gone over the retainer in my billable hours, but I called it even. The poor woman didn't need more things to worry about. I didn't want to drive her over the edge.

Especially if it might be the same edge Collin had gone over.

The next day, as I so richly deserved, I slept in. Yoko wasn't happy that breakfast was delayed. I took his objections under advisement by carefully burying my head far enough under the covers that he couldn't paw at me.

I was now gloriously unemployed. There were plans for meeting Kali for lunch. Other than that, I could stay in my pyjamas until I ran out of savings.

For once, I was in my bedroom getting dressed when my phone signalled an incoming text message. I wondered if something had come up, and Kali would be delayed.

Instead, the text was from an unknown sender:

Don't be fooled.

That was weird. I didn't know you could get a text from an anonymous source. Where would the reply go?

I replied anyway, hoping that the telephone company would somehow sort it out.

By what?

The reply came back within moments of me pressing the send button. Whoever was on the other end was a fast typist.

Not what, whom. Alyssa Blakeway.

Who are you? I typed.

Surely you can't have forgotten me already.

Wonderful. Somebody who thought it was cute to be mysterious. I was typing something particularly rude when another message arrived.

Go tonight, while she's trolling. Her husband left you a present in their basement.

Trolling?

What do you mean?

There were no more messages. I wondered if somebody was playing a joke on me. If so, it wasn't funny. Assuming that Sitri was keeping his end of the deal, I could only think of one possible culprit.

The bell above the door of BhadraKali tinkled cheerfully as I entered. Keith was perched behind the counter on a stool. I immediately headed for him, my face grim.

"Hi Veronica. Are you taking the boss away so I can slack off?"

His smile seemed innocent enough, but it could be an act.

"In a minute. Right now, I'd like to talk to you about the texts you sent me an hour ago."

"What texts? I don't think I've sent you any since the wedding."

He looked sincerely puzzled.

"Do you know of any way I could get an anonymous text?"

"Sure, that's easy. There are some web sites where you can do it, or if you know the person's phone provider, you can send an e-mail to their phone number at the provider."

If he was lying, it was an award-winning performance. I decided to believe him.

"Crap. Okay, I'm curious. How is it possible to reply to such a text?"

He looked surprised, like I should have known the answer. Techies are like that.

"Did the sender include a phone number or an e-mail address?"

"No, there was nothing. No phone number, no e-mail."

"Then you can't. It's strictly one way. I suppose that, technically, a provider could set something up, but I don't know of any who do."

"Double crap." The bead curtain behind the counter rattled and Kali appeared. I was startled to see her in jeans and a blouse instead of a Romantigoth gown. Regardless, her colour scheme hadn't changed. Everything was black except the blouse which had a red Peter Pan collar and buttons that matched the colour of her hair tips.

"Is anything wrong?" She asked.

"Nothing that can't wait until after lunch."

It was another beautiful autumn day in Calgary. We walked up the street to a nearby Thai place.

"How does it feel to be unemployed?"

"Wonderful. I slept in..."

"No difference there."

"...and it's nice to put this case behind me. There will be another one soon enough. Maybe this time someone will want me to find a missing soup spoon."

An older gentleman was coming out of the restaurant as we approached, and held the door open for us. I've known some women who think that implies that they are considered helpless. I figure that the courtesy is better than getting it slammed in my face. I hold doors open for guys, too.

"Spit it out. What's wrong?" She said as soon as we sat down. Damn it, it was like trying to keep secrets from Mum.

"I'm not sure. I got some weird texts just before leaving my place."

I got out my phone and showed her the messages.

"That is weird. Who sent them?"

"I wish I knew. Obviously, somebody who thinks that I should remember them."

"I know what 'trolling' means online. Does it have another meaning?"

"In real life, it means fishing from a moving boat. I can't see Alyssa being involved in either. There aren't many fishing spots around Calgary."

"At least this doesn't have anything to do with Sitri."

"I'm not sure about that. According to Keith, I shouldn't have been able to send a reply to these texts. There's something fishy going on."

"Maybe that's what the sender meant by 'trolling'."

"Very funny."

"I thought he promised not to show up again for a hundred years?"

"If he keeps his promises. After all, he's a demon."

I wanted to change the subject, so I told her about my visit with Alyssa.

"What are you going to do about her?"

"I don't know. In some ways she seemed suicidal, in other ways not. I'll have to see what happens."

"What kind of present could her husband have left for you? He didn't know you existed until the night he kidnapped you. Even then, you didn't tell him your name, did you?"

I let out a deep sigh.

"No, but he could have looked at my business cards. Do you have any idea how little I like unanswerable questions?"

"It isn't unanswerable. All you have to do is look in the basement."

"I doubt that Alyssa would let me poke around her house. Besides, I'm not all that anxious to see what the crazy, homicidal, evil sorcerer left me as a present. I'm still alive. Just this once, I think that I'll quit while I'm ahead."

She poured us each a glass of water from the pitcher on the table.

"Who are you, and what have you done with Veronica?"

CHAPTER 20

Presents of Mind

I f it hadn't been for the growing feeling of unease in my gut, I'd have felt like a complete scumbag. As it was, I only *mostly* felt like a scumbag.

Binky and I were sitting down the street from the Blakeway house. I was spying on a woman who had just had her life destroyed, and I was doing it on my own time. At one point she walked in front of the living room window and adjusted the drapes, so I knew she was home.

My firm resolution not to look into the "present" that Collin was supposed to have left for me lasted through lunch, and all afternoon. By supper time the curiosity was gnawing at me. By the time I'd finished eating, I'd convinced myself that it wouldn't hurt to take a look. Whoever had sent the texts must have counted on the raging sense of curiosity that had led me to become an investigator. It annoyed me that I was that predictable.

Just before seven o'clock, a cab pulled up in her driveway. A moment later she came out. I used my binoculars to get a better look.

Holy crap, talk about FCM. She was wearing the littlest Little Black Dress I'd ever seen. The front had a plunging neckline that showed her navel. The bumps of her nipples were obvious on either side of the neckline, and were certain to make a personal appearance if she did anything except stand perfectly upright. The hem line had to be less than a hand span below where her legs met. I was impressed by her ability to walk on strappy sandals with heels that high; I would have broken my ankles. As she got into the cab, the dress pulled even tighter than it already was. That glimpse made me almost certain that the dress and sandals were her only items of clothing.

From her Victorian demeanour when I'd first met her, I would have bet real money that she didn't own any clothes like those, and wouldn't have known what to do with them if she had them. She looked like she was on her way to a club, and I suddenly knew what the anonymous texter had meant by trolling.

Three days after his death, it looked very much like Alyssa was out fishing for a replacement for her husband.

That afternoon she'd acted like a zombie. There was no way that Alyssa should have been able to throw off her grief and PTSD to be this functional so soon unless I was missing something unbelievably major.

I very much wanted to follow her, to see what she was really up to. However, tonight I had a date with the secrets that Collin had allegedly left in the basement. Unless she found Man of Her Dreams 2.0 tonight, I could always follow her another time.

I gave the cab ten minutes after it pulled away, just in case she'd forgotten something. I walked to the house in case a neighbour saw my strange car parked out in front. I had my hands in my pockets to hide my fashionable pair of blue nitrile exam gloves that would keep me from leaving fingerprints.

I performed some basic counter-surveillance by taking a stroll through the neighbourhood before approaching Alyssa's house. There was nobody sitting in a vehicle within sight of the house. All the roof lines were clean. All the windows that faced Alyssa's house had closed drapes.

Pictures of me breaking and entering would not have been good for my career, so I headed for the back yard. Whoever had sent the texts had all but told me to perform an illegal act, and I had no idea what the texter's motive was.

The side gate was still locked, but was easy enough to climb. It was also completely in shadow. I wish I'd done this last time.

One thing I'd noticed when I'd been in the yard before was that the Blakeways had no concept of domestic security. There was no bar on the sliding glass door, just the factory-standard key lock. I had it open within two minutes, even while wearing the gloves.

There was no alarm company sign outside, or a control panel inside, so I just walked in. Alyssa was the type to leave a light on when she went out at night, so I didn't have to fool around with flashlights, or grope around in the dark. A flashlight moving inside a dark house is a great way to attract attention of the wrong kind.

The closed door to the basement was by the kitchen. Just on general principles I opened it cautiously. For all I knew there could be a claymore mine attached to the door handle.

A thought occurred to me. I headed upstairs instead.

The master bedroom wasn't hard to find. Nor was Alyssa's closet. In it I found two very different wardrobes.

On one side, taking up about three quarters of the space, was her staid, mousy wardrobe. Everything on that side was knee length or longer. Tops were either pullover with a crew neck, or buttoned up to the top. There were a few pairs of sensible shoes on the floor.

Despite the volume of clothes, at the moment they were pushed far to the side so Alyssa could access the other quarter of the closet.

In that collection, there were gossamer lingerie items that would conceal nothing, and cost a fortune while doing it. The shoe collection was much larger, tending toward stiletto heels and strappy sandals. The dresses were all similar to what I'd seen her wear earlier. All in all, it was the wardrobe of a woman whose sexuality made mine look like that of a shy nun.

The Alyssa with whom I had spoken earlier was not the Alyssa who had just left.

After being counselled by Trinity, I'd done some reading about psychology. In this case I was sure that I was looking at a case of dissociative identity disorder. Although it was rare, DID, also known as a split personality, explained everything. I knew that, when it did happen, it was said to be caused by long-term abuse, so that fit as well.

While I was there, I made a quick check of the rest of the room. There was nothing unusual on the closet shelf, nor in her dresser. The underwear drawer confirmed what the closet had told me. She had a collection of sensible, cotton underwear at the front of the drawer, and a smaller collection of sexy underwear at the back.

The surprising thing was the other closet and dresser. They were completely empty. She'd probably just gathered up all his things and thrown them out. As far as she was concerned, Collin was dead, and that was the end of it.

I checked the master bathroom as well. Again, there were feminine products in one drawer, and the other one was empty. There was only one toothbrush in the holder.

Curious, I went down to the living room. Sure enough, the pictures of their wedding were gone from the mantel. They'd been there the last time I'd visited. Collin might as well never have existed.

When Alyssa got over somebody she didn't fool around. There was no hint that another person ever shared the house with her, let alone that she'd had a husband.

It was time to check out the basement. The stairs were covered with carpet, so my descent was quiet. There were no sounds downstairs. The light shining through the basement windows was minimal, but it was good enough for me to scan the area, and confirm that I was alone.

There was a slight, unusual, pleasant odour to the basement. It wasn't

a normal basement smell. More like somebody had been burning
something aromatic, with a chemical floral scent on top.

The windows all faced the side or back of the house, so I risked turning on the lights.

The basement was divided into three rooms. The main part was a social area complete with a bar. There were no bottles on the shelves. The
chairs and couches surrounded an area rug, and were positioned away
from any of the walls. The larger of the other rooms was used for storage. The remaining one was the furnace and utilities area.

Once I knew the layout, I made my search plan. Covert searching is
one part technique, and two parts obsessive-compulsive behaviour. I had
no idea what I was looking for, so I would have to look everywhere. If
there was a drawer, I would examine all the contents, trying to keep
them in the same positions so nobody would know I'd been there. I'd also
examine the sides, back and bottom of the drawer, as well as looking at
the drawer slides inside the desk with a flashlight. I'd tap the bottom, as
well as measuring the inside and outside depths to detect a false bottom.
Anything was in the least bit misplaced or unusual has to be investigated, including sections of floor, walls or ceiling that looked or sounded
different. Anything that could be taken apart would be disassembled, ex-
amined, and then re-assembled. It takes a long time to do a good job.

If Alyssa was out clubbing, I probably had at least three or four hours
before she would even toy with the idea of coming home. Assuming that
she came home at all that night.

The furniture in the main room was pretty standard. Not as good as
upstairs, but modern, and in good shape.

One thing that didn't fit the decor was an antique steamer trunk
against one wall. That seemed like as good a place as any to start my
search.

I went over the outside of the trunk without finding anything. It was
wasn't that heavy, so I carefully picked it up so I wouldn't scratch the
concrete floor. There was nothing underneath. I gently tipped it a bit,
and scanned the bottom with my flashlight. Nothing.

The fastenings on those trunks are ward locks, the kind that has been
around since Rome had an empire. My biggest problem was finding a
pick among my set that would move the mechanism in the right way.
The latch finally popped free, and I opened the lid.

Well, what do you know?

The trunk contained a variety of items that could only be magical
tools. There was a dagger, similar to Collin's athame, but with a white
handle covered in symbols. Unlike an athame it looked to be razor sharp.
Four big candles sat firmly in metal dishes to catch the drips. This must

be where Collin kept his spare tools before he had the rental property.

It wasn't exactly breaking news that Collin had a stash of magical tools. My mysterious texter must want me to find something else, unless this was all a game.

The smell was stronger in the trunk, and lacked the floral overtones. I recognized it as incense. I picked up a plastic bag with small rocks in it: frankincense. Someone had tried to cover the scent in the basement with air freshener.

That led to another weird implication. Unless Collin threw Alyssa out of the house while he did his rituals she would have been home, and must have known about it. At the very least she must have wondered why the basement smelled the way it did.

A small, blue velvet bag sat in the bottom of the trunk. Inside was a ring. It was silver, with the words "ANEPHENETON MICHAEL" and "TET-RAGRAMMATON" carved in it. Unless he wore it on the end of his pinkie it was too small for Collin. There was also a small brass jar with two handles. It was about the size of a perfume bottle, and had writing around the middle in Hebrew. The lid had a weird seal on it, consisting of some squiggles around the circumference and a picture in the middle that reminded me of a radio telescope. I took pictures of everything in the trunk.

A hard-cover notebook contained at least a hundred pages of hand-written notes. A few early pages were in English, the majority were in some alphabet I wasn't familiar with, so I snapped a couple of pictures to show Kali. I couldn't recall ever seeing Collin's handwriting, but this looked feminine to me. Maybe he'd bought his magical tools from someone else.

The only other items in the trunk were some metal pendants. They were asymmetric, almost random looking sigils similar in style to Sitri's demonic seal. I took pictures of them too. One of them looked familiar. I was almost certain I'd seen it before.

After locking the trunk again, and making sure it was in its original position, I looked around the rest of the basement very carefully.

The social area was next. I found it odd that two people who seemed to have little or no social life had a party room. I looked under the furniture, beneath the cushions, unzipped the cushion covers, and ran my hands down into the depths of the seats. Apart from a small amount of change, some old, lint-covered candies, and the usual unnameable stuff that seems to accumulate in sofas, there was nothing.

There were no obvious lumps when I walked over the carpet, but the easiest way to find out what's under a carpet is by looking. There could be a floor safe, or single sheets of paper. One sofa was on wheels, so I moved it back, and started rolling the carpet aside.

I should have guessed. There was something under the carpet, all right. Painted on the concrete floor was a ceremonial circle. As far as I could tell, the circle was identical to the one Collin had in his hideout. At least, before I'd changed it. Why would Collin need to rent a place for his rituals if he had a ready-made ritual space at home?

There was only one reasonable answer. I had a nasty feeling that I'd been badly fooled.

Collin wasn't the original sorcerer in the family. Alyssa was. No wonder she wanted the magical tools back.

This changed everything, and explained very little. At least I knew why the ceremonial robe Collin had worn looked like it was too small for him. He'd stolen it from his wife rather than wasting time making his own.

This was disturbing to say the least. Alyssa had successfully presented herself to me as a mousy, conservative type who was being bullied by her abusive husband. Mousy and conservative don't fit the profile of someone who forces demons to do her will. Neither did it fit with her clubbing clothes.

What it did fit with was my theory that she had multiple personalities. If she did, how many did she have, and what did each of them want? Which one was the original? Which one had I met?

The who and how were becoming clearer, even if the what and why weren't.

Alyssa stayed at home most of the time. It gave her all the time she needed to research the summoning rituals, create her tools, paint her circle on the floor, and cover it with a rug so Collin wouldn't know. Under the rolling sofa I found some pieces of cardboard that were the perfect size to fit into the windows. As long as Collin wasn't home, she could work down here day or night with no chance of being observed.

Already I had more questions than answers. If Alyssa was the sorcerer then what was Collin doing? Was this a shared hobby between them? That didn't make sense. Why would she hire me to see if he had a mistress if she knew what he was doing? Maybe one of her personalities did, and another one had hired me. The possibilities made my head hurt.

I put the carpet and sofa back the way they'd been. So far I'd found Alyssa's things. There was still no sign of the "present" that Collin might have left behind.

The storage room was full of the miscellaneous junk you'd expect: Christmas ornaments and lights, a dusty exercise bike, stacks of boxes containing the old financial records of Collin's clients. That made covert searching a lot more difficult. I examine everything without leaving smears in the dust.

Most of the stacks were almost ceiling high. One of them was not only shorter, but somehow didn't look right, as if it had been moved.

Behind the stack an extension cord was plugged into the wall. The cord ran behind the boxes, and by pressing my cheek to the wall I could just see where it disappeared into a small hole had been roughly cut in the dry wall. The debris from the cut was still on the floor. That seemed unusual enough that I decided to follow the wires.

On the other side of the wall was the utilities room: furnace, electrical panel, gas and water meters. The cord entered near the floor, ran up the wall, across the ceiling, and ended where another cord plugged into it. The new cord continued across the ceiling, and disappeared above a heating duct.

There was a short step ladder in the storage room. I brought it in, and climbed up so I could see what was going on.

Near the ceiling was an air vent. There was no duct behind it, so it must be there only to allow air circulation in and out of the utility room.

The mystery cord was plugged into a video camera that was set behind the vent. I left the furnace room, and looked at the vent. Sure enough, I could see the lens, but only if I was close, and knew exactly what I was looking for. Nobody would notice it if they didn't know it was there.

The camera was pointed toward the area where the circle was. I wondered who had put it there: Collin or Alyssa?

It seemed strange that Alyssa would record her own rituals, unless she wanted to critique herself. Either her summonings had been successful, or she was recording the failures to see where she went wrong. But why hide the camera? From Collin? Why not just put it out in the open, and hide it when she was done?

Perhaps Collin had found out about Alyssa's magical hobby, and bugged the basement to find out what she was doing. That was believable, given his controlling nature. If I believed the text messages, this was almost certainly Collin's "present."

I unscrewed the vent with my multitool and extracted the camera. It was still running. The camera wasn't just plugged into its charger. It also had a USB cable running to an auxiliary disc drive. A big one.

If I was lucky, that drive could answer a lot of questions for me. I had to decide whether I dared to take it with me.

If Alyssa had placed the camera, then she would eventually discover that her disc was missing. On the other hand, she wouldn't know that Collin hadn't taken it. If it was placed by Collin, then I was safe.

I had another thought. If it was Alyssa, she'd have a nice record of me peering curiously at the camera. That made it easy. The video had to come with me.

I turned the camera off, and took the disc. Although I hadn't really expected to bring home any souvenirs, it fit nicely into my hoodie pouch.

The vent cover went back into place easily. Since I'd been distracted, I went back to the storage room to continue my search. There was nothing else of interest.

I hit another jackpot when I moved back to the furnace room. After looking inside the furnace (the filter needed cleaning), I noticed that the old humidifier attached to the outside was dry. That was common with that type. The motor burned out, or the drum became coated with lime from Calgary's hard water, and people just turned it off instead of getting the humidifier fixed. I opened it up.

Lying on the bottom of the tray was a stack of DVDs in thin plastic cases. Each disc was labelled in marker pen with what appeared to be two dates. The oldest label was six years ago, some time after Alyssa and Collin had married. The writing looked masculine.

They joined the hard drive in my pouch. It was getting late, so I called it a night.

After a look around to make sure I'd put everything back exactly where it had been, I turned out the lights, went up stairs, and left. It took me a couple of minutes to re-pick the patio door so I could lock it again from the outside.

I looked around. The back yard couldn't be seen by neighbours. I swarmed over the fence, and dropped down into the shadows. There were no obvious watchers.

Binky and I quietly left the neighbourhood.

CHAPTER 21

Show Time

I brutally crushed my curiosity, and refused to look at the videos that night. There were twenty five DVDs. If they were full, that added up to about a hundred hours of video. Besides, even if they weren't Collin's porn stash, I wanted the sun to be up when I watched them. Whatever had happened, or was still happening, in that basement wasn't something I wanted to experience during the dark hours.

Don't look at me like that. You'd have some quirky fears too if you'd almost been eaten by a demon.

At an utterly unreasonable hour the next morning I found myself staring at the ceiling, unable to sleep. Yoko Geri stayed in bed until he heard the sound of kibble hitting his bowl. If I didn't get to sleep in, neither should he.

It had not been restful night. Honestly, I should have just gotten up, and looked at the discs. They could still be harmless, but this case had a nasty habit of handing me unwelcome surprises.

I was about to get a bowl of kibble for myself when I decided that I de-served a real breakfast: a toasted slice of heavy bread I'd baked a few days previously, creamy scrambled eggs, and sauteed mushroom caps with prosciutto.

Ah, the joys of comfort food in troubled times.

I sat in my comfy chair, and started by cataloguing what I had.

I did some online research, punched some numbers, and estimated that the hard drive would hold about 100 days of HD video, assuming that it had been running 24 hours a day. That was an interesting number, being just over fourteen weeks.

There were twenty five DVDs, each marked with dates that were ex-actly 14 weeks apart. There was no DVD for the current period. It was safe to assume that Collin hadn't had a chance to transfer the video from

the hard drive yet. I wondered how he'd managed to compressed 3000
gigabytes of video onto a four gigabyte disc.

There should be about 78 days of video currently recorded on the
three terabyte drive. When I plugged it into my computer I found exactly
one file. This was going to take a while to review.

The video started by showing the empty basement. I hit fast forward,
and settled in with Yoko watching me from the sofa.

For a while, the only motion was the rhythmic waxing and waning of
the light through the windows as the days passed. It was almost hypnot-
ic.

The first bit of real motion turned out to be Collin. He came down
stairs with a file box like the ones I'd seen. He went into the storage
room, then came out without the box. Instead, he was carrying the step
ladder. He passed out of sight beneath the camera. A few seconds later,
the camera moved slightly. He must be checking his installation.

When he re-appeared, his face filled the whole screen as he checked
the vent. It was creepy seeing the dead man who had tried to kill me
looking out of the display at me.

Once Collin was gone, there was nothing for a very long time. I turned
off the video.

That was how he'd gotten all that video stuffed onto DVDs. He'd cut
out the parts where nothing happened.

I tried the first DVD that was dated over six years previously. It contained several video files. The file names appeared to be dates.

The first one opened with a moment of empty basement, followed by
Alyssa coming down the stairs in a pink baby doll that hid nothing. She
looked a little younger than the Alyssa I knew. From the light coming in
the windows it was morning.

She started by putting the pieces of cardboard in the windows. The
camera adjusted itself to the lowered light level.

She moved the sofa, and rolled the carpet aside. She unlocked the
trunk, and brought out the same selection of tools I'd seen in Collin's
hideout. That suggested the solution to another minor mystery. Collin
hadn't had to make his own tools. He'd borrowed or stolen his wife's.
Were the tools left behind ones he didn't need for what he wanted to do,
or did he not know how to use them?

The way she set up the candles around the circle had nothing to do
with the alignment of the room's walls. Maybe she was setting them to
the compass points. After getting out the tools, she took off the baby
doll. She recited a prayer as she put on the robe that fit her so much better than it had him.

"By the figurative mystery of these holy vestments, I will clothe me

with the armour of salvation in the strength of the highest, Ancor, Ama-
cor, Amides, Theodonias Anitor, that my desired end may be effected
through the strength of Adonay to whom the praise and glory will
forever and ever belong, amen."

Wow, talk about run-on sentences. My grade-twelve English teacher
would have failed her for sure. I guess if you are summoning demons you
don't get credit for good writing.

One major difference between her and Collin is that she didn't use the
book. Apparently, she had it memorized. Alyssa was one impressive lady.

Scary, but impressive.

Another major difference was that her triangle wasn't painted on the
floor. Instead, it was made of embroidered cloth that she could lay out
where ever she wanted it. I guessed that she didn't limit herself to one
demon, and the various demons must require the triangle to be placed in
different locations.

Ceremonial magic was mind-bogglingly complex. I prefer point and
click technology. Or in the case of my baton, click and point.

I couldn't hear the next part, as she walked around the circle with her
athame, and said something too quietly for the camera to pick up. She
then put one of the sigils around her neck. I couldn't see which one it
was. It was the next act that raised the hair on the back of my neck.

"I invoke and conjure you Beleth and being with power armed from
the supreme Majesty, I thoroughly command you..."

Oh hell no. Not again. This was not fair.

She was invoking *Beleth*? After everything else, this could *not* be happening to me.

I stopped the video, and spent the next while pacing around my
apartment while Yoko watched me from the sofa. This was the moment
that a fictional PI would pour a double shot of whiskey.

I'd gotten drunk once in my life. It didn't solve any problems. Instead,
it lowered my inhibitions, my raging hormones took over, and I made a
fool of myself.

I don't like to think about it, much less talk about it. Alcohol was no
answer. I'd just have to cope.

I went back to the computer, fast-forwarding until something appeared in the triangle, then reversed to the beginning of the manifesta-
tion.

Just like with Sitri, Beleth was heralded by a swirl of mist. This time,
however, instead of a perfect man with a leopard's head and Pegasus
wings, there was a trumpet hovering in mid-air that played a slow or-
chestral fanfare with lots of wind instruments and drums. It sounded familiar. I thought that maybe I'd heard it on TV, but I had no idea what it

was called. It was one of those tip-of-the-tongue things.

The fanfare went on for several minutes. The trumpet dissolved, and a mighty king appeared seated upon a pale horse. Everything was perfectly proportioned, but the horse was pony-sized so it would fit in the basement. The king was, as they say in the books, of terrible countenance. Somehow, he made his voice echo in the small room. If this was Beleth, it wasn't a side of him/her that I'd seen before. He pulled out a sword and waved it aloft, being careful not to damage the ceiling.

"Tiny human, how darest thou disturb me, I who am a king, mighty among all the legions of Hell? Thy death shall be long in coming, and infinitely sweeter to thee for its arrival, a thousand lifetimes hence. I have had mortals tormented for all eternity by my ministers for lesser offences than thine."

I take it back. It did sound somewhat like Beleth.

"O mighty Beleth," Alyssa said, raising a wand before her, "I thank thee for thy previous service in securing for me a husband. Now there is another service that thou mayest perform."

Beleth turned to mist. The horse vanished and the demon reappeared as an extremely pretty little girl. Little, as in a bit over a metre tall, not as in young. She had brown eyes, and chestnut hair to her knees held back in a pony tail. The only reason one would have for not thinking that she was eight years old was that she had a figure that a porn star would kill for. That was apparent from her cutoffs and muscle shirt. Her crown was still perched on her head at a jaunty angle. This was more like the Beleth I knew and didn't love.

"Very well, Alyssa, thou hast constrained me in thy service."

Yeah, right. Just like our various attempts had "constrained" Sitri.

"My husband's manner is too mild. He showeth his love in tenderness and forbearance, yet if he truly loved me, he would take care of me by delivering me from the need to plot my own course."

"Thou wishest me to make him more – forceful – in his affections?"

"That, and to be in command as a proper husband should."

"Very well, it shall be done by thy will."

What the hell was I hearing? Collin was a sweetie, so Alyssa summoned Beleth to dial up his assholeness to eleven? That didn't make any sense to me.

I replayed the sequence, from first appearance to final dismissal a few more times, trying to figure out Alyssa's motives. I also made a separate recording of the audio. I had the feeling that I would need to consult with other people later.

My insight into Alyssa's mental state was becoming both slightly clearer, and a lot murkier. I went through the rest of the recording. Over the next year Alyssa kept summoning Beleth to fine tune the way Collin was abusing her.

I remembered how disgusted I'd been with myself when I realized that I'd let my first boyfriend turn me into "Adam's girlfriend" instead of "Veronica who had a boyfriend." When Collin had seen this, he must have been horrified.

If I understood the time line, Alyssa had summoned Beleth to make Collin fall in love with her. Once they were married, she used Beleth to turn Collin into a mean, abusive SOB who treated her like a slave. In other words, the man of her dreams.

I'd been deeply concerned when I thought of how teenage boys with no conscience would act if they got hold of the ritual Collin used, and summoned Sitri to turn girls into their own personal love bunnies.

Now I saw the flip side of the coin: Lonely, or manipulative, girls summoning Beleth to turn boys into their ideas of the perfect boyfriends. Or to punish those who didn't treat them "properly."

Welcome to Stepford, Connecticut. Population: Alyssa and Collin. I hoped.

It was early evening when I stopped making notes. Consulting a whole series of psychology websites had given me the clues I needed to make some sense of Alyssa's mind. As minds went, it was not a good place to visit.

Despite appearances, she was actually the dominant member of the relationship, having snared a basically nice guy to use as raw material, then summoning a demon to make him "perfect." Her version of love, however, was more like an unhealthy obsession with controlling her every thought and action with no consideration for her as a person. She wanted to be used and abused, physically, economically, psychologically, and sexually. She seemed to get off on having no control over her life, and used Beleth as her proxy to control Collin into controlling her.

I guessed that Alyssa's control of Beleth didn't count for her, since Beleth wasn't human. It was by far the wackiest reasoning I'd so far encountered in my life.

If the nice guy Collin was still in there, underneath the demonic control, it was no wonder to me that he'd gone mad toward the end. I began to feel sorry for the poor abused bastard who'd tried to kill me.

Had our binding spell had contributed to his demise by providing a three cornered fight: Beleth's changes, original Collin, and the binding? I wondered what it was like with all of them trying to modify his behaviour at the same time.

It was a perfect example of why such bindings were seldom done in Wicca, and only when necessary. In this case, we hadn't had all the information we'd needed. We did what we thought was right at the time, and it was far too late to worry about it now. I'd keep it to myself. Kali and her group didn't need the guilt.

Collin's actions also became clearer. Somehow, he'd discovered Alyssa's dirty secret. Maybe it was the lingering incense, or he'd come home at the wrong time. To get away from her, he'd decided to do his own rituals with her tools, and make his own sex slave who couldn't control him. I wondered why he'd chosen Prince Sitri instead of a demon of higher rank. Maybe he thought that King Beleth wouldn't allow it.

As evil plans go, it wasn't a bad one. After he stole her tools, in theory she wouldn't be able to do any rituals to stop him.

My subconscious had been worrying about the trumpet when she arrived, so I Googled "fanfare." One of the suggestions jogged my memory and suddenly I remembered the name of the music it had played: Aaron Copeland's *Fanfare for the Common Man*. That fit exactly with what I knew of Beleth's twisted sense of humour.

My perennial big question in this case was still with me.

What was I going to do now?

CHAPTER 22

It's Never Simple

My first stop was the land titles website where I ordered the title for the Blakeway house. That told me that Collin had bought the house eight years ago, and it was still in his name.

Alyssa's notes said that they'd been married six years ago. She must have done her first ritual sometime before that, and forced him to ask her to move in.

When she'd slipped up, however that happened, he'd put the camera in the basement to find out the details of whatever he suspected. We'd never know what that was now that he was dead. Obviously, it wasn't that she was being unfaithful, otherwise he'd have put a camera in the bedroom.

Unfortunately, by the time he knew what was going on, it was far too late for him.

I'd been played all along. Alyssa knew that if I investigated her husband, eventually I'd stumble across his rituals. All she wanted was her magical tools back. Whether I lived or died in the process was of no concern to her. That pissed me off.

Damn it, it was time to send up the bat signal again.

I got the phone from my night stand and texted: *Request dossier on Alyssa Blakeway, Calgary.*

If this was anything like last time, I should be getting a response just about...

Send whatever information you have on the individual to cgaf7p7jya6un-9@NTEENJ643.com via encrypted e-mail. How urgent is this?

I wondered what the urgency rating for "imminent major demonic attack" was. I settled for texting back *very*.

I scanned the documents Alyssa had given me into the computer, then appended a note explaining that I needed a full dossier on her family, life prior to six years ago, and anything suspicious regarding any-

body in her life. If you are going to ask a spooky organization for information, you might as well go for the full meal deal.

Once the e-mail had been sent there was nothing to do but wait. I hate
waiting.

There was, however, one promise I could break immediately.

"Detective Shuemaker."

"Hi Danielle. It's Veronica. Have you had lunch yet?"

"No, I'm just finishing a report. Why?"

"Unless you have something pressing to do I'll be there in 20
minutes."

"Don't I get a say in this?"

"Nope. I'm buying."

"Fine, twist my rubber arm."

Sometimes it was hard to believe that I'd met Danielle three years
ago. Every once in a long while I still had a dream about her, lying in the
slush bleeding while a psycho druggie tried to kill us.

A couple of things had come out of that incident. Some were positive:
increased self-confidence for one, and Danielle feeling like she owed me
for saving her life for another. Both of us had also developed a healthy
awareness of traffic at intersections. At least we pretended that it was
healthy, and not bordering on a phobia.

I'd dealt with all the major psychological effects of that incident.
There was one little thing remaining, and I was going to use this opportunity to address it for both of us.

The District Four station where Danielle worked is at the end of a cul-
de-sac. Miraculously, there was usually parking on the street only a few
metres from the front door.

There were two officers at the front desk when I came in. One was
talking to a man on my side of the counter. He appeared to be explaining
how to fill out some kind of form. The other officer looked up as I came
in.

"I'm here to see Detective Shuemaker," I said.

"Is she expecting you?"

"You'd better believe it," Danielle said as she came out the security
door. "She said she's paying for lunch."

Danielle looked much the same as last time I'd seen her. From the
bulk of her brown hair, it looked like her French braid would be mid-
back length when she combed it out. There were a few more silver hairs.

"Keeping busy?" I asked her as we got into Binky.

Her snort was quite unladylike.

"Are you staying out of trouble?"

"Touché."

I drove back to 16th Avenue and turned west. We were waiting to turn south at Edmonton Trail when she asked the question.

"So, where's this three-star restaurant we're going to?"

"I thought we'd have the lunch you promised me three years ago," I said, feeling nervous. At Edmonton Trail I turned south, then immediately turned right. I could sense her stiffen beside me. She was quiet while I pulled up behind the last car in line. The only sound in the car was the engine, and muted traffic outside. Finally, she spoke.

"I haven't been here since before our – incident."

"Neither have I. It seemed like it was time."

Danielle blew out a long breath.

"You're right. It's stupid to avoid the place because we had an MVA on the way here. I'll have a double cheese, rings, and a banana shake."

The line edged forward. Peters' Drive In is very busy at noon. It's not the best time to go if you are in a big hurry. I wasn't.

We got up to the intercom, and I gave the disembodied voice our order. With mine I included a large order of fries. Danielle raised her eyebrow at me.

You have to understand, the large order of fries at Peters' is not the little cup you get at other places. When I was an intern, six of us from Calgary had taken two of the American delegates to the police conference out for lunch. My mother was driving, and included a large order with everything else. The two American cops decided they also wanted a potato fix. She just smiled, and repeated their request to the intercom. I was going to say something when Nick put his finger to his lips.

They were expecting the usual "large" you'd get at any other fast-food place. What they got was a big box, filled to overflowing, with the bulging lid taped over the top to keep them mostly under control. Each box would feed a family of four all by itself.

I think they were eating fries for the rest of the conference.

In a remarkably short time, Danielle and I had our food, and were parked in the big lot next door. The weather was still nice enough for us to grab some grass under the trees.

"So what have you been up to lately?" I asked, "Apart from keeping the peace."

"I have a new boyfriend."

"Really? How long? Another cop?"

"He's a fireman named Riley. I've been seeing him for eight months."

"How's the sparkage? No pun intended."

"At the risk of handing you a straight line, it's hot. Better than that, he's an amazing guy who's been all over the world, doing all kinds of interesting things. On our first date I brought him home, and we spent the next five hours sitting on the couch just talking."

"He sounds like a keeper."

"That's my plan. Keep your mitts off him."

I stole one of her onion rings. She stole a handful of my fries.

"Are you seeing anybody?"

"Not at the moment," I said. "There was a guy a few weeks ago, but it didn't work out."

"Oh?"

"He was an MMA fighter, and didn't like losing to 'little girls'."

"He actually called you that?"

"In front of Nick Holley and Stan Watkins. Then he went postal, and tried to hurt me. I put him down, and the boys took him away in cuffs."

"You know how to pick 'em."

"I'm trying a new strategy now. I've sworn off jocks, and men who are crazier than me."

"Sounds like a good start. Kind of limits the pool, though."

We ate in silence for a minute.

"I was wondering..." I started.

"I knew it! I bet Bryon Strother twenty bucks you'd ask for a favour."

My curiosity overcame my hurt feelings.

"Where have I heard that name?"

"He was in the Mountain Bike Unit for One District. Now he's with us."

"Right. Late twenties, dark hair, tall?"

"That's him."

"Danielle, I didn't just buy you lunch to bribe you. Apart from the other night, we haven't seen each other in almost a year. I admit that I need your help, but I could have called someone else if that was all."

"Sorry, but you have to admit that it looks like stereotypical PI behaviour."

"My feelings would be a lot more hurt if I wasn't so desperate. This is as serious as it gets."

Either the look on my face or my tone of voice got through to her. She dropped her smile.

"What do you need?"

Despite how many times I'd rehearsed this in my head, this was not going to be easy.

"I need some property to get held up on its way back to the owner."

"Are you freaking insane? Property handles that, unless I request them to wait. How would I justify that? Does this have anything to do with your near miss the other night?"

"I know that it's a lot to ask, but this is important. I have some clues that the wife is the real bad guy, and her husband and I were fallout. If she gets the stuff back that was in the rental unit, she'll start the whole thing again with other people. I just need the return of the property to be held up for a couple of days while I investigate."

She stared at me like she was trying to read my mind.

"What's her game?"

"I'm not sure yet. Believe me, if I had solid proof I'd turn it over, and let you handle it."

"All right, what do you suspect?"

Crap, I did not want to get into the whole demon thing with her.

"I think she's a black widow, and somehow drove her husband insane. Since she wasn't there the other night, as far as you are concerned there's no reason to even think of starting an investigation of her."

She thought about that for a while, idly pilfering my fries while she did so.

"You're right. Looking at her would be a tough sell."

More of my fries disappeared while she thought more.

"You know, I have a gut feeling that we're missing something in this case. Blakeway doesn't seem capable of overpowering someone with your skills. He might have had an accomplice that you never saw. I think we should go over the physical evidence again."

"Thank you. Can you play the gut feeling card without getting into trouble?" She smiled.

"I'm a woman. I'm supposed to be intuitive." I snorted.

"Right. Seriously?"

"I can make it work. Probably not for more than a few days, though. Just keep me in the loop about your investigation."

"Believe me, if I find something on her that you can use I promise that I'll be on the phone to you so fast that the other shoe won't have finished dropping."

She picked up her last onion ring, and looked at it critically.

"You know, this was a good idea. I hadn't realized exactly how twitchy I was about coming here after our incident until I saw where we were going."

I looked at the fries. We'd eaten almost half the pile and I was stuffed. There would be no supper for me tonight.

"Do you want to take these back to the station?"

"Sure. I'll put them in the lunch room. I'll be more popular than I already am."

"So, Bryon thought my motives were pure, did he?"

"Yup. Foolish lad."

"Maybe I should give him a call."

"Leave the poor boy alone. He got engaged since last you saw him."

"Damn. Missed again. You're right. Having standards limits the pool."

There was no word about the dossier the next day. I puttered around doing not much of anything until six, when I headed over to Alyssa's house for another fun evening.

Again, Alyssa left around seven. Again, she was wearing her FCM dress. This time, I was in clubbing clothes too, though not as extreme as hers. My feminine essentials, including baton and cuffs, were in a shoulder purse.

It wasn't difficult to follow the cab in the thinning post-rush-hour traffic. Once we got out of Ranchlands we headed down Sarcee Trail to Crowchild, then east on Seventeenth Avenue.

Seventeenth heading east quickly became the usual nightmare of slow, congested traffic, and people wandering across the street without looking. I knew that there was a BDSM club around here, and wondered if we were heading there. At this point nothing would have surprised me. A few more turns, and the cab stopped in the middle of the lane. After paying, Alyssa got out, and entered a building that looked like a condemned warehouse.

With that architecture, it had to be a trendy club.

I managed to find a parking spot only three blocks away, which around there was a minor miracle.

There was no visible advertising on the outside of the building until I got within a few metres. In keeping with the building style, the club had an old industrial door that looked like it had been salvaged from a boiler room. It was guarded by a bouncer. Screwed to the brick wall next to it was a sign about the size of a license plate in brushed steel. The lettering itself was difficult to make out, but was somehow brushed differently so that it was prismatic in the street lighting against the matte background.

It read TWERK, except that the E was fashionably backwards. As names of clubs went, it was probably the most honest one I'd ever encountered. The building shook with the bass line that was playing inside. I began to wish I'd brought ear plugs.

There were two couples entering just ahead of me. As the bouncer heaved the door open for us, one of the women glanced at me, and gave me that quick eye flick and lip curl that translates as "I have longer legs and bigger boobs than you do, and you will never get the hot men I will." I ignored her. I could have knocked her senseless with one hand. Besides, she was probably only with her pretty boy because he drove a BMW. My new dating standards gave me a great sense of superiority.

Once the door was open, the rest of the music started to filter out. It reminded me of why I don't go to clubs. Sure, spending a few hours drinking and dancing your brains out with random hot guys until you select the one you were going to use that night sounded like it could be fun – in theory. In practice, I always got a headache from the airport runway noise levels. I'm certain that bartenders must read lips, because I can never hear what anybody is saying unless they are yelling into my ear. Then there's that whole standards thing again.

There was a sign just inside saying that the cover charge for women was waived all month. This must be a new club that was trying to build a following. All the better for me.

When the inner doors were opened, I almost staggered from the sound level in the main dance area. Despite the early hour, people were already crowded on the floor. Some were dancing upright, and others proving that they'd come to Twerk for the name.

I had to push my way through the gyrating bodies. The heat level from the perspiring patrons increased considerably the further I went from the door. I was heading for a flight of stairs that I could see at the back of the club, so I could look down on the crowd and spot Alyssa.

Occasionally I'd smell something sweet, vaguely like nail polish remover but with a bite to it. I got a particularly strong whiff as I was passing one girl who was holding a cloth over her face as she danced. Poppers. I'd have to let my friends in the drug unit know about this place.

I was almost there when a guy grabbed me around the waist, spun me around into his arms, and tried to kiss me. There was a revolting moment of domestic beer breath, then his tongue hit my firmly closed lips. I jammed the tip of my forefinger hard under his jaw, about three centimetres forward of the hinge. He made a gagging sound, and his head jerked back. The hug loosened, and he tried to paw at the finger. I stepped around him so my foot was behind his. With nowhere to go, and his head tilted back, he fell backward on a girl who was rubbing her butt against the guy behind her. She lost her balance, and dumped the guy behind her who fell into more twerkers.

It was the best entertainment I'd had in weeks. By the time the drunk and stoned dominoes had stopped falling, there were at least a dozen people on the floor. All of them were too out of it to understand how they had gotten there, and several of them were trying to hide their lack of underwear, or body parts protruding from zippers, depending on gender. After the sloppy attempted kiss, I was incredibly grateful that I had a bottle of hand sanitizer in my purse. I put a blob on my hand, and scrubbed my lower face with it. It stung my lips, and I would have to remember not to lick them before I got a chance to wash properly.

The stairs led to a balcony. I stood half way up looking for my ex-client.

It took longer to spot her than it should have because she was almost directly below me, under the stairs. The fact that she was in a heavy make out session with some guy hid her face for a while. It wasn't until she tilted her head back as he licked her throat that I recognized her. Fortunately for me, her eyes were closed, so I remained unseen.

My hands clenched the stair rail, and I fought my anger back into its box until later. Collin was mourned more by the person he'd tried to kill than by his wife. Even the man he'd become didn't deserve that.

I hadn't really thought this through. Like a dog chasing a car. I had her, now what was I going to do with her?

I retraced my steps, this time without anybody grabbing me. After the heat of the club, the air outside felt cold and I shivered. It also smelled really good as I left the drugs, booze, and body odour behind.

I was glad to get into Binky, and turn on the heat. Walking around outside dressed like your only goal in life is to get laid isn't as much fun on an autumn night as it is during a summer day.

It took a couple of trips around the block before I found a parking spot where I could see the club entrance.

She came out almost two hours later, draped over a different guy. I guess the one I'd seen her with hadn't measured up, assuming that she had any standards at all. Why have standards when you can mold him to fit your dreams?

A few minutes later a cab pulled up and they left, pursued by Binky. I would have expected the cab to go to his place. Instead, they ended up at hers. Again, that made some kind of weird sense. Why worry about a potential crazy stalker knowing where you live when you have a demon to clean up any problems for you?

At least he paid for the trip. There was no possibility of mistaking what her intentions were. The moment they were out of the cab their behaviour was one step short of ripping each others clothes off on the front lawn. His hand was under the back of her dress, revealing to everybody in the neighbourhood that she really was naked underneath.

A few moments after the door closed behind them, the downstairs light went off. The bedroom light went on, but only for a minute. Confirming what was going on upstairs wasn't of interest to me.

The rest was hidden by darkness. Some of it was due to the lights being off.

The next afternoon I got a response to my information request. There was no message, just a massive attachment. A minority of the information in it was public domain. The rest was data that I clearly shouldn't have, and that nobody should have been given without a fist full of court orders. I wondered how big the price tag would be when Trinity finally asked for my help.

Alyssa's story was not a happy one.

Her father was listed as unknown. Barbara, Alyssa's mother, was almost sixteen at the time, and already had two children, two year old fraternal twins named Keith and Nina. The unknown father might not have known she was pregnant.

Sometime in the next two years, Barbara got religion of the fanatic, extremist kind. Her high school record showed multiple disciplinary incidents from starting fights with other students because of their "godless" ways. These replaced the fights she'd started with other students over accusations of stealing boyfriends. There was nothing on her home life during this period until she turned eighteen and left, taking her children with her.

There also was no record of how she supported her family once she left home. That in itself was not a good sign. If she'd gotten a legitimate job there should have been employment records. Instead, she'd been off the grid for almost ten years. By that time the twins were fifteen and Alyssa was thirteen.

Nina killed herself the next year. The medical examiner's report pointed to long-standing depression caused by abuse from her mother. According to the report from child services, Barbara had renounced sex, and believed that God would not have let her children hit puberty unless they were evil beings who were in league with the devil. The case worker strongly suspected that she was schizophrenic, but Barbara refused to have a psychological evaluation.

Keith died a year later, after he and Alyssa had been taken away from their mother. His death was attributed to a drug overdose.

Alyssa, now fifteen, survived. She was in foster care for a year, then left. Although she was on her own she managed to stay in school, and make enough money doing part-time jobs to share a basement suite with a 32-year old named Cyrus Hullett. She lived with Hullett for three years, and had one child during that time. She gave up the boy at birth.

Hullett was the cause of the drunk driving incident that killed him. By then, Alyssa had enough skills to support herself doing miscellaneous office jobs.

Her medical records showed that she picked up several cases of crabs, chlamydia, and gonorrhoea in the next three years. It was probably a miracle that she avoided HIV. Again, it didn't take a genius to figure out that she was rebelling against her mother's anti-sex attitude, and therefore unknowingly walking in her early footsteps. During this period, she also had several convictions for drunk and disorderly after being at parties that were raided by the police.

Everything changed when she hit 22. She became engaged to a Joe Costillo for several months, then broke it off. She then became engaged to Max Hewett, and again broke it off after a few months. Two months later, she was engaged to Elias Pinkert. That lasted only a few weeks.

By the time she was 28, she'd been engaged to no fewer than 17 men. I had a suspicion, so I used a program to plot the engagement time line. The program was kind enough to fit a curve to the points which made the trend clear. Over those five years, the amount of time between engagements was steadily decreasing. So were the lengths of the engagements. She was obviously looking for something that she wasn't finding, and getting more desperate about it.

There was a gap of almost a year, and then she met Collin. This time she moved in with him almost immediately, and married him a few months later. The gap must have been when she found out about the Key of Solomon, made her tools, and laid her trap.

Part of the report was further information on Collin, and it agreed with some of what I'd already suspected. He had an abusive father who beat him with a leather belt for every tiny infraction. As a result, he bonded more with his mother and seemed to have had an unremarkable dating history. His ex-girlfriends all agreed that he was basically a nice guy, even if shy about his body. Several had remained friends with him after their breakup. All of that had changed six years ago when he met Alyssa.

The whole tragic mess made sense to me. Fairy tales are full of people making wishes that don't turn out the way they expect. In the stories, there is a strict limit on the number of wishes. Fixing the situation requires luck and cleverness, and usually results in things going back to their original state, with the wisher learning a moral along the way.

As far as anybody knew, demons would grant an endless supply of wishes as long as you jumped through the right hoops. When Collin turned out to be a nicer guy than Alyssa wanted she just called up Beleth, and modified her husband's behaviour.

By any rational definition, Alyssa was guilty of horrendous crimes against her husband, and was an accessory to my assault and attempted murder. The only difficulties with bringing her to justice would be finding sections of the Criminal Code that applied to what she'd actually done, and finding proof that a court would understand and accept.

If only spectral evidence was admissible these days. It was almost enough to make one long for the Massachusetts legal system of 1692.

CHAPTER 23

Meeting with an Old Friend

By supper time I'd finished reading the dossier. I now had a better understanding of the forces that had shaped Alyssa's life. What I needed was a way to stop her.

Kali wasn't answering her phone, and I remembered that George was in town for a visit. She probably wouldn't be out of bed until tomorrow.

I needed to talk to somebody. The choice wasn't conscious, and I was a bit surprised at myself as I listened to the phone ringing.

"Hello?"

"Hi Andrea, it's Veronica. Have you had supper yet?"

Again, I mostly supervised while Andrea cooked.

We started by preparing the porchetta, then cooking it in the microwave oven on low. There's nothing shameful about using a microwave oven, as long as you know what you are doing. Most people still think that its main use is to cook food quickly, and that it only has a "high" setting.

While that was cooking, we prepared roasted potatoes seasoned with garlic, basil, oregano, salt and pepper. Those went into the conventional oven.

Steamed broccoli florets with an Asiago d'allevo cheese and wine sauce rounded out the menu. I intended to drive home, so I brought only one bottle each of my best red beer. I wasn't going to repeat the drunken time that we'd had before.

"I suppose you heard about my favourite employer," she said while I savoured a bite of porchetta. Cook it long, and cook it slow. That's the secret.

"I was there."

"Oh, did you kill him?"

She'd spoken while I was taking a sip of beer, and I almost choked.

The look of outrage on my face must have been spectacular. She started laughing.

"I'm kidding. I heard he died in a car crash. Were you really there? I assume you are all right since you walked in here without crutches."

"I wasn't in the car. He tried to kill me before his accident."

"Oh my God. You have to tell me all about it. If you don't mind, that is."

"First, a question for you. You mentioned that your family were Benadanti. Exactly how much involvement do you have in that?"

Her startled look was replaced by caution.

"Why do you want to know?"

"Believe me, it's relevant to my story."

"Now I *have* to know. My father is more involved than I am, but I've done a bit."

"Good enough."

I told her the whole story of Collin, his demon summoning, and my near death. The only things I left out were the new facts about Alyssa's involvement.

"You aren't joking, are you? You were going to be eaten by a demon? A real demon?"

"Unfortunately, I'm completely serious."

"You lead a much more exciting life than I do."

"I'll trade you."

"No thanks. Not that I'm complaining, but why tell me?"

"Your family has a history. I knew you'd listen to me without immediately thinking I was crazy."

We were quiet for a few minutes. I was thinking about how my world had changed.

"Do you still dream about it?" Andrea asked very quietly.

The dream about Sitri came smashing back into my consciousness, and brought all its emotional baggage with it. The tears came before I was aware of what was happening. What the hell was wrong with me? I was ashamed that I was sobbing, completely out of control, and for no reason at all, in front of a woman I'd only met a few days before.

She grabbed a box of tissues and put them on my lap, then held me like an infant in her arms. I cried harder, humiliated that I was acting like a child. I was also scared, because I had no idea what was going on.

After a very long time, I managed to regain a little control.

"I'm sorry, I don't know what came over me."

"I do. Something similar happened to me."

I looked up into her face. "You were attacked by a demon?"

"In a way. When I was fifteen, three boys from school invited me to a party. It turned out that they'd stolen a couple of bottles of vodka from somewhere, and we were going to a new housing development to drink them. They broke into one of the houses, and when the vodka ran out, one of them tried to kiss me. I'd never kissed a boy before, and at first it made me feel grown up. I was too drunk to understand what was happening. He stuck his fingers in me and it hurt, but he kept telling me that I was so pretty. I was confused. I remember wishing his friends would leave so we could kiss some more." She drew in a deep breath, and let it out slowly. "All of them had sex with me. I was so out of it that I'm not sure how many times it was, but I think all of them had me more than once. I woke up, cold, sore, and naked the next morning. All the boys had left. I was lucky that it was Sunday, and nobody was working there."

My protective instincts took over. It was my turn to hold Andrea. It made me feel a little better to be comforting her instead of the other way around.

"I was so ashamed, I didn't tell anybody what had happened. I felt like it was my fault. Every time I saw one of the boys at school I was terrified that it would happen again. I felt completely powerless to do anything, and my grades slipped. My parents were angry with me, but I couldn't tell them what was going on. I didn't really know myself."

"After that, I didn't trust boys. When I was seventeen a girl hit on me, and I felt safe with her. I would have nightmares about what had happened, and she took part of the pain away."

I was overwhelmed by her story. Although I'd never experienced anything similar, for some reason I could strongly relate to what she'd been through. It must have been terrible.

"When I was eighteen the dreams became so bad that I went to a therapist. She helped me to understand what I was going through, that I'd bought into the lie that it was somehow my fault. I thought that I'd given them permission by not fighting them, but if I had they would have hurt me, and then done it anyway."

She took another deep breath. This time it shuddered as she let it out. I could see tears forming in the corners of her eyes.

"I'm still seeing my therapist, and I'm getting better. I still like women, but I think that some day I might want a relationship with the right man. I'm getting comfortable that I'll probably always be bisexual. Now I'm more angry than afraid, and the dreams are going away."

She was silent for a minute. We held each other, and occasionally sniffed. I felt close to her.

"I'm sorry, Andrea. I'm glad you told me."

She turned to look at me. After a moment she smiled sadly.

"For a private investigator, you can be pretty dense. I didn't tell you so you'd feel sorry for me. I told you so you'd know that I understood what it meant for you to be raped too."

If she'd said that under normal conditions, I would have violently denied it, but with my emotions in such a raw state, the word echoed through me.

Oh my God, she was right. I'd been raped.

My experience was both better and worse than Andrea's. There had been no actual contact, so I had no pregnancy or health concerns. The physical damage had been straight assault by Collin. I didn't feel physically soiled by my attacker.

What I did feel was a deep sense of helplessness. I was used to being in control. I had a black belt in Krav Maga, and had recently beaten a man who outweighed me at least 30 kilos in a serious fight. I had years of experience in keeping my sexuality under control, at least most of the time.

The demon had taken over my mind; the most private place we have. It was not a fight. I couldn't pretend that I might have won if I'd been a bit faster or luckier. One moment everything was normal, and the next I *wanted* to give myself completely to a demon.

It was terrifying, horrifying, and sickening. It was an attack against which there was no defence. I would never feel completely safe again.

"I was..." My throat locked up. I couldn't say it. Andrea stroked my hair.

"You are afraid of the word because you think it defines you. It doesn't. It only defines the demon."

I was so confused. I thought that I'd put the incident behind me, but it was obvious now that there were bad things going on in my subconscious. Until they were resolved, my life would be ruled by fear and self-doubt.

"I think I'll call my psychologist tomorrow."

"It would have been a lot better for me if I'd told someone right away. I'd hate to see you go through years of torture like I did."

I gave her a long, intimate, final hug, then gently pulled away.

"Thank you. I knew that something was wrong, I guess, but I didn't know what. Maybe I was hung up on the usual definitions. What happened to me didn't really fit them."

"Some definitions are useful, others aren't. We just have to figure out which are which."

I gave her hands a squeeze.

"You're a good friend."

We sniffled, and blew our noses. I tried to be discrete about mine, although my nose had completely stopped hurting. Hers was like a trumpet. We started giggling. For once, I didn't mind giggling. It was far better than what I'd felt before. She recovered first.

"Before you go back to saving the world, I believe you said something about making a chocolate souffle for dessert?"

Yoko Geri and I were still in bed when the phone rang. He stretched and yawned as I fumbled on the nightstand. The clock said 8:17 A.M.

"Chandler Investigations."

"Ms. Chandler, this is Detective Shuemaker at Four District. I wanted to let you know that we have finished our investigation, and your client's property is being returned to her."

Damn.

"Thank you, Detective. Can you let me know when she picks it up?"

"My pleasure. Have a good day."

Obviously, someone was listening on Danielle's end. Alyssa would probably be back in the demon raising business by tonight.

I'd learned my lesson after my run in with Collin. I called Kali, and didn't bother with pleasantries. I told her what I'd discovered about Alyssa.

"She's getting her tools back sometime today. I bet that she'll be back to summoning by tonight."

"What are you going to do about it?" she asked.

"Stopping her would be nice."

"I'm going with you."

"That's why I'm calling. The demon can only kill me once. I'm not sure about you."

"Any other time I might be insulted. In this case, you have chosen wisely."

"Can you be here by noon?"

"No problem. I'm also going to tell the rest of the group in case we need back up."

"No objection here. I'm tired of being pushed around by demons and sorcerers."

There was a pause.

"Did I just say that out loud?"

After breakfast I called my therapist, Dr. Trinity MacMillan, and made an appointment for the next day. She felt that this was an emergency and wanted to see me today, but I told her I'd be busy with something at least as important. She wasn't happy about it. Neither was I, but there was nothing I could do about it.

I was just finishing making lunch when Kali arrived, and let herself in.

"What's the plan?"

"We go in hot, blow them to hell, and get back to the barn in time for tea."

"Veronica, I think you've been playing too many video games."

"I wish I had that kind of time to waste. Honestly, I have no idea. The problem is that, short of killing her, I don't know how we can stop her. I'm hoping you have some ideas."

Kali flumped down on the sofa. She did not look happy.

"Is something wrong?"

"I'm scared of what's happening to us. We used to be nice people. Okay, sometimes you beat the crap out of people, but you always had a good reason and they were always bad. Now we've manipulated a man's will, you broke into someone's house, and we're talking about killing someone if they don't do what we want."

I sat beside her, and tried to keep an emotional distance from what I had to say. Like removing a bandage, if I said it quickly maybe it wouldn't hurt as much.

"There's something you need to know about the night I almost died. Sitri raped me." My voice stumbled a bit over the word.

"Oh my God, Veronica. I didn't know. I – oh my God."

"It wasn't physical. You know all those stories where some force is trying to control someone, and they struggle against it. Sometimes they get away and sometimes they don't, but they always struggle, right?"

She nodded.

"It was nothing like that. If I hadn't been bound hand and foot, I would have ripped my own clothes off, and attacked him. I'd have let Sitri do whatever he wanted to me, no questions asked."

"Veronica..."

Damn, this was more difficult than I'd thought. I could feel myself losing it.

"The only reason why nothing happened was that he let me go. The lust got dialled back, and the fear took over instead. If he hadn't done that, I'd have to live with having given myself to him without any thought of protest. I was completely powerless."

The tears poured from me, and I couldn't stop them. Maybe it was time for me to learn that keeping control wasn't always a good thing. The best I could do was to hope that Kali could understand what I was trying to say while crying.

"That's what we're fighting. Collin wanted to turn somebody into his plaything, and Sitri could have done it for him without effort. Alyssa has already driven one person insane, and is shopping for her next victim. The police can't touch her because there's no proof that a court would accept. She's like a combination of a drug addict and a serial killer. Every time something isn't exactly they way she wants it to be, she takes another hit of magic to fix it. If somebody is in her way, they are removed. We've tried being more or less nice by using traditional magical defences. None of them have worked. If we're nice we won't survive. It bothers me too, but it's as simple as that."

Kali hugged me, and I let the remaining tears out. I felt wetness on my shoulder.

"All right, *hermanita*. Let's kick ass and take names."

I couldn't help it. I laughed. I had a mental picture of Kali, wearing a Romantigoth gown, firing an assault rifle while wearing a beret. For some reason, she also had a cigar dangling from her mouth.

I hoped that Sitri was at least as disturbed about being inside my brain as I was sometimes.

"I still don't like the idea of killing her," Kali said.

"If she tries to sick a demon on us there won't be much choice. I've come to the conclusion that I actually have very little problem with killing someone in self defence. I just hope for your sake that it doesn't come to that."

"How about if we just tell her that we know what she's up to, and we'll turn her in if she doesn't stop?"

"The problem with that is that she has to be rational, and a bit gullible. Pretend that you're psychotic, and somebody threatens your only method of finding happiness on your terms. What would you do?"

"Shit," Kali replied. "I see what you mean. If we can get her to retaliate conventionally without first attacking her, we can have her charged with assault."

"And if she responds magically?"

"We either have to kill her, or we'll end up dead. Or worse. Come to think of it, we could threaten her, she could agree to stop, and then summon a demon to take us out later," Kali said.

"We could insist on taking her tools. From what I've read, it takes at least several months to make new ones."

"That might work as long as she still believes that she needs them. You said she's memorized the ritual, so taking her book won't do anything. Anyway, she can get another copy. The athame was deconsecrated, and Collin's circle was spoiled, without any effect. If she finds that out, she could do the ritual any time stark naked using her finger as a wand."

"That's what really worries me. The only thing that keeps us safe so far is that she thinks that she needs the tools. Once she realizes that she can summon demons without them, we're completely screwed. For that matter, if we believe what Sitri said she doesn't even need the ritual."

Kali doesn't drink coffee, and I wanted something more substantial than tea. I made us my special hot chocolate as comfort food. As I took a gulp, and something else not nice occurred to me.

"There's another possibility. As long as the demons play the game, it takes hours to summon one. Before she can invoke one we could just take her down, and claim that she was trying to kill us. Maybe plant a weapon on her for proof."

"That's not bad, except that I'm a terrible liar. I don't know if I could pull it off, regardless of how evil she is."

She sipped her own chocolate.

"I'm not sure I could either. It was just a thought."

"We don't have much time to come up with something that'll work."

Around four that afternoon the phone rang. My personal telephone curse must be slipping: I was just going to make more hot chocolate. Kali had a meeting with a distributor, and had left half an hour before.

"Good afternoon Ms. Chandler. This is Detective Shuemaker. I thought you'd like to know that your client was able to pick up her property this afternoon."

"Thank you," I said, matching her tone in case someone was listening. "Is she there now?"

"No, she came by about an hour ago while I was occupied."

"Thank you, Detective."

Shit. I called Kali's cell phone.

"*Hola.*"

"She has the gear. We need to get over there right now."

"Damn, the distributor should be here any moment."

My stomach knotted, but I made the offer anyway.

"I can do this by myself."

"Don't even think about it. I'm coming. I'll just have to brief Keith on what I want. How about if I pick you up on my way past?"

"You have no idea what a relief it is that I won't have to face this alone. Call when you get here."

I spent the next fifteen minutes wondering what to take with me, and then fretting about what we were about to do. When I'd planned to confront Collin, I knew exactly what I was going to do, but had no idea what I was getting into. This time I had no plan, and knew exactly what I was getting into.

I settled for my basic kit: my duty belt with baton, handcuffs, multitool, and lock pick set. The thought kept sneaking in that it was overkill for Alyssa, and useless if we had to deal with a demon. I took a breath, and tried to relax.

The phone rang. I was answering it, and locking the door behind me, before the first ring ended. So much for relaxing.

The trip to Alyssa's house was very quiet. There was no sense in going over everything again when we didn't know exactly what we were going to find when we got there.

The doorbell rang cheerfully. There was no answer.

"Maybe she isn't here yet."

We went around to the side of the house. I got down on my hands and knees and peered through one of the basement windows.

All I could see was cardboard.

"Shit, she's already started the ritual."

We ran back to the front door. I had no hope that it would work, but I tried the knob anyway. If a miracle happened, it would save a lot of time.

A miracle happened. The front door was unlocked.

I took out my baton, but didn't extend it.

"Stay behind me," I said quietly. "If she throws a fireball or something, run screaming and hide. Maybe it'll distract her long enough for me to whack her."

"Fireball?" Kali said dubiously.

"Or whatever. I'm tired of being surprised."

We moved as quietly as possible to the top of the basement stairs. We could hear Alyssa in the basement. She seemed to be in the threat portion of the ritual. We had to move quickly.

I stomped down the stairs, hoping that the sound would distract her. When I got to the bottom, she was looking in my direction.

"Alyssa, I need you to stop what you're doing immediately."

Although she was looking in my direction, her monologue never faltered for a second. I flicked my wrist, and the baton extended with a satisfying riff of clicks.

"Alyssa, I'm not going to ask you again."

Her flat expression never changed. The words kept pouring from her mouth.

I wasn't sure if I was going to stuff a rag in her mouth, slap her, or nail her with my baton. It would depend on how she reacted.

I took a step forward. Mist formed in the triangle of evocation.

The floating trumpet appeared, this time playing First Call. Given Beleth's previous association with horses, that was both appropriate and creepy. From that alone I would have expected Beleth to be on her way.

I would have tackled Alyssa anyway, hoping that taking her out would disrupt the demon's appearance. The bugle solo this time was so short that I didn't have time to make the decision and move.

Beleth appeared, the great king seated on his pale horse. I had an urge to try tip-toeing away, but she'd already seen me. Either she'd ignore my presence or not.

"O mighty Beleth," Alyssa said, raising a wand before her, "I thank thee for thy previous services. Now there is another service that thou mayest perform."

Beleth leaned forward, resting his forearm on the high pommel of his saddle. I could smell the musky scent of the horse.

"I don't think so."

Alyssa looked shocked. Apparently this had never happened before.

Behind me, Kali was on the bottom step. She leaned close to my ear.

"What's going on?" She whispered.

"I think the rules have changed again," I whispered back.

Our Disaster Train had left So Screwed far behind, and was now approaching Total Shit Storm.

CHAPTER 24

Sorry for the Inconvenience

The mighty demon king Beleth sitting astride his horse shimmered, and the mist shrank to become the female dwarf Beleth, who casually wandered out of the triangle of evocation. She waved and smiled in our direction.

"Hi Veronica. How's it going?"

Alyssa gasped, then grabbed her book and started flipping pages. I took it that this was not what was supposed to happen.

I no longer had the courage of ignorance on my side. This time, I knew that this tiny, smiling woman was a real demon. Regardless of her apparent friendliness, the best I was hoping for was a few more seconds of life for myself and Kali, so being polite seemed like a good stalling tactic.

"Hello, Beleth. Long time no see. Been busy?"

"This and that. Nothing as exciting as the time you've had. Aren't you going to introduce me to your friend?"

We knew that demons didn't follow the rules we had thought they did, but I didn't know if the tradition of "names have power" still worked.

"I don't think so."

"Whatever," she said, walking past me, and holding out her tiny hand. "Hello, Kali. I'm Beleth. Nice to meet you."

Kali froze, unsure whether it was better to let the demon touch her, or to risk being impolite.

"How did you know..."

"Oh, come on Veronica. It's not like you don't mention her often enough."

Crap.

"You've been watching me."

"Oh yes. Like one of your reality shows, but with more reality and less stupidity. You have quite a following."

I opened my mouth to speak, then decided I didn't need the distraction right now. Reality show? Following?

I felt the heat in my face as I wondered how much of my life was open to demonic surveillance. Did it include my night with Brian? No wonder demons traditionally knew all of a person's secrets. How many were watching? Were we on display right now?

"Any friend of Veronica's is a friend of mine," Beleth added. What exactly did that mean? If we were friends, what was that worth? There was so much I needed to know now, and almost no way of finding out unless Beleth mentioned it. Instinct told me I didn't want to start asking questions and reveal my ignorance. In the background, I could hear Alyssa incanting threats to try to control the demon.

"So," I tried to ask casually, "what are your plans for the evening?"

"Just hanging around. Having fun. Why? Did you have anything specific in mind?"

"No. I was just asking."

"Too bad. I'm getting bored by Alyssa's games. I'm looking for something new to entertain me."

Beleth was sauntering around the basement as she spoke. Kali and I turned in place to follow her, like sunflowers following the sun. Or rabbits following a wolf.

"We could always go for a pizza," Beleth said. "I've never done that before."

Alyssa had given up on her book, and put it down.

"This isn't fair," she said. "I did everything right."

Beleth laughed, and actually slapped her knee. I'd never seen anyone do that in real life.

"Did everything rite. That's a good one."

"You can't do this. I command you to return to the triangle."

Beleth looked at Alyssa for a moment, then carefully placed her right thumb on the end of her nose, wiggled her fingers, and blew a professional-grade raspberry at her. Alyssa looked stunned. It wasn't what I expected either, but after my previous meeting with Beleth, I wasn't as surprised.

"Did I do that right?" She said to us, with a look of concern. "I always worry that I'll use the improper idiom, and send the wrong message."

"That was probably exactly what you meant to convey," Kali said. I could hear a tremor in her voice.

Alyssa, still standing in her circle, raised her arms above her head. I have to admit that, by candle light and in her embroidered robes, she looked impressive.

"Oh thou wicked and disobedient spirit, because thou hast rebelled and not obeyed nor regarded my words which I have rehearsed, they being all most glorious and incomprehensible names of the true god, maker and creator of you and me and all the world, I by the power of those names which no creature is able to resist do curse you into the depths of the –"

"Oh, be quiet," Beleth said, cutting her off in mid-curse. "I don't have to listen to any more of your nonsense." She turned back to me and smiled prettily. "Now, where were we?"

"I believe you said you were bored." I said.

"And that you wanted pizza," Kali added.

Keep her talking. As long as she's talking, nobody is dying.

"Thank you. Yes, Alyssa bores me. All she wants is for me to take a good man, and turn him into a bad man. Where's the fun in that? I mean to say, I've had some wonderful fun with men in my life, and the best ones were the naughty ones. But, abuse? Humiliation? Some days I really wonder where my research is leading me."

The first time I'd met Beleth, she said that she was experimenting on men; turning them into human dressage horses. I'd never learned what the point of the experiment was. Maybe there was no point, like kids who pull the wings off flies just for fun. If she thought of herself as a re-searcher, maybe there was some way of handling her.

"That's interesting," Kali said. "What is the topic of your research?"

Yes! Go Kali!

"I'm studying human sexuality in this world," Beleth said happily. "It seems like there's so much to learn, and it's all so weird."

"Like the dressage experiment," Kali prompted.

"Oh, you heard about that? Of course you did. After all, you and Veronica are BBWs."

I blinked. We were *what*?

"I think you mean BFFs," Kali said. I'd have to ask later if she knew what a BBW was.

"Of course, thank you. BFFs."

I was keeping one eye on Alyssa, and saw her frustration building. It seemed like she didn't like being ignored. Before Beleth could get back to describing her research, Alyssa fished a silver ring from her robe and put it on. She also brought out the brass jar I'd seen earlier. Alyssa pointed the ring at Beleth like she thought she was a member of the Green Lantern Corps.

"By the power of the Most High, and his all His Angels, and by the will of Solomon the King, whose ring this is, I hereby command you to enter into this vessel, even as Solomon, in his might, commanded Asmodeus."

Beleth threw her hands up in horror, and giving off a thin, wailing sound, dissolved into writhing mist. Alyssa kept the ring pointed at the cloud which darted around the room, trying to get away. After a moment it stopped moving around and hovered in midair. Pulsing like a heart with tiny lightning strokes inside, the mist slowly moved toward the mouth of the brass vessel. It gave the impression of being reluctant, but Alyssa kept commanding it to get inside.

I was trying to figure out what to do. One the one hand, Alyssa the human would be easier to deal with than Beleth. On the other hand, maybe Beleth would be thankful if we saved her from imprisonment.

The last of the mist entered the magical prison, Alyssa slapped the engraved lid down on the opening. Holding it in place, she left the circle, and grabbed a pair of pliers from the steamer trunk. She used them to crimp the edge of the lid over the bead at the top of the vessel.

I heard a whisper beside me. "What's she doing?"

"I think she's trying to seal Beleth into the jar," I whispered back. I looked toward Kali, who was looking down with wide eyes.

"I don't think it'll work," Beleth whispered again, as she leaned against the wall next to me. "Everybody knows that the seal should be lead, not brass."

"Would that actually work?" Kali whispered. I wasn't sure why we were whispering now.

"Of course not, but at least it would be more traditional."

Alyssa looked up at the sound of the whispers. Her eyes widened, and she dropped the pliers.

"No, you have to obey me!" She shrieked.

It was time to end this.

"We won't allow you to harm anybody else," I said. "You don't have to be like this. We can get you help."

Her face showed nothing of the pretty, docile woman I'd first met. It was all anger and hatred. I wondered how I could ever have been fooled by this woman. She pointed her finger at me, and screamed at Beleth.

"Destroy her! I command you to destroy her!"

Beleth looked down, and carefully studied the fingernails of her left hand. Then she looked at Alyssa.

"Sorry for the inconvenience, but I'm not playing with you any more."

Alyssa stood there, her chest heaving as she breathed heavily. Slowly her raised hand lowered to her side. I turned to speak to Beleth.

Kali's eyes widened, and she tackled me.

Alyssa hit us just as Kali knocked me aside. For a moment the force of being tackled from two directions threw me off balance. I fell free of them both and rolled.

Kali was struggling with Alyssa. Kali pushed her away, and Alyssa bounced off the wall. Kali sank to the floor.

"This is all your fault!" Alyssa screamed as she came at me again. She had her white-handled knife in her hand.

I rolled backward, and heard a sharp metallic sound as the knife dug into the floor right where I'd been.

Alyssa was crouching on the floor as I regained my feet. She looked up, and was about to spring at me. My foot was already heading for her face. She tried to cut it with the knife, but my leather boot was tough, and brushed it aside.

I connected with Alyssa's face, and was sure for a moment that I'd broken my foot as it was jammed into the toe of my boot. Damn, I really needed to practice kicks. Alyssa toppled backward and didn't move.

"Shit," I said with feeling, as I limped forward to check on her.

Kali was lying on the floor, breathing hard and watching me.

"Do you want me to dispose of her for you?" Beleth asked. "Really, it's not a bother."

"No, thank you. That won't be necessary." I kicked the knife out of range, then got out my handcuffs and pulled Alyssa's arms behind her back. I was not gentle. There was no way I was letting that homicidal bitch anywhere near either of us again.

"As you wish. You might change your mind in a moment."

"Are you okay?" Kali asked. Her voice sounded weak.

"I'm fine," I said, looking up. "How about you?"

"Yeah, I just need to rest." That's when I saw the blood pooling under her.

I knelt beside Kali, and gently rolled her over on her side. My arm was wet where it had touched her back.

There was a big gash in her lower back where the knife had sliced through her clothes and skin. I'd been right; the white knife was razor sharp.

"Is something wrong?" She said. Her voice was unsteady, like she'd aged eighty years.

The wound was off-centre, at the base of her rib cage. It had missed her spine. The bad news was that it was right where her kidney should be, and blood was pouring out of it.

The only thing I could think to do was to grab the cut with both hands, and tried to hold it closed. My fingers kept slipping from all the blood. There wasn't enough flesh for me to get a good grip on her, and the blood kept welling out.

I was going on pure instinct, and before I could figure out what to do next, I felt something behind me.

"Interesting," Beleth said, looking over my shoulder. "How do you treat something like that here?"

I had to call an ambulance. With one hand, I wrestled with my pocket trying to reach my phone. The phone came out, but my hand was covered in blood, and the phone skidded out of reach. I was barely able to hold the wound closed, even with both hands.

Kali must be running out of blood, and I couldn't afford to let go for an instant. If I didn't do something right away Kali would bleed to death.

I looked around. There was nothing I could see that would help.

"Would you like some assistance?"

I met Beleth's brown eyes. The demon seemed genuinely concerned, but then that's always the way they are in stories until they go all -- demonic. I looked around again. There was nothing I could do by myself to save Kali.

Once more, I was helpless. For a moment, I teetered on the edge of the cliff. This was how people lost to demons – by making a deal when they thought they had no other choice. But Kali's blood was covering my hands, and a growing amount of the floor.

"Help her," I said. "Please."

"As you wish," Beleth said.

She reached over, and put her hand on Kali's blood-soaked back beside mine.

I waited for a miracle to happen. There was no glow, no tingling in my hands, no weird sounds: none of the things we expect in this age of computer-generated movie effects. It looked like Beleth was doing nothing.

My face itched where my tears were running down it, but I couldn't let go of Kali. My hands started to cramp from the strain of holding her wound closed, but I couldn't let go of Kali. My arms shook, but I had to hang on to Kali. The cut, and my precarious grip on it, were the scope of my world.

"Please, do something," I said.

"I am."

I could barely see through my tears, as random thoughts bounced around in my head. It was so unfair. Kali came here to keep me safe. I should have kept my eyes on Alyssa. Why wasn't Beleth doing something? Kali's sister had been blown up by terrorists. Her parents had died in a senseless car accident. What would I do if she died? What would I tell Mum and Dad?

I almost didn't hear Beleth when she said "you can let go now." Oh God, was Kali dead? I couldn't breathe.

I wiped my eyes as best I could against my upper arms. The blood had

stopped gushing from Kali's back. There was so much of it. It was everywhere. Was there any left inside her? Still not daring to hope, I gradually
relaxed the pressure I'd been putting on her skin. My fingers were
cramped, and refused to straighten on their own. I had to bend them
outward against my thighs.

The wound was still there, but the blood had mostly stopped. For an
eternity I waited while Kali laid on the floor unmoving. I looked at Beleth, and she looked smug. I wanted to scream, to smash Beleth's face in,
to do something to express the horror, and sickness, and pain that was
inside me.

Then I saw a small movement as Kali took a breath.

"You probably want to get her to whatever passes for a doctor around
here," Beleth said. "You'll want this." She handed me my phone.

It took both hands, and three tries, before I manged to dial 9-1-1 cor-
rectly.

Sometime during the call, before I could thank her for whatever she'd
done and find out what her price was, Beleth vanished.

I didn't even see her go.

The paramedics were the first on the scene. I heard one of them calling out upstairs.

"Down here." I yelled. "Hurry!" I trusted EMS, and I knew that telling
them to hurry was stupid, but I couldn't help myself. Kali was so pale and
quiet. I had to cradle her in my arms to convince myself that she was still
alive.

I didn't want to let go of her, but I made myself move aside while they
got to work, doing all the incomprehensible things that medical people
do to try to keep your loved ones from leaving you. I prayed to Kali's
gods that their magic was stronger than Alyssa's.

"Are you injured?" One of the paramedics said. I didn't understand
why he was asking me when Kali was the one who had been stabbed.

She made me sit down on the sofa, and ran her gloved hands over me.
When I didn't react, she asked again.

"Are you hurt anywhere?"

"No. Will she be okay?"

"We're doing everything we can. What about the other woman?" She
indicated Alyssa.

"She's the one who did it. She's just unconscious."

She quickly checked Alyssa, who was still lying on her stomach. Then
she went back to help her partner with Kali.

I could see the knife across the room where it had landed after I
dropped Alyssa. *There's blood on it,* I thought. Then I realized how stupid

that was. There was blood everywhere.

It was probably only a minute later that I heard other footsteps upstairs. One of the paramedics went upstairs to guide the police down, and to get the gurney from where they'd left it.

Alyssa woke up just as the first constable came into view. She started writhing around on the floor trying to get out of the handcuffs. When she saw me she wriggled toward me like a sidewinder. I'd knocked out several her teeth. The ones she had left were covered with blood. I think she intended to bite me. I almost kicked her in the head again. Instead, I just pushed her away with my foot.

I was dancing on the same edge I'd experienced when I caught Adam and Ashley in school. It would have been so easy to smash the life from her, but then I'd be taken away, and Kali would be alone. That thought was all that allowed me to stand aside so the constable could deal with my prisoner. He removed my cuffs and substituted his own. He also sat her in a chair across the room.

Alyssa was screaming about how I'd ruined everything, and she was going to kill me.

I sat back down on the sofa; not giving a rat's ass that I was also covered in blood that was soaking into the upholstery. It was Alyssa's sofa; let her clean it up. The one thought I clung to was that the paramedics were still working on Kali, and had started a pair of IVs. They wouldn't be doing that if she was dead, would they?

Shortly after, a plainclothes cop I didn't know came down the stairs.

"I'm Detective Bissett. Can you tell me what happened?"

My mind wasn't as sharp as usual, but I tried to give a proper report. I indicated the raving woman across the room.

"That's the owner of the house, Alyssa Blakeway. I'm a private investigator, and until recently she was my client."

"You're a PI?"

I brought out both my investigator's license and, for good measure, my baton license. He copied down the information.

"If she was no longer your client, what were you doing here?"

"My sister and I came here tonight to talk to her."

"Is your sister also a PI?"

"No, she owns an occult shop." That raised an eyebrow.

"What did she have to do with your client?"

"Alyssa recently lost her husband. She was becoming increasingly unhinged with talk about summoning demons. I brought Kali over here for advice, and to back me up while I tried to talk her into getting help."

The detective looked at the still-lit candles, and the circle painted on the floor.

"I take it that it didn't go well."

"When we arrived she was doing some kind of ritual. She tried to stab me with that knife. Kali pushed me aside, and Alyssa cut her instead. Then she came after me again. That's when I decked her and cuffed her."

While we were talking the paramedics were putting a bandage on Kali, and lifting her onto the gurney. Our parents were due back in a couple of days. How would I tell them about what had happened?

"One last question. Were you the only ones here?"

I looked him straight in the eyes as I answered.

"Yes. I'd like to go with her to the hospital, if that's okay."

"Sure. Go ahead."

I was certain that Beleth would have left no forensic evidence of her presence, so it was a safe lie. Everything else I'd said was the truth, as far as it went.

The constable who had control of Alyssa had to keep pushing her back into the chair. She helped my credibility a lot by screaming that her demons would kill us all, and generally acting like I'd described her: a homicidal psychotic. She tried to bite the paramedic who was examining her for a concussion, then spat in his face. Two burly constables led her away, still kicking and screaming. I was done. Let the justice system deal with her.

I convinced the paramedic to let me ride in the ambulance with Kali. I could call someone later to pick up Kali's car. There was no way that I was going to leave her side until she no longer needed me.

One way or the other.

CHAPTER 25

Life Changes

The ambulance howled through the dark streets while I fought the urge to scream along with it. It wouldn't do Kali any good, and it probably wouldn't make me feel any better. There was nothing more that I could do

"Her blood pressure is up to eighty over sixty," the paramedic said after a while.

"Is that good?"

"It's a lot better than it was."

"What's normal?"

"One twenty over eighty, more or less. Don't worry. She's doing fine as she is."

The bleeding appeared to have almost completely stopped. Her condition was as stable as it was going to get before we got her to the hospital. We were just keeping an eye on Kali as her partner drove.

I sat on the bench near the foot of the gurney, physically holding on with my hands, and mentally holding on with my eyes. My only comfort was that I could see Kali's chest rising and falling as she breathed through the oxygen mask. She looked a lot paler than was usual for her.

It was fifteen minutes from Alyssa's house to Foothills Medical Centre. My only view of the outside were the flashes from streetlights through the front window. I knew that we were hurtling down Crowchild trail, but t felt like we were just sitting still waiting for Kali to die.

The siren abruptly cut off as we approached the hospital. The emergency entrance is inside a garage so nobody has to be outside in bad weather. The ambulance quietly glided inside, and came to a stop.

The back door was wrenched open, and somebody in a white coat guided me outside, out of the way, as a crew of people removed the gurney, and swarmed around Kali. Doctors, nurses, orderlies, I had no idea who they were, but they seemed to know what they were doing.

Various people started calling out incomprehensible orders to each other. The whole mob of them started moving indoors, Kali at the centre of the activity. I felt a hand on my arm. It was the driver.

"Come with me."

I looked toward the double doors where Kali was disappearing.

"I know you want to be with her, but you'd only be in the way. Let them do their jobs."

He was right. I couldn't do anything for her except to be there. I let him lead me toward the waiting area.

Hell began anew.

There were other people in the waiting room. Every time somebody came out of the doors to the surgical suites, everybody looked up like ground squirrels looking for a predator, hope on their faces followed by disappointment.

Two hours went by. A doctor wearing a surgical mask on his forehead stepped through the doors.

"Ms. Chandler?"

I snapped out of my worry daydream as he sat in the chair next to me.

"Unless there are any complications in the next while your sister is going to be fine," he said.

I didn't care that tears were streaming down my face. He ignored them. He probably saw crying relatives several times a day.

"When can I see her?"

"We had to do some surgery to clean and close her wound, so she'll be out for another half hour or so. I'll send someone to show you where to go, and you can visit her for a few minutes.."

"Thank you," I said quietly.

"She's a very lucky woman," he continued. "The knife nicked the hepatic artery, but the blood had mostly clotted by the time we got to it. There were no problems closing the wound. Give her a couple of weeks and she should be good as new. The wound was a clean slice, so the scarring should be minimal."

The relief was more poignant than the worry had been. I couldn't stop crying. I could feel the tears dripping onto my chest. Through the blur I saw him stand up, and I grabbed his hand before he left.

The surgeon smiled, and went back to save another life.

No matter how hard the staff tries, hospitals always seem to smell like a combination of sick people and disinfectants.

Kali was lying in a little bay, walled in by white curtains.

She looked so pale, lying in her bed, surrounded by IV stands, and various monitors. The pale blue gown they'd put her in didn't help. I thought I recognized the tracing on the screen that represented her heart beat. As far as I could tell, it looked strong and regular. Blood was flowing into her, and the numbers that looked like they might be a blood pressure said 98/72. That was higher than it had been in the ambulance. I carefully held her hand, trying not to disturb some kind of clamp on her finger.

After a while, she opened her eyes. I could tell it took her a moment to focus. I'd been there myself, so I gave her all the time she needed. I resisted the urge to throw myself at her and hug her.

"*Hola, hermanita,*" I said quietly.

She made a small sound, like somebody who isn't awake yet, licked her lips, and tried again. I looked but there was no glass of water for her nearby.

"*Hola.*" Her face screwed up. "What happened?"

"Some idiot tried to save my life by throwing herself in front of a crazy woman with a sharp knife."

"Oh. Is that what happened? That was stupid of her."

"I thought so. They stitched you up, and you're going to be okay."

She finally took in where she was.

"Hospital?"

"Yes. Foothills."

"What about...?"

"The police will probably be here any minute to take your statement. Alyssa is under arrest. She was ranting about getting demons to kill us all, which is why we went to convince her to see a therapist."

"Oh." She thought about that for a minute. "Was anybody else there?"

"No, just us. She attacked me; you got in the way; I put her down. End of story."

A nurse came in and checked the machines.

"Hello, Liliana. How are you feeling?" Kali looked annoyed.

"She prefers Kali," I said.

"Sort of numb," Kali said.

The nurse made a note on her chart.

"Okay, you should rest." She looked at me pointedly.

"I'll see you later." As the nurse and I left I saw a cop coming in to take Kali's statement. It was a good thing we'd gotten our stories straight.gwr

The place looked no better in the morning. After they moved her out of recovery I wanted to stay with Kali. The nurses wanted to throw me out. I made such a fuss that they let me sleep in a chair in Kali's room overnight.

When I awoke I didn't move in case I disturbed her. After a while, Kali opened her eyes.

"*Hola.*"

Her voice sounded hoarse and weak. This time there was a glass of water on her bedside table. I held it for her while she slipped. I could see the relief on her face. I'd been there, too.

"Did it work?"

"Did what work?"

"My thrilling heroics. Did I save you? Or is this the afterlife?"

I put my arms around her very, very gently.

"I thought she'd killed you. Please, promise me you'll never do that again."

"Would you have done the same thing?"

"I have training. You don't."

"Would you have done it if you didn't have training?"

I didn't answer. She wasn't supposed to be so logical at a time like this.

"What about Alyssa?" She said, then frowned. "Or have we talked about this?"

"I told the police everything that happened, except for motivations, and our little friend." I lowered my voice and moved closer. "There's no evidence that Beleth was there. Do you remember giving a statement last night?"

Kali nodded weakly.

"I just gave the basics. There were a few gaps, but I blamed them on being stabbed. We'll have to testify at Alyssa's trial."

"I figured that. She's one person I won't mind getting off the streets."

A doctor came in to check on her. He seemed pleasantly surprised by the recovery she was making.

"You'll have to take it easy for a week so you don't pop any stitches. If there's any bleeding come in immediately. You should be healed in a few weeks."

"The doctor last night mentioned scars," I said.

"There will be a scar, but it shouldn't be too bad. If it's a problem, you can get a plastic surgeon to fix it later. All in all, you're a lucky woman. The artery had started to clot by the time the paramedics got to you. That probably saved your life. We had to give you four units of blood once you got here, which is a lot. You'll probably be tired for a week or two. Get lots of sleep, fluids, and food. Are you vegan?"

"No," Kali said.

"Treat yourself to lots of steak, or liver if you like it."

After the doctor left I thought about what he'd said. Kali was lucky.

They just didn't know how lucky.

Neither did Kali. I wondered how to tell her that a demon had some-how saved her life without mentioning what the price would be.

The next day Kali was looking a lot better. The doctors had originally thought she'd be ready to go home after a week or so in hospital, as long as she didn't do anything but rest when she got out.

Now they were revising that estimate downward. It seemed that Kali was healing a lot more quickly than they'd expected. Again, a doctor said that she was a lucky woman.

Was this something unrelated, or had Beleth done something to her? I wished that I knew.

For now, as long as Kali recovered, I wasn't going to look the gift horse in the mouth. Especially if it was doing dressage.

I took her home the next day. Her doctors were shaking their heads, and still attributing the whole thing up to her being lucky, being young, and having a good metabolism. They still recommended rest for a week or two before she tried moving around. I promised to stay with her, and take care of her.

By the time Mum and Dad returned a week later, Kali was out of bed and puttering around her house. On the day we were to go to the airport, I found her in her bedroom looking at her back in the mirror. She'd taken off the bandage.

"What do you think you're doing?"

"Admiring myself. What does it look like?"

"Are you trying to kill yourself?"

"Have a look."

Instead of an angry looking wound with stitches that could pop open at any moment, there was a thin line that was slightly less pink than the rest of her skin. The stitches were loose, and obviously doing nothing useful. I wasn't an expert, but it looked to me like it had been healing for a month. I felt the area gently. Kali said there was no pain at all.

"That's spooky."

"You're just jealous because I'm tougher than you thought. Shall we go?"

It was nice to have a brief moment in our lives where the biggest problem was dealing with finding a parking spot.

We were standing by the arrival doors, waiting with a sizable crowd for the flood of people to come through.

Out of the blue, she said "how much do you want to tell them?"

I'd been thinking about that, and I still didn't have a good answer.

"I don't know. It's a lot to take in, and I'm not sure I'd know where to start."

"Remember the Great Santa Claus Scam?"

"Duh. I'm the one who told you about it."

"You didn't tell Mum until you had built a complete case, right?"

"Are you suggesting that we don't tell them anything yet?"

"Do you have a better idea?"

"No. I guess we'll stick to the official versions for now."

The doors opened and passengers started trickling through a few at a time. Mum and Dad came through a few minutes later.

I hugged Dad while Kali hugged Mum, then we switched.

"How was the trip?" I said as we waited in the crowd for the baggage carousel to start turning.

"It was fun," Mum said. I waited for her to say more.

"All right, out with it. How did you do?"

"A gold and a silver," Dad said.

We proved that, despite all that had happened, we were still teenage girls by squealing, and jumping up and down. It wasn't until later that I realized the significance of Kali happily jumping up and down. It looked like her wound really was healed.

"What was the gold medal for?" Kali asked.

"Pistol marksmanship."

"And the silver?"

"Solo take down."

I had an idea what that might involve, but Kali just looked baffled.

"It was the police equivalent of calf roping," Mum said. "We had to subdue bad guys, and handcuff them in the shortest time."

"And you only got a silver medal?" I taunted.

"Have some respect. You should have seen the size of the last guy she drew," dad said.

"Big?"

"Freaking huge," Mum said. "They must have found him unemployed in Greenland. The thing that cost me the gold was the time it took to flip him over so I could cuff him. It was like trying to move a dead moose by myself."

"Veronica did something similar while you were gone," Kali said. Mum gave me her single eyebrow Mother Look.

For a moment I thought she was talking about Collin. Then I remembered Brian. That was all right. Mum in particular needed to hear about that from me as soon as possible, before Stan and Nick started exaggerating the details. The stories already going around One District would be bad enough.

"I met a guy who said he was an MMA fighter, so I invited him to an Abuse Club meeting."

"Did you break him?"

I looked at Dad in surprise. Normally he likes to pretend that his Princess is a gentle soul.

"Stan and Nick had to rescue him," Kali said. I gently punched her arm.

"Quiet, you. He wasn't too thrilled with being beaten up by what he called an 'amateur.' After I was through with him, Stan arrested him for trying to punch Nick."

"Is that where you got the head wound?"

"Of course not. He never touched me." Oops. I'd fallen into that one. I touched my forehead. My hat wasn't quite low enough to cover the lowest butterfly closure. You can imagine what it was like trying to get away with anything when I was a child.

"That's from my most recent case. The one you already know about."

There was a silence while Mum gave me The Look, and Dad grabbed the luggage that had just appeared.

"You might as well tell her," Kali said.

Bugger. She was right again.

I gave them the long version of the case, leaving out both demons, Alyssa's involvement, and that whole "nearly being eaten" part. It was quite thrilling enough without those minor details. Of course Mum already knew that I'd been assaulted, but she'd allowed me to be skimpy on details during our long-distance phone conversation. Now she kept asking me pointed questions to get to any details I might have "forgotten" to include. She'd have had the whole story out of me if I hadn't been experienced with interrogation.

I deflected part of it by telling them more about my fight with Brian. I also succeeded in giving them the impression that he and I hadn't gotten around to any kind of relationship yet. Would I ever come to terms with my sexual frenzy that night? Maybe. Someday.

Kali unwittingly helped deflect attention by being properly horrified that I'd been interested in Judy White's brother. Great, now I'd have to keep my frenzy from her too.

I also dragged Andrea across the conversation as a red herring. Dad was interested in her idea of me giving cooking lessons, and suggested that if I wanted to pursue it I could use the restaurant as a classroom on Sundays when it was closed.

Eventually, the conversation returned to Mum and Dad's adventures.

We spent the evening hearing about Ireland. True to my instructions,

Dad had shot videos of all of Mum's matches.

The pistol competition was really interesting. The first part was a normal shooting range with silhouette targets and regular ammunition. Mum's shots consistently chewed through the centre ring. At that level of competition it only took one hit outside the ten ring to lose.

The second part was far more exciting. It was like a live action video game. Everybody wore armour and face shields. They used Simunition, which is basically a low-load cartridge with a paint ball instead of a bullet, to prevent serious injuries and shoot-throughs. The contestants went through one at a time, having to clear a house without being shot by the bad guys or killing hostages. Of course, Dad couldn't be there to take pictures, but each contestant got a DVD of their performance, recorded from the in-house cameras.

I gained new respect for my mother's combat skills, as well as setting a new bar for myself. She was like a machine, clearing each room without exposing herself, shooting the obvious bad guys, catching bad guys faking being hostages before they could get her, and saving all the hostages including the ones who were having hysterics.

The last bad guy was waiting for her in a closet on the left side of the hall by the exit. If she'd missed checking the closet he'd have shot her in the back before she was through the door to safety. If she had just pulled the door open, he'd have shot her point blank.

We watched her stalking down the hall, her Glock held low in both hands before her. It looked like her eyes were fixed on the exit, a mistake that two of the other contestants had made before her. She said to us that the slats on the closet door made her suspicious.

As she approached the door, she hugged the left wall. Without breaking stride, she put her left foot in front of the door, then pivoted gracefully on it so she was on the other side facing back up the hall. The door burst open, and before the bad guy could lock onto her position, he found himself with her gun literally touching his face shield. His bug eyes were clearly visible, and her words were picked up clearly by the microphone in the hall.

"Go ahead. Make my day."

My family is freaking awesome.

Dad poured small glasses of a nice Chardonnay so we could toast Mum's medals. I was about to finish my glass when Mum said, "By the way, we met a friend of yours in Ireland."

I paused with the glass in midair. "Who? I can't think of anybody I know who would be over there."

"She said that her name was Belle. I think she was German."

"Now I'm really confused. I don't know anybody named Belle."

"I'm trying to remember her last name. It was right after the shooting competition, and things were a little confusing. Do you remember, Quin?"

I swallowed just as Dad said, "I'm pretty sure she said it was Eth."

Wine sprayed across the room. The rest went into my lungs. It was at least two minutes before I stopped coughing. Everybody, myself included, were afraid I was going to choke to death.

"She wasn't by any chance really short with long black hair, was she?" Kali said while I coughed.

"That's her," Mum said. "Oh shit. Beleth. The woman you had me looking at last year for your first case."

"*Mierda*," Kali said.

"That's her."

Mum looked at her watch.

"I'll have to call my contact with the PSNI in the morning. Maybe they can get a line on her."

"Don't bother. If previous experience is any guide, she'll be long gone by now, let alone by the time you call."

"Did you ever figure out who she is?"

"No. Not a clue."

Mum looked at me, then shifted her stare to Kali. I could almost hear Kali blush. Her poker face sucks.

"All right, but someday I want the story you aren't telling me."

"I look forward to it," I said, lying like a rug.

Kali and I left around ten to let Mum and Dad try to get some sleep. I stopped at the curb to take a deep breath of night air.

"How's your nose?" Kali asked.

"A lot better. They must have been wrong about it being broken."

I took another deep breath, and then got in the car.

"I hate lying to them."

"I know," Kali said. "It won't be for long."

"I suppose. Mum's going to be pissed. I'm not sure how Dad will react."

"He'll be overly protective."

"Yeah, I suppose there's no surprise there. You know, I'm seeing a pattern here. Months of missing teapots and fake disability claims followed by days of intense terror, and near death experiences at the hands of demons."

Kali squeezed my hand in hers.

"There's one good thing about all this."

"Really? Please, tell me what it is, because I must have missed it amid all the fighting, deaths, and insane people. Not to mention a demon who seem to have become fond of me."

Kali gave me an ironic smile as she drew away to open the car door. "We don't have to worry about being bored."

A REQUEST

Thank you. Yes you. It means a lot to me that people read, and even more when it's one of my books.

Book reviews are a critical part of getting the word out about new books. Please consider letting others know what you think of this one by leaving an online review. If you really liked it, you might also consider raving to your friends about how good it is.

If the place where you bought book this doesn't give you the ability to leave an online review, please consider leaving one on GoodReads (http://www.goodreads.com/), or another book review site.

Thank you again.

GLOSSARY

Buona salute (Italian) – good health!
Ciao (Italian) – Hello or goodbye
Comprende? (Spanish) – Understand?
De nada (Spanish) – It's nothing.
Eres una molestia, miquita (Spanish) – You are annoying, monkey girl.
Guarde silenco (Spanish) – Keep quiet
Hermanita (Spanish) – Little sister
Hola (Spanish) – Hello
Muy estúpida (Spanish) – Very stupid
PSNI – Police Service of Northern Ireland
Sono felice di conoscerti (Italian) – I'm pleased to meet you.

Hijueputa Verónica. No me salgas con esas estupideces. ¿Que mierda te pasa? ¿Es que no te importa nada la gente que te quiere? ¿Es que tu vida no vale nada o que? ¡Reacciona! Tu sabes que me moriría si te hubiera pasado algo hoy. ¿COMPRENDE? (Spanish) – Son of a bitch Veronica. Do not give me that crap. What the fuck is wrong with you? Don't you care about the people who love you? Isn't your life worth anything or what? Talk! You know that I would die if anything happened to you. UNDERSTAND?

ABOUT THE AUTHOR

G. W. Renshaw is a writer, martial artist, Linux druid, and actor who lives in Calgary, Alberta, with his lovely wife, and the twin cats Romulus and Remus. He has a wide range of interests, from flint knapping to quantum cosmology. He will happily watch just about any film with tentacles in it.

You can connect with him at:

Website:
www.gwrenshaw.ca/

Facebook:
www.facebook.com/GWRenshaw

Twitter:
www.twitter.com/GWRenshaw

Made in the USA
Charleston, SC
30 May 2016